Die
Diehl, Stanford.
Angel in the front room,
devil out back : a$ 25.00
novel

 W9-CLU-865

ANGEL

IN THE FRONT ROOM

DEVIL

OUT BACK

A NOVEL BY

STANFORD DIEHL

LONGSTREET PRESS

Atlanta

ANGEL
IN THE FRONT ROOM
DEVIL
OUT BACK

Published by
LONGSTREET PRESS, INC.
2140 Newmarket Parkway
Suite 122
Marietta, GA 30067

Copyright © 2001 by Stanford Diehl

All rights reserved. No part of this book may be reproduced in any form or by any
means without the prior written permission of the Publisher, excepting brief
quotations used in connection with reviews, written specifically
for inclusion in a magazine or newspaper.

Printed in the United States of America

1st printing 2001

Library of Congress Catalog Card Number: 00-111987

ISBN: 1-56352-643-3

Jacket and book design by Burtch Bennett Hunter

To Nicholas and Jordan —
I couldn't have dreamed up two better boys.
To my mother, who was always there for me —
even when I really screwed up.
And to Tara, always.

I wish to acknowledge the people who read early drafts of this book and who gave to me their ideas and feedback: Cathy Kingery, my sisters Cathy Lovern and Melissa Pestel, Virginia Leonard, Karen Kellogg, Sonya Cobb, Linda and Bruce Dodge, Joe Gallagher, Laura Ellis, Peter Gethers, and William Diehl. I couldn't have done it without you. Additional thanks to William Leonard, Leola Rosser, my great aunts and uncles, my brother Bill, and my good friend Yvonne Diehl. I also want to thank my son Nick, who first listened, patiently and thoughtfully, to his dad's crazy idea for a novel.

And special thanks to my wonderful agent, Helen Breitweiser, for her encouragement, her diligence, her good judgment, and – most of all – for believing in me.

ANGEL
IN THE FRONT ROOM
DEVIL
OUT BACK

JULY 17, 1978
SOLOMON'S ROCK, GEORGIA

L onnie Brim emerged from a path that led down from
Bosco's Bar and Grille and sauntered beside the railroad
track. His face was gaunt, the skin tight, as if stretched thin over high,
protruding cheekbones. His deep brown eyes were cautious and darting. He held a brown paper sack in his hand.

A white man appeared out of the darkness and walked toward
Brim. As usual, the man looked distinguished and proper in a char-
coal gray, three-piece suit. The chain from his pocket watch looped
down from the vest pocket and glittered in the moonlight.

The man came up to Brim and nodded curtly. Brim handed over
the sack. The man turned and headed back toward the darkness.
Brim watched him go as he pulled out a pouch of tobacco and rolled
a cigarette. When he was done, he stooped down and struck a wood-
en match on the rail beneath him. His face, dark as a bruise, glowed
in the match light. He lit the cigarette and stood up, blowing gusts of
smoke up toward the bright stars. He admired the night and dreamed
of the day he would be done with this business: paying off white men
and serving up whores to the coloreds.

He turned quickly when he heard steps approaching from the far
end of the track. "Evenin', Lonnie," the man said as he emerged

from the darkness.

"Jesus, Mr. Slats, you scar't livin' shit outta me. What the hell you doin' out here anyways?"

Slats held up a bottle of whiskey as if to toast. "Just enjoyin' this fine evenin'," he said.

Brim laughed. "Well that's just dandy, but you need to find yo'self..."

Brim never saw it coming. In one quick motion, Slats swung the whiskey bottle up and around, shattering it across the side of Brim's head. Brim staggered backward, the sharp smell of whiskey flooding his shocked senses. Slats kicked him in the belly, hard, then delivered a solid punch to his right temple. Brim collapsed to the ground. As the white man towered over him, Brim fought for consciousness. He believed that should he pass out, he would never wake up again.

Marvin Slats nudged Brim with his foot, trying to roll the man over. But Brim grabbed the foot and pulled it upward with a grunt and a jerk. Slats flipped backward onto the track, his head thumping onto the wooden ties. Brim scrambled up and tried to run away, but Slats dove on to his back. They rolled across the track and down the gravel bank on the other side. Slats shoved Brim aside and got to his feet. Slats kicked Brim again – three, four times. Brim lay in a heap, surrendering. He had been taught from an early age never to fight back against a white man. But what if the man was going to kill you? What if it was pure survival?

Slats grabbed a tuft of Brim's hair. He pulled the black man's head up and put his face an inch from Brim's ear. "I got every right to kill you, boy. You understand me? I got every goddamn..."

Lonnie Brim didn't know what else to do. He turned his head, opened his mouth wide, and clamped his teeth onto the fat of Slats's right cheek. Brim bit down with all his might, stealing away the menacing words pouring out of Marvin Slats's mouth. Slats screamed until his voice broke.

Brim probably would have bitten that man until his jaws gave out or until the cheek tore away in a mass of bloody tissue, had not the club come down across the back of his neck.

Slats scrambled free. "Jesus Christ!" he cried. "What took you so goddamn long?"

On the ground, Brim heard a second voice now, a young man. No more than a boy. "You told me to stay hidden until you knocked him out."

"Jesus Christ, man, the motherfucker bit me!"

"Yeah," the boy agreed. "You're really bloody."

Brim wondered if they were going to kill him now, but his body would not respond, and his mind was drifting away.

"I think you killed him," Slats said, cautiously approaching the body. "You won't s'posed to kill him."

"He's not dead," the boy said. "I can see him breathing."

The man laughed. "Maybe he ain't dead, but he's gonna wish he was."

The last thing Brim heard before he faded out was the crass laughter of Marvin Slats.

Lonnie Brim had no idea how much time had passed when he woke up again. He was still beside the track, face down. He managed to roll over onto his back and look around. He was alone. He was alive. What the hell was going on?

Brim looked up into the night and noticed a strange unearthly glow pulsing through the darkness to his right. At first, he thought it was the effects of the beating or the blood streaming down the side of his face. But when he worked his way up to one knee, he saw the fire, rising up from the other side of the woods. Tongues of red flame flicked out above the trees, and billows of coal-black smoke gushed up into the night sky, blotting out the moon and stars. Bosco's Bar and Grille was burning.

For a moment, Brim hesitated. It was all too strange to comprehend. Where were the white men? Why hadn't they killed him? Brim got up and ran toward Bosco's, staggering at first as the pain of the beating pounded within him but then picking up speed as he came to fully realize that his livelihood was burning away.

Brim emerged from the woods into the back parking lot of Bosco's. The flames were raging now. They engulfed the old building, seared across its walls, and exploded through the roof in torrents. Lonnie Brim ran to the front door, peered into the bar, and – with an arm over his face – slowly made his way in. There was nobody there. No one burning. No one dead. Had they all made it out?

Then, above the howl of the savage flames, Lonnie Brim heard the distant screams. They were guttural screams of anguish, but the cries barely rose above the roar of the fire. Upstairs, Brim realized. He knew he could never reach them. He rose his arm higher and looked up the stairs. He saw a single figure. The boy. He was on the second floor, trying to work his way up the flight of stairs to the screams above him.

"Billy!" Brim screamed. "Get your ass out of here! You won't make it!"

The boy turned and looked at Brim, dead in the eye, just as if there wasn't a fire raging around him. "My mama," the boy said with words only he could hear. "She up there."

"Goddamn it, Billy. You won't make it!"

The boy never heard him. The stairway collapsed in rivers of fire and burning wood. It swept down and across Brim and knocked him off his feet. He felt the intense heat steal away his breath and scorch the right side of his body. He was down now, the hot smoke rolling over him. He knew he wouldn't make it back out. They all would die here. Him, his girls, the boy, everyone who had come that night to Bosco's Bar and Grille.

It was then that Brim realized someone was pulling him. He tried to look up, but his eyes wouldn't focus. A figure pulled Brim across the floor, back out into the night. Brim looked up but could only see the glare of the fire, like a dragon above him, belching flame and smoke into the darkening sky. The third floor collapsed, and a row of windows on the ground floor shattered. Brim sat up, looked around, saw no one. Whoever had saved him was gone.

Slowly, Lonnie Brim crawled away from the fire. He didn't remember rising to his feet and beginning to run. He didn't remember racing through the streets and lawns of Solomon's Rock with the fire at Bosco's bar billowing up in great columns behind him. He didn't hear the police sirens or the fire trucks arriving. He heard only the faint screams crying out far above him and the sound – like the whoosh of a huge wave breaking and an endless roll of thunder – of the boy falling into the pit of flames.

1

TWENTY YEARS LATER

Jackson Moon cut through a cornfield that led to a three-story house. He had gotten the address from a skeletal white man smoking crack at the abandoned train depot in Solomon's Rock. Twenty bucks had gotten Jackie the location of the house as well as the description of a black man in his early forties who had lived and worked there for as long as the crackhead could remember. It was all Jackson had to go on. He had to start somewhere, and Jackie assumed that no one would be running drugs in the county without Michael Grant being involved. Grant was the key to what had happened twenty years before. Jackson was sure of it.

As he walked through the towering stalks of corn, a full moon disappeared behind a bank of black clouds, and large drops of rain began to fall around him. The night came alive with the slapping sound of water striking the thick green leaves. The second story of the house was brightly lit, and silhouettes moved across the thin drapes covering the windows. Occasional bursts of laughter rose above the sound of the rain and the relentless beat of loud rap music that thumped from the house. A dim light, perhaps from a single lamp in the front room, filtered through the lower story. A porch light splayed across the front lawn and illuminated a single tall oak, casting a shadow over the driveway and into the darkness of an open field beyond.

Jackson stopped at the edge of the cornfield and crouched low. His heart fluttered with anxiety and anticipation. He had returned to Solomon's Rock after twenty years to make a stand, to get to the truth that had stolen away his life. He had spent a single night trying to make his way into his father's secret society, and another twenty years running away from what he had found. As he did almost every day, he remembered that night again, a night so long ago and yet as fresh as frost. Crouched in the bushes beside the railroad track, much as he was crouched now in the cornfield, he had watched Lonnie Brim fight for his life. He had emerged from his hiding place only to strike Brim with a wooden club. He remembered the guttural laugh of Marvin Slats and the fire rising up from the bluff above the man with Slats's bloodied face shrouded in the unearthly red glow of the hungry flame.

He could no longer run from the images of that night. He had tried to run, but the nightmares had always tracked him down: on the long road to southern Florida, in the old church on Runyon Street, at the senior citizens' home where he tried to pay his penitence, and in the state penitentiary where he had spent the last five years of his life. Here, now, at this house, was where he would make his stand.

As he came out of the corn and into the mounting rain, a light came on in the bottom story of the house. The light flashed on in the back room and struck Jackson like an escapee in a searchlight. He froze in the rain and watched the window. He saw the shadows of two men as they passed in front of the curtain and sat down at a table. Jackson bent over and trotted to the edge of the house. He slid below the lit window and pulled his knees to his chest. The rain was pounding down. It soaked his clothes and hair and poured down his face in rivulets. He could not hear the men in the back room.

Jackson edged along the siding and flattened his back against the door. He eased up and peered below the valance. The two men sat on high-backed chairs, a snow-white pile of powder on the table between them. They sat in a kitchen. Stacks of dirty dishes filled the sink and the counter beside it. Next to the sink, six black bags full of garbage and beer cans sat like a flood barricade. Moths fluttered around the fluorescent light above the sink. One of the cabinet doors stood open, the counter below it smudged with grease and a glob of peanut butter. Jackie heard a telephone ring. He ducked down as one of the men went to the front of the house to answer the call. Jackson sat in the rain, took a deep breath, exhaled slowly through his nose, and slicked his hair back away from his face with both hands.

When he rose back up, he saw the man sitting at the table. The man held a razor blade between his thumb and index finger, cutting up the big pile into smaller ones. He snorted a long line through a rolled-up ten-dollar bill. His brown face was long and thin, the eyes sunken, the lips drained of color. His hair was cropped close to the skull, and he wore the heavy fatigue jacket that the crackhead inform-ant had told Jackson about. He was the right age, too, as far as Jackson could tell. Early-to-mid forties. The informant had called him Stomp. If Stomp didn't know anything about the fire at Bosco's, he would know something about the underground Grant operation in Solomon's Rock, something for Jackson to go on.

The other man returned to the kitchen and stood by the counter behind Stomp, probably updating him on the call he had just taken. The two of them laughed about something, then the second man bent over the table and took a snort with the rolled-up bill. He straightened up and cocked his head back so the liquefied powder could drip to the back of his throat. Stomp pointed to a boombox on the counter, and the second man slapped a button on the device. Rap music erupted from the box as the second man moved his hips to the beat. Stomp bobbed in his chair and pulled a wad of bills from the fatigue jacket. He licked his index finger and began counting the money.

Jackson wrapped his left hand around the doorknob, held his breath, and slowly turned it. The door was unlocked. He looked back into the kitchen. The two men were belting out the chorus of the song. Jackson pulled a snub-nosed .38 from the waist of his jeans and held it against his chest with his right hand, the left still on the knob. He turned the knob a full rotation until the door clicked open. He let out a breath as he watched Stomp continue to count the bills. The second man bent over the table for another snort. The rain beat furiously against the windowpane, and as Jackie slowly eased the door open a sliver, the music slipped out into the night, sweeping Jackson into a shared environment with the two drug dealers. The point of no return. He blew out another deep breath and rushed through the door.

Both men turned to the door as it clattered open. The second man, a white rock still clinging below his nose as he straightened up, cried, "What the…" just as Jackson brought the butt of the .38 around, smashing the second man in his left temple. He fell across the counter, slinging a sugar bowl across the floor as he dropped down to the linoleum himself. Stomp reached for a gun in his coat pocket, but Jackson already had the pistol pointed at Stomp's face. He cocked the hammer back.

"Don't move a muscle, Stomp," Jackson ordered, and the black man froze with the stack of bills in his left hand and the handle of a semiautomatic in his right.

Jackie held the .38 dead steady, aiming at the bridge of Stomp's nose. "Let go of the gun and bring your hand out of the coat. Very slowly."

"You crazy, man. You know who you fuckin'…"

"Shut up, Stomp."

"How you know…?"

"Shut the fuck up." Jackson enunciated each word, driving his point home.

Stomp watched as Jackson pulled the revolver back slowly, raising the barrel toward the ceiling. Stomp's eyes flared open as the butt of the gun rushed toward him, slamming against his forehead. The chair careened back on two legs, then jerked forward as Stomp collapsed on the table, the white powder puffing up around his head, the stack of bills fanning out over the table surface and onto the floor. Jackson rushed around the table, scooped Stomp over his right shoulder, and carried the black man out into the storm.

The man was thin and light until the rain soaked into the fatigue jacket. Jackson carried him into the cornfield. He bolted down one row then cut across the field, the wet leaves of the stalks slapping the two bodies as they passed. Thunder rumbled above Jackson as his breath grew heavy and hoarse. He came to a gully at the far edge of the field and threw Stomp onto the muddy earth. The black man coughed hard and came up on all fours. Jackson punched a knee into Stomp's back and drove him onto his stomach. Jackie crooked an arm around the dealer's neck, jerking his face up out of the mud but keeping one knee on the small of his back. The man cried out.

"Shut up, goddamn it." Jackson put the pistol to Stomp's right temple. "Nobody will give a damn about a black dealer shot dead in a cornfield."

"The man go'n care," Stomp spat out.

"The man? Who's the man, Stomp? Who is the man?"

Stomp shut his mouth in an attempt at staunch silence.

"Screw that. You don't need to tell me what I already know. Michael Grant runs all the dirty business in this county. I know that."

"Then you know you fucked up royal. The man go'n have your…"

Jackson shoved Stomp's face down into the puddle of water pooling up in the gully. When he let it up again, Stomp fought for breath and coughed violently. Suddenly, Jackson heard a commotion back at the house. Men were shouting. Soon their voices were outside. "Stomp?" they called. "Where are you, Stomp?"

Jackson pulled the man's head back and croaked into his ear. "How would you like to drown in three inches of water? I hear it can happen.

I just want to know about the fire at Bosco's bar. I want to know what went down that night."

Stomp actually laughed. Jackson jerked his head back to shut him up. "Man, you fuckin' wit' me, right? I don't even know what you talkin'...."

Jackson stuffed Stomp's head back down into the puddle. He heard footsteps rushing along the rows of corn, splashing loudly in the mud, men calling out. "You best let Stomp go. Let him go 'fore we track you down and skin you alive."

Jackson pulled the man's head back up, his ear against Jackson's lips. "You been around a long time, Stomp. I know that. You may not have been in on anything back then, but you sure as hell know something. Are you telling me you never heard about the fire that killed fourteen black folks and a Georgia state senator?"

"Yeah, I heard about it, man. That's all. I just heard some shit."

Jackson wrapped his arm back around the man's throat, squeezing his larynx. The footsteps were getting closer as the men scouted the rows of the cornfield. They methodically moved toward the gully. The rain exploded around Jackson and Stomp like a hail of gunfire. Lightning throbbed through the clouds. Corn ears shuddered from the rain and stalks cracked from the men who trampled through the field.

Jackson ducked Stomp back down in the trough of muddy water. He held him as the man squirmed wildly like an epileptic breaking into spasms. Finally, he lifted the man's head up. His eyes were clamped shut and mud drooled from his face. His mouth fell open and brown water gushed out of it.

"What did you hear, Stomp?" Jackson growled. "Last chance. Next time you won't come up for air."

"There's a guy," Stomp wheezed, water still gurgling at the base of his throat. "They call him Red Eye. Red Eye Barnes. Word is he survived that fire. The white folk don't know why he's all scarred up. They don't think anybody got out of there alive. But Red Eye made it.

He was only a boy back then. That's all I know."

Jackson remembered standing in the doorway of Bosco's Bar as the fire raged, Lonnie Brim calling out to the black boy on the stairs, the steps collapsing...."

"Where does this Red Eye live?"

"Over near the train station. Back in the woods off Depot Street. He lives in a little shack back in there. I swear, man, I don't know nothin' else."

Jackson brought the pistol up over his head and slammed it across the back of Stomp's neck. The black man collapsed into the mud. Jackie rolled him over onto his back. The footsteps were two rows over now, louder even than the sudden boom of thunder.

Jackie bolted away from the cornfield, toward a stand of pine twenty yards away. He had almost made it when he heard a voice call out, "There he is! Heading for the trees! Get a light over here!"

Gunfire popped behind Jackson. He dropped into the mud, as a bullet splintered a tree ten feet in front of him. He rolled once and came up into a crouch. He slipped once in the mud as a bullet struck a stream of water to his left, making a deep *spalunk* sound. Another bullet thudded into a dirt bank to his right. He dove into the stand of trees and came up running hard, swerving between the pines. The acrid smell of pinesap stung his eyes as he stooped forward and galloped. He came to an eight-foot drop-off and slid down the bank as the gunfire roared behind him, thumping into bark. He ran along the bank to his left until he neared a dirt road cutting east through the wood. He huddled against a thick pine, his gun against his heaving chest, and stood as still as he could. The rain slackened, but another shock of lightning strobed in the dark forest.

The men were still yelling, some distant, one as close as thirty-five feet away. They had found Stomp at the edge of the cornfield. Jackie could hear the other man from the kitchen, the one he had first knocked out with the butt of his gun, cursing up near the house.

"Don't nobody kill the motherfucker!" he called out. "I got first crack at him, goddamn it!"

The rain was now a random patter against the pine needles. Jackson heard a branch break close by, maybe fifteen feet to his right. He stayed statue still, his back flat against the wet bark. A bug leapt from the tree onto Jackson's chin, but he let it crawl slowly up his cheek. A white man with short red hair, a red mustache, and dark stubble on his neck stepped into Jackson's line of sight. Jackson turned his head slowly to take the man in. The man held a Luger in his right hand and walked in tiny, purposeful steps, his eyes narrow and focused, his senses alert. He resembled a cat with its ears pricked up. Jackson turned his right shoulder against the tree and held the .38 up in front of him with two hands.

"I don't want to shoot anybody," Jackson stated as the man froze. "Just toss the gun over here and lay down on the ground."

The man made a motion as if he were going to throw the gun, but instead he swung it up and yanked off a wild shot in Jackie's direction. Jackson hit the dirt, and rolled sideways to the other side of the tree. His assailant took another shot that ricocheted off the tree and cracked through the woods. Jackie rolled to his stomach, the gun propped on the ground out in front of him, and squeezed off a single shot that ripped into the mustached man's left thigh. The redhead cried out and collapsed into the needles. A roar of voices sprang up and footsteps stampeded toward Jackson. He dashed across the dirt road, turned right, and sprinted through the trees. *Where is it? Where the fuck is it?*

Suddenly, the barrel of a shotgun dipped down in front of him like a metal guard dropping at a railroad crossing. The barrel slammed into Jackie's chest, and his feet flew out from under him. He hit the ground hard. A young white man with long black hair spilling out from under a plaid hunter's cap pointed his shotgun at his fallen prey and called out "I got him, boys. . . . "

Jackson threw his right leg up against the barrel. The shotgun jerked upward as a shot roared off into the branches above. Jackie sprang up, his shoulder pounding into Longhair's midsection. Jackson got his legs under him and drove the man into a tree trunk. He felt the air gush out of Longhair, and the shotgun dropped to the ground. Jackie thrust a tight right uppercut into the man's chin, bolting his head backward into the tree and flipping the cap away. As the man fell, Jackson picked his pistol up off the ground, turned toward the approaching footsteps, and fired four shots into the trees. He heard the footsteps scatter and bodies diving for cover. Jackson turned and started running again at full tilt. His lungs burned and a sharp pain tore into his ribs. The footsteps fell in behind him again and voices called out "Johnny! What's going on?" Jackson felt like the fox being chased down by hounds and horses.

Then, finally, he saw it. His rented blue Neon hunched in a turnoff. He rushed to the car and pounced up on it, his boots pounding across the hood as he crossed to the driver's side. The car was just as he had left it, purring softly in idle. He jumped in, threw the car in gear, and spun out toward the road, a geyser of brown water spewing up behind him.

He fishtailed out onto the main road, two men appearing in the rearview mirror. Gunshots popped madly, and just as Jackie assumed he was out of range, the back window exploded. Glass darted into his headrest; rain and wind gusted through the car. Jackson tried to maneuver around a sharp left bend but the car fishtailed again, hopped an embankment, and slammed into a tree. The passenger door crumpled as the car shot back across the road and swung around. When it stopped, Jackson was staring straight ahead at the men who were running up the road toward him. He had a notion to drive dead-ahead at them, but instead he cocked the stick into reverse gear, backed around the bend in the road, punched it into neutral as he swung back around, and dropped directly into fourth as he slammed the accelerator to the floorboard. Within five seconds, the car was in overdrive and didn't slow down until it slid out onto intrastate 121.

2

Noxie knew the newspaperman would come. Blue Furman had made a career out of exposing the crimes of Noxie's father, Michael Grant. From the time Grant had taken over the nightclubs and strip joints around Solomon's Rock, to the early days of the Grant pornography empire, to the unleashing of the grand plan for a Civil War theme park that would be the perfect conduit for Grant's dirty money, Blue Furman had been there, right on top of it, telling the story in the black-and-white pages of the *Atlanta Journal*. So when Noxie told Furman he had some juicy information and then whetted the newsman's appetite with stories only an insider would know, he had Furman hooked.

Noxie had rented an old apartment on Atlanta's east side, using an assumed name. The landlord was happy to get an advance and didn't ask many questions. The rundown tenement didn't spark much rental interest. It looked like it had been abandoned for a long time. The entrance was on an alley off Carson Street. Cracked wooden stairs led to the second floor. There was another apartment across from Noxie's, presently vacant. The spot was perfect.

Noxie noted the suspicion in Furman's eyes when he showed up at the door. The newsman wore jeans and a coffee-stained white shirt with a button-down collar. His shoulders slumped under a gray tweed jacket that was frayed along the lapel and reeked of cigarettes. He had a motley muss of brown hair that was randomly streaked with gray. And Noxie knew Furman also had a twinge of fright in his gut, but he couldn't resist the bait. Couldn't resist an opportunity to tear down Noxie's father even more. Grant was in prison now, but that wasn't enough for Blue Furman. All he cared about was another story that would further build his reputation as a reporter. Word was that Furman's exposé of the porn trade in the Southeast would one day earn him a Pulitzer.

The apartment was furnished with a scarred kitchen table, a beat-up couch and chair in the living room, and a single bed – a cot really – in the bedroom. Noxie didn't plan to stay. There were no towels, no sheets on the bed, no curtains on the windows. Noxie offered Furman a seat at the kitchen table, then took two beers out of the six-pack in the refrigerator and popped the tops. Furman kept a sharp eye on Noxie as he took a swig of the beer and lit a Winston Light.

"So what have you got for me?" Furman asked anxiously.

Noxie smiled. "I've got a story that will make your career, Mr. Furman."

Furman put on a scowl. His career was already made, and he resented the idea that some lowlife thought it wasn't. Under the table, Noxie reached into his pants pocket and slowly pulled out a hard metal ball. It filled his palm, half the size of a baseball.

Noxie and Furman stared at each other for a moment. Noxie rubbed the ball with his thumb.

"Well?" the newsman asked. "What have you got for me?"

Noxie got up and made his way around the table. "It's about Grant's son. Not much written about him."

Furman thought about it. "Way I heard it, the guy's all messed up. Some kind of mental defect. His mother tried to kill herself. Locked herself and the kid in the garage with the car running."

"That the way you heard it?" Noxie asked, the anger slipping into his voice.

The ire caught Furman's attention. He turned in his chair and started to rise. He saw the fist coming at him. Something round and silver in it. The metal ball clocked him in the side of the head, a solid blow to the left temple. Furman went back down on the chair so hard it toppled over backward. He was out before hitting the floor, a purple welt swelling on his head like a fist pushing out of his skull, the cigarette still burning between the second and third fingers of his right hand.

When Furman woke up, he was back at the kitchen table. His mouth was gagged. One end of thick rope was tied tightly to his right wrist, the other end of the rope was tied to the far table leg, stretching Furman's arm across the surface of the table. His other arm was behind his back, tied to the chair. His feet were tied to the chair legs. Furman had to strain to look up at his captor.

Noxie looked down at the newsman with concern. He had a meat cleaver in his hand.

"You write with your right hand, don't you, Mr. Furman?"

Noxie saw the realization come into Furman's eyes, the shock of total fear. It gave Noxie a sudden rush. He felt the blood rush to his penis. He opened his arms as if taking in the wave of satisfaction. He had a high forehead with widely spaced eyes and a square chin. His fine hair was cut short, and he was often kidded about his effeminate nose and smooth chin. He only had to shave every few days and then only to remove the light fuzz that puffed out on the tip of his chin. He carried his six feet, three inches awkwardly, like an adolescent adjusting to a sudden burst of height, and he didn't seem to know what to do with the thin long fingers that dangled to his knees. He would wiggle them, rub his chin with them, scratch his thigh, lace the fingers together, or rub them briskly as if warming them up in the July heat. His voice, too, rung pubescent, rising and falling, crackling out, scratchy and uncertain. But he had developed a knack for putting on a deep, menacing tone when he had to. He delivered threats well. It was only then when he felt in control. He felt a new personality rising within him, taking shape in his chest and searing up his throat. He savored the look of fear he could drive into a victim's eyes. They would ignore him on the street or laugh at him behind his back, but when he was armed, when he put on the voice, they could not ignore him. They could only fear him. Noxie liked it like that. It was what he had come to live for.

"Mr. Grant's son does not have a mental defect," Noxie said dreamily. "My only real weakness is that I love my father too much. I can't stand to see a man tear him down. A cowardly man who can't face my father man-to-man, but has to resort to words on a page." Noxie looked down at the newsman. Sweat poured down Furman's face and stung his eyes. He wiggled frantically in the chair and tried to pull back the arm that was stretched across the table.

"Yes," Noxie said. "I remember now. I saw you on television once. You were writing on a little pad. It was your right hand. That's the evil one."

And the cleaver came down. It sank into Furman's wrist, just to the right of the rope. The newsman's scream seemed even more agonizing, muffled by the rag stuffed in his mouth. It took four chops to take the hand off.

Noxie watched Furman's head loll. His right arm was now free from the rope, though the severed hand was still tied at the wrist. Furman's head rolled back in the chair, the eyes glazed in horror and pain. A high-pitched whine escaped from his throat and pierced through the gag. Noxie watched for a moment, then he went into the living room and reached under the couch cushion. He pulled out his nine-millimeter Glock and brought it back into the kitchen. He set the pistol on the table, next to the hand, as if daring the severed hand to grab hold of the gun. He smiled at the irony: the gun right next to Furman's hand but the hand no longer attached to the newsman's body. Furman glared at the gun, then at the hand, as if willing his lost body part to pick up the Glock and kill his tormentor.

Noxie took one of Furman's Winstons, stuck it in his mouth, and lit it. He would let the man suffer a while. Let him realize what his life of harassing Michael Grant had finally come to. Long moments to reflect and repent. By the time Noxie had finished his cigarette, Furman had passed out. Noxie would wait to see if the man woke up again, let him realize that his awful nightmare was indeed true, before putting a bullet through Blue Furman's brain.

3

Jackson pulled the damaged Neon into a parking spot on the courthouse square. The storm from the night before had calmed, but the sky remained dark with clouds. Just as Jackie got out of the car, a blast of sunlight streamed through a leak in the cloud cover and glinted off the gold-plated dome of the courthouse. Jackson was planning to visit the registrar of deeds when a big black Chrysler New Yorker took a sharp turn toward him, screeching into a parking slot, its tires bumping the curb. Tinny country music clattered out of the open windows. Jackie shaded his eyes with his palm and peered in at the driver of the car.

"Cecil?" Jackson said to his old cellmate. "What the hell are you doing here?"

Cecil Blanks cut the engine and poked his head out the driver's side window. The country music played on as Cecil yelled over it. "My main man Jackie. I knew you were heading back this way, right into a world of trouble. I'm here to cover your back, man. It's the code of cons."

Jackson arched an eyebrow. He wasn't sure he wanted to be bound by the convict's code. "Well, that's awfully touching, but I really don't need any help."

"Bullshit, buddy. I know what you're getting yourself into, even if you don't. Ghost Grant, Jake Marston…"

Jackson strode up to the window and held up a hand. "Keep it down. Those aren't the kind of names you want to be tossing out around here."

"My point exactly," he said.

Jackson peered inside the huge New Yorker. He could smell the stench of stale cigarette smoke, sour beer, and Cecil's Aqua Velva cologne. Four empty beer cans were crumpled on the passenger side floor. The ashtray mushroomed with cigarette butts and discarded globs of gum. Above the ashtray, a useless air freshener – a bikini-clad redhead straddling the hood of a GTO – dangled down from the rearview mirror. There was a mass of free wires poking out a hole where the car radio once lived. On the car seat beside Cecil sat a cheap boombox with a clutter of tapes next to it. One of the cassettes, labeled "The Women of Country," had brown tape bunched out of it like a Christmas bow.

"Can you turn that damn thing off?" Jackson said, jabbing a thumb at the boombox.

Cecil punched the top of the tape player and the music died.

Jackson's eyes wandered to the black woman who was passed out in the back seat of Cecil's car. Her red miniskirt was hiked halfway up her butt, and her long legs were bent at the knees, the black high-heels resting on the back door handle. The left side of her face was stuck to the black leather of the seat, and purple eye shadow drained down her cheek.

"Who's your date?" Jackson asked.

"Oh, her," Cecil said, as if just remembering that he had a passenger in the car. "I stopped by a strip club in Atlanta last night. The Back Room. You ought to go there, man. It's a hot joint."

Jackson looked back at the woman. "I'll mark it on my calendar," he said.

"I think I met The One, Jackie. Girl by the name of Starry. She dug me, man. Sat on my lap all night long, didn't even bother to put her shirt back on between songs. I asked her out to dinner and she took down my number."

Jackson nodded doubtfully. "Make sure you invite me to the wedding."

Cecil smiled broadly. "You'll be the Best Man, partner." It never failed to amaze Jackson how sarcasm utterly escaped Cecil. The little man took a box of Camel cigarettes from the dashboard, and offered Jackson one. Jackson shook his head before Cecil stuck the box to his mouth and drew a cigarette out with his lips. He lit the smoke with a silver Zippo lighter. His silk shirt, as black as the car's interior, was unbuttoned below his chest, exposing a tuft of scraggly hair. His dark hair was slicked back from a round baby face. Cecil was still a juvenile delinquent at heart. He wanted Jackie to call him "Cecil the Shark," claiming it was the name they gave him in prison. He was thirty-six years old, five-foot-six, and pudgy, like a doughboy. Jackie's boxing coach behind bars, a bear of a man named Clarence, once told Jackie that he had a nagging urge to poke Cecil's tummy and make him giggle. Jackson had laughed but Clarence held a stern gaze, as if disturbed by the notion.

The woman in the back seat squirmed and moaned, her black heels banging against the back window.

"Look out back there," Cecil said. "You're gonna scuff up the windows."

"What the…?" The woman groaned as she sat up in the seat. "Where the hell am I?"

"Solomon's Rock, Georgia," Cecil reported like a tour guide proudly announcing a historic sight. "Cradle of the redneck South."

"Who the fuck are you?" the stripper demanded.

"The name's Cecil Blanks."

"Who the…? What am I doing in your fucking car?"

"You were passed out on the curb at the club. I figured I'd save you from wandering serial killers."

"She'd probably be better off with the killers," Jackson put in.

"And you brought me to Solomon's Rock? What's wrong with you? I live three blocks from the Back Room."

"Don't sweat it, Missy," Cecil told her. "I'll be heading back up there in a couple of days...."

"A couple of days? What the hell am I supposed to do until then?"

Cecil smiled. "We'll think of something, darlin'."

The black stripper let loose a warrior cry and clawed at Cecil, her long fingernails reaching up from behind and scratching four red lines on either side of his neck. Cecil screamed and drew away, putting his hands up to the bloody marks. The girl took another swipe at Cecil as he cowered away. Jackson opened up the back car door and wrapped a hand around the girl's upper arm.

"I'll take you to the bus depot," Jackson said, "and give you the fare home. How's that?"

She glared at Cecil, but let Jackson help her out of the car.

"C'mon now," Cecil said. "Least you can do is take off your top."

"Excuse me?"

"I'll drive you to the depot," Cecil offered. "You can sit up here in front, take off your clothes, and I'll stick some bills down your panties."

She took another swing at Cecil through the driver's side window, but Cecil pulled back and laughed. "You're a frisky one."

"Goddamn it, Cecil," Jackson said. "If you're going to hang out with me, you've got to learn some restraint."

"I got restraint," Cecil claimed. "I just needed to release some sexual tension. You know what I mean? It's been a long time. I don't go for none of that homo prison shit."

It was then that Jackson looked up and saw Sheriff Bailey Sump standing on the sidewalk. He stood six-four, two-sixty in his pressed uniform. The sun glared from the sheriff's star pinned to his tan shirt. A shiny stripe ran down his black slacks. The usual implements hung from his belt: handcuffs, service revolver, and a polished billy club. His arms bulged from the short-sleeved shirt. He was surveying the scene, his steel blue eyes glaring with distaste from beneath the rim of his trooper's hat.

Bailey had played right offensive guard and defensive end for the Solomon's Rock Spartans, the only player in the history of the high school to make all-state at two different positions. He was the hero of a team that won an unlikely state championship. Bailey made the game-saving tackle at the two-yard line, leveling the Valdosta fullback as he lunged for the goal line in the final seconds. The team carried Bailey off the field.

Bailey played a year for the University of Georgia before blowing out his left knee. He still favored the knee, and a pouch now poked over his belt, but every year he was invited to the Spartan homecoming game, where he was always saluted at the fifty-yard line with a reverent ovation.

"I heard you were back in town," the sheriff said to Jackson.

Jackson nodded. "Bailey," he said cordially. "I was just taking this lady to the bus depot."

The sheriff nodded. He liked Jackson. They had been friends in high school and ran in some of the same circles, Bailey as the son of a sheriff – one of the most powerful men in Solomon's Rock – and Jackie as the son of a distinguished lawyer. Bailey had hoped they would meet up again under better circumstances. He stepped down from the curb and moved up next to Cecil's car window. He stared into the car.

"You takin' this lowlife to the depot with you, too?" he asked Jackson, pointing a thumb at Cecil.

"I'm just here to visit with my buddy Jackie for a while," Cecil said.

"So you're a con, too?" the sheriff asked.

"Ex-con," said Cecil.

"Whatever," grumbled Bailey. He pushed his hat back on his head and bent over to look around in the car. "You going for a record here? See how many parole violations you can break on one sitting?"

"Nah," Cecil said. "I ain't goin' for no records."

The sheriff eyed him wryly. "We got laws here," he pointed out.

"Well, hell, I know that," Cecil said.

"We don't allow loud music in the square, nor open beer cans in an operational vehicle."

"I picked them cans up off the highway," Cecil said. "Doing my civic duty, you might say."

"Uh huh," the sheriff grunted. "Most important of all," he went on, "we keep our hookers out of sight."

"I'm not a hooker," the woman objected. "I'm a dancer."

Bailey looked up at her for a moment. "Whatever," he said before turning his eyes back to Cecil. "I would run you off to jail right now if I didn't have more important things to do than take out the trash."

"Hey!" Cecil said before Bailey lifted his index finger to quiet him down. "You keep it clean in this town. I only give one warning."

Bailey looked over the car again, then moved out of the window and over to Jackson.

"I'm sorry about this, Bailey. I had no idea...."

Bailey put up a hand, waving it off. "Listen, Jackie. My father wants to meet with you. I guess he wants to talk over a few things."

"The commissioner?" Jackson said, unable to hide the anxiety in his voice.

"No big deal. He just wants to chat. Why don't you stop by his office later, after you've taken care of the girl here?"

"Okay," he said tentatively.

The sheriff nodded, said, "Good to see you, Jackie," as if embarrassed to admit it, then walked toward the courthouse. He stepped up on the curb before turning back around. "You make sure she gets on that bus," he said. He put a finger to his hat and bowed slightly before moving off, his southern manners refusing to lapse even in present company.

"I resent his implications," the stripper said, cocking her chin up with pride.

Jackson just shook his head. "That was a great way to meet up with my old friend the sheriff."

Cecil started up the New Yorker. "I'm going to check in to the General Lee," he said. "I want to get washed up and settled in. I'll see you later, Jackie."

"Thanks for the warning," Jackie said under his breath as he took the stripper by the arm and led her toward his car.

"Wash off that smelly cologne while you're at it," the stripper yelled at the car. "That's some nasty shit you got on."

"Hey, Missy," he called back, "maybe I'm trying to attract a different class of lady."

She tried to go at Cecil again, but Jackie held her back. "Ignore him," he said. "The guy can't help himself."

At the Solomon's Rock terminal, Jackie gave the stripper her bus ticket back to Atlanta and waited for the departure with her. The terminal was dark and cool, with high-backed benches and a marble floor. Bus terminals, train depots – they always transported Jackie back to some distant era when the world moved to a slower beat. Even the smells seemed ancient, like the pages of an antique book. Sunlight slanted through the cathedral-style windows, shifting through wisps of dust that drifted down and settled on the curved wooden bench where the two sat patiently. The dancer had washed her ruined makeup off in the bathroom when they arrived, and now she pulled out a compact and applied eye shadow and lipstick while peering into the small round mirror. Jackie watched her with unusual contentment until they announced her departure.

"Sorry for the trouble," Jackson said.

The stripper shrugged. "Guess a girl deserves what she gets, passing out on the curb in back of a strip joint."

"Yeah well. Just stay out of strange cars next time."

The girl put a hand on Jackson's cheek. "You a nice man. A fine-lookin' man. You way too fine to be hanging out with that loser Cecil. You look like you should be a doctor or a lawyer or something."

"My brother's the lawyer," Jackson said.

She smiled. "You ever come back to the club, you ask for Lady Blue, you hear me?" Then, as she turned to go, she added, "But *you*, you can call me Sandy."

Jackson nodded to her, bowing his head slightly. She had taken half a dozen awkward strides on her black stilettos before Jackson called to her. "Sandy," he said, and she turned back around. "You take care of yourself now."

She felt moved by the concern in the sad eyes. "You, too," she said before spinning away with a final glance over her shoulder.

Only then did Jackie realize that he needed to heed the advice more than she did.

Jackie was in the bathroom of the bus station, splashing his face, when a big black man with sunglasses and a felt hat came in. His large purple nose drew in currents of air in long, slow pulls. He wore brown trousers, a vest with thin purple stripes, and a suit coat that fit too snugly. He took off his hat and sat it on the radiator next to a sink. "Gonna be another hot one," he said. He was looking in the mirror when Jackie reached up and grabbed the back of the man's head. He slammed the man's face against the mirror, shattering the glass. The man cried out as Jackson took him down on the floor.

The man was on his stomach against the tiles of the bathroom floor. Jackson growled at him. "You should take some lessons on following people. You really suck at it."

"What the fuck?" The man was wheezing as Jackson wrenched his head to the side.

"You can tell me why you're following me or I can break your neck," Jackson said.

The man reached out his right arm but it flailed helplessly in the air. "I'm with Marston," he said.

"Marston? Why the hell is Marston following me?"

"He's interested in this Grant fellow. That's all I know."

Jackie twisted the man's head until his back creaked.

"I swear I don't know nothin' else," the man said. "I just follow orders."

"Yeah, I know how that is. It's the same thing the guards at the concentration camps said — just following orders."

The man looked confused. "I don't know nothin' about no camps."

Jackie wanted to hit the man just for being stupid.

"Listen. You tell Marston I don't have anything to do with Grant. Nothing at all. You got that?"

"I got it."

"I don't know what he wants with me anyway. I've been out of this town for twenty years. There's nothing I can do for him."

The man tried to shrug. "I don't know shit, man. I'm telling you...."

Jackson stared down at the man for a few moments, then reluctantly let him up.

"Motherfucker," the man barked as he pulled a knife from his coat pocket. He snapped out the blade, took a wide swing at Jackson. Jackie jumped back as the blade swished by. He stepped inside of the second swing, digging his shoulder into the crook of the man's arm so the knife couldn't get to him.

Jackie brought a knee up into the man's gut, then swung his left elbow around in a tight arc, blasting the man in his right temple. The man staggered back as Jackie came across with his other elbow, busting open the man's lip. The man fell against the bathroom stall.

Jackson moved in, placing a hand on either side of the stall doorway. He jerked his head forward, butting the man between the eyes. The man flew backward, his butt splashing down into the open toilet. Jackie picked him up out of the commode, spun him around and dunked his head into the water, pulled the head out, dunked it again, jerked it out, and leaned into his flooded ear. "You give Marston the message. Tell him to keep off my ass." He dunked the man's head one more time and left him lying in the stall. "Don't forget to flush," he said as he headed for the door.

A man in a black suit came into the bathroom as Jackie was heading out. The man looked down at the legs that were sprawled from under the stall door.

"Must've had a rough night," Jackson said as he passed by.

4

The first unpleasant thing Ellis Moon experienced when he walked into the prison meeting room was the bright lights that stung his eyes and made him squint. The second unpleasant thing was the sight of Michael "Ghost" Grant in his blue prison uniform and close-cropped hair, eyes darting about as if looking for a way out of a trap. The guard led Moon in, then walked back out, locking the door behind him. The guard stationed himself outside the room, peering in through a small square window. As attorney and client, the two men were guaranteed a private consultation.

In the center of the room was a metal table. Moon placed a notepad on it, next to an ashtray. Moon tried to push away the sour look on his face as he sat down at the table across from Grant. The prisoner had a small goatee and sideburns. His hair was so short that he looked bald from a distance. Up close, Moon could see the hairs sticking up like pins jabbed into Grant's head. Ellis Moon couldn't keep from imagining that he was the one slowly sticking pins into Grant's scalp. Every time he saw Grant, he tasted bile at the edges of his tongue. He heard a little voice telling him it was time to get out of this racket.

The most disturbing thing about Michael Grant was the way his eyes were constantly jumping and darting. Moon wondered what the hell the man was looking at. It was a small room, gray, with no redeeming features. And yet the eyes moved constantly, taking in the upper corners of the ceiling, the blank wall, the gray door. Moon found himself following the man's line of sight, expecting to see something there. Sometimes he would even jump and spin around when Grant's eyes would flare open in apparent surprise. Moon would jerk around to stare only at the wall behind him, a rush of adrenaline singeing his nerves.

"Whatcha got for me?" Grant blurted. The words came out fast, staccato. "Show me whatcha got."

The voice jolted Moon out of his reverie. As much as Ellis dealt with Grant, he was still unsettled by the man's frenetic bursts. After a session with Grant, he felt totally burnt out, wired from bursts of fight-or-flight juices. "Well, we've lined up some excellent experts on the definition of pornography and on the statutes regarding pornography law. We're going after this damn community test. By its very nature, it's an arbitrary standard...."

"Fuck that," Grant barked. Law arguments bored him. He had no patience when Moon tried to explain the subtleties of his defense. "What about Farmer? Farmer and that other fuck – the cop."

Moon could only sigh. "We're working on it. We need some time."

"I ain't got no time, goddamn it!" Grant seethed in his chair. Moon watched the eyes settle down, only to stare out into empty space. "Farmer is yours, Moon. Your responsibility." The eyes flicked onto Moon then darted off.

Moon nodded slowly. Farmer. Grant's aide who had turned state's witness. "It's not that easy, Ghost. They move him around...."

Grant's hand slammed the table in front of him. The crack echoed off the walls. The guard peered in with a wary eye. Grant flashed a stare at the guard, then returned a stern look to Moon. They were killer's eyes, empty and hard.

Grant leaned into Moon. "You too soft, Moon?" he whispered.

"Can't handle the job? You run my business, you got to take care of business. You hear what I'm saying?"

Moon shifted in his chair and looked down at his notepad on the table. "We'll get to him."

Grant reared back in the chair. The eyes started moving again. "You get to him, goddamn it. Nobody fucks with me. That's the message. That's the fucking message. Farmer has to pay. You get me out of here, and I'll kill him with my own bare hands, the cocksucker."

Good idea, thought Moon. He'd get Grant clean of the pornography rap just long enough to prepare for his murder trial. "We'll get to him. That's all I can tell you. We'll get to him."

"Get Cracks on it," Grant ordered. "He'll take care of it for you."

Moon nodded. "Okay. I'll talk to him."

"And the cop?" Grant blurted, his mind darting as quickly as the eyes.

"We're working on the detective. We may have some dirt on him."

"Fuck the dirt," Grant demanded. "Kill the bastard."

Moon looked over at the guard in the window, then back at Grant. The eyes met him straight on. "We don't need to kill anybody. We can get you out of this thing. We just need to keep calm, follow the strategy. We'll get you out of here."

Grant burst out of the chair and started pacing beside the table. He could take no more than six or seven steps before turning around and pacing back again. He pulled out a cigarette and lit it. Moon took a deep breath. Grant was never interested in the legal strategy, the motions, the research, the prospects. He just wanted to shut people up. In a way, Grant made the defense very simple: Just kill everybody.

"There's another matter," Grant said. He blew out torrents of blue smoke and watched it collect against the ceiling. "There's this little shit in here – name of Creeks – I think he's got some Indian in him or something. I guess he's some big badass behind bars. He's been fucking with me. Nobody fucks with me, Moon."

"Jesus," Moon whispered. "You want us to take out somebody in here?"

"He's getting out. That's what I'm telling you. End of the week sometime. He's been all high and mighty about it."

"So he won't be bothering you anymore." Moon knew it was a hopeless gesture.

"You're goddamn right, he won't be bothering me. Him or no other fuck around here," Grant scoffed. "I want him to go down hard. I want the message to get all the way back in here. Loud and fucking clear. You got me? Nobody fucks with me, not on the outside, not on the inside, no-fucking-where. You understand me, Moon?"

There was no use in arguing about it. "Sure, Ghost. I got it."

5

Cecil watched the waitress from the phone booth outside the diner. Few things better in life, he was thinking, than a small-town waitress with nice legs, wearing a short black skirt and a white blouse you could see her bra through.

"Yeah," Cecil said when the phone was answered. "This is Cecil."

"What do you have for me, Mr. Blanks?"

"Nothing really. Not yet. I'm working on it, though. I'll be on the inside of this gig before you know it, I can sure tell you that. Nothing to it."

"You should only call for a good reason, Mr. Blanks. Where's your friend?"

"My friend? Oh, you mean Jackie. He had an errand to run. I'm at a pay phone."

"You shouldn't be taking these chances. It isn't wise. A man will get in contact with you."

Cecil didn't like the sound of that. "Well, you see, the thing is, I need some more cash."

Another silence. Cecil waited this time. "You certainly went through your allowance quickly. I am not financing some kind of freedom celebration here. The good times must be rolling for you."

Allowance. Like he was some kind of little kid with his hand out. "It's not like that. Not like that at all. It's just that I need to spend some money on the guy, get in his good graces you might say. Loosen him up a little. Get him talkin'. Hell, I ain't even seen him since we were inside. I got to get him to trust me."

"Get him to trust you more cheaply, Mr. Blanks."

"Yeah, okay. I'll take it easy this time."

"A man will be in touch. He'll have some money. Don't do anything stupid. I don't want you robbing some family grocer. You hold out until my man gets to you."

"Okay," said Cecil. "I got it. I'll keep an eye out for him."

"No. You keep a low profile. My man will find you. Don't raise suspicions."

"Nah, man. You don't have to worry about me. I'm smooth as a cucumber. I've done this kind of shit before."

"Yes I know. I've seen your record."

"My record?" Cecil said. "What are you talking about?"

"Don't call me, Mr. Blanks...."

"Yeah, okay. I've got a room at the General Lee. You can call me there."

"Make sure only you answer the phone."

"Why's that?"

"What if your friend Jackson was at the hotel with you? It wouldn't do for him to pick up the line, now would it?"

"Right," said Cecil. "I didn't think about that. Maybe we should have a secret signal, you know what I'm saying? Let it ring twice, hang up, then call right back."

"Just answer the phone at your hotel room. It's a simple request."

"Hey, I'm just trying to cover the bases."

"Don't you think that if someone else were in the room, they might find a secret ring suspicious?"

"Yeah," Cecil admitted. "I guess you're right."

"I know it's a strain for you, but let's try to think these things through."

Cecil rubbed his chin. "What's your point?"

The voice paused in exasperation. "Goodbye, Mr. Blanks. Don't call here again."

"Yeah, yeah. I got it. And about that 'Mr. Blanks' shit?"

"Yes?"

"My friends, they call me Shark. Cecil the Shark."

More silence. "Don't disappoint me, Mr. Blanks. I don't like to be disappointed." The voice was still calm, but the message had been delivered. The line went dead.

Cecil walked down an alley between the C&S Bank and a building marked *Dade and Sanders, Accountants*. He chose the back entrance, so he could enter Thomas Dade's office without passing any other doors. He mounted a single flight of wooden steps, turned to his right, and stepped through a door that was ajar. He eased the door shut behind him.

Thomas Dade looked up from his desk and wrinkled his brow at the sight of Cecil Blanks. A shelf of dirty blonde bangs poked over Dade's receding hairline. He wore designer eyeglasses, an expensive gray suit, and a slate blue tie. A personal computer sat on a small table that was angled in the far left corner; to the right of the desk sat a high-backed brown leather chair, faced toward the door. Dade's desk was uncluttered except for a single folder opened in front of the accountant, a black phone with a keypad and two rows of call buttons, three stacked trays marked "in," "pending," and "out," and a single rose in a thin porcelain vase next to a wooden humidor.

"Hi Tommy," Cecil said with a broad smile.

"Do I know you?" the accountant asked.

"You know the man I represent," Cecil told him.

"Oh?" Dade said, leaning back in the plush desk chair. "And who would that be?"

"His name is Mr. Marston. Jacob Marston?"

Dade's eyes froze. He placed a single piece of typewriter paper back in the folder on his desk and closed the file. He rose up unsteadily, crossed the room, and opened his door just enough to peer out into the hallway.

"I took the back entrance," Cecil said. "No one saw me."

Dade closed the door and locked it. He walked back behind the desk and lowered a set of beige blinds. He twirled on a cord and clicked the blinds closed. The room darkened. Dade then flipped a light switch and surveyed the black-clad man in his office. Cecil smiled at him again, exposing two crooked front teeth.

"What do you want?" Dade whispered.

"It's not what I want, Tommy. It's what my boss wants."

"And what is that?"

Cecil sauntered over to the blinds and peeked through them. "Mr. Marston has decided to call in his marker."

Dade's mouth fell open. He looked across his desk as if looking for a pile of cash. "I … He can't.… I don't know what you're talking about."

"Wrong answer, Tommy. Look, it ain't my concern how you got into this mess. Drugs, girls, fancy cars. I understand how it goes. But now it's time to pay the piper."

"It wasn't anything like that," Dade protested. "I made a bad investment. There was no one else to turn to.…"

"Bad investment." Cecil giggled. "I made a bad investment in Vegas a coupla times."

"Look. I don't have the funds right now. Mr. Marston knows…"

"Mr. Marston," Cecil stated, cutting the accountant off, "doesn't expect you to pay from your own pocket."

"I don't understand…," Dade began, then his eyes looked up at Cecil. "Oh no. You can't expect me to steal from Grant."

"Why not? You're his accountant. It ain't like you haven't done it before. That's how you got into the mess in the first place."

"Yes, but Grant's strapped for cash right now. His legal bills…"

"That's the beauty," Cecil said. "Marston has some good information that Grant is about to go to the laundry. He needs cash for his legal troubles, and he's ready to make a big transfer through TOI." Cecil took a slip of paper from his front shirt pocket and approached the desk. He unfolded the paper and laid it out on the desk surface, pushing it over so that the accountant could have a good look. "Here's an offshore account number where you will transfer the funds. Mr. Marston is a very generous man. He's giving you 10 percent. He figures that'll make a million or so for you. All you got to do is find a nice island to retire to."

"That's absurd. You want me to steal ten million dollars? Grant will have me killed."

Cecil smiled at the thought. "First of all, Grant would kill you if he found out you stole a five spot. Might as well make it worth your while. Second of all, if you don't do it, if you try to run, I'll personally tell Grant about your past indiscretions. Grant will have a pistol pointed at your belly, Marston will have one aimed at your head. It will just be a question of who can pull the trigger faster."

Dade's shoulders collapsed. He put three fingers to his temple. Cecil wondered if he would start sobbing.

"Jesus, Dade, what did you think?" Cecil said. "You steal from Michael Grant, lose the money, then borrow it back from Jake Marston. You thought you'd just skip away home?"

"I thought...," Dade said as he tried to form an explanation. "I thought I could pay it back. I thought...."

"You thought, you thought," Cecil waved his hand in the air. "Hey, I thought I'd be a major porn star by now. You take what I think, what you think, and a throat full of phlegm, and you got yourself a hock wad on the sidewalk. You know what I'm saying?"

Dade looked over at Cecil as if he were a wild mongrel let loose in his office. Irritation flushed redness into the whites of Cecil's eyes. The smile was gone. He walked in front of the desk, directly across from Dade, put his flat palms on the oak surface and leaned over into the accountant's face.

"What I'm saying," Cecil said, enunciating each word, "is that it don't matter what you think. I'm just the messenger. What matters is that we come to an understanding. I need to tell Mr. Marston that we have an agreement here."

"You don't understand. I can't…"

Cecil slapped the desk with both palms and leaned in closer to the accountant. Dade could smell the cigarette smoke in Cecil's clothes and the beer stench in his breath. The smell of cheap cologne was so strong that Dade almost gagged on it. "This quiz ain't multiple choice, Tommy-boy. You keep your eyes on those accounts. When the money rolls in, you roll it over." Cecil tapped on the slip of paper with the account number on it. "Right into this here account. End of discussion. I will tell Mr. Marston that the message has been delivered."

Cecil leaned back. He took two steps to the corner of the desk, opened the humidor, and withdrew three cigars. He smiled as he lifted the cigars up and waved them at Dade. He smelled one deeply and sighed.

"You have yourself a fine afternoon," Cecil said pleasantly, then he turned toward the door, stuffing the cigars in the pocket of his shirt.

6

Jackson sat at a back table of the Tin Roof Diner, twirling his coffee cup in slow circles, dreading the meeting he had to keep with Commissioner William Sump. His back to the front door, he looked out the window at the drizzling rain that had blown in from the east. It spat and slackened, gathered and swirled like light snow in a strong wind. The rain shimmered off the metal roof of the diner and sluiced down the roof in rivulets, pouring in even streams above the window. Behind the diner, a rusted railroad track cut through a kudzu-draped dale and bent off to the right, under an old suspension bridge that had been closed to automobile traffic. Beyond the tracks, a group of teenagers huddled together in the side parking lot of Sal's Quickie Mart, smoking cigarettes and laughing. Two girls stood beneath the market awning, sheltered from the downpour, while the boys stood in the rain as if impervious to weather.

A van pulled into the store's front parking lot. An old woman got out of the driver's seat and opened a red umbrella. She tightened the bonnet beneath her chin and walked to the other side of the van. She slid open the side door and pulled out an aluminum walker, placing it carefully by the passenger's door. She then pulled a step stool out of the van and held out a hand to an old man in the back seat. The old man's eyes flared open at the prospect of dismounting the van. He leaned heavily on the woman as he brought his foot down to the step stool, wavering his shoe in the air for a moment, inches above the stool, like a man with vertigo searching for the top rung of a ladder. He gripped the walker tightly, and his whole body trembled. His mouth hung open and his vacant eyes stared out into open space. He slid the walker forward a couple of inches, shuffled his feet up to it, then shoved it ahead again. The woman watched him patiently, taking a slow step each time he moved forward, keeping the umbrella above them both.

Jackie was so lost in his memory that he had not noticed Cecil come into the diner. He slid into a chair across from Jackson and watched him for a moment.

"I never knew kudzu was so goddamn interesting," Cecil said.

Jackson spun around slowly and stopped cold. Behind Cecil, a woman entered the diner. Bridgett Baines came in and eased the door shut behind her. She leaned against the panel, her hands bent behind her, still clasping the cool brass knob, her eyes set on Jackson. She smiled slightly before approaching the table. It was a pure vision to Jackie. Bridgett's blonde hair, wet from the rain, hung to her breast. She had a small nose, bright green eyes, and soft subtle lips. Her spirit and kindness shrouded her like a halo. She wore a short black skirt and a white blouse. Her fingers innocently toyed with the button clasped between her breasts.

"Bridgett," said Jackie, rising up out of his chair. "It's good to see you." He came around the table and kissed her cheek, then pulled out a chair for her. She sat down and he went back to the seat next to her.

Jackson watched her for a long moment as she settled in and ordered a cup of coffee. Bridgett Baines was beautiful and smart. She had gone to work for Thomas Dade, the accountant in town, because it was one of the few firms that could use her expertise. Dade was the numbers whiz, Bridgett a genius with computers. The biggest firms in Atlanta had actively recruited her out of Emory University, and she still got calls from headhunters a few times a month, but she wanted to keep her home in Solomon's Rock. It occurred to Jackie, as his old girlfriend pushed a long strand of hair away from her face – completely oblivious of her amazing sensuality – that he could sit there and watch her for hours.

"I've been out in the world for a while now," Jackson said, "but you're still the prettiest thing I've ever seen."

Bridgett looked up casually and smiled. "I'm not sure how flattered I am," she replied, "considering a good portion of that time you spent in jail."

"Some of those female guards are pretty damn hot," Cecil broke in. "Once you get past the mustache."

Jackie turned to Cecil and eyed him for a moment. "Bridgett," he said finally. "This is Cecil."

"A pleasure," she said.

"You have no idea."

"That's enough, Cecil," Jackson warned him.

Bridgett turned back to Jackson and smiled. "If I'm so damn pretty, why'd you run away from me?"

"It was never you I was running from," Jackson said.

Bridgett studied the sadness creeping into his eyes. The enigma always surprised her. Jackson Moon was a man who could take care of himself. Tall, rugged, square-jawed, a sly smile. But a single one of his little-boy looks made you want to fold him in your arms, mother him, let him know everything would be okay. Bridgett found herself wondering if Jackson was ready for someone to care for him, but she quickly realized that there were things he had to resolve first, things he had to do on his own.

"You okay?" Bridgett asked.

He smiled weakly and the eyes started to clear. "Yeah. It's just strange, you know, coming back here."

"How's your Aunt Frank?"

"She's hanging in there. I'm going out to see her later."

"Must be hard on her, losing her land. It happened to my father, you know."

"Yeah, I know," he said, the eyes softening in sympathy. "Eminent domain. It's a hard thing to explain, how a town can buy off your land in the public's interest, whether you want to sell it or not."

"Especially when the public interest is a Civil War theme park, of all things."

Jackie shook his head. "A Civil War theme park financed by a pornographer. Go figure."

"I guess I can't be complaining. In an indirect way, I work for the guy. Not much call for a woman with a background in computer finance around here."

"You do what you have to do."

"I suppose," Bridgett said, not really believing it.

"My brother Ellis wrote me in prison about Frank's house and land. He set it up for some movers to take the whole house – lock, stock, and barrel – over to Maple Street. He figured it would be less stressful for her. Problem is, she keeps thinking they already moved the house without telling her. I guess they've picked her up wandering around town, asking folks where they hid her house."

"I don't know what it is about land and my father's generation. It's something mystical. My father ended up in a nice little house with a beautiful yard. What did he need with ninety acres of forest anyway? But after they took his land away, it was as if they ripped his heart out of his chest. He was never the same. He died less than three months after the move."

A silence fell as they listened to the rain patter off the tin roof. The silence seemed to hold regret within it. It was a silence full of lost time. Bridgett reached across the table and cupped Jackie's right cheek in her hand. "I have to get back to work. I just wanted to say hi."

"You're gorgeous" was Jackson's reply. His words were draped in amazement.

"You sound surprised."

"I mean you're even more gorgeous than ever."

She smiled. "I was just a kid when you left."

"And you certainly grew out of it."

"Jesus, Jackson. It's only me."

"Indeed it is. But 'only' is not the word I'd use."

Bridgett laughed. Her spirit glowed from the disarming smile. "Flattery will get you nowhere. It's going to take some industrial-strength groveling to win back my favor."

"I could crawl under the table," Jackie suggested, "and kiss your feet."

She granted him a little moan. "That sounds pretty intriguing."

"Hey," Cecil broke in, tired of being left out of the conversation, "you get one foot and I'll take the other."

Bridgett and Jackson both stared at Cecil until he shrugged.

"Unfortunately," Bridgett said, obviously losing interest in having her feet kissed, "I don't have the time. I've got to get back."

Jackson rose up as Bridgett did. She started to leave but then looked back over her shoulder. "How about a drink later?" Bridgett asked.

"I'm at your service. You know a place?"

"There's a little club I know of. The clientele is a bit suspect, but they play some great blues there."

"Crawdaddy's," Jackson said.

"It'll be just like old times," said Bridgett.

"I can only dream."

Bridgett smiled again, her face lighting up. "I'll pick you up around eight?"

"I'll be counting the seconds."

"Just don't run off anywhere before then." Bridgett knew she had made a mistake when she saw Jackie's eyes darken. She took in the sudden rush of Jackie's regret and, at the same time, recalled what the man could do to her heart. She studied the heavy black eyebrows that arched gracefully on his forehead and dipped just below the corner of each eye, the hard jaw and full lips, the intoxicating depth of his emotion. To conjure a smile to Jackson's lips, to turn him playful and alive – it seemed like a special gift to be afforded the honor. She placed three fingers on Jackie's left cheek and coaxed his gaze up to her.

"It's okay, Jackie," she told him. "You're home now."

The corners of his lips turned slightly upward, as if granting his mouth something it didn't deserve. "And I'm not going anywhere," he said firmly. "Not this time around." The voice turned dreamy and the wispy sensation of lost time fell again.

The yellow blouse. It was just like the one Jackson remembered from the night they had lain together in the grass beside a still pond in early August. They were in their junior year of high school, two months before the fire at Bosco's bar. He had brought her to this place. There was no moon out and the sky was clear, so the night grew black and the stars blazed above them.

Jackie put his head back in the grass and looked at the galaxies above him. Nothing seemed to matter now. He was alone in the woods with Bridgett Baines, both of them lying down in the grass, staring up at millions of stars. They were still for a few moments. Jackie reached his hand over, grasping for some part of her, but she grabbed the hand and put it on his own thigh.

"I thought you said something was going to happen," she said and, after Jackson laughed, added: "I mean something unusual. More than a teenage boy getting horny."

Jackie felt hurt and rejected for a moment, but he shrugged it off. The night passed slowly. He felt her body next to his, inches away. He could hear her breath, smell her skin. He groaned.

"Hush now," she snapped playfully. "You said we were supposed to concentrate on the stars."

"On the heavenly bodies you mean?" Jackie said. "That's what I'm trying..."

And that's when they saw it. A streak of light blazed across the sky.

It burned a bright white and arced across the dome of night. It made Bridgett gasp. The milky trail behind the shooting star faded away.

"You saw it?" Jackie asked.

"I've never seen a shooting star before," Bridgett admitted.

"It's a meteor, really," Jackson pointed out. "It's not a star at all."

Bridgett started to speak but another light flashed, this time in the western part of the sky. It passed so fast that Bridgett wasn't sure she really saw it. In her peripheral vision, she saw Jackie pointing, and she tilted her head in time to see another orb of light, as bright as any star in the heavens, falling more slowly this time. Down toward the rim of earth, it dropped like a flare, leaving behind it a long streak of gray.

"My god," said Bridgett. "How long have you known about this?" It was as if he were awakening her to some secret revelation of the universe. This magical place where the stars fell out of the sky.

Jackson laughed. "A couple of weeks. You didn't read about it?"

"About this spot?" she asked.

Jackie laughed again and nudged her. "Not the spot, Bridgett. It's a meteor shower. You can see it every year around this time, but it's really spectacular this year because there's no moon out. You can see the meteors a lot better."

Another meteor streaked across the night sky. And another. Flash, flash, and gone. By the time Jackie pointed, it was over.

For a long moment, there was only the sky, awash with stars. Quiet. Then another bright light flared and streaked, and both of them gasped. More moments passed. Jackie now savored even the times between meteors, when both of them waited in anticipation, gazing at the same sky, sharing the same moment. Another slow one fell off to their right and they both turned their heads to see it. Jackie studied Bridgett's profile as she looked back up. Then she turned to him and smiled. She took his hand in hers. Bridgett looked back up just as two meteors flared up and crossed paths.

"Incredible," she whispered. The night seemed to grow blacker, the stars brighter, and the blaze of meteors more dazzling. There was only the night and the stars and the brilliant show of light and the boy on the ground next to her.

Jackson looked back up at the sky and felt the softness of Bridgett's hand in his own. He saw another meteor flash directly above. He wondered how many wishes he would get on a night like this and how many would come true.

Jackie heard Bridgett rise up from the ground and walk over to the pond's edge. When he got up and walked over to her, she was watching the stars reflected in the pond. It was another breathtaking sight to Jackie, stars now above and below them, the meteors falling in symmetry together, one in the heavens, the other a streaking arc of light painted on the pond's surface. Neither of them talked. They just watched the glittering of light in sky and in water.

It was a hot night. The breezes had stilled. They heard a lone dog howling in the distance but not much else.

She smiled, looked out across the pond. "Go for a swim?" she asked, and before Jackie could answer, he saw her in the pond's reflection, wiggling out of her jeans. When he turned to take Bridgett in, she dove from the pond's edge and disappeared, with the slightest splash, beneath the black water. She popped back up, half way out into the pond, her yellow blouse clinging to her skin. Jackson looked down at her jeans on the ground and noticed her underwear lying there with it.

It took a split second for Jackie to react. He tugged at his own shirt, caught it for a moment on his head, and jerked it frantically up, ripping one sleeve. He peeled one pant leg off but was too frantic to gracefully remove the other leg. He hopped about at the pond's edge until finally losing his balance and splashing sideways into the water. In the pond, he finally got his pants off, and then his underwear, and threw them up on the shore. He looked for Bridgett in the water. She was on the other side of the pond now, her head just breaking the surface.

"The idea was not to get our clothes wet," she told him.

"Oh," Jackie said. Of course, he had other ideas entirely.

Jackie tried to calm his heart and began to knead the water slowly, working his way out into the middle of the pond. Bridgett stroked her arms below the water's surface, her eyes peering out like a water snake's. She moved effortlessly, arcing a wide circle around the boy in the water.

Jackie made broad circles with his arms, treading the water in the middle of the pond. The occasional slosh of his arms breaking the surface made a crisp, sensuous sound. Jackie watched as Bridgett circled around him, slowly closing in.

Jackie could now hear Bridgett's breath on the surface of the water. He kept his place in the center of the pond but rotated slowly to keep his eye on the beautiful girl who was encircling him. He saw only the top of her head: her eyes, her nose, her hair dipping down into the water. But even if she had exposed more, it was the eyes that had him captivated. The eyes studied him, considered him, enticed him, seduced him, but he kept his place in the center of her circle, being patient, savoring the moments as she closed in, feeling the water and the slow-moving currents that both of their bodies shared.

She came closer, circling, circling, the eyes considering. Jackie gazed into the eyes with a growing anticipation. Finally, Bridgett was so close that he could touch her with an outstretched arm, but his arms continued to stroke the water's surface. She was like a wild animal to him now. A sudden move, and she would be gone forever. He just watched her as she circled around him.

"Remember that night, Jackie, when I offered myself to you?"

"Oh yes," Jackie groaned.

"It was the sweetest, gentlest, most giving thing a boy has ever done for me."

Jackie didn't answer. For perhaps the hundredth time, he relived that night months before when Bridgett had taken her shirt off, the night he had frozen, the night he was unable to touch the perfect breasts of Bridgett Baines. It had not seemed sweet or gentle or giv-ing to him. Stupid, that's what it was. He had gotten his chance to fondle an angel's breasts, but he had stood as if handcuffed, unable to move.

"You knew I was vulnerable," Bridgett whispered. "You knew I wasn't fully giving myself to you. It wasn't pure, and you knew it. That touched me, Jackie. You touched me that night."

She kept her distance now, just over an arm's length away, circling, circling. As Jackson remembered it, he *hadn't* touched her that night.

"Tonight, Jackie. Tonight, I'm not vulnerable anymore. Tonight, I want you."

And then, her breasts, the perfect breasts erect beneath the blouse, brushed his chest below the water. He felt her hand slide across his skin, along his chest and down to his hip, and his eyes closed. His breath came in short gasps. Now she was moving slowly away from him, but her eyes were still on him, inviting him. Jackie reopened his eyes and was amazed that the vision of Bridgett was still there.

Jackson moved toward her now, cutting through the water an arm's length from the body that he desired more than anything on this earth. She led him closer to the water's edge, and when he could touch bottom, she moved into him, pressed the length of her body against his, and wrapped her arms around his neck, her ankles clasp-ing behind his waist. Her body was weightless to Jackie as he gently placed his hands on the small of her back. He felt her fingers running up through his hair, gently pulling his head toward her.

The first kiss was simply two sets of lips touching. Jackie felt his entire body tremble. She smiled, even laughed a little, and ran a fin-ger across his upper lip and around to the lower one. Then she placed her lips on his again and kissed him deeply. Jackie pulled her to him, pressing her breasts against his chest. Bridgett reached her hands up between their two bodies and slowly unbuttoned her blouse. Jackie's breath caught in his throat as she pulled the blouse apart and slid it down her arms. The blouse settled in the water, then drifted off toward the shore. The next kiss was long and hungry and probing. His tongue danced across hers and then she pulled his tongue deep into her mouth, sucking and kissing it. She bit his upper lip and groaned when he kissed her chin, her neck, the space between her breasts. She guided her left breast to his mouth but he pulled back, flitting his tongue across the hard nipple. Slowly, he carried her through the water, toward a dipped depression of shoreline, a scooped-out hollow of moist red clay.

He placed her there as he tasted the other breast, and she sat on the rise of red clay, in two inches of pond water. Bridgett cupped Jackie's head and brought his lips back up to hers. She had to rise up to him now, as he loomed above her, standing in water to his waist. His erection jutted out of the water and Jackie could feel it straining within the skin. He was so hard it hurt.

Bridgett was kissing his chest now, sucking on his nipples. His mouth fell open and he groaned as the tip of her tongue circled his belly button and touched the head of his penis. Jackie felt as if his desire might rip him open, but then she took him in her mouth and his longing dissolved in a rush of pure ecstasy. The dog's howl he heard in the distance could easily have been his own.

When Jackie could barely handle the pleasure any more, Bridgett took her mouth from him and fell back on the shelf of clay. She lay on a slight incline, her head on a tuft of grass, her body sloping down into the shallow water. Jackie stood above her, drinking in the sight of her luscious body oozing in the red clay. Droplets of water, silver in the starlight, shimmered on her breast. He touched a wet finger against her nipple and ran it down her ribs, over her tummy, and down into the water, across her inner thigh. Bridgett's eyes closed as his lips followed the path of his finger, kissing her breast, the curve of her body, the bone of her hip that rose out of the water. His finger moved slowly across her thigh and touched her gently. Bridgett squirmed in the clay and brought her feet up onto the scoop of shoreline, pushing her waist up out of the water. Jackie stroked her with his finger, kissing her breasts and her hips and her tummy, until she felt a rush of blood surge below her skin and her chest flushed red. A high-pitched moan rose from her mouth.

Jackie stood fully now and she rocked her hips against him at the water's edge. She held his hardness in her hand and gently guided it into her. Jackie reached down into the warm water, tucking his hands under her then running them up the back of her thighs until his hands pushed lightly up against the back of her knees, sliding her to the edge of the shelf where she pressed against his hardness. His eyes rolled up into his head as he moved slowly inside of her, then out of her slightly, then in again, and each time she took in more of him, until finally, with a thrust of her hips, she took the full length of him, and – with an unbearable explosion of pleasure – she felt him touch the deepest part of her.

They moved together as she lifted her arms over her head, palms up, and watched him rocking above her. He stood in the waist-deep water, eyes glazed as they savored the body that lay in the wet red clay. He arched his back and looked up into the heavens above him. And he swore that every single star fell out of the sky.

7

Jackie left the Tin Roof Diner through a back door, walked
down the kudzu-draped hill as the vines grabbed at his
ankles and pulled at his wrists, and came up into a slim alley on the
far side of the Dairy Joy. He pulled off his leather belt as he walked.

The Toyota was still there, backed into a parking slot across the
street from the diner. Jackson opened the car's rear door, slid in, and
had the belt around the driver's neck before he could turn all the way
around. The driver threw his hands up to his neck – too late – and
the coffee he was drinking splashed across the inside windshield,
dousing it creamy brown. Jackson pulled the belt taut just as the driver gasped in a breath. The driver's long ears flushed scarlet and his
ruddy complexion darkened.

Jackie leaned up into the man's ear. "You tell Marston that if I catch
any of his goons on my ass again, I'm going to stop being so gentle."

Jackson held on tight to the belt. A dry cackle rose out of the driver's throat.

"You got it?" Jackson asked.

The driver tried to grasp the belt around his neck, but Jackie
tugged it harder.

"Got it?"

The driver managed a nod. Jackson held the belt for a few more counts to emphasize the message. He let the driver feel the sensation of breathlessness. Then he loosened the grip on the belt but left it around the driver's neck. "That must've been your friend I left in the stall at the bus terminal," Jackie said matter-of-factly.

The driver wheezed. "Jesus Christ," he bellowed. "You put Jamaal in the damn hospital, man."

"Oh yeah? What was wrong with him?"

"What was wrong with him? You beat the crap out of him. Hell, as many times as you dunked him in the toilet, he probably needs a fucking enema."

"Not even an enema's gonna help you if you don't start talking."

"I don't know nothing. Keep an eye on you and the little guy. That's all I was told."

Jackson tightened the belt again. "Just give me something to go on. What does Marston have planned around here?"

"Goddamn it. I ain't got a clue. My guess is it has something to do with Grant."

Jackson had to laugh. He loosened the belt. "Well now, there's an insight. You guys. Jesus Christ. Does it actually say 'Goon' on your business card?"

"You want, I'll show it to you."

Jackie shook his head. "Doesn't it interest you? What you're in the middle of?"

"I just follow orders. The less I know the better."

"Well, let me clue you in. The C-4 is about to hit the fan around here, and you're gonna need a flak jacket to stay healthy. If I were you, I'd polish up the resume." Jackson was still shaking his head as he got out of the car.

8

Thick. Dense. Slow. His father had many words for it, but they all meant "stupid." Noxie wasn't so stupid that he didn't know what his father was talking about. Noxie realized he would never take over his father's businesses, the Ghost Grant empire. He didn't expect that. He had a problem with numbers, and he didn't read very well. But he had become good at what he did. His father had always said Noxie would never be worth anything to anybody, but as it turned out, he was worth a lot to his father's operation. All he wanted in the world now was to hear his father say it. To say that Noxie was good at what he did. To say he was proud of his son.

Noxie's thoughts always seemed to return to his father while he was waiting. After coming into the apartment through the window, he had meticulously prepared the place to wait, freeing up enough room for him to lie flat. He had eased down into the space below the floorboards, and his thoughts began to meander, but they always returned to his father. He wished his father could see him here, waiting with the kind of patience that few men had. It was one of the qualities that made him so good at his job. He could wait hours, days. He once waited in a basement crawl space for four days without eating, without speaking, only moving slightly to keep his muscles from cramping.

Of course, it made sense that he couldn't see his father. It came with the job. "Deniability" was how Cracks put it. Best if they didn't associate with each other, Cracks would say. It protected both him and his father. It was easy enough for people to believe that he and his father didn't get along, what with the suspicious death of Noxie's mother and the alleged involvement of his father in the accident.

Cracks – that was Frank Crackson, a close aide to Michael Grant – never called him Noxie. He called him Edward, his God-given name. Edward's father first started calling him Noxie, but would never tell his only son what the nickname meant.

Noxie's orders always came directly from Cracks, no one else. It was Cracks who had helped Noxie out, had given him purpose. Noxie hungered for a purpose early on. He would sometimes listen to his father's phone conversations, or press his ear to the door when his father was talking to other men in his study. He knew, on that day two weeks after his eighteenth birthday, that his father wanted Ulster Graham dead. Graham had moved into his father's territory. It was Noxie's big chance. He could do something for his father to prove his worth. He took the .38 his father kept in the glove compartment of his Lincoln and shot Graham right on the street as he was coming out of a downtown bar. Somehow, Noxie had simply walked away.

His father beat the hell out of him for that one. Called Noxie a moron. All kinds of names like that. It was Cracks who took Noxie under his wing, taught him how to do it right.

"Come on now, Michael," Cracks had told Noxie's father, "He's got the balls for it. He proved that. He doesn't have a wife, kids. He can relocate at a moment's notice. Move into a new neighborhood, no strings attached. Keeps to himself. Doesn't talk much. Seems to have some kind of knack for making himself invisible. Another ghost, I guess. Hell, he figured out what you were up to. And you know he's loyal...."

His father just grunted. "But he's a goddamn idiot, Cracks. Jesus, anybody can see that. He'll shoot his fool head off."

But Cracks had somehow convinced Michael Grant, and since that first clumsy hit, Noxie had killed nine more men over the next seventeen years. Salvador Creeks, the convict who had messed with his father in prison, would be Number Ten.

It was two hours later when Noxie heard the sound of keys jangling in the hall, the lock turning, the apartment door swinging open. Noxie felt the adrenaline flowing. "You need to act when you feel that charge," Cracks once told him. "Don't come down from it. You want to be charged up, on edge. Block everything else out. Emotion, even hatred. It's a job, Edward. A very dangerous job."

Noxie waited. Creeks opened the refrigerator, pulled out a bottle of beer and twisted the top off of it. He grabbed a bag of chips from the counter and walked into the living room. Noxie held his breath as the man walked right over him, but he did not move. Not a muscle.

The apartment was small: a kitchen, living area, bathroom, and one bedroom just big enough for a single bed and a dresser. Creeks clicked on the television and it crackled to life. He turned the channel to an old rerun of *Gilligan's Island*, then collapsed into a black lounge chair that faced the TV set. Noxie knew he could emerge and approach Creeks from behind.

Noxie waited a few more moments, making sure Creeks was settled in. He had slipped on white latex gloves before coming in through the bathroom window, and now the rubber helped keep a firm grip on the boards as he pushed them up and over. He had spent two hours the night before honing his switchblade to razor-sharpness. In his left hand, he held a leather strap. Creeks had to suffer before he died. It was part of the message.

Creeks sipped his beer, stuffed chips into his mouth, the chip crumbs falling down his stomach, into his lap. What a slob, Noxie thought, no pride at all. And he had no idea. No clue that his killer was in the room. Noxie smiled. Again, he wished his father could see him here, in total control of his prey, so skillful that the man didn't realize, even now, that Noxie was preparing to strike. Creeks watched the television, sometimes nodding his head and grumbling with laughter.

Just then, Creeks dropped the remote control to the television set. He cursed as he fumbled around for it, poking his hand in the chair cushion, chips falling on the floor. "Goddamn it," he barked, as if his biggest problem in the world was a lost remote control. He jabbed his hand down into the cushion hard, hitting the remote down in there, and the television suddenly clicked off.

Creeks looked up at the blank screen. And reflected there, like some unearthly vision, a man was rising up out of the floor – rising up, up, up, and coming forward as if floating across the room. The vision came right up behind Creeks, and he was so enraptured by it that he didn't even turn around. He just watched the reflection as it loomed above his chair.

Noxie had the blade of the knife in his teeth, an end of the leather strap in each hand. He prepared to swing the strap down over the man's throat when Creeks suddenly let out a terrified scream and threw his hands up. Noxie snapped the strap down, in front of his victim's rising hands, pulling the leather taut over the man's neck. Creeks gagged as Noxie pulled harder, jamming Creeks back against the chair. The man sputtered, a high-pitched whine squealing up out of his throat. Noxie kept pressure on the strap. Almost there. He didn't want to kill him – not yet – just put him out.

Suddenly, in a spasm of panic, Creeks threw the full force of his body backwards, against the chair, and the lounger toppled over, knocking Noxie off his feet. Creeks popped free of the strap that now dangled harmlessly in Noxie's hand.

Noxie landed on the floor as the lounger crashed down on top of him. A rush of air gushed from his lungs, driving the knife out of his teeth. The knife clattered across the wooden floor and slid against the far wall. Noxie was pinned by the chair, so Creeks was up first, tumbling sideways, out of the lounger and across the floor. Noxie threw the chair off of him and went for the knife but Creeks got there first.

"Son of a bitch!" Creeks roared as he came up with the switchblade in his hand. He swung furiously at Noxie as the killer dodged backward, inches from the blade of the knife. Noxie slammed into the kitchen table, and the next swipe of the blade sliced open a gash on his forearm. Noxie ducked under the next slash and spun into the kitchen, snapping the leather strap at Creeks like a whip. The leather slapped against the convict's dirty left cheek and he cried out in pain. Noxie came back with a backhanded swoop and the strap cracked across Creeks' right ear.

Creeks screamed again, and he kept screaming as he came at Noxie in a fit of rage, the knife grasped above him in both hands. Noxie rolled at his attacker's feet, and Creeks went down as Noxie tumbled across the kitchen and sprang up. Before Creeks could rise, Noxie kicked him hard in the belly. Creeks grunted and rolled back, coming up to his knees. It was then that Noxie kicked him full force under the chin. Creeks bolted backwards, his arms and head flying up, and the switchblade sailed through the air and clanged into the sink.

Noxie went for the knife, but Creeks got hold of his left leg. Noxie was trying to drag the man across the floor when Creeks sunk his teeth into Noxie's left calf. Noxie squelched a scream in his throat and fell backwards, against the kitchen counter. He flung his right arm back and somehow flipped his body over. His hand slammed down into the sink, breaking a glass.

Creeks let loose of the leg just as Noxie grabbed hold of the knife handle. Noxie turned around, the knife out in front of him. The glass had sliced his hand right through the glove. He knew he was breaking one of the rules that Cracks had taught him: Never leave anything behind. Not anything belonging to you, not a single fingerprint, not a drop of blood.

By the time Noxie turned with the knife in his bloodied hand, Creeks had made it to the door. He was turning the knob when Noxie lunged across the kitchen and buried the knife into the man's right shoulder. Creeks tried to scream, but Noxie got a hand over his victim's mouth, turned him around, and drove Creeks down to the floor. Noxie dropped a knee into the center of the convict's back, scooped up the leather strap and wrapped it around the man's face so that it crammed into his mouth. He tied the strap off as Creeks gagged. Noxie had to act quickly. He had very little time. But the job had to get done. The message had to be clear.

When he was through with Creeks, Noxie went to the bathroom and wrapped the cut on his forearm with a towel. Then he stuck the gloves in his pants pocket and wrapped a washcloth around his right hand. He washed off the knife, popped the blade into its handle, then stuck the switchblade into his back pocket. When he came out into the hall, a door slammed shut on the same floor. Somebody was nosy, but not nosy enough to get too involved. Noxie took the single flight of stairs and then calmly walked the three blocks to his car.

The apartment building was in a bad neighborhood, the kind of neighborhood where people minded their own business, and where a few screams at night weren't all that unusual. A domestic disturbance, no doubt. Only two nights earlier the police had been called to 6D after a woman hit her husband upside the head with a toaster. Three people in the apartment building admitted to hearing the screams to the police, but none of them saw anyone leave the apartment.

The body had been stabbed seventeen times, but none of the wounds killed Salvador Creeks. He bled to death during the thirty-seven hours between the time of the attack and the time his sister found Creeks in his apartment, soaked in his own blood.

And at Riverside Correctional, they got the message: Nobody fucks with Michael Grant.

9

Every time Jackson came upon the courthouse square, the memories flooded through his head. The square itself held icons from the past – the tiny movie house, the corner library with its flight of marble steps and the regal lions guarding its entrance, the C&S bank, the grocer displaying bins of fresh fruit on the sidewalk – but it also exposed ruptures from the present: a small CD store, an arcade advertising virtual-reality helmets, a new Dunkin Donuts. At the very center of it all, the courthouse stood stout, resolutely refusing to change with the times. Even the trees shading the building seemed ancient and knowing, as if blessing the block of earth with a quiet timelessness, a place to rest and to reflect and to seek haven. The grass was the deepest green God ever made.

As Jackie stepped along the courthouse walk, the image of Alfred Sachs formed in his mind. The young senator would saunter along the same walk, an easy smile on his face. Young children would rush up to him, and he would laugh, pulling from his suitcoat pocket a bag of peppermint gumdrops. He offered the paper sack to every child who approached. The children dug their hands in and drew out fistfuls of the peppermint gumdrops. Jackie remembered watching him from a park bench and was surprised that day when the senator moseyed up to the bench and sat down on it. He offered Jackson a gumdrop – the peppermint aroma washing over him as the sack opened – but Jackie refused.

Senator Sachs popped a gumdrop into his own mouth and asked a question, to the wind it seemed to Jackie.

"You believe in genes?" he asked.

Jackson looked around, then studied his pants. "Jeans? They're all right, I guess."

The senator smiled patiently. "I'm not talking about blue jeans," he said. "I mean them fancy genes that the scientists talk about. They say it's the genes what makes you who you are." The senator looked over at Jackie's blank face. "Now I don't much cotton to all that college talk, but I think they got a point. We all got ourselves a gene what tells us who we ought to be. Some of us got a banker gene, some of us got a politician gene, some of us got a musician gene...."

Sachs looked over at the boy. Jackie nodded knowingly, even though he had no idea what the senator was talking about.

"The point is," said the senator, "you may not have yourself a lawyer gene."

That caught Jackson's attention. He looked over at Sachs with renewed interest. The man knew something.

"Fact is," he went on, "I got to think you don't have one of them genes. Don't matter what your daddy wants or your mama or nobody else. If you ain't got the gene, it ain't go'n happen."

The senator ate another gumdrop. Jackie looked at the deep green grass of the courthouse lawn. His head was nodding again, this time with understanding.

"Your job," said the senator, "is to find out what sort of gene you got. You're the only one that can figure that out. You figure out your gene, son, and you go'n be happy."

The senator offered the gumdrop bag again, and this time Jackson took one. He popped it into his mouth. Best thing he'd ever tasted.

Jackson entered the office of the county commissioner through an open door. The office was spacious and flush with the spears of sunlight streaking through the clouds. A huge oak desk sat in the middle of the room, a U.S. flag on one side of it, a confederate flag on the other. Bill Sump, the sheriff when Jackson was last in town, held the phone to his ear. He pointed at a seat and Jackson walked over to it. Bill Sump pivoted in his chair, away from the visitor, as Jackson's steps echoed across the hardwood floor.

The air was dusty and hot. A large ceiling fan hung from the ceiling but it did not move. The stench of stale cigar smoke clung to Jackie's skin. He had never remembered feeling so cramped and claustrophobic, even in a jail cell. There were three large pane-glass windows in the office, looking out on the square. Pictures lined the walls, images of Sump over the years, accepting commendations, shaking hands with governors and police officers and celebrities. He had some awards up there, too. Jackson thought about getting up to peruse the wall hangings, but he didn't want to seem too casual, not under the circumstances. You deferred to Bill Sump. Jackson remembered the crooked finger Sump had pointed at the chair. And he remembered the sheriff, twenty years ago, on Lonnie Brim's lawn, a shotgun in his hand, lifting the sight to his eye.

Sump hung up the phone and swiveled in his chair. The commissioner was tall and slim, but his brute strength was stuff of Solomon's Rock legend. He had never lost an arm-wrestling match and probably never would. He had not been challenged since the day he slammed Bull Markem's fist to a table, breaking two bones in the big man's hand. Sump's arms hung long from a short-sleeved shirt, knots of muscle bunched against the bone. He wore a bland brown-and-white striped tie that hung only three inches below his chest. He dressed like a buffoon, but no one ever made the mistake of underestimating the man – at least not twice. The steel-toed boots he wore also inspired legend. Sump supported castration for sex offenders. The story went that he had exacted justice with the boots on more than one occasion.

His hair was close-cropped and white, and his forehead shelved out over sunken eye sockets. The skin beneath both his eyes was puckered, as if swollen from wasp stings, and the eyelids were heavy and veined purple, leaving little space for the pinprick pupils. His beaked nose arced over his upper lip, and a weak chin sloped into a long bony neck. The effect was disturbingly reptilian. Jackie imagined the commissioner's tongue flicking out to grab a circling fly.

Sump's voice held menace like a satanic message hidden in a heavy metal rock song. His low, purposeful words were often disturbing enough, but there was something beneath the words themselves that reeked of desolation. Sump glowered over at Jackson, and it took Jackie a moment to realize he had stopped breathing.

"Well, I just had to see it with my own eyes," Sump said in his gravelly voice. "A wayward son returned to us."

Jackson tried to smile but it didn't work. He felt perspiration prickling on his shoulders and the back of his neck, like small crabs crimping onto him. A bead of sweat rolled from his hairline to his eyebrow. When he inhaled, it felt as if he was drawing a wool blanket into his throat.

"I am sorry to hear about yo' daddy," Sump went on. "He's a fine man. A fine man. I'm just sorry he wadn't treated better over his lifetime. Some things hurt him mighty bad. Some things he just never got over." Sump walked slowly to the back of the room and lowered the blinds on the third window. As he did, the dark clouds outside – as if in acquiescence – blotted out the shards of sunlight. The room darkened.

"I wouldn't know about that. I just..."

"'Course you wouldn't know about it. You went scadaddling off somewheres, leaving that poor man on his own. He wanted to teach you, boy. He wanted to groom you. He was proud of you, told everybody how you had become a man, how it was time for you to take yo' place." Sump shook his head sadly, picked up a cigar as he walked back past his desk. "You sure did disappoint him, son, runnin' off like that. Didn't even tell him where you was off to. He never heard another word from you, did he, boy?"

Jackson looked down at the floor. Drops of sweat speckled the wood below him. "No sir."

Sump bit off the end of the cigar and spit it in the wastebasket. "He's been sick for quite a spell, you know. Ain't been nobody there to nurse him proper, 'cept yo' mama and Leola, and both of them need extra care theyselves. And then there's Ellis, yo' baby brother. You left everything for him to take care of, didn't you, boy? You only come back now to see what might get left behind – that the idea?"

"No sir," Jackson said, looking up. "I don't want a thing. I just came, well... I'm not sure why I came. I just thought if my daddy died before I saw him again – well, I would regret it some day."

"Well, ain't that thoughtful of you." Sump put the cigar in his mouth and approached Jackson. He bent over the chair and leaned his gaunt face in. Jackson could feel the heat rising off the old man. He could smell the tobacco and a hint of liquor on his breath.

Jackson started to blabber. "If you're worried about me, Sheriff, what I might say or something, I can tell you right now..."

Jackson didn't even see the hand come up. It was the commissioner's right hand, whipping up from the arm of the chair and driving across Jackson's left cheek. Jackson heard the sharp crack of the slap as he spilled out of the chair and hit the ground. The chair toppled on top of him.

"What the hell are you talking about, boy?" Sump barked.

"Nothing!" Jackson said. "I'm not talking about a damn thing."

Sump drove his boot into the pit of Jackson's belly, gushing the air out of him. Jackson wheezed, and the room started to spin. He gasped for breath. "Jesus Christ."

In one motion, the commissioner raked Jackson up, threw him back down on the chair, and leaned into him again. Hot breath, the smell of tobacco and liquor. Jackson felt dizzy and nauseous.

"Now you listen to me, you yeller-back scumbag," Sump growled.

"I ain't worried about you or nobody else. You understand me?"

Jackson nodded hard, keeping his eyes to the ground. He just wanted out of there.

Sump put his mouth onto Jackson's ear, speaking in a low hiss. "This town has done just fine without you for over twenty years," he said. "Nobody cares nothin' 'bout what happened all that time ago. It is laid to rest. Nobody cares nothin' 'bout you, nobody cares nothin' 'bout what you have to say. All they know is you is the little yeller fuck who ran off and broke his daddy's heart. Now, some of us, we got lots of respect for a man who cared for this town and took pride in it, and I won't stand by while some cowardly convict tries to tear down everything that man stood for." Jackson tried to speak, but Sump slapped a hand over his mouth. "Now I don't know what you have in mind, so I'm go'n tell you how it will be. You go and see yo' daddy, you lay him down proper when the time come. You listen nice and respectful to the good things people have to say about him, you nod and you thank them, you take care of what business you have to, then you go crawl back into the hole you climbed out of." Sump kept the hand on Jackson's mouth, letting the words sink in. "You understand me, boy?"

Jackson nodded, and Sump removed his hand. He glared at Jackie again before sidling casually across the room.

"Now get the fuck out of my sight," he said, and Jackson did.

Cecil took a parking spot on the courthouse square and waited in the New Yorker, smoking a cigarette and looking out through the waves of heat rising from the hood of the car. He had seen Jackie's car at the diner and assumed that Jackson had walked up the square to keep his appointment with the commissioner. He wondered what the commissioner wanted with Jackie.

Solomon's Rock was a strange place. The way Cecil heard it, Ghost Grant's operation started out of the small town and spread to Atlanta once Grant had the machine running smoothly. Cecil gazed around the square. It looked like a place frozen in time: an old single-screen movie theater showing a Disney flick, a Belk's clothing store with mannequins in the window, a hardware store with two guys sitting out front on lawn chairs, a library on the corner with stone lions guarding the door.

Cecil watched some old geezer, a big white man wearing overalls, stand up from his checker game on the courthouse steps. He started walking, very slowly and with a bit of a limp, through the deep green grass and the heavy shade of the oak trees growing in the courthouse square. Right toward Cecil's New Yorker. The old man looked like walking was a Herculean effort. He limped right up to the driver's side window of Cecil's car and stuck his wrinkly head in. His breath stunk – from some cheap Mad Dog, Cecil supposed. Cecil pulled his face back from the window, and the old man propped his elbows on the door, sticking his hands into the car.

"What the hell?" Cecil barked.

The old man just peered at him. His eyes were so dark they looked like holes in his head.

"What you staring at, old man?"

The old man shook his head. "Tell the truth," he said. "I ain't so sure. If I had to guess, I'd say I'm starin' at a real asshole."

"What the fuck?" Cecil said.

The old man just smiled, showing off brown teeth, then he dropped something on Cecil's lap – an envelope. When Cecil looked back up, the old man was walking back toward the checkerboards. Cecil picked up the envelope. It was full of money.

Cecil got out of the New Yorker and stuck the bills in his pocket. He found a place called Jimmy's, just off the square. They had some big fat hotdogs, rolling on the grill. Cecil got his dog all the way: mustard, onions, relish – the works. He walked up to the unattended register. The cash drawer was open. A man sitting at the lunch counter reading a newspaper spoke up. "The dog's a buck-twenty. You need change?"

Cecil fished around in his pocket. "All I got is a twenty."

The man at the lunch counter sighed, got up and came over. He didn't even bother to ring up the sale. He simply pulled the drawer open a little more and counted out the change, then stuck the twenty in.

"You Jimmy?" Cecil asked, trying to be friendly.

The guy looked up and scowled. "Who wants to know?" he asked.

"Name's Cecil." He held out a hand, but the man just looked at it as if Cecil's palm was covered with a rash, then he walked back to the counter. "Nice day to you, too," Cecil said as he walked out.

When Cecil got back to his Chrysler, Jackie was in the passenger seat. He was punching the dashboard, slamming his elbow into the door, cursing up a storm.

"Have some respect for the automobile," Cecil said.

Jackson seemed near tears. His eyes sparkled as he looked out at the courthouse with gritted teeth. "Bastard," he mumbled.

Cecil had other things on his mind. "You know Jimmy? The one with the store over on the square? Guy don't even keep his register closed up. Just sitting there wide open, nobody within twenty feet..."

"Don't even think it," Jackie snarled.

"I wadn't thinkin' nothin'," said Cecil. "I just notice stuff like that. Pick things up real quicklike. Can't even help myself. You might say I got a gift in that area. A real eye for detail."

"Just keep your detailed eye off Jimmy's cash register."

Cecil shrugged as he stuffed the hotdog into his mouth. A clump of relish fell onto his shirt. "I just got myself an eye for that sort of thing. That's all I'm saying."

"Let's get out of here," said Jackson. At the moment, he didn't have the patience to deal with Cecil's strange ways of viewing the world. "I need to go visit my aunt."

10

Cecil wondered why they called her "Aunt Frank." Her name was Frances, so why not call her that? Aunt Frank — it sounded like some kind of cross-dresser. But when they came upon the house, Cecil could see why Frances loved it so much. It loomed among the tall trees like an ancient plantation manor. Cecil could almost see women out front in ornate hoop dresses and sun hats the size of tractor tires, men in their finest duds smoking cigars and sipping drinks, nattily clad slaves at their beck and call. Land stretched out behind the house with thick woods beyond. But when you got closer, you could see that the grand old place was showing signs of wear: fine cracks in the fancy columns, the porch starting to sag, one of the shutters unhinged, a couple of the trees around it starting to die out.

The old lady opened the door with the chain still on it, peering out through the crack. Jackie told her who he was and she said she knew. She asked about chocolates. "I done paid for them," she told Jackson. Then she slammed the door in his face.

Cecil whistled through his teeth while Jackson thought it over.

"I sold her some candy bars, back before I took off. It was one of those charity things, you know. Baseball or something. I think I sold them but was never around to hand them out."

"You tellin' me she remembers that?"

"Sounds like it," said Jackie. "She wants the chocolate bars she paid for."

Cecil thought Jackie was crazy, but they went over to the store and picked up five Nestle bars. When they got back, Frank opened the door again with the chain still on it and peered out. Jackie held the candy bars up so she could see them.

"That ain't the kind I bought," Aunt Frank said.

"It's all I have."

She stood there a few seconds considering it. "It'll have to do," she said and opened up the door.

Jackson and his Aunt Frank reminisced about old times, back when Jackie was a child. The old woman's face lit up as they talked. She would make a merry "O" with her thin lips and clap her bony hands together joyfully. Her skin was gaunt and yellowish, but her delightfully expressive brown eyes bulged out of the sockets. Gray hair would have fallen to her knees had it not been piled up in buns on top of her head. Jackie had seen the hair down only once, and its length and strange luminance had left him slack-jawed. She wore a white cloth dress with purple flowers printed on it, and a single silver chain around her neck.

They talked about the time Frank took Jackie and his brother Ellis down to the Water Works. There was a playground there: swings, see-saws, picnic tables, a merry-go-round. When they drove up, the park was closed. A big log blocked the entrance to the park. Frank had turned the car around and was heading out when, suddenly, she said "Pooh!" and turned the wheel so sharply that Jackie and Ellis fell over on the seat.

Frank turned right off the entrance road, banged down a little gully, and started barreling across a big field. Jackie and Ellis were screaming and laughing as Frank's old Chrysler bumped across that field toward the playground.

She drove all over the park that day. Along paths that were only meant for walking, down alongside the creek, *through* the creek a couple of times, across the base paths at the baseball diamond.

They were up by the reservoir, eating a picnic lunch, having the day of their lives, when they saw the sheriff's car down below with the lights flashing. It was exciting stuff for a couple of young kids. Next thing Jackson and his brother knew, Frank was back in the Chrysler, cranking it up and heading out. It was an old-time Chrysler, late forties, with running boards beneath the doors. Jackson and Ellis hopped up on the boards as Frank spun out in the dirt. A getaway right out of *Bonnie and Clyde*.

They drove along the fence to the far end of the reservoir, bolted over a ridge, and careened wildly down a grassy hill. It was a steep hill that went down a bit, then leveled out, then went down some more. It made for a wild roller-coaster ride. Jackie could still remember Aunt Frank's look as she drove the car down that hill – the eyes wide and expectant, as if she were just along for the trip, not steering the automobile. At the bottom of the hill, they came up on Highway 3, and Frank laid rubber right in front of a family station wagon as the car slid across the road, hooking west. Frank took that highway at eighty miles an hour until they got to Clearwater Pond, the two brothers hooting and hollering the whole way. And Aunt Frank, her mouth in a little "O" of pleasure, seemed as young as a schoolgirl who had just gotten away with skipping class.

Cecil and Jackson were sitting out on the porch. Frank insisted on feeding them bacon and eggs, so she was in the kitchen cooking them up. Cecil told Jackie that somebody should put the old girl in a home before she hurt somebody, maybe even herself.

"Nobody's putting her in a goddamn home. You got that?"

The sharp words took Cecil aback. "What you got to say about it?"

Cecil wanted to know. "Hell, you ain't even stickin' around yourself, Jackie."

Jackson snorted. "I'll take her with me if I have to. She can live with me."

Cecil laughed. He couldn't help it.

"What are you laughing about?"

"It's funny, that's all. Family shit. I had you figgered as this guy without no roots, no relations to get you all fucked up. Now you been here less than a day and you're all confused. Funny how family can do that to a man. Same with yo' brother. In the end, you don't have no say-so about it. He's yo' brother, man, and...."

"This has nothing to do with my brother. He's an asshole. My Aunt Frances, she's good people. She doesn't deserve this shit."

"What shit, Jackie? Gettin' old? What?"

"I'm talking about throwing her away, locking her up, just because her mind is a little off kilter."

"Shit, Jackie, I'd say her mind fell right off the kilter and hit the floor."

"Just forget it, okay."

Cecil thought about the psychiatrist he met on his last hitch. One of his patients started beating on him so the doctor hit the patient with an antique lamp. The psychiatrist ended up inside for it. Cecil tried to remember what the shrink had called it – the reason why the patient had started hitting the doctor – transfers, transferring.... "Transferments," Cecil said. "That's what's happenin' to you."

"What are you babbling about now?"

"It's what you call a psychotic term. This shrink told me about it once. You see, you all mad at yo' daddy cause he's dyin', or maybe you mad at yo' brother cause he's a hot-shot lawyer, or could be you just pissed off 'cause everybody got all old on you. Hell, who knows? Point is, you take it out on me. Transferments. You can't go in there and get all pissed at yo' aunt – hell, she wouldn't even know what the fuck you were talking about. Not much point in yellin' at Daddy. Yo' brother, he'll just tell you to fuck off. So you get pissed at me instead. Transferments."

Jackson glared over at him. "Don't try to act smart, Cecil. It only makes you sound dumber."

To Cecil, the remark simply proved his point. "Transferments," Cecil said, turning his chin up and crossing his arms.

When they came back inside and walked into the kitchen, Jackson noticed that the burner to the stove was off. Nothing was cooking.

"You want somethin' to eat?" Frank asked. "All I got is eggs."

Jackie looked helpless. "No, Frank. We aren't hungry."

She went to the refrigerator, but Jackie beat her to it. He leaned over his aunt.

"Frank," he asked her. "Would you like to come with me? I mean if you had to. If they were going to put you away."

"Put me away?"

"You know, if they were going to put you in a home or something...."

"Why would they do that?" she asked, like she couldn't think of one good reason that they might.

"Well, Frank, I hear you keep wandering off, looking for your house, wondering where they hid it on you. Now there's one reason they might use."

"Well, if they'd stop moving it, then I wouldn't have to go looking."

"But they haven't moved it. They're going to, but they haven't yet."

She was trying to figure that out. "They sure did move it. Last week, they moved it clear over to Alabama."

Jackson gazed into her eyes, trying to hold her attention. Frank looked scared, as if wondering why a strange man was staring her down. "Just tell me. Would you go with me? If they were going to put you away, would you come with me?"

"To the Grand Canyon?" she asked.

"The Grand Canyon?"

Cecil laughed.

"You know," Frank said, "you can find yo'self these donkeys, ride them right down in there."

"Donkeys? I don't know about that, Frank."

"It's true, though. The girl down at the grocer, she showed me pictures. She was on top of one of them donkeys, carried her right down into the Grand Canyon."

Jackie was getting frustrated. He thought he might actually cry. "Just tell me, Frank. Would you go with me?"

"You find me one of them donkeys," she said. "I'll go with you."

Maybe it was dealing with the dementia of his great aunt, or maybe it was the abuse he took from Sump, but Jackson was fed up. When they drove back through town, he ordered Cecil to park on the square and wait for him. Then he hopped out of the car. He took the east entrance and mounted the steps of the courthouse to the chambers of Judge Tomey. The secretary, a middle-aged woman with thick black glasses, tried to keep him out, but when she announced Jackie on the intercom, the judge told her to show Jackson in. She opened the double doors to Tomey's office.

Between Jackson and a huge oak desk lay a full thirty feet of hardwood. The judge peered out of his floor-to-ceiling window, out across the courthouse square. He turned fully toward Jackie, sunlight splashing across the rugged face. Even in the bright light, a black shadow still seared down the deep scar running from the corner of the judge's right eye to his jaw line, one of the few things Jackie had left behind. Tomey's face was weathered, pockmarked, much older than his forty-one years. The judge had finally gotten what he wanted, Jackie realized. He had paid the devil and gotten his judgeship. Just like he had told Jackson to do twenty years before.

"Mr. Jackson Moon," the judge announced, his voice echoing in the huge room. "I'm honored." Subconsciously, Tomey touched a finger to the scar Jackson had given him.

"Sure you are," Jackson said as he began the walk across the room. The chamber was stark, almost forbidding. A single painting of the judge's father adorned the side wall. A brick façade stood behind the oak desk. A file cabinet, a single red-velvet chair, a small glass-fronted bookcase, a standing lamp, and a regal American flag – all seemed randomly placed about the office. Open space dominated the atmosphere. Open space and the judge himself: black eyes, dark hair slicked straight back, large ears and pursed lips, a huge Adam's apple that bulged out over the gray tie, the dark suit of a shade the judge always wore as if perpetually in mourning.

"To what do I owe this pleasure?" asked the judge as he smiled, showing a row of straight, perfectly white teeth.

"I'm not sure it will be a pleasure, Judge."

"Is that so?" said Tomey, undaunted. The smile did not waver.

"I need to talk to you about some things that happened a long time ago."

The smile broadened. "That right? You want to talk about old times, Jackie? You remember that Fourth of July parade? The one when Old Chief Waters drove his fire truck smack into Monte's storefront? Knocked out the glass and tore out a whole row of shelving. That was something else, wadn't it? The Atlanta news stations even filmed that one. Those city folk got a good laugh, I'll bet. Damn hicks can't even drive a fire truck straight."

"Yeah, that was something," said Jackson without cracking a smile. "But I'm not here to talk about fire trucks."

"You ain't? How about the big game against Valdosta? You recall that? State championship. Not one paper gave us a chance in hell. 10–6, I think it was. Our boys held them suckers on fourth-and-two at the goal line. Holy God, that was sweet. Only state championship Solomon's Rock ever won."

"I'm not here to talk about a goddamn football game either,"

Jackson growled. "I think you know what I want."

The judge's eyes narrowed. The smile was gone. The lips were set. "You listen to me, Jackson, because I won't say this again. Nobody wants to hear about some shit that happened twenty years ago. You understand me? We all got over it. We moved on even if you couldn't. Now you best take care of yo' business and get on out of here. Maybe get yourself one of them fancy city doctors, one that can look inside your head and work shit out for you. But you ain't gonna work stuff out 'round here, my old friend. You'll just find a whole world of hurt. I can sure promise you that. You up against more than you know." Tomey met Jackson's stare. The scar's shadow seemed to darken. Then, as suddenly as the darkness came into his eye, it fled again. The judge laughed out loud.

"You always were a bit dense, weren't you, Jackson? Never quite figured out what the hell you got yourself into. But you were there, just like the rest of us. You might be stupid, but you sure as hell ain't innocent."

"I know that. I just want the truth. That's all."

Tomey shook his head and laughed some more. He went over to his desk and fished out a cigar from a walnut humidor. He offered Jackson one and then closed the box when Jackie refused. He carefully cut the cigar with a small pair of silver scissors, then lit it with a gold lighter. He turned back to the window.

"They say the truth is a relative thing, ain't you heard that? The townfolk, we've settled this thing. Nobody wants to go back. You know what they *do* want, though?" The judge turned back toward Jackson, moving close into him, the darkness returning to the hard eyes. "They want you to go away. Go on home."

"I am home," Jackson said.

"No," Tomey said flat-out. "No, no, no. It don't work that way. You had your chance. You were in. You were family. But you made your choice. I warned you about that. Hell, I begged you not to walk away. But you made your choice, and now you got to live with it. This ain't your home no more. Never again."

With that, the judge turned to the window and fell silent. Sunlight streamed through the wafts of cigar smoke. Jackson watched the judge for a few moments, remembering the man of twenty years ago, remembering the shovel that he swung through the air, the sharp edge slamming upside Tomey's head.

"Maybe I ought to gash your face with a shovel again, give you a scar on the other side to match the one you already have."

Tomey just gave Jackson a broad, shit-eating grin. "I wasn't expecting it last time. I thought you were my friend back then. This time, I'll be watching you every second. You won't get the drop on me."

"I think you ought to tell me what that night was all about. I may just dig up more than you bargained for."

The judge's eyes narrowed sharply and the ridged creases around the eye sockets deepened. "I'll make yo' job a little easier," he said in a low, gravelly monotone. "You go digging at the Rock, you won't find a thing."

Jackson held the judge's gaze. "If I can't dig up any bodies," he said, "maybe I'll have to bury some."

"You're messing with some dangerous people."

Jackson didn't blink. "But I got one thing they don't."

"And what would that be?"

"Nothing to lose," Jackie told him.

The shit-eating grin returned. "There's always something to lose," he said.

Suddenly Jackson laughed.

"What's so damn funny?"

"I was just thinking about you in prison," Jackie said. "The way you go along to get along? They'll be passing you around. Probably give you some kind of cute nickname. Judge Fudge Packer, something like that."

The grin disappeared.

"You know," Jackson went on, "maybe you should start cramming a big pole up your ass. Loosen it up down there. It'll be less painful when the time comes."

"Fuck you."

Jackson drew back, both hands in the air. "Hey now, I ain't into that shit myself. It was a suggestion, not an offer."

The judge took a long draw from his cigar, reclaiming his composure. "You ever hear of a little thing called the statute of limitations?" he asked.

"Not for murder," Jackson said.

"I didn't murder nobody."

"Tell it to a judge," Jackson said. "A real judge."

Tomey looked up at him, his eyes flaring with mischief. "If it ever comes to that," he said, "I've got my ace in the hole."

Jackie wondered what the words meant. He took in the smile that emerged again on Tomey's face. The judge waved him off. "Get the hell out of here," he said.

Jackson turned around and left the room, letting loose a belly laugh as he swung open the big doors and walked through them. But as he descended the single flight of stairs, back out of the courthouse and onto the street, he knew he had nothing to laugh about.

11

Jason Farmer was waiting for the FBI. It was time to move again. The agent was due around 9:00 or so. Hopefully, Farmer would get a nice place this time. The last two weeks had been hell, holed up in a cheap motel. He opened the door to his second-story landing, a glorious view of the parking lot.

Farmer walked out on the landing. The plain-clothes cop was on a chair a few feet down. His head was cocked back.

"Hey," Farmer called out to him. "Sleeping on the fucking job? You s'posed to be protectin' my ass, mother...." As Farmer approached the cop, he caught sight of the perfectly round bullet hole in his forehead. With his head cocked back the blood flowed into his hair, congealing in it. Stunned eyes stared up in apparent warning. Fright shocked through Farmer. He had to get out.

He headed for the kitchen. The FBI wouldn't let him keep a gun, but he was determined to find a knife, a hammer, some kind of weapon.

As soon as he entered the door, he stopped cold. A man stood in front of him, early thirties at most. The man steadied a gun at Farmer. It looked like a cannon.

"You don't fuck with Michael Grant," the man told him.

Farmer fell to his knees. "Please, man. I won't talk. I swear it. I'll do whatever you say. Whatever you want. Anything, man. I'll do it."

From his knees, Farmer looked up at Noxie. Tears streamed down the man's face. If only Noxie's father was there to see it. He would be amazed at the fear Noxie could drive into this man. The eyes pleading, terrified. That was the look Noxie wanted his father to see. The look of terror that proved just how good Noxie was.

"You know what my father thinks they should do to a man who steals?" Noxie asked Farmer. "They should cut his hand off."

Farmer stuttered. "I ... I ... I never stole nothin'."

Noxie just shook his head slowly. Farmer didn't get it.

"So what should I do to a man who talks?" Noxie asked, proud of himself for being so cool, so slick, driving home the message. Cracks had spent a lot of time teaching Noxie how to deliver the message. The message – the fear – was as important as the hit.

"Open your mouth," Noxie ordered, waving the Colt in Farmer's face. Noxie liked the feel of his Glock 17 better, but this was a job for the Anaconda. The long barrel. Power practically purring from the beast. It could blow over a refrigerator from fifty feet.

"What? What are you...?"

"Open your fucking mouth." Voice low, firm.

The man shook his head. "Please ... Please ... I'm begging you...."

"Open...your...mouth." Noxie had the perfect voice for menace. Slow and steady. Almost a monotone. The man was sobbing as he opened his mouth and Noxie calmly placed the barrel of the gun inside of it.

"So what do you think?" Noxie inquired. "Should I cut your tongue out or just blow your mouth clean off?"

The man had lost it. He just closed his eyes and heaved tears. Noxie left the gun in there so Farmer could taste the oily polish. Then he slowly pulled the gun back out of Farmer's mouth, and the man collapsed to the floor, his face buried in the carpet. Noxie didn't want to shoot Farmer in the mouth. It would mess up his plan.

When the FBI showed up, twelve minutes late, Farmer's chest had been obliterated by three bullet blasts. The first agent on the scene grimaced at the bloody sight. Her eyes were strangely attracted to a bloody object placed on the floor next to the dead man's left ear. She took out a pen and, with morbid curiosity, prodded the object, half expecting the thing to suddenly scamper off. Then her face clouded over with a look of revulsion. Slowly, she placed the pen between the dead man's teeth and propped open his mouth. Only then was she sure that the object on the floor was the tongue that had been sliced out of Jason Farmer's mouth.

12

"Hi, Ellis," Jackson said into the telephone receiver. "How are you doing?"

"Holy shit," said Ellis. "Jackie? I can't believe it. Where are you?"

"I'm home."

There was a short silence as Ellis took the information in. "You're in Solomon's Rock?"

"That's right."

"I don't believe it. What are doing there?"

Jackson shrugged. "I belong here. Always have."

"Well, sure. That's great. Listen, I'm sorry I didn't visit you in prison, but I tried to call you when you were down in Florida. Mom gave me a number. You never called back, so...."

"I was trying to distance myself from some things. Sorry about that."

"Did you get my letter?"

"Yeah, I got it. Thanks for writing. I should have sent a letter back...."

"Forget about it. I understand." A short silence followed before Ellis spoke in an almost reverent tone. "I've missed you, brother."

"I've missed you, too, Ellis. I've thought about you a lot. I hope you're staying out of trouble."

"Hey," Ellis said. "I'm a lawyer for Michael Grant. When Grant is your business, trouble is your line of work."

Jackson took that in, then said: "I think my business and yours might be crossing paths."

"Don't talk like that, Jackie. You scare me. I don't want to see you get hurt."

"We're all scared, but we can't let that stop us from doing what we have to do. I'm not going to run away anymore. Maybe I'll have to be scared, maybe I'll have to get hurt. But I'm not going to run."

"I hope you know what you're getting into here."

"I called because.... Well, because I want you to know I'm not trying to hurt you. Whatever happens, that's not what I'm after. I just hope you don't get caught in the crossfire."

"Jesus Christ, Jackie. What the hell...?"

"I'm not looking for trouble. But what I am looking for ... well, trouble will probably follow right behind it."

"Look, why don't you just lay low for a little while until I..."

"I've been laying low for twenty years. I think that's long enough. Like I say, I know this could put you in a tough spot, but I've got some facing up to do. There was a time when I blamed you – hell, I blamed everybody – but this has nothing to do with you now, at least not from my point of view. I want you to know that."

"All right," Ellis said tentatively. "I just hope you know what you're doing."

"I'm doing what I have to do. That's all."

"Jesus, take care of yourself then. And if you end up needing a lawyer...," Ellis paused as he thought about his words, "...you can probably find a hell of a lot better one than me."

They both laughed, and the tension broke.

Jackson's voice went soft. "You watch yourself, little brother. You hear me?"

"You know what they've always said: Angels follow me wherever I go."

"Except when you're around me," Jackson said. "Then you got a demon on your tail:"

They laughed again, and Ellis felt teary for the first time in a long, long while.

"I'll be talking to you," Jackson said.

"I'd like that," Ellis said. He could almost see Jackie nodding as he hung up the phone. Ellis put down the receiver gently. Emotions flooded through him. He wondered just how much trouble his brother could dredge up. A whole hell of a lot, he figured. A whole hell of a lot.

13

Jackson walked east along Greenville Street until he could
see his father's house through the trees. Jackie stood out
on the sidewalk a few moments before deciding that he wasn't ready
to face his father yet. Instead he walked down to the Carters' and cut
through their backyard to the woods, then headed back behind his
father's house. He ducked through the brush and followed a path that
was barely distinguishable until he saw the small cabin hunched
between two low, moss-covered mounds. He had looked upon the
cabin many times, though he had never been inside — he had never
been allowed as a boy and had never dared even when challenged by
his friends — and only now did he realize how the two small hills
looked like ancient burial mounds. He stopped short and eyed the
cabin as dusk descended.

Slowly, the cabin door opened and a thin black woman moved into
the doorway. To anyone else, she would have seemed frail, the bones
so thin it seemed they might snap, the skin stretched tight over them
like Saran Wrap, the eyes gaunt, ghostly, buried deep in the sockets
so that they peered out of a darkness deeper than a face as black as
new asphalt. Leola's laughter cackled in the wood. "My eyes must be
deceiving me," she said from the doorway.

"No ma'am," said Jackie as he smiled broadly. "I don't believe they are."

"Well, what you doin' standin' there like some kinda scarecrow? You come over here and give your Leola a hug."

Jackie looked down at his feet. They seemed to be frozen. He looked up, almost helplessly.

"What's the matter, boy? You still think you cain't come inta my house. You a growed man now. Least ways, it sho' looks that way from here."

Jackie laughed nervously and then took a single step, as if into a ritual circle. He approached the old slave cabin where his father's maid had always lived, a house just beyond the edge of the wood in the Moons' backyard and yet as far away as another world entirely. Jackson stepped up on the single stair and Leola took him into her arms.

"My Lawd almighty," she said. "I been waitin' for the day, Jackson Moon. I been sittin' right'chere, just waitin' for the day...."

The woman was not tall, and yet she seemed to cradle Jackie up like a mother nurturing her baby. Jackson's head lodged into her chest, and she slowly stroked his hair. He felt suddenly safe and comfortable, and yet tears welled behind his eyes as the woman held him firm.

"You come on in now. You come on in and set a spell with your Leola." She led Jackson into the cabin, into the small lamp-lit living room, down onto a wooden, wicker-bottomed chair. Leola backed up then, her eyes glowing with the lamp's flame until she settled into her high-backed rocker. "My little Jackson finally found his way back home."

Jackie looked around the cabin. It was a place that had always lain just beyond the brittle wooden walls, and yet a place he had never before seen. He took in the smell of blackberries and pepper-mint tea and crushed pecan shells. A bunch of wildflowers, gold and purple and white, sat in a jelly jar on the table along with three lit candles. Silhouettes of a younger Jackie and Ellis hung on the wall, etched on black construction paper and carefully cut around the outline, then mounted on off-white newsprint and laid in hand-made frames. Across from Jackie, there was a small couch, covered in a blue quilt with tiny flowers stitched on it. Photographs were everywhere: on the table, hanging from the walls, crowded on a hearth to Jackie's left. He recognized a picture of his mother with Leola, but many of the photographs he didn't recognize. Young black children, a solemn black man in a crisp army uniform, a younger Leola with a long slender arm loped around her shoulders. Photographs from a life he didn't take part in.

Beyond a double ceiling beam huddled a small kitchen and through a door to his far left was the bedroom, but Jackie's eyes were drawn inexplicably to a stark cotton curtain that hid away a third room. Jackson stared hard at the curtain, as if by force of will he might look right through it.

"What's back there?" Jackson heard himself ask.

"In good time," Leola said, nodding as if glad about his interest. "All in good time, boy."

Jackson shook his head, breaking out of the trance. "What do you mean?"

"What you need to know," Leola said. "All in good time."

Jackson shrugged. "I don't need to know anything, Leola. I'm not here for that."

Leola laughed easily. "And what you think you here for, Jackson?"

"I'm here to see my daddy, before he dies."

"That ain't all you here for, boy. That ain't even the most of it."

Jackson looked away and tried to laugh. "You think you know what I'm here for, Leola?"

"I don't know much," Leola said. "But I always knowed you'd be back here, Jackson Moon. I knowed you'd be sittin' right in that very chair. I knowed you'd come back and I always knowed why."

Jackson met her stare. "So you tell me," he said. "Why did I come back?"

A broad smile stretched out across Leola's face. Jackson sensed the secret behind the gleam in Leola's eyes "Redemption," she said simply. "You here for redemption, son."

That made Jackson laugh. "You think that's what I need?"

"We all in need of it, boy. Every single one of us."

"Ain't that the truth."

Jackson's lightheartedness was suddenly driven from him by the piercing stare of Leola's bottomless eyes. The stare nabbed a breath as it rose up Jackie's throat. "We all in need of it, boy. Ain't no doubt of that. But you, Jackson Moon, you the one that gots the chance. Ain't many a'tall who gets that. Not many a'tall. You got the chance for it, boy. Only you."

Jackson walked along the long backyard toward his father's house. On each side of him was a row of pecan trees, their limbs arcing over like marines crossing swords above him. His legs grew weary, as if weighted down by the humidity on his shoulders. He sat down in the tall grass and drew in the lemony smell of flowering alyssums and the tangy aroma of silver thyme. Slowly, as if sedated by the summer air, he stretched his body out until he lay fully on his back, feeling the earth below him. There was much in Solomon's Rock that Jackie still wanted to run away from, but as he felt the earth below him, he knew he was finally home. He knew he belonged here, on this spot of the earth, among the green grass and the dandelions.

14

As Jackie walked into the kitchen, a wash of bright light flooded through the windows, drowning everything he saw in white. His mother turned to him and in the light, she looked as young as when Jackie had left.

Then the light dimmed and scattered. Shadows seeped into his mother's skin, spreading deep wrinkles across her face. She seemed to age in front of his eyes. The eyes darkened and faded, sinking down at the corners. The lips cracked and thinned, turning the bright smile into a forced echo of joy.

"My little Jackie-Jack," she whispered as they hugged.

"Hi, Mama."

"It's been so long, my sugar angel. Too long."

"I know," said Jackson softly.

They pulled away from each other.

"Your daddy's upstairs," his mother said as she returned to a sink full of dishes. Jackie had expected the aging of his mother, but something else struck him even deeper. A light had gone out. Her boundless energy had died away. Slowly, she went back to washing dishes, as if it were the only thing left on this earth for her. It was the first time Jackson realized, or thought he realized, the toll his leaving had taken on his mother. Jackie felt tears welling up. A single tear broke from the rim of his eye and rolled down his cheek. He wiped it away with the back of his hand.

"Does he know I'm coming?" Jackson asked.

His mother shrugged. "I told him, but he didn't say anything. Every time you called on the telephone? He hadn't wanted to talk to you. I always made excuses, told you how he was out and such, but he just never would pick up the phone."

Jackson had called his mother two or three times a year since he left and always his father was out. Maybe fifty calls over twenty years, and not once was his father available to talk. "I kind of figured that out, Ma," he said. His mother turned and gave him the forced smile.

"He's very sick, Jackie."

Jackson nodded. "I know."

Jackson slowly mounted the steps, his nose full of musty smells that made him think of ghosts. It was the only time Jackson ever believed in spirits. They were surely in this house. They smelled of dry dust and the faint scent of mothballs. Their sound was the slow methodic ticking of the grandfather clock at the base of the stairs. They swirled up into the high ceilings and crouched in the corners like spider webs. Jackson could feel the weight of them as he mounted the steps to his father's second-floor bedroom. He could hear them whispering a strange language that he couldn't quite distinguish. An ancient language, perhaps, or just echoes that had reverberated too long. He stopped on the stairs and his shoulders sagged. He turned his head and looked down at the hallway below, remembering the story of his father breaking his leg when he leapt from the stairway landing onto a pile of blankets in the hall. He saw himself and his brother Ellis running up the porch steps and bursting through the front door, home from school, dropping books in the foyer, without the slightest sense of a haunting past.

Jackson walked into the first bedroom on the left. His father was on his cushioned chair, one foot on the ottoman, smoking a cigar. Swirls of thick smoke hung in front of the old man's face. Jackie stood still in the doorway, studying the man: the brooding eyes hooded by heavy gray brows, the thick scowling lips, the jaw still square but the jowls hanging. Slowly, the eyes started to turn as the head rose only slightly and the old man brought Jackson into his line of sight. His stare didn't change noticeably. Jackie got the uncomfortable feeling that his father had been expecting him. For twenty years, he had been waiting in the chair, ready to move his head in just that way, turning an eye to his lost son.

Jackson walked into the room. The eyes followed him. He stood in front of his father and nodded, but the old man just stared.

"What do you want?" the father growled.

Jackson shook his head and looked toward the open window. "I don't want a thing."

"Why are you here?"

Jackson looked down at the man on the chair. "I came here to see you, Daddy. I heard you were sick."

The eyes squinted. "'Course I'm sick," he mumbled. "They used to call it 'consumption,' you know, back when my father got it. I was just a boy. When they said he had consumption, I figured he just ate too much."

Jackie laughed a little, but his father didn't crack a smile. The uneasiness settled in the room. Jackson stammered. "So how are you?"

He glared up at the boy. "How am I? When I go to the toilet, I get a pan crammed up under my ass. On a good day, I can walk from the bed to my chair. This," he said, lifting up the cigar, "is all I got left to live for. Two cigars a day. That's the bone they've thrown me. That's how I am."

Jackson backed to the edge of the bed. Might as well get it over with. "You know, I never wanted to run off. But the stuff that happened..."

"Oh no!" his father boomed. "You ain't comin' in here after twenty years and get me to talk about any of that. All those years ago, boy, that was the time to talk to me about it. Not now. You made your choice."

"That's what I'm trying to tell you. There wasn't much choice...."

"I ain't talkin' about this, boy. I looked for you that night. I drove up and down that highway, searched out around the Rock. I was never sure what happened to you. We could've talked, figured it out, but you had your own notions. Not a word to one soul. You just walked away – from me, from the town, from your friends, from your family. You got no right, boy, no right at all, to come back now lookin' for answers. That's all in the past. The answers you want, they buried back there, too."

His father didn't look at him. He peered straight ahead, his jaw set. He wasn't going to talk.

Jackson moved away from the bed, leaned down toward his father's face. "That's the problem. It's not left in the past. It's still going on."

But his father's expression didn't budge. The eyes stared dead ahead, giving up nothing. He was done.

Jackson sat on the edge of the bed and studied his father until early evening lengthened shadows across the side yard. Jackson's father, the cigar stub dead in his hand, nodded off. His face seemed to melt as sleep took him. He became softer, older, vulnerable, the bitterness rising away as his lips parted slightly and his eyes closed. Jackson looked away, gazing around the room. His eyes fell on an object on his father's dresser. A set of keys. He walked over to them, looked down at his sleeping daddy, back at the keys, down again. One last long look at the ring of keys, and he swept them up, then headed for the door.

As he passed his father, the old man stirred, then spoke: "I coulda helped you, boy. Back then, we coulda done somethin' about it. But not now. Ain't one goddamn thing any of us can do about it now."

"Maybe you're right," Jackson conceded, and as he stepped toward the door, his father's eyes cracked open. A weak hand touched his son's arm.

"Jackson," he said, barely audible.

Jackie stopped.

"Your mama," his father wheezed. "She's cared for me over forty years. It ain't her job anymore. You got to get her to leave."

"Leave? Daddy, I can't tell her..."

"Get her to go, Jackson. I don't want her to see me like this. I don't want her to watch me die."

Back in the kitchen, Jackson said, "He's really sick, isn't he?"

"Yes," his mother agreed, "He's very sick."

"Maybe we should find a nurse to watch him. You could go visit your sister...."

She turned and gave him a look that stopped his words. "I'm not going anywhere. My husband needs me now."

Jackie looked at the floor. "Mama?" he asked. "Back when I ran off – did you know what was going on? We never really talked about it. About why I left."

She just shook her head. "I don't want to know. That was the men's business, not mine."

Jackie stared at his mother, as if trying to unlock a mystery. "I was your business, wasn't I? Your own son?"

Her look softened before she turned back to the sink. "Don't make me take sides, Jackie. You might not like the one I choose."

15

Jackson was deep in thought as Cecil turned the New Yorker down Depot Street. Cecil had to park the car by the railroad tracks, and they walked the rest of the way. The shanty of Red Eye Barnes looked like some kind of fort that kids would build out of plywood and two-by-fours. It hunched down on the far side of a mossy slope, as if hiding there.

"Who the fuck is this guy?" Cecil asked.

Jackson had avoided Cecil's questions on the ride over, but he was going to find out soon anyway, so Jackson finally answered him. "You remember that fire I told you about?"

"The one that burned up them colored folk and the state senator?"

"Yeah," Jackson replied wryly, as if he had been involved in dozens of fatal fires in his hometown. "That's the one."

"What about it?"

"This guy we're going to see – he was there."

Cecil whistled through his teeth as they walked along a set of half-buried stones that made up a walkway. The blue spring flowers of carpet bugleweed snaked between the stones, and a splash of light played across the white and lavender Johnny-jump-ups planted along the front wall of the shack. A fat black bumblebee settled on a flowering zinnia at the corner of the structure. Jackson knocked twice on the door.

The door cracked open, and a small black man peered out. Half his face, a single eye, filled the space. A tiny Chihuahua yelped madly at the foot of the door, occasionally driving its snout into the open slot. "What you want?" the man asked.

Cecil looked over at Jackson.

"We just came over to talk to Mr. Barnes," Jackson said. "Billy Barnes."

"Talk about what?" The little dog barked crazily from inside the shack.

Jackson looked away from the door, up through the branches of an elm tree, out to the blue sky beyond. "We're here to discuss a fire, Mr. Barnes. A fire that happened a long time ago."

"I don't know nothing about no fire," Barnes said through the crack.

"I've heard differently," Jackson said. "Stomp sent me over here. He said you should talk to me."

"You a lyin' dog," Barnes said.

Jackson sighed. "I'm not here to hurt anyone. I just need some answers for myself. I was there, Mr. Barnes. I was at the fire that night. I saw you on the stairs."

The eye looked at Jackson with renewed interest, then over at Cecil. Barnes pulled open the door, turned around, and walked back into the house. Jackson and Cecil followed him in. The Chihuahua squirmed between Red Eye's legs, growling at the intruders but keeping a safe distance from them. The smell of green beans and bacon wafted through the room.

The man stood next to a rocking chair against the far wall. There was barely enough space for the occupants of the room: the three grown men, the dog, a rocking chair, a beat-up sofa, and a table with a small black-and-white TV on it, a coat hanger stuck in the antenna slot. The floor was covered with carpet remnants. A small kitchen with a portable gas stove arched off to the left of the main room. Steam rose from a pot on the stove. Barnes eyed the men suspiciously. It was immediately obvious where he got the nickname. His right eye was sunken and dead, a black pupil surrounded by a burst of red veins. Around the eye, the man's face was stained red, dark blue, and a purple so deep it was almost black, like a permanent bruise. The bad eye seemed to turn in on itself. The good eye was wary, uneasy, like that of a trapped animal.

Jackson held out a hand in greeting. "My name is Jackson," he said. "Jackson Moon."

Ignoring the outstretched hand, Red Eye studied Jackson with his good eye. "You a Moon? Is that what you're tellin' me?"

Jackson nodded. "That's right. Jackson Moon."

"You here to kill me?"

The question took Jackson aback. Kill him? He looked over at Cecil, but Cecil just shrugged.

"Of course not. Why would I want to kill you?"

The man just sneered, as if Jackson had asked the silly question. The little dog growled, then let loose a barrage of quick barks. "I been waiting for this day, you know. Figgered you'd come for me."

"Look, Mr. Barnes... I don't know..."

"Who he?" Barnes snapped, thrusting a finger at Cecil. "He one of yo' — what you call them? — one of yo' clients?"

"My clients?"

"You know what I mean. He hire you to keep him out of jail?"

Cecil laughed. "I *met* Jackie in jail," he said. "What you talkin' about?"

Red Eye glared at Cecil, then back at Jackson. "You been in jail? I thought you was a lawyer. What you doin' in jail?"

Finally, understanding dawned on Jackson. "I see," he said. "You think I'm Ellis Moon, the lawyer. Nah, man. I'm his brother. I'm sure as hell no lawyer. Like I said, I'm not after anything from you."

Now Red Eye understood. He turned fully to Jackson and looked at him hard, took him in. Jackson swore it was the right eye, the ruined one, that really studied him.

"You the older one," he said. "The one what kill't Mary Brim."

"Goddamn it," Jackson said. "I didn't kill anybody."

Red Eye nodded, as if whether Jackson killed the woman or not didn't really matter much to him. "'Course you didn't," he said. "What, you and Mary, you had somethin' goin' on. You lovers, that it? You run off together that night?"

Cecil laughed out loud.

"No, we weren't lovers. Where did you hear that?"

Red Eye smiled. "Around," he said. "I hear it all around, boy. Kind of funny, tha's all. How you both disappeared on the same night."

Barnes acted like he was ninety years old. Jackson tried to pin his age, realizing the scar added some years. Jackie figured the man couldn't be more than thirty. He was small but wiry, his skin gaunt.

"You heard some shit," Jackson said.

Red Eye laughed a little as he sat down on his rocker, off his guard for the first time since they had come to the door. The Chihuahua jumped up into his lap. "Musta kill't her then," he surmised.

"You don't hear too well, do you, Mr. Barnes?"

Red Eye settled in his rocker and studied the two men again, Cecil with a quick glance and Jackson with a longer stare. The dead eye was downright spooky to Jackie. It seemed like the eye was taking in information that no good eye could pick up on.

"You and me," Barnes said. "We got somethin' in common then."

Jackson had to nod. "I guess we do."

"I was just a eight-year-old boy," Red Eye said as if unloading a weight from his shoulders. He had held his secret for years to protect himself, but he longed to tell it to this man because he knew the guilt of it would bind them together. Somehow he knew that this Jackson Moon would feel indebted and that Red Eye's guilt – a guilt he knew did not rightly belong to him – could be passed on to the man in his parlor. "I heard them folks burnin', saw Mr. Brim come in through the flame. He call't out to me, just before the steps fell through. Last thing I saw was you...." Barnes turned to Jackson suddenly, just as he said the words. Jackson swore his heart stopped for a moment, and that the ruined eye looked right through him, back to the night long ago. "Not sure how I saw it, but I did. It was you – in the doorway. Musta been you what pulled Brim out that fire. You won't but a baby yo'self – fifteen, sixteen-year-old?"

Jackson stared back at him, the horror and guilt from twenty years before returning to his eyes.

"You boys, you was just coverin' for that senator. Ain't that it? Somebody kill't him, somebody with money and power. Somebody who could get away with it. That's all it was."

Red Eye confused Jackson. "No," he said. "We were.... Those men, they were just cleaning up the town." It was a helpless gesture. Jackie realized he was just spouting the party line.

Barnes erupted in laughter and slapped his knee. The dog leapt from his lap and dashed into the small kitchen. "Holy Christ, son. I hope you ain't really believin' that bullshit. That is the biggest cow pie I ever had dumped on my doorstep."

That got Cecil to laugh, too. Jackson glared at him, but softened when he looked back at Red Eye Barnes.

"Damn, boy," Red Eye went on. "You white boys, you the ones that ran the goddamn house. Ain't you figgered that out? Brim delivered reg'lar payments. You coulda closed that bar any ol' time you wanted to. They won't no need to burn the place down."

Jackson remembered his father, meeting Brim on the railroad track, taking the sack.

"We were just cleaning up the town," Jackie said dreamily, echoing the words that had been fed to him, but not really believing them. "That's what my daddy told me. We were ridding the town of a terrible sin."

Red Eye just shook his head. "You a real prize, boy. I cain't figger if you is full of shit or just a plain idiot. Got to be one or the other."

Jackson watched the man rock in his chair. "Why don't you tell me then, Mr. Red Eye Barnes? You tell me how it was."

Barnes looked up at Jackie, considering it, then he looked out the single window as his gaze drifted off. And then his mouth began to move....

Over time, Billy Barnes had become invisible. At first, his mother had kept him up in the closet while she worked. Billy would sit quietly or lay down on the quilt his mother had made for him, listening to the grunts and wheezes of the men and – sometimes – the soft cries of his own mother. His mother had nowhere else to take Billy, and when she had no clients, she would sit on a chair by the closet door and read him stories. Sometimes, she would read long passages from the Good Book.

Lonnie Brim found out about the boy, but he let her keep him there, as long as he stayed out of the way and none of the customers complained. After a while, Billy ventured out of the room, making his way down into the bar where he would hide under a vacant back table. Or he would crawl up under the stairs, into a small nook, where he could watch the men on barstools, drinking bottles of beer and shots of pure whiskey. Then one of the men would lead a woman up the stairs, tramping right over the spot where Billy hid, the man swatting the girl's fanny and the woman laughing about it.

Billy would crouch up farther under the stairs when a white man came into the bar. Different white men would come, now and again. They wouldn't dally in the bar like the colored men did; they would pick out a woman quickly and take her upstairs without saying a word, except for maybe a curt order: "Get on up there, girl," or something mean and nasty. But then there was one white man – a senator, as Billy found out – who came regularly. He would even sit with the black men sometimes, drinking whiskey and dark beer.

And when he went up the stairs, he always took Angel. He wasn't like the other white men, disrespectful of the colored girls, grunting at them and ordering them up the stairs with ugly words and swears.

He would approach Angel slowly, just like you might come upon a real angel, and he would hold out his hand like a gentleman, ask if she would honor him with her presence. She would take the hand and rise up with a smile. Of all the women, Angel had the nicest dresses, the nicest shoes, the nicest hair – the senator made sure of that. After a while, no other man could take Angel up the stairs. Only the senator.

I gots to think that senator-man fell in love with Miss Angel. I gots to believe it. And I think, after while, she came to love him, too. One night, Angel didn't come in to work no more. Word was that the senator, he had taken her on home. Her and her little bundle – that's how the men would say it – Angel and her little bundle. I never see'd Angel again, the senator neither – not until that night.

Billy was up under the stairs again, wrapped in his quilt and growing sleepy from the murmur of voices, the clinking of glasses, and the pillows of rising tobacco smoke. The smoke settled in soft waves, like dunes of sand, up around the ceiling light. Billy had wedged up into the corner of the space beneath the stairs, his eyes easing closed when the white men stormed in, crashing through the door as if it were locked from the outside. Billy Barnes snapped fully awake and gasped aloud as the white men barged in, their eyes full of hatred and violence.

At first, four men stomped into the bar. Two of the white men had shotguns cocked and aimed at the crowd in the bar; the other two wielded clubs that they beat back the crowd with. Billy cowered back into his corner. He didn't recognize the men, but he didn't venture into the white neighborhoods very much. Shouts and screams rang out from the barroom, but the men with the sticks ordered them to quiet down. One of the men at a side table wanted to know what the hell was going on. One of the stick-men turned and, without warning, slammed his club against the man's forehead, blowing him out of the chair and flat to the ground. Screams welled up then, but the fourth man quieted them with a fierce crack of his club against a table.

Next in, behind the first four white men, walked the sheriff of Solomon's Rock. Billy had seen him before. He had even taken a girl up the stairs on occasion. He was the meanest of all. He would grab the girl's arm and thrust her up the steps, kicking her if she fell. But this was no social visit. Billy's heart raced and he heard a strange, low whine rising in his throat. He stuck a corner of the quilt into his mouth and clamped his teeth down on it, but he couldn't keep the tears from streaming down his face.

"Now we go'n do this nice and orderly," Sheriff Sump said. "Nice and orderly and nobody gets hurt. We need you folks to get on upstairs now. We got some business to tend to."

The customers in the bar looked at each other with questions in their eyes. But when the white sheriff shouted "Get!" and pulled out his own club, folks started moving up the stairs, up over Billy, some of the women starting to cry.

"What's this about, Mr. Sump?" Darrell asked from behind the bar. From his perch, Billy could see Darrell's side of the bar and, on a lower shelf, the shotgun that Lonnie kept back there in case of trouble.

"It ain't none of yo' affair, boy. You get on up them stairs with the rest of 'em."

"It is my affair, Sheriff." Darrell tried to stand tall and hold his ground. "Mr. Brim ain't around, so I got charge here."

The sheriff slammed his stick across the bar. The boom of it caused Darrell to jump.

"I am in charge here, boy," the sheriff roared. "You got that? All you got to do is get on up them stairs 'fore I put this club upside yo' head."

Darrell hesitated. Billy watched him move slowly down the bar until he was standing beside the shotgun. The sheriff glared at him for a few moments, then he turned away, nodding at one of the white men behind him. Just like that, the white man fired the shotgun. The blast boomed like a bomb going off in the small bar. Billy lost his breath. He heard screams above him, and he saw Darrell fly backward, slamming into a shelf of liquor bottles, his chest blown open. The bartender was still for a moment, propped against the shelf, as his head rolled back. He seemed to look at Billy with eyes that were dying out, as if pleading to the boy for help. Then the shelf gave way and Darrell hit the floor, the shelf tumbling atop him. Bottles smashed to the floor.

The sheriff waved at the dead man behind the bar. "Get him on up there," he ordered two of the men. To the other two, he growled, "You boys get the body out of the car. Hurry on up, now."

Billy watched in horror as the two men carried Darrell up the stairs. Blood poured through the stair slats, splattering on Billy's quilt, but the boy dared not move. He kept flat against the back wall, eyes wide. For a moment, the bar was empty except for the sheriff, who lit up a cigar while waiting for the other two men to come back. He sucked on the stogie, puffing it lit, before taking a long, deep drag and blowing out currents of thick blue smoke. As the sheriff looked around the bar, Billy held his breath. For a moment, everything seemed to stand still.

Them other two men came back in. They was carrying that senator, one aholt to his arms, t'other to his legs. He was wrapped in a blanket, and blood was soaking through it. That man was dead as hell, I can surely tell you that. Dead as holy hell before that fire was ever set. They were carrying him like a sack of potatoes. It was dead weight under that blanket. Ain't no life there a'tall.

The two men carried the wrapped body up the stairs. Half way up, just above Billy Barnes, one man lost his grip and the dead man's head slammed down on the wooden step. Out of the folds of the blanket, a single eye glared at Billy. All the boy could see was the iris, shrouded in shadows like a marble at the bottom of a dark pool, and a pupil as empty as dreamless sleep, cold as a deep cellar.

"Jesus Christ, Zach, watch what you're doin'," one of the men said.

"Son-of-a-bitch is heavy," said the other.

"Come on. Just pick him up and let's get the hell out of here."

The head rose up again as the second man picked up his end. The steps above Billy bowed as the men carried the body up. The sheriff followed after them. The steps creaked from the strain of all the men. Suddenly, the sheriff stopped on the step directly above Billy's head. He stopped cold and, once again, Billy's whole world went still. What was the sheriff doing? Why had he stopped? Had he somehow sensed Billy just below him? Billy came close to crying out or dashing for the door, just to break the suspense of the white man standing still on the stair above him. But then Billy heard a match strike up, the sheriff puffing on the cigar again, blowing out smoke. Then, slowly, the sheriff made his way on up the steps.

Billy could hear the sheriff calling out orders. "Get on up there, now. C'mon. Sure was a shame about Darrell. We don't want another accident like that, now do we?" Billy could tell that the white men were herding people into the upper attic, no more than a crawl space above the third floor. It had a door that pulled down from the ceiling and old wooden steps that folded out. He heard the door squeak open and the stairs snapping into place as they pulled them down. Women were screaming and crying, men were struggling against the men who hit them with their sticks. They screamed once, all together, as the white men grunted and the sheriff said, "Get them legs up in there now." Billy imagined the two dead bodies getting shoved up into the attic. He heard the door close up, followed by the muffled cries of people locked in the attic.

Three men dashed back down the stairs and out the door. They ran back in carrying five red barrels, maybe two feet high and as big around as a bicycle tire. Billy could smell the acrid odor as they carried the cans up the stairs. He heard liquid being sloshed on the floor above, then all five of the white men clamored back down the steps, pouring gas behind them. Billy huddled into the quilt as the gas streamed down through the steps. One of the cans banged down the stairs and rolled across the floor. The men splashed gasoline over tables and across the bar, throwing the cans against the wall as they emptied them.

One man stayed behind. The sheriff took a last look in the bar from the doorway and said, "I'll let you do the honors, Marvin," to the man who was left. The man's face was bleeding, his shirt ripped, the clothes smeared with dirt. From the darkness of his eyes, a sparkle of delight danced as he walked slowly to the doorway, drawing in the fumes through his thick nose. He stood on the threshold and smiled like a demon, striking up a lighter and holding it high over his head as if observing some sacred ritual. Billy could hear the wind brushing against the tiny flame, louder even than the muffled cries, louder than Billy's heartbeat. Then the man opened his palm and the fire fell. It dropped toward the floor, suspended for a moment – it seemed to Billy – over a puddle of gasoline that reflected the spark. A frozen moment before the end of the world.

All I recall after that is the flames and the heat. I came out from under the stair, them screams cryin' out up above me. Sounded like heaven dyin'. Heard my mama up there, burnin' to death. I started on up. Somehow I made it to the first landing. That's when Mr. Brim came through the door. He shouted somethin' at me, but I couldn't hear nothin'. I remember yellin' at him how my mama was up there. That's all I cared about. I was gonna go on up there and get her down.

"That's when I saw you," Barnes said, looking up at Jackie. "I saw you in the doorway, looking in at Brim. The stair collapsed. Next thing I recall was waking up down in the cellar, half burned up."

Jackson had not moved during the story. The images came back to him now. The smells, the sounds, the searing heat in the doorway of the bar. Slats had left him down at the track to keep an eye on Brim, to make sure Brim didn't get up to the bar before the fire was set. Jackie had heard the shotgun blast and, a little later, saw the flames rising up. Brim stumbled up from the tracks, made his way groggily to the bar. Jackson followed Brim up the slope, heard Brim yelling something as he entered the doorway. When Jackie made it to the door, he saw Brim in the burning bar. When the stairs collapsed, waves of heat blew Brim to the ground. The black man was motionless on the floor as Jackie made his way among the flames. He remembered the roar and crackle of the fire as he grabbed Brim by the ankles and dragged him out. Worse than the sound of that fire was the silence in the cabin of Red Eye Barnes after he had finished his story and left his good eye set on Jackson Moon.

"You're telling me you survived that fire?" Jackson asked him finally, looking up at the disfigured black man.

Red Eye smiled. "Amazin', ain't it? One of them things cain't nobody explain. I don't remember much after the stairs went out. There's a black man, name of Collins, he tol't me once that it was him what found me down in that cellar, little boy half-dead. Other folks, they say I just wandered out of there. Say I ended up in the colored section, moseyin' down the street all burnt up, not even knowin' what happened to me. Folks took me in, here and there. Passed me around, you might say. Took care of me. They always tole me to keep quiet about it, too. They knowed it wouldn't do me no good, white folk findin' out how I walked off from that fire. The black folk, they knew I could tell some stories, maybe get myself kill't or worse."

"Don't the white folks ask you about that eye of yours?" Cecil asked.

"I just say it was a accident. Gas tank blew up in my face. Colored folk, they know the truth. White folk, those that even care, they figger me for another dumb-ass nigger what blew his silly self up."

Jackson looked up at Red Eye Barnes. He studied his scars, found himself shaking his head slowly. "I'm sorry," he managed to say.

"You all sorry," Red Eye snapped. "And don't think I don't know why you pulled Brim out of there. It wouldn't do for him to be kill't in the fire. Hell, he was the one they blamed for settin' it. You pulled him out so they could chase him down later and shoot him while he was holed up in his own house. They planted that gun on him, boy. You know that. It was all a bunch a nonsense, Brim burnin' down the bar then shootin' at a bunch of white folks on his front lawn. Silliest notion I ever heard tell of."

Jackson was shaking his head as if warding off demons. "I don't know about any of that. They didn't tell me what was going on. I didn't light that fire. It wasn't me."

Red Eye just shook his own head sadly. He was petting the dog that had returned to his lap. "Yes it was, Mr. Jackson Moon. You didn't pour the gasoline, but you might as well've lit the match."

16

"Who is this?" asked Ellis Moon.

Cecil finally had the lawyer on the phone. He had gone through an operator and two receptionists. They kept telling him Moon wasn't at the office. Cecil threw enough names around – Jackson, Ghost Grant, Red Eye Barnes – that he finally had Ellis Moon on the other end of the line.

"My name is Cecil. Cecil Blanks. My friends, they call me Shark."

Silence. "And how may I help you, Mr. Blanks?"

"I was thinkin' more in terms of how I might help you," Cecil said. Maybe this was his way into the Grant operation. Might as well cover his bets. If Grant and the lawyer Moon came out on top of all this, Cecil wanted a piece. He'd take something simple: look after some of the whores, maybe run a strip club, whatever.

"I don't understand," said Moon.

"Well, you see, I've been hanging out with your brother here in Solomon's Rock. Let's just say there's some interesting stuff going on. Stuff you should probably know about."

"Is that so?" The lawyer acted nonchalant, but Cecil knew he had him hooked. He would give him a taste.

"You ever hear of a guy called Red Eye Barnes?"

Moon thought about it. "Seems like I recall ... A black man, had some sort of accident...."

Cecil wasn't sure if Moon was playing it dumb, or if he really didn't know the story.

"That's what he tells people," Cecil said, "but that ain't how it went."

Silence, then: "Yes?"

"This Barnes fella, he was in the bar that night, the whorehouse. He saw it all, Mr. Moon. He says Lonnie Brim didn't set that fire. Bunch of white folk did." Cecil paused for effect. "Bunch of important white people."

"Is that what he said ... this Red Eye?"

"Sounds like he might be telling the truth. The guy says that senator, the one that got killed, he was dead before he ever got to the colored bar."

A long silence. Moon was taking it in. Cecil knew he had taken the bait.

"Anything else?" Moon asked.

"Yeah, well, maybe so. I think we should meet. Talk about how I might be able to help you folks out."

"Us folks?"

"You know. You, Grant, the operation. I got skills, Mr. Moon."

"Skills? What type of skills."

Cecil had to think about it. "Well, you know, I been in prison."

"Prison? What, they teach you how to make chairs?"

"Chairs? Man, I'm talking about knowing my way around. I could take care of business. Maybe watch after your girls, make sure they stay out of trouble. Anything you need."

Ellis Moon placed the phone receiver on the desk for a moment and rubbed his temples. Who was this guy? He got hold of some interesting information, no doubt about it, but "watch after your girls"? Was the guy selling services as a pimp? What did he really want?

Ellis picked up the phone again. "I think you've got the wrong idea about me," he said.

"Hey, I'm just saying I'm flexible, that's all. For now, I could be your eyes and ears around here. I think you need that. Some shit's going down, man. You don't need no surprises – am I right?"

"Well, maybe you could be helpful."

"That's all I'm saying. I just want to be helpful. If you like my style, maybe you could give me a regular job."

"Hmmm. We'll have to see about that. But you're right. I don't get a chance to go down to Solomon's Rock very often. Maybe you could keep your eyes open."

"There you go. That's why they call me Shark. I keep my eyes open, prowl the waters you might say, smell for blood."

Smell for blood? Ellis wondered if the guy was for real.

"What do you say?" Cecil Blanks asked. "Maybe we should meet."

"Maybe so."

"How about this? I'm planning a little trip down to Atlanta anyways. You know that little place over on Forsythe, two blocks up from Five Corners? The Back Room, I think it's called."

"You mean the lounge?"

"Right. The strip club. We could meet there."

"Why there, Mr. Blanks?"

"I got a friend there, that's all. Her name's Starry."

"Starry?"

"That ain't her real name," Cecil pointed out.

"Oh, her stage name. I get it."

"Right. Her stage name. Starry over at the Back Room. You know the place?"

"Yeah. I know it."

Cecil's imagination started galloping again. "'Course you know it. Shit, like preaching to the choir. You probably run the fucking place – am I right?"

"I'm a lawyer, Mr. Blanks."

"Yeah, right. I know that. But Grant – he own the place or what?"

Ellis found himself pinching the bridge of his nose. "He has an investment, yes."

"Damn, I knew it! You probably go there after hours, right? Get a personal show, a little overtime action."

"It's a business. There are laws...."

"Laws, right. I'm sure that's a major concern."

"As a matter of fact..."

"Hey, you don't need to get all uptight with me. I'm with you, man. Got to keep up the image. I'm nothin' if not discreet."

"That was my immediate impression."

"You know, I could help you at the club. I know the strip routines up and down. I could help the girls, show 'em what the guys like. Pump up the tips, if you know what I mean. Work out a few extras. I got all kinds of ideas."

Ellis was losing patience, but knew it was best just to humor the idiot. "Well, maybe we can discuss some of your ideas when we meet."

"Yeah, sure. That'd be great. Tomorrow night?"

"That would be all right. How about nine o'clock?"

"I'll be there."

"Good."

"How will I know you?" Cecil asked.

"You just talk to the girl out front, tell her the Shark's in the house. I'll get the message."

Ellis could almost see the numbskull beaming. "Hey, I like that."

"I thought you might."

Moon hung up with Cecil Blanks and massaged his temples. His next call was to the Back Room. He asked for James.

"James. It's Ellis Moon."

"Hello, Mr. Moon. How you doin'?"

"Fine, James. Listen, I need a favor. You got a stripper there, stage name of Starry?"

"Well, sure. Nice girl. But now won't that make Belle a little jealous?"

"She's not for me. I just want to talk to her."

"Sure, whatever. You need a private room?"

"A private room to *talk*, James. I want you there, too. I need both of you to keep an eye on a guy. I guess he's a customer."

"Well, sure. You're the boss."

"Let's meet at eight. I need to go over some things."

"You got it."

Ellis started to hang up. "Oh, and James?"

"Yes, sir?"

"You might as well set Belle up for me, too."

"There you go, sir. Now you're talking."

Moon hung up. He couldn't believe what he had to deal with. There was still one more unsavory call to make – to the courthouse at Solomon's Rock.

17

Noxie was excited about working with Cracks. They had done a job once before, Noxie's second after the Ulster Graham hit. Cracks broke into the house, talked to Grant Longely and his wife as they lay in bed, and then left Noxie to shoot them both in the head, the wife first. Afterwards, Cracks smiled and patted Noxie on the back. "Good job, Edward," Cracks had told him. "I'm proud of you." Noxie imagined that it was his father who said the words.

Together Cracks and Noxie took the elevator and got off one floor above Casey Hart, the cop who was now the prosecution's star witness against Michael Grant. Cracks had gotten good information on Hart. He was in Room 306, and the rooms on either side of and across from Hart were locked down and deserted. A 24-hour guard was placed in front of the hotel door. There were two, sometimes three, cops or FBI in the room with Hart at all times. And, of course, unlike Farmer, Casey Hart was himself a policeman, licensed to carry a gun and trained to use it. The job would be Noxie's toughest one yet. A moment of truth for him. Proof of his abilities. He was glad to have Cracks along. They walked up to the door labeled 406, both of them dressed in dark blue suits and red ties. Cracks rapped on the door.

A man opened the door and looked out. "Yes?" he asked.

"We're with hotel security," Cracks told him. "We need to check your room."

"The police were already here...," he protested.

"Yes sir, I understand. It's for your own protection."

The man shrugged and walked back into his room, leaving the door open behind him. He was wearing a gray suit, the tie pulled loose, no shoes. The television was on a local news program. Cracks walked into the room first, and before Noxie had fully closed the door behind him, Cracks had stepped behind the man and slit his throat. Noxie turned just as the thin line of the razor slice began to spit blood. The man fell forward, first to his knees, then flat on his face. A gurgle rose up, from the man's mouth or from the cut, Noxie wasn't sure. Cracks threw a bedspread over the man and went straight out to the balcony, slipping on his rubber gloves.

"What the fuck is that?" Noxie asked. Cracks was strapping some weird thing on. It looked like one of those get-ups you would put a baby in, hang it in a doorway so the kid could spring up and down. It looked like Cracks was wearing a big diaper. Noxie giggled until Cracks whacked him on the side of the head.

"We'll laugh about it later, Edward. We got a job to do now."

Cracks clipped one end of a rubber cord to the diaper thing, the other end he clamped to the balcony rail, then he stepped over the rail and held on.

"Soon as you hear the glass shatter," he told Noxie, "you got to take out the hall man. I'll get to the door."

"And I'll come in, guns blazing."

Cracks gave him a wry look. "Just remember: Your buddy Cracks will be in there, too."

"Right," said Noxie, sorry now that he made the guns-blazing comment. He had to subdue some of his enthusiasm, Cracks would often tell him, channel it into total focus.

"Timing is everything, Edward."

Noxie nodded solemnly, but Cracks eyed the boy a little longer before nodding back. When Cracks leapt backward off the balcony, the rubber cord pulled taut, then stretched out, lowering Cracks slowly like a yo-yo descending. Cracks floated down to the lower balcony and, as his feet touched ground, he grabbed the rail and looked up at Noxie. Noxie removed the clamp and dropped it down to his mentor. Cracks placed the rubber cord on the ground, slipped out of the diaper-thing, and waved back up to Edward. It was a go. Noxie walked back across Room 406, past the dead man wrapped in the bedspread, toward the door. He checked the clip in his 9mm Glock 17 and pulled on his gloves. Cracks had an old Thompson. Thought he was Al Capone or something. The Thompson still had it though. Nothing like a reliable submachine gun when you needed to take out a room full of law.

Hart and the two FBI agents were playing poker. Hart was up almost fifty bucks and in a good mood. The one agent, Colby, was dour and terse, a heavy smoker, but Hart liked Agent Steele. He was big and gruff, deep-voiced, and funny. He had a sleepy, casual way about him, but he noticed things that the other agents missed: an unlocked closet on the floor, a man in the lobby with a suspicious satchel, a slight twitch at the corner of Colby's mouth when he was bluffing.

Hart enjoyed the Colby/Steele shift and usually stayed up late with them, playing poker, watching a game, telling stories. The other agents bored the hell out of Hart: Stevens with his beady eyes, always standing by the door; Martin watching TV all day, even the soaps; Alexander on the phone, checking in with his wife every goddamn hour. Steele was a man's man, and a good agent. He respected Hart for what he was doing, understood what kind of balls it took to go up against the Grant machine.

Hart was pissing into the toilet when the balcony's sliding glass door shattered. His heart leapt into his throat, and he cursed himself for leaving his gun on the table. He had to be a big shot, sitting the gun next to his winnings like some goddamn Wild-West outlaw. Now he was standing in the bathroom with his dick in his hand.

Cracks riddled the glass door with bullets as he barreled through it, rolling into the heavy curtains and coming up on one knee in the middle of the floor. Colby was fumbling for his gun when Cracks stitched a line of bullets across his chest, blowing him off his chair. The second agent dove to the floor as gunfire riddled the wall behind him. Steele got off two shots from his Magnum. One bullet thumped into Cracks below the left rib. Cracks screamed as he fell back and blew off another rally that split open Steele's head.

Hart rushed out of the bathroom, closed and locked the bedroom door, and picked up the phone as Cracks struggled toward the door to let Noxie in. Noxie had come out of the third-floor stairwell with his semi-automatic leveled. The guard didn't have a chance. Noxie shot him four times as the agent stumbled backwards down the hall. Then he heard the glass shatter. Perfect timing.

His heart raced when he heard Steele's pair of metallic gunshots. He tried the door. Locked. He started to fire at the knob, when Cracks opened the door, his white shirt soaked in dark blood.

"Damn it, Cracks," Noxie cried, rushing into the room. "What happened?"

"He's locked in the bedroom," Cracks wheezed. "You've got to take care of him."

Noxie walked directly at the bedroom, blowing bullets into the wooden door. The door splintered and cracked as Noxie pummeled it with bullet holes.

Noxie crashed through the door and rolled on the floor into the bedroom, still firing. He rose up as the bathroom door slammed shut and the lock clicked. Noxie popped a new thirty-round cartridge into his Glock, just to make sure, and came at the bathroom door, obliterating it with a hail of gunfire. When he kicked open what was left of the door, Hart was laying in the tub with his chest torn open, the shredded shower curtain draped over him.

Noxie wrapped the body in the shower curtain and dragged it back through the hotel room and out onto the balcony. "You don't fuck with Michael Grant," he proclaimed as he strung the rubber cord around Hart's neck, tied it to the railing, and rolled the body over the rail.

Back in the room, Noxie stepped up to Cracks. Cracks was wheezing hard. "Help me up," he pleaded.

"The job is the thing," Noxie stated, quoting the words of his teacher. "You got to take care of business."

"Goddamn it, Edward, what are you babbling about? We've got to get out of here."

"No emotion. No regrets. Do what you have to do." It was Noxie, still proudly quoting the man who had taught him how to be a professional.

Cracks looked up at him, first with confusion, and then with the fear Noxie had come to love. The ultimate measure of respect. The teacher looking at the student, granting him the look of terror. "Come on now, Edward," he pleaded. "What the fuck...?"

No emotion. Do it when you still have the charge. Noxie admired the respect one more moment and wished he could see it in his own father's eyes. Then he blew a hole in Crackson's forehead.

He left the room and headed for the stairwell. By the time the police showed up, Noxie was out into the night, walking calmly down the streets of Atlanta.

The police found a hotel security guard on the second floor landing, a bullet in his throat. They found Armond James, an insurance salesman attending an industry conference, in his room on the fourth floor with his throat cut. In Room 306, they found two dead FBI agents, one with a line of bullet wounds across his chest, the other with his head blown open. Frank Crackson, a known henchman of Michael Grant, was there, too, shot once in the ribs and once squarely in the center of his forehead.

And Casey Hart – the star witness in the prosecution's case against Grant – was bobbing from the balcony, his chest ripped apart, a rubber cord around his neck, blood drooling down to the sidewalk below.

18

Even in half-sleep, in that wispy moment before the mind comes fully awake, Durlen "Sweets" Malloy realized that there was a presence in the room. He rolled over in the bed and tried to make out the figure. He couldn't see him, but he knew he was there. Tucked in the shadows that the moon formed in the dark room. Sweets sat up in bed. He knew the smell of the man who was sitting in a corner of his single-room apartment. It was a smell he feared.

A match blazed up in the darkness. The man touched the match to the end of his cigar and puffed greedily to get the cigar going. He waved the match until it died, leaving only the ember of the cigar tip to light up the man's lean, hard face. Sweets recalled a friend who told him about a book on dinosaurs that his son had checked out of the library. The friend swore one of the pictures was of Commissioner Sump in a former life. They took to calling Sump "Terrible Lizard" or "Lizard Man," and it always made Sweets laugh. Except when the Terrible Lizard was sitting in a chair less than ten feet away from him.

"We got us a problem, boy," Bill Sump stated. "You know I don't like problems."

"Yes, suh," Sweets answered. "I know you don't."

Sump puffed the cigar. "How come you never told me about this Red Eye fella? I thought we was friends, you and me."

"Red Eye? I never saw no need..."

"No need, Sweets?" Sump broke in calmly. "No need? We got ourselves a fella that knows some stuff he ought not to. We can't have a boy like that runnin' his mouth off, now can we?"

"He won't talk, Mr. Sump. I can promise you that. He ain't never said nothin'...."

"Well, I know that ain't true," Sump said. "He is most surely saying somethin' now. I got the word from a very reliable source. He is sho' 'nuff talkin'."

Sweets didn't respond. He watched the man smoke his cigar. He wished the old commissioner would drop dead right there, just drop out of the chair, clutching his heart. Sweets wondered how he had ever gotten indebted to the monster. The man could wring out his weaknesses, feed his fears, unlock his deepest shame. And now Sweets was trapped.

"You should have told me, boy," Sump went on. "You should have told me about this Red Eye fella. I had heard some stories here and there, but I never did know how much that boy saw. He's got quite a story to tell." In the light of the cigar ember, Sweets saw Bill Sump's pinpoint eyes staring at him.

Sweets tried to say something but couldn't. He was scared, and he knew anything he might say would be a lie. He didn't want to make Mr. Sump madder by lying to him. "I's sorry, suh. I ... I didn't think he was fool enough to talk."

Sump's bony head nodded slowly. "It ain't yo' job to think, son."

Sweets sat still on the bed.

Sump sighed, as if letting Sweets know that he regretted what had to be done. "If that boy can't keep his mouth shut, somebody's go'n have to shut it for him." Sump leaned into the moonlight. "You understand me, boy?"

Sweets nodded. His hands were trembling so hard that he clasped them together.

19

Jackson still wasn't sure if he had heard the foreman right. The construction crew had come to move Frank's house, and the foreman was having a problem with Jackie's aunt.

"There's an old lady here," the foreman said. "She's chained to the house."

"Excuse me," Jackie said into his parents' phone. "What do you mean?"

"I mean just what I say. She's chained up to the house."

"Well, can't you unchain her?"

"It ain't my job to be removing folks from the premises, Mr. Moon. Especially a kooky old broad who's chained herself to a pole."

"Right. I see your point."

Frank was supposed to be staying with her friend Mrs. Lott, but driving over to the property in the beat-up Neon, Jackie knew it could only be Aunt Frank. When he got to the house and crossed the lawn, he saw his aunt sitting on the porch floor, a heavy chain wrapped around her three times and around the porch column twice. The foreman shrugged, then held out his arms, palms up, as Jackie approached.

Jackson stood next to the foreman, both of them looking at the old woman wrapped in the chain. Aunt Frank looked at the foreman, then at Jackie, then back at the foreman, then back at Jackie. She wore a gray print dress and flat-bottomed canvas shoes. Bolts of long gray hair were bundled up on top of her head.

"Why did this man chain me to my house?" she asked.

"Hey, I didn't…"

Jackson put a hand on the foreman's shoulder. "It's okay," he said. "I'll handle it."

The foreman walked away, shaking his head, and Jackie sat down on the porch next to his aunt.

Frank looked at the chains on her with basset-hound eyes.

"Why did that man chain me to my house?" she asked again.

"That man didn't chain you to the house, Frank."

"He didn't?"

"No. He didn't."

"Then who chained me to this pole, Jackson?"

Jackie looked over at her, glad that she at least knew who he was. "Well, let's take a close look at that. Who do you think chained you to the pole?"

She looked at the chains for a long time. Just when Jackson assumed she had forgotten the question, she answered: "I did?"

"That's right. You did."

"I did?"

"Uh-huh."

"Are you sure?"

"Yeah. I'm sure."

She kept looking down, her long face scrunched up as she strained to figure it all out.

"Why did you chain yourself to the house, Frank?"

She thought about it, then looked over at Jackson. He could see, like a cloud clearing, the understanding dawning on her face.

"Did you know I was born in this house?"

To Jackson, the question felt like a dagger to his heart. "No," he said softly. "I don't think I knew that."

"It's true," she said. "I was married in this house, too. My only child, she died in this house. I thought she was just sleeping in the crib. My husband, he spent the last day of his life sittin' on the lounge chair in the front parlor. He watched the baseball game, then told me to take him to the hospital. He never came home."

"I'm sorry," was all Jackie could think to say.

She looked away. Jackson could smell the ripening figs from the tree in Frank's backyard. The rich smell hung in a passing breeze.

"You're not losing the house. These men are here to move it. The lot on Maple Street – remember?

She looked at Jackie, then away again. "I can walk out back there, through the woods, far as Helms Creek." She turned to look at her nephew, to make sure the creek's name sunk in. It was her husband's name, her name. "Helms Creek," she said again, then looked back at the path through the woods. "I can walk all that way and never leave the land that belongs to me. Cain't nobody say nothin' to me about it. They do and I'll tell them, 'This here land beneath my feet, it is mine. It belongs to me.' I can walk across it any time I please. All the ways to Helms Creek."

She looked back at Jackson.

"I understand, Frank."

"It belonged to my father," she said dreamily. "My father's father."

Jackie didn't know what to tell her. Perhaps the truth. "I'm sorry, but the land doesn't belong to you anymore. The county took it and sold it. It's called 'eminent domain.' They can buy your land if it's for the greater good. You'll get a lot of money."

Jackie sighed. For Frank, money wasn't the thing. Not this time. "You know what, Frank? There's a place in Florida, out near where I used to live. I can take you there. You can walk across the sand, right along the surf, until you can't walk anymore, until you are purely worn out. Just as far as you can go, right along the beach, and not one soul can tell you any different. You can look out at the ocean, look out as far as the eye can see, and you can say that water, every drop of it, belongs to you and no one can say it doesn't."

"I could walk barefoot?" she asked.

"Sure you can."

She thought about that. "They got donkeys you can ride?" she asked.

"No donkeys," said Jackie.

She nodded. "They got those at the Grand Canyon."

"Yeah, I know."

"Can ride them right down in."

"Right."

They were quiet for a few minutes. Jackson sensed that his aunt was drifting off. He put a finger on her cheek and turned her eyes slowly to him.

"A long time ago – I must have been twelve, thirteen maybe – we were walking, just you and me, coming across my daddy's backyard. Beautiful spring day. I remember the sun coming down through the trees and the shadows dancing through the grass. You stopped me, Frank, dead in the middle of that yard. Looked right in my eyes, and you know what you made me do?"

"I made you promise," she said clearly.

Jackie looked at her, surprised at what she could remember. "That's right. You made me promise. Even back then they worried over you. They weren't sure you could take care of yourself, and Uncle Rufus was already awful sick. You made me promise, right then and there, that I'd never let them put you away."

"You promised," she said, just above a whisper.

"It's a promise I intend to keep."

She nodded slowly. "Okay," she said.

"But you've got to remember where your house is. You've got to keep things in your head. You've got to try."

"I'll try, Jackson."

"I'm going to take you over to Mrs. Lott's now. She said she would look out for you until your house was all settled in over on Maple."

Frank looked concerned.

"What's wrong, Aunt Frank?"

"They ain't takin' it to Alabama?"

"No. Not Alabama. It'll be right over on Maple Street."

"You sure about that?"

"I'm sure."

Frank nodded. "All right."

"All right," Jackson said, looking back out at the road.

"Jackson?"

"Yeah, Frank?"

"Can you get this chain off of me?"

20

Ellis Moon met with Grant in the small meeting room, just before the prosecution team arrived. Cigarette smoke was already dense in the stagnant air.

"Well, Ghost, they will be moving you soon. Sometime over the next couple of days. Out to Forsyth County, as we discussed before."

"Change of venue," Grant leered, as if the ploy was an ingenious scheme.

"I still don't think it's a good idea," Moon pointed out. He thought they would be better off with a jury close to Atlanta. A big-city jury would be more tolerant of pornography, Moon reasoned. More open-minded. But Grant had insisted. The prosecution, of course, had no problem with the change.

Grant waved Moon off. "So what're those assholes comin' here for?" he asked, referring to the prosecution.

Moon shrugged. "I doubt they want to go to trial now. Not without any good witnesses. All they really have is the truck driver, the one running the porno, and he didn't even know your name until the police brought it up. They've got to go after you with the community test. That will be a lot harder for them. The interstate rap was a solid charge."

Grant laughed. "They ain't got shit on me now. The stupid fucks."

Moon nodded. "They'll go for the community test, Michael. Whatever the community finds offensive is pornographic. It's an ambiguous law. I don't think the prosecution has any interest in running with it. They knows it will just turn you into a martyr for the free-speech guys. They'll want to deal...."

"No deal," snapped Grant. "No fucking deal."

Moon held out a hand. "Don't worry. We're holding the cards now. Maybe they're desperate. Maybe they'll offer you a suspended sentence, probation. We should at least listen to what they have to say. We've got nothing to lose."

Grant grunted. "No fucking deal."

"No deal," said Moon, trying to calm the man down. "Nothing that will keep you in prison. We're going to get you out."

Grant nodded, peered around the room. He was looking away from Moon when he asked suddenly: "What about your brother?"

"My brother?"

"Yeah. The one making all the trouble."

"Jackson? What about him?"

Grant put his hands on the table and leaned over to Moon. "You got to shut him up. He's raising a ruckus down there."

Moon was always surprised at how much Grant knew, even locked away in prison. He often wondered how he got his information. "I'll tell him to lay off. He doesn't want any trouble. I'm sure of that. I've tried...."

"You don't try, goddamn it! You do it. You're his own blood for god's sake. If you can't control your own brother, how can I expect you to control my whole fucking operation? Jesus, Moon. Shut the guy up."

"I will, Ghost. I will." Grant pulled away slowly and started pacing the room. He lit another cigarette and blew a swirl of smoke up around the bare light bulb. Ellis remembered the Cecil Blanks character who had called him. "I've got a guy to keep an eye on Jackson down in Solomon's Rock. It's under control."

"The business comes before everything. Remember how I told you that? Family, friends, God. The business comes first." He shot a menacing glare at Ellis Moon to drive home his point. "My daddy once bit off his own brother's ear. Bit it off, Moon. Spit it in his face. He did that for the business. His brother, he didn't listen too good, so he lost an ear. You understand me?" God, the ear story. Every time Grant told Moon about his uncle's bitten-off ear, he seemed to relay a different message with it. It was like a parable by Jesus. The Prodigal Ear. "Yeah, I got it."

Grant stopped in his tracks, glared again at Ellis. "I don't think you do," he claimed. "You got to take care of your brother. Do whatever it takes. Take care of him, or I will."

Now Moon got it. He felt a touch of nausea. All of this was getting out of hand. Was Grant telling him to kill his own brother? "Jesus Christ. Slow down. Jackson isn't going anywhere with this stuff. He won't find anything, and even if he did, it was twenty years ago."

"You want all that shit to come out? Shit about your own daddy? We all in this together, you know that."

"Yeah, I know."

Grant sat back down at the table. "Look here, I know about family. But this is for all of us. Just take care of it. For all of us. Take care of it."

Moon nodded. "It's under control," he said again.

"That's all I want to hear." Grant drew hard on his cigarette and sighed out billows of smoke. He studied Moon as if he were deciding what to do about him. "I don't know why I ever got mixed up in that small-time shit. Pain in the fucking ass, you ask me. It wasn't such a bad idea – get the whorehouses goin' in the cow towns, then let the locals run 'em. We get plenty of cash without the hassles, right?" Grant scoffed. "I was a young stud back then. Fucked up royally on that one. Local yokels can't handle this shit. Smallest problem, they come runnin' back to us. Want us to take care of it. It just ain't worth it. Good money, I suppose, but it ain't fucking worth it, far as I'm concerned."

"So why don't we get out?" Ellis asked.

Grant shrugged. "Hell, I don't know. It's kind of fun havin' the local fucks under my thumb. Besides, what would these poor hicks do without us? We provide a valuable public service. Keep those boys satisfied, know what I mean? Otherwise, they'd be out fucking with the cows. Makes the milk taste funny." Grant laughed hard and slapped the table. "We keeping them cows safe, Moon. Think of it that way. Shit, some of them boys, they never go back to women. You understand what I'm saying? They wives in bed, wantin' some attention, and the boy is out in the barn, serenading the cattle."

Again, Grant burst into laughter. Such was his opinion of anyone living outside the city, a funny stance given that Grant himself grew up in Solomon's Rock and got his start there. Grant even wanted to start a magazine dedicated to sex with animals, target it at the cow towns. God, Moon could just imagine the legal troubles that would spark up. Here in a state where oral sex with your own wife was still illegal, Grant wanted to sell pictures of men having sex with dogs and sheep. The guy was out of control. Problem was, Moon realized, the damn rag would probably pull in a mint.

"What about this Marston fuck?" Grant asked, suddenly bringing up the man who was trying to move in on his business.

"He can't touch you, Ghost. You know that."

"Way I hear it, he's got some fuckers trying to work the inside. I didn't get where I am by being lax."

"Okay, okay. I'll get a couple more guys on that, see if we can dig up anything about Marston's operation."

Grant nodded slowly. "That brother of yours," he growled. "You think Marston might have his mitts on him?"

The question surprised Ellis. "No," he said. "Hell no. My brother wouldn't want any part of that. That's why he ran in the first place. He doesn't have the stomach for that kind of stuff."

Grant kept nodding. His whole body swayed. It was a slow, hypnotic, menacing movement.

"This Marston? If he gets a finger – a fucking pinky – into my business, I'll hold you personally responsible. You got that?"

Moon studied the eyes. "I got it," he said.

The guard rapped on the metal door. The prosecution had arrived. When the guard swung open the door, a small, chubby man appeared – five-foot-six, forty-eight years old, thinning blond hair combed to the side, blue eyes, nervous smile. It was the assistant prosecutor, Harold Rains. His arms were full of notebooks and papers. Grant's growl was audible. Rains came from one of those cow towns he despised. He was a competent lawyer, but not an outstanding one. He had been passed over three times for lead prosecutor, most recently by the man who followed him into the room. At six-foot-three, Caleb Jordan towered over his assistant. He wore an immaculate navy blue suit with a silk paisley tie. Early forties, he had a long face and square chin, brown eyes, and jet-black hair. He was tough, competent, no-nonsense, but he didn't especially like the limelight. He was only interested in getting the job done. Grant called them "the hick and the dick."

The hick spoke first. "Ellis," he nodded. "Mr. Grant."

"Harry," said Moon, nodding back. "Hope you are well."

The dick said nothing. He sat down, opened his briefcase, and pulled out a small folder. Rains started sifting through his pile of documents.

"What's up, gentlemen?" Ellis beamed. He didn't really approve of Grant's murderous tactics, but it sure left the defense in an enviable position.

Rains looked up from his papers. "We thought we would compare notes. Talk about the charges against your client. Maybe come to an agreement."

"An agreement?" said Moon.

"That's right. We think it's time to talk about a deal."

Ellis smiled. "Well, that's interesting. You weren't talking deal earlier."

Jordan broke in, exasperated. "Oh, you mean before your client killed off all our witnesses?"

Grant started to bolt up from his chair, but Moon placed a hand on his knee. "Now, Caleb, that's a vicious charge. I hope you can back that one up better than you can back up the current charges against my client."

A smile broke out on Jordan's face, the kind of shit-eating grin that sent a chill down Moon's back. Jordan had something up his sleeve.

"Let's just put it this way," Jordan preened. "If I were your client, I would take whatever Mr. Rains here is offering."

Moon sat silently. What could they have? "I'm listening," he said.

Rains nodded, sifted through some more papers. "We drop the pornography charge," he said. "Your client pleads guilty to extortion and the interstate transportation rap."

"What the fuck?" Grant blurted. He started to stand until Moon got a hand up on his shoulder.

"I think my client has the right question," Moon said. "The pornography rap is your weakest charge. It's not going to hold up. And you want us to plead guilty to everything else? That's not a deal, that's a mugging."

"But wait," Jordan said, the smile still on his lips, "there's more."

Moon turned back to Rains.

"We also agree not to charge your client with witness-tampering, prostitution, and first-degree murder."

Now Grant was up. "What the hell are you two goons blabbering about?" he demanded.

Ellis stood up and put his hand on Grant's shoulder again. "Settle down, Michael. They don't have anything. It's all a bluff."

Jordan just kept smiling, then he winked at Moon. Winked! It was the strangest thing Ellis had ever seen Jordan do. He would never over-play a bluff that much. Moon figured Jordan might really have some-thing. Maybe he wasn't worried whether Grant took the deal or not.

Ellis turned to the hick. "What the hell is going on, Harry?"

Rains held up his palms. "That's our deal," he said. "Take it or leave it."

"I'll take it and cram it up your fucking..."

"Michael, Michael," Moon pleaded. "Let's just calm down. We aren't going for any of this crap. Don't worry about it."

Grant growled as he sat back down.

Moon studied the two men. "You don't even have a case against my client," he stated.

"We've got a new witness," Harry revealed, his eye now set on Ghost Grant. "He's a good one, Mr. Grant. Right up at the top. He's going to give us everything."

Jordan leaned over the table toward Grant. "Everything," he slowly repeated.

Grant just frowned.

"If you've got a witness, you've got to give it to us," Moon said. "We need to prepare our case."

Jordan just laughed.

"The judge has discretion on that," Rains pointed out. "At this point, anonymity is crucial for our witness. For his own protection. The judge is giving us leeway here, Ellis. You don't get him. Not yet."

"And once you do get the name," Jordan said, still focusing his gaze on Grant, "it will be too late. The deal will be off the table. We go to trial, and we tack on the other charges. You're looking at the chair, Mr. Grant."

"Fuck you," Grant replied.

"I tend to agree with my client," said Moon. "This is a waste of our time. Unless you're willing to give us more specifics about these new charges, we've got nothing to go on."

"You know what your client did," Jordan pointed out. "You know he's a crook and a killer."

Grant was up again, reaching for Jordan. Caleb Jordan rose up to his full height and swatted the hand away. "You don't have your goons in here. You better think about that. You're just a weak old man."

The guard was in the room now, drawing his stick. "What's going on?" he demanded.

Jordan held a hand out to the guard. "It's okay," he said. "We're all done here." He collected his folder from the table and put it back in his briefcase.

Harry Rains shook Moon's hand. "We'll be in touch," he said softly. He held Ellis's hand for a couple extra beats, smiling broadly. Moon wondered what the hell they were up to. These guys were acting downright strange. Who could they have in their pocket?

"We ain't dealing," Grant barked.

Jordan shook his head and snickered. "You can't kill everybody. Sooner or later, it will catch up to you." Jordan nodded at Moon as he picked up the briefcase and left the conference room. Rains followed after him. A second guard escorted the prosecutors out as the first guard stood by the open door.

"Don't worry about this," Moon said to Grant. "They're bluffing. They've got to be."

"And what if they're not?" Grant snapped.

Ellis looked over at him. He had no answer. Instead, he headed for the door. "I'll be in touch. I'll figure this out."

Grant lit a cigarette as he watched Moon leave. A scowl was planted on his face. He blew out a cloud of smoke and squinted his eyes. "Somethin' ain't right," he observed. Slowly, he took another long drag and exhaled into the room. The guard stood motionless by the door. Grant took three more pulls on the cigarette, thinking about the meeting with the hick and the dick, remembering what he had heard and seen, considering his options. Finally, he stubbed the cigarette out in the tin ashtray.

"You keep your ears open, check your sources. Something's up with Moon."

Above him, almost imperceptibly, the guard nodded.

Harold Rains waited for Jordan to remove his suit coat and lay it across the back seat. After his boss settled in the passenger seat, his shoulder belt fastened, Rains pulled the dark blue Grand Am away from the curb, cutting in front of a cab. The cabdriver honked and thrust a fist out the window. Rains ignored him. He rolled up his window, turned on the air conditioner, and eased a Brahms CD into the slot on the car stereo.

Jordan had a brown file folder open on his lap, and a highlighter pen in his right hand. He put a hand to his mouth and cleared his throat. "So we know the guard's dirty, right?"

"We know," said Rains. "He's in Grant's pocket."

"Good," said Jordan as he massaged his chin. "Now we just need to leak the line to him."

"Shouldn't be hard," said Rains. "We have good people in the facility. Get them to talk about Moon, make sure the guard's in earshot...."

"We've got to be careful about it. The guard might be an idiot, but Grant isn't. The leak can't be too obvious."

"Right," Rains agreed, a bit bothered that Jordan didn't trust him to do it right.

"This feels good, Harold. We sink Grant *and* Moon. Perfect."

"If Moon agrees to talk," Rains pointed out.

"Once Grant thinks Moon has turned on him, Moon's got no choice. He'll have to come to us for protection, or he'll run. Either way, we bring Moon down."

"He'll be pretty pissed off at us, setting him up like this. He may even be able to convince Grant that it's all bullshit. A Fed setup."

"No way. Grant's too cautious. He can't afford not to be, in his business."

"I still say Moon will run."

"So let him. It can only help us. If he runs, it will shake Grant up, make him look vulnerable, wedge a crowbar in the gear shaft. As long as people believe this 'ghost' shit, they think he's invincible. We start to crack away the façade, maybe we scare some mole out of the woodwork."

"I caught the wink," Rains said. "Nice touch."

As much as he hated to, Jordan had to smile. "A little heavy-handed, but I couldn't resist. I want to see Moon squirm, the cocky bastard. I've got a hard-on, Harold, and it's time to fuck the son-of-a-bitch."

21

On the way back through town, Jackson pulled his rented Neon into a slot on the square. He helped his aunt out.

"I need to check on something real quick," he told her.

They walked through a glass door between Belk's and the TrueValue. Above the door was a small sign, no more than a plaque, that read "Jackson Moon Jr. Attorney-at-Law."

They mounted the steps and came to the door of his father's old office. Jackie tried each key on the chain he'd taken from his father's room. The third key he tried unlocked the door. Frank came in behind him, walked through the small reception area, and into the main office. She sat down on the cushioned chair across from an old desk. Being chained to her house had tuckered her out.

Jackson sat on the roller chair behind the desk. He looked around, not sure what he was after. He pulled open the desk drawers, shuffled through some papers. Apparently there was still a case open. Looked like a property dispute. Probably his father's last case.

Jackson walked around the office. He opened the closet door. There was a suit coat in it and a full-length herringbone, some boxes on the upper shelf, a pair of rubber boots on the floor. He closed the closet door, then looked behind each of the four paintings on the wall. No safe that he could see.

"You lookin' for the lockbox, ain't ya?" It was Frank, watching him from the visitor's chair.

"What are you talking about?"

She smiled coyly. "They both had one. Yo' daddy and his brother. They liked keeping the cash apart. My husband still made me keep all the records in order though. He was very particular about that."

"What cash?"

"From the town businesses. You know what I mean. Any time a business wanted to start up a new store or maybe they were needin' a new addition. They had to pay the fees, you know."

"They had to pay the Planning Commission," said Jackson.

"'Course they did."

"And you kept the records?"

She nodded. "Rufus said he wouldn't trust no one else."

Jackie eased himself back down in the roller chair. "Where is your lockbox, Frank?"

She peered up at him. "I'm sure that's none of your business."

He nodded. "You're right about that. You're surely right. It's just that I'm looking for a particular transaction. It has to do with a property settlement."

Frank nodded. Jackie wondered if he was losing her.

"Do you remember a name in the records? A Michael Grant?"

"Grant?" she pondered. "I don't remember. I heard of him, though. Heard his name. Maybe I saw it. I don't remember."

"How about Twelve Oaks? Twelve Oaks International?"

She shook her head. "I don't think we had any business with them. Not that I recall."

"That was another name for Grant's business," Jackson pointed out. "Twelve Oaks International. That's the company that owns the big theme park. The one gobbling up all the land around here.

Bridgett, my friend who works for Grant's accountant, she says TOI shows up…"

That perked Frank up. "TOI?"

Jackson straightened up, crossed his hands across the oak desk. "That's right. T-O-I."

"I surely remember them. TOI: that's the name Rufus gave me for the register. Them folks, they musta had a whole lot of business with the town. They were awful generous, them folks. Yes, sir. TOI. Awful generous folks…"

Jackson studied his aunt as her mind drifted away. He wondered if she would ever understand the irony. The very people who had so dearly paid off her husband – the generous folks of TOI – were the very same ones who had taken away her home.

She was still mumbling. "Awful generous folks…"

B ack in his room at the General Lee, Cecil picked up the phone on the third ring.

"Hello, Mr. Blanks."

"Look, if you don't like 'Shark,' why don't you just call me 'Cecil'?"

"How is the project progressing?"

"Fine," said Cecil. "Everything's fine."

"So you have Jackson on board?"

"Well… That's the only…"

"Mr. Blanks, there isn't much time. We need our patsy."

"I know, I know. I'm working on it."

Silence. All Cecil could hear was some crackling on the line.

"You sure no one's listening?" Cecil asked.

"I'll take care of this end. You take care of yours."

Dial tone.

22

Red Eye looked up at the coal tower rising above the train tracks. This was crazy. How far would he go for a bottle of good Tennessee bourbon?

"Hey, man!" Sweets Malloy called out from above him. "Come on up!"

"You crazy, man. Why the hell you want to be up there, anyways?"

"Just like when I was a kid. I love this old tower, man."

"You fucking crazy," Red Eye repeated. "Now you done had yo' fun. Come on down here and bring that whiskey wit' you."

Sweets laughed into the night. "I'm staying right where I am, brother. If you want this whiskey, you best come on up and get it."

"Damn," sighed Red Eye. He looked up again at the tower that spread out over the tracks like a giant granddaddy long-legs. He examined the pulleys and knew it would have been black men that once lifted the coal into the tower so that the train engines could pull up beneath it and load up with coal. Slowly, Red Eye mounted the ladder, grumbling obscenities all the way up.

When he reached the top, he gingerly scooted into the belly of the tower and pulled himself against the back wall, as far away from the opening in the bottom of the tower as he could get. Sweets sat on the edge of the opening, dangling his feet above the tracks far below.

"Come on, sit yo' ass over here. You ain't go'n fall, man."

"Fuck you, Sweets," Red Eye replied, clearly disgusted with the whole affair. "I ain't no schoolboy out for cheap thrills. I done got my jollies out a long time ago."

"Damn, boy. You act like you is a ninety-fucking-year-old man."

"And you act like you is a ten-fucking-year-old child," Red Eye replied, as he watched Sweets drop a stream of spit down onto the tracks. "Now you give me the whiskey and shut yo' ass up."

Sweets laughed as he handed over the bottle. Red Eye took three large gulps and relaxed a little. Two more gulps and he laughed, too. "You one crazy motherfucker, that's all I can say."

They sat in the tower and drank. Far away, they could see a train on its long approach to Solomon's Rock. Sweets swallowed hard and his stomach fluttered. He knew it was time. He moved closer to Red Eye Barnes, who was drawing again from the bottle of bourbon. Sweets gripped a solid oak club hidden beneath his right thigh.

"You stay clear of me," Red Eye warned, but his voice was more playful now. "You ain't movin' me one inch closer, if that be yo' notion."

Sweets' reply came as a whisper. "I'm sorry, Billy, but I got me no choice. I really am sorry, man."

Red Eye's good eye went cold. "What the hell you whisperin' about, son? I cain't hardly..."

Red Eye's words were cut off as the club came rushing out of the night and struck with a deathly thud across his face. He heard his nose crack and tasted a gush of blood in his mouth. He tried to scream, but the club came again, slamming into his ribs. Three of the ribs snapped, and all the air whooshed out of his lungs. The third blow smacked dully against the side of his head, driving every thought out of his brain and leaving him senseless.

He came to in a groggy haze as he was being dragged toward the tower opening. His body refused to resist. Somewhere deep in his soul, he urged his body to take life. Slowly, Sweets slid him over the edge, and Billy Barnes fell.

Red Eye's arm sprang out, grabbing hold of Sweets' leg. Red Eye held on in some savage death grip as Sweets pounded him again and again with the club. Red Eye would not let go. Death would not take him easy. He had seen too much, been through too much. When death had taken his mother and a state senator and thirteen other black people, he had somehow risen from the fire and lived. He had been beaten before. They had tried to steal his spirit and his soul. Now he hung above the railroad track and refused to let go.

Sweets panicked. The train approached. His plan was flying apart. Red Eye had to be on the tracks when the train rushed through. If they could ever identify him, there would be no problem believing the deformed man had wandered onto the track in a drunken stupor. But now Sweets could only think of freeing himself from the death grip of Red Eye Barnes. He didn't care about alibis or explanations. He pulled the pistol from the back of his belt. The first shot glanced off Red Eye's shin, tearing away clothes and skin. Still, the man clung to Sweets. The second shot tore away Red Eye's left shoulder. His arm flailed away, and the body fell. Sweets watched as Red Eye sailed down, as if floating, and landed with a booming thud, face up, on the railroad ties.

Sweets gasped for breath and scrambled up into the tower. The train was racing toward the body. He tried to regain his composure. Sump could cover up the findings if they discovered bullets in the body. But there would be no body to speak of. Sweets looked at the approaching train, then looked down at Red Eye Barnes. Suddenly, both eyelids shot open. The good eye and the bad eye glared up at Sweets Malloy. Sweets screamed in horror. He was certain both eyes were looking at him. Both eyes saw.

The train thundered down the tracks. Somehow, Red Eye arose. Even with the left shoulder torn away, Red Eye lifted both of his arms in one last act of superhuman defiance. He let out a roar that Sweets would never forget. It ripped through his skin and seared down his chest, his stomach, his groin, his thigh. He would never be sure if the scream had come from his own throat or from the mouth of Red Eye Barnes. He only knew it continued to cry out, even as the train, its whistle howling and its engines roaring, slammed into the body of William Barnes and hurled its pieces into oblivion.

23

Jackson kept his head down as he walked up the walkway to the courthouse. The morning had blossomed bright and clear, and the yellow sun glared from the courthouse dome. The aroma of magnolia blossoms and daffodils flitted through the air. Jackson took the east entrance to avoid the commissioner and the sheriff. He mounted the steps, passing by the old men playing checkers. One of the men nodded to Jackie before spitting brown juice into a paper cup. Jackie entered the building through double doors. A slight breeze swept down from the high ceilings, and a coolness rose from the marble floor. Jackson walked through the first door to his left, into the office of the registrar of deeds. He placed his palms on the wooden counter, and pinged a silver bell once.

"Just a moment, please," came a call from the rear of the office.

Jackson looked at the rows of dusty records behind the counter. They were neatly placed in manila folders, meticulously catalogued, and stored in eight sets of high shelves. Two larger binders sat on the counter to Jackson's left. The faint smell of Lemon Pledge couldn't mask the scent of aging wood and old paper.

"Well, I'll be," cried Mrs. Wells as she made her way through one of the aisles of shelves. "Jackson Moon. Now aren't you a sight for sore eyes."

"Hello, Mrs. Wells. Awfully good to see you."

The woman stepped around the counter, sizing Jackson up. She wore a knee-length gray skirt, and a ruffled maroon blouse blossomed around her neck. A glittering hummingbird broach, pinned above her left breast, steadied its beak beside the ruffles, intent on pollination. A pair of thick black-rimmed glasses hung from a thin chain around her neck.

"How is your Aunt Frances?" Mrs. Wells asked. Jackie's aunt had helped out around the courthouse for years, filing and typing.

"She's just fine, ma'am. As good as can be expected."

"Oh, don't I know it. I was so upset to hear about her problem. That mind of hers was as sharp as a tack. The good Lord most certainly is mysterious in his ways."

"You are right about that," Jackie said, forcing up a smile.

"You should go back out to the Home," Mrs. Wells suggested. "You were always so good with those children."

"Maybe I'll do that," he said.

"Now are you just here to visit, or can I help you with something?"

"As a matter of fact," Jackson said. "I did need to check on a few things."

"That's what we're here for."

"I need to look at a couple of maps, a current one and one from a few years ago, before they started building this theme park."

"Oh yes. That monstrosity. Is this about the freeway taking your aunt's land?"

"Yes, ma'am," Jackson lied. It was a good cover. He didn't want to raise Mrs. Wells's suspicions to the point of gossip. "I just want to see what they've got planned and who's land got taken up. Just trying to get my bearings again."

"Well, that's nice. I hope you can do something about your aunt's land. A freeway, for goodness sake. The only reason they're going to build it is to make it easier for all those tourists to come to that park. It will be the ruin of this town."

"I think so," Jackson agreed.

Mrs. Wells led him behind the counter and down an aisle of shelves. She set him up at a table out back and retrieved a pair of maps, one dated a month back, the other dated August 1978. Jackson spread the first map out on the table and noted the boundaries of the TOI land. He then compared it to the earlier map and wrote down the names of the deed holders who had sold out to the Twelve Oaks theme park. As he scribbled the names out in his reporter's notebook, he heard the voice of the commissioner out front. He held his breath and hoped Mrs. Wells would not mention that Jackie was looking at maps at the back of the room.

"How we doing this morning, Alice?" Commissioner Sump said, his low voice rumbling to the back of the office.

"Just fine, Commissioner. It is a fine day. Glad we got rid of that awful rain for a while."

"Ain't that the truth," the commissioner agreed. "I lost a hibiscus, you know."

"Oh, that is such a shame."

"Don't work too hard, Alice," Sump said as he started to leave.

"You know I won't."

The commissioner was heading out the door and into the cool hallway when Alice called out to him. Jackson froze. She was the type of lady who would think it rude not to let the commissioner know that Jackson was out back. Mrs. Wells spoke to Sump in the doorway, too low for Jackson to hear.

"I'll do that," Sump said as he walked away. Jackson took a deep breath and went back to writing down the names.

Jackson was heading out of the courthouse when a voice spoke his name behind him. He turned to Bailey Sump. "You got some business here?" the sheriff asked.

"Just saying hello to some old friends," he said.

Bailey walked down the three steps to the walkway and cut across the grass to a pair of cast-iron chairs on the lawn. The chairs were shaded by a huge magnolia tree. The sheriff sat down on one of the chairs and patted the other one, inviting Jackie to sit next to him.

Jackson sat down. "Something I can help you with, Bailey?"

Sheriff Sump took off his trooper hat and sat it on his lap. He ran a hand through his thinning hair. "Why don't you just let this thing drop, Jackie?"

"What thing would that be?"

The sheriff smiled tolerantly. "All this business about the fire. Leave it to the past. I'm saying this as a friend, not as a sheriff. You're just going to end up screwing yourself up again."

Jackson looked out across the lush green lawn.

Bailey pressed on. "Ain't it about time for you to settle down? You should look up Bridgett Baines. She's still available, you know. You two had something special."

"Until folks in this town tore apart everything I believed in."

Bailey shook his head. "Let it go, friend. All that bitterness is just gonna eat your insides out."

"I've got to figure out some things. Then maybe I can let it go."

"You'll never figure it out," Bailey said wistfully. "You'll just end up driving yourself crazy over it. You know, I got curious myself a couple of years back. My daddy always kept me out of his business until I became sheriff myself. Hell, he still keeps me out of his business, but I got to wondering about that mess at Bosco's, so I looked into a few things."

Jackie looked at his old friend. "What did you find out?"

"There wasn't anything *to* find out. That's what I'm telling you. I went through the evidence and the statements, double-checked some things, but when it came to talking about it with folks, nobody would say the first word about it. I finally dropped the whole thing. There was nothing left to dig up."

"So when folks won't talk about a crime, your inclination is to drop it?"

Bailey passed a hard look at Jackson, then his face softened around the eyes. "I just couldn't see the point of dragging it all back out. I couldn't see what would be gained by it."

Jackson thought about it. He remembered the times before Jackie's father had opened a new world to him on a single long-ago night. He and Bailey would talk about their fathers, both wondering about the professional lives their fathers lived. They would try to piece together some rough composite from stories and assumptions they both had gained over the years, but in the end, they realized that their fathers had refused them entry into the mechanisms of Solomon's Rock.

"We're in the same predicament, aren't we, Bailey? Both of us grew up thinking our daddy worked for the good. A lawyer and a sheriff. We figured they were the good guys, right? What do you do, Bailey? What do you do when you find out different?"

The sheriff seemed to think about it. His reply came in a low, thoughtful voice. "I just pray that the good Lord, in His infinite wisdom, judges me only for my own sins."

Jackson frowned. "Your own sins? Keeping quiet, letting it go on. We're not just talking about the past here. I think they call that a sin of omission."

No answer. Bailey put the trooper hat back on his head.

Jackson said, "You know, they say a boy doesn't become a man until after his daddy dies." He wasn't even sure why he said it.

Then Bailey said, almost below his breath: "Or until the boy finds the balls to stand up."

Jackson looked over at Bailey. Instead of a sheriff, he saw his old school chum, peering back up at him like a child. Jackie remembered a game they used to play. They would knock their fists together as if clinking beer mugs and make a toast to their dreams and wishes: *Here's to balling Sue Anne Griffin.*

Jackie smiled and held up a fist. "Well, then," he announced. "Here's to finding the balls."

Bailey held up his own fist and knocked it against his old friend's. "To finding the balls," he said.

After his talk with the sheriff, Jackson tracked down the names of the old deed holders. Two of them told him, as politely as possible, that their property transactions were none of Jackson's business. Mr. Tobble was more considerate but he seemed to be reading his responses from a script. It was a line Jackson would come to learn by rote. The Twelve Oaks theme park was good for the economy of Solomon's Rock, and they sold the land out of a sense of duty and commitment to the greater good. No tales of high pressure or of Grant's goons perhaps paying a visit out of professional courtesy.

Jackson hoped to have better luck with the Brasches. Clement Brasch had not sold his land right off. He had apparently held onto it as long as he could. Virginia Brasch was Jackson's third-grade teacher. She had always liked him. Jackie hoped it would be his ticket to the truth.

Mrs. Brasch led him out to the back patio, sat him on a white wicker chair, and brought him some iced tea with lemon. Sun filtered through the healthy oak, maple, and white ash trees, streaming cones of shade across the long back yard. Fiery red and orange yarrow, toned down by purple fountain grass, ringed the white cement of the patio. The smell of rhododendrons and roses coursed through the light breeze. Clement Brasch joined them on the porch and took a chair begrudgingly.

"I don't got time for this, Ginny. I got work to do."

"Now, Jackson is an old student of mine. I expect you to show him some courtesy."

"Well, what is it you want to know?"

Jackson leaned forward in his chair. "I'm just interested in the sale of your land to Twelve Oaks International."

"Interested how?"

Jackson shrugged. "Did anything unusual go on?"

"What do you mean? I sold my land. Who the hell wants an amusement park in their backyard? Not me."

"But you didn't sell right off. You held out."

Clement looked away, out past the garage filled with lawn tools. "I loved that piece of property, but it didn't make no sense after while, holding on to it."

"Anybody pressure you, Mr. Brasch? Maybe force you into the decision?"

His eyes flared with passion. "Nobody forced me to do nothin'. You got that? I make my own decisions."

The response seemed too defensive to Jackson. And he noticed the look of disgust on Mrs. Brasch's face as she glared disapprovingly at her husband.

"Did Senator Sachs make an offer? I hear he was trying to stop that park from being built."

"Nobody made an offer 'cept those TOI folks. That's all I know about it. Now I got to go back to work. Ginny, why don't you show this boy the door." He got up and walked out toward the garden.

Jackson got up and shrugged. "Sorry," he said. "I didn't mean to hit a nerve."

They walked around the house to the front lawn. Mrs. Brasch put her hands around Jackie's upper arm, escorting him.

"We tried not to sell," she said as if she were discussing the nice weather they were having. "And the senator did make an offer. The way Clement put it, Grant's folks would hurt us if we didn't sell to TOI, but they'd kill us if we sold to Sachs."

"Grant threatened you directly?"

"My husband first, but he ended up telling me about it. He was scared. Then one day, this huge man in a black suit drove up our driveway with my daughter. Can you imagine that? I was horrified. He said he saw her walking home from school and he was concerned for her safety. The next day we sold."

Jackson opened his car door and stepped in. "Thanks for your help," he said.

"Anything for my favorite student."

Jackson smiled and started the car. He watched his old teacher walk back toward the house. She carried herself with pride. She had come clean.

From the outside, the Sachs house looked the same as Jackson remembered it, except for a granite sign out front reading The Alfred Sachs Memorial Library and Museum. The three-story structure was freshly painted in eggshell white with slate blue shutters and a gray roof. Six steps led up to a large front porch and a pair of polished double doors. Sweet pea and striped petunias blossomed from a red clay pot at the base of the stairs, and flower boxes stuffed with pink and white perennials lined the low outer wall of the porch. The wooden green porch swing swayed gently in a light breeze. Slender curtained windows edged the front double doors on either side, and ivy swirled up the porch columns. The grounds were immaculately tended, as they always had been when the senator was still in residence. Jackson mounted the steps and knocked on the door.

A tall man in his mid-fifties answered the knock. He wore spectacles and a gray three-piece suit. He lifted his head slightly to examine Jackie through the glasses.

"There's no need to knock," the curator told him. "This is public property."

"Right," Jackson acknowledged as he passed by the man and stepped into the entrance hall. The house smelled of fresh paint and cut flowers. A huge portrait of the senator hung majestically at the end of the entrance hallway, a long red runner seemingly laid out for him. A banister twirled upward to Jackie's right and at the base of the stairs, dogwood branches with white blossoms stood in a polished brass floor vase.

"Is there some way I can be of service?" the curator asked formally. A few strands of graying hair swept across his bald head, and he assumed the air of a haughty intellectual.

"I just wanted to look around," Jackson said.

"Certainly," said the man. "If there's any way I may assist, simply ask."

Jackson thanked the man, who then disappeared down the hallway, turning sharply to his left. Jackie followed after, entering a large sitting room at the back of the house. Antique red velvet chairs were placed in a circle in the middle of the room. Waist-high ivory ashtrays stood beside each chair as if waiting for an opportunity to serve. A small plaque explained how the senator often entertained powerful guests who sat in the circle to discuss the issues of the day. A huge picture window took up most of the back wall, looking out onto the Sachs property. Jackie came to the window and gazed out. Beyond a tulip garden below the window, the lush green land sloped down to the right, meeting a small pond of blue water quilted with lily pads and lotus buds. A black man, holding a long-handled net, swept leaves from the pond's surface. Further off, over a rolling grass hill, rose the mechanical arm of a crane. Black smoke puffed up into the blue sky. TOI at work.

"Ironic, isn't it?" said the curator as he stepped up behind Jackson. "The very project that Senator Sachs had tried so hard to stop now grovels at his doorstep."

"He didn't have much luck, did he? Stopping Twelve Oaks, I mean."

"He claimed one very important victory," the man said proudly. "They will never get his land. He made sure of that. He willed this museum and the grounds to the county. In perpetuity."

Jackson nodded slowly. It was the one thing he couldn't understand. Why would Grant kill Sachs for land he could never get his hands on? It made no sense. "Unless he didn't know," Jackson said absently.

"Pardon?"

"I was just thinking," Jackson said, turning from the window.

"Maybe Grant – maybe the TOI people didn't realize that Sachs had willed away his land. After all, Sachs had no heirs."

"Well, they must have had their collective heads in some very deep sand."

"Why is that?"

"It was a big event," the curator explained. He showed Jackie to an exhibit along the right side of the room. The walls were covered with images of the senator, accepting awards, winning elections, delivering pronouncements. One of the pictures showed Sachs on a bandstand in front of his house. A banner read "Future Site of the Alfred Sachs Memorial Library and Museum." A row of high-school students stood in a line below him. "He held a press conference and then had a reception on the grounds." The man pointed at the row of kids. "These young students were the first recipients of the Alfred Sachs Scholarship of Service. The grants are given each year to students who show an interest and aptitude for local government."

Jackie studied the picture. "Maybe they pressured him to abandon the will. Maybe they were trying to scare him and they went too far."

The curator stared at Jackson as if he were an imbecile. "First of all, sir, Senator Sachs was not one to be bullied. Let us not forget that he, and he alone, stood up to this … this Civil War amusement." He said the words as if they were something rancid in his mouth. "Secondly, you are presuming that the senator was killed under suspicious circumstances."

Jackson raised an eyebrow. "He was killed in a black brothel, in a fire supposedly set by the proprietor. You don't consider that suspicious?"

The curator cleared his throat and adjusted the spectacles on the bridge of his nose. "This facility relies on the generous support of benefactors and sympathetic institutions. It would be a great disservice to the senator and all his good work to dredge up insinuations from the past."

"Yeah, I keep hearing that. Only never quite so eloquently."

The curator sighed. "I've heard the stories, sir, and I will tell you this in confidence. The senator was not generally enamored of Negro prostitutes. He was genuinely in love with a specific woman."

The comment surprised Jackson. "Is that so?"

"Indeed it is," the curator said. He was not comfortable with the topic of conversation, but he refused to appear ignorant of any facts or innuendo surrounding the senator. "In any case," the man went on, "Senator Sachs wasn't at the bordello for pleasure. His lover was no longer employed by that establishment."

"But he wasn't there to close it down either," Jackson stated.

"Perhaps not," the curator admitted. "But I can assure you, sir, that no one could have taken this land away. Senator Sachs had already turned it over to the county, with the agreement that he and his family could live in it until their deaths. The papers had already been signed and sealed."

"His family?" Jackson said.

The man closed his eyes slowly and opened them again. "His family, as it were," he said solemnly.

"The black prostitute," Jackie said tentatively. "The senator's lover."

The curator sighed heavily, obviously put off by Jackson's lack of discretion. He did not answer.

Jackson smiled awkwardly and looked over the exhibit. Below the photographs was a large oak desk with a computer monitor, a mouse, and keyboard on it. The screen displayed a picture of Senator Sachs below a shaded box that contained the words of a stirring eulogy by the speaker of the Georgia House of Representatives. A button at the lower right of the screen read "Next Entry."

"You folks are up with the modern technology, I see," Jackson said.

"The grant is very generous. It supports upkeep of the house and grounds, the scholarships, and maintenance of the museum."

Jackson placed his right hand on the mouse and clicked on the "Next Entry" button. Another eulogy of the senator appeared.

"Is that all there is? Eulogies?"

"The senator was a beloved man," the curator said. "These are the eulogies placed in the public record by state and national officials. But the computer houses many articles. Just about anything written by or about the senator. It is quite extensive."

"May I?" Jackson asked, motioning at the desk chair.

"Be my guest," said the curator, pulling out the chair for Jackie to sit in. He then walked across the room and through a door with "William Colright, Curator" on it.

Jackson began cycling through the various entries in the database. He found a Search function and entered "Grant" in the dialog box, only to get "No Records Found" in response. He had to chuckle. He wondered if Mr. Colright had meticulously removed any reference to the pornographer. Next, Jackie tried "Twelve Oaks" and got twenty-seven hits. He began browsing through the entries returned.

He found numerous articles chronicling the senator's battle against the theme park. The articles were careful to name Twelve Oaks as the combatant, never Michael Grant. At each front, Sachs had been rebuked. Owner after owner sold their land off to TOI. None of them held out, none of them sold to Sachs. Jackson also came across an article about a commission headed by Sachs that investigated fraud of local government contracts. The article had speculated that the commission might delve into the Twelve Oaks property purchases, but Sachs vehemently claimed that TOI was not, and would never be, the target of his commission. Jackson wondered if maybe he was investigating the planning commission and its system of payoffs for building contracts, but he doubted if the senator would expose the duplicitous sins of his beloved town.

Jackson performed a search on the "Investigative Commission on County Construction Fraud" and came up with multiple hits. The investigation did not seem to involve TOI or the planning commission in any way. The last entry in the database was a small article that announced the closing of the investigation. No wrong-doing had been found.

Jackson spent the afternoon researching the database. It covered

Sachs's childhood, his rise to power, his election victories, the many infrastructure and educational grants he had won for the county, and finally his tragic death and the crescendo of praise for the senator that followed. He picked up a lone story in the mix: the sale of Virgil Stone's property – the land abutting the Sachs stead – to TOI. Stone had been the last holdout keeping the theme park from encroaching onto the lip of the Sachs boundary markers. It was the Stone property where the crane now sat, eating away the precious land in huge chunks.

Jackson returned to the window and watched the crane in the early evening haze.

Mr. Colright emerged from his office. "Did you find what you were looking for?" he asked.

"Maybe," Jackson said. "The land they're digging on now – it belonged to Virgil Stone?"

"That's correct."

"I've been talking to some of the owners who sold to TOI. Mr. Stone is a hard man to track down."

"He moved away from Solomon's Rock. That's all I know."

"And he was the last holdout. The barrier between the Sachs land and the theme park."

"I suppose that's so," said the curator.

Jackson watched the huge mechanical arm turn. The thick treads of the crane began to move, slowly creeping in the direction of the Sachs Memorial Museum, its ugly exhaust stack spewing black filth into the air.

Noxie placed his semiautomatic Glock and the Colt Anaconda in a blue gym bag, along with a couple of shirts and some clean underwear. Next he pulled out the razor he had taken from Frank Crackson's body. Noxie remembered the hotel room above Hart, the fine line slashed across neck of Armond James. He touched the razor's edge, ran his finger along it until a drop of his own blood bubbled up. He snapped the blade back into its sheath and packed it away. He considered packing his fancy boots before deciding it was best to pack light for the short trip to Solomon's Rock.

24

Sweets Malloy knew it was all ending, his short stay in paradise. He still had a good high, but he felt the pangs of it all fading out, and he didn't have much time left with the girl. He sat in a large open room above Crawdaddy's bar, his back against the wall. The heavy blues music thumped the floor he sat on and throbbed in his muscles like a rhythmic massage. The girl, she called herself Kaila, sat close to him on the floor. She touched the skin above his wrist with her fingertips, rippling a current of desire up his arm and across his breast. A wave tingled across the crown of his head. As if in a dream, he turned to her, and she filled his world with her large brown eyes, full lips, and coffee-colored skin.

Sweets leaned back against the wall and very slowly rocked back and forth, back and forth, as the music rumbled below him. The girl loaded the pipe with the last rock and lit it for him, then took a hit herself. Sweets leaned into the girl and smelled her rich, earthy skin. The smell sent a shock of desperation through him, and as he held onto the girl, he thought of Billy Barnes dangling from the coal tower, grasping Sweets in a death grip. That's how Sweets felt holding the girl, as if he might fall forever if he ever let go.

He studied her skin. The color of coffee with two splashes of cream, he decided. "Two lumps," he murmured, laughing a little. She just smiled and giggled. He fell into her eyes. They were exotic, almost Oriental. Her black hair hung straight down, the bangs pushed off her forehead.

Leaning against Kaila's full body, his cheek brushing her hair, Sweets reached out his hand and touched the flat of his palm against the fabric of Kaila's shirt, gently stroking her firm breast. She closed her eyes and moaned. The moan vibrated inside of him. The girl's nipple hardened to his touch through her thin green tee-shirt. Sweets reached up under her shirt and felt her naked breast. It filled his hand.

Kaila ran a single finger along the inside of Sweets' right thigh, up over the bulge straining against his trousers. A shock of desire shivered through his penis, into his belly, up his chest, and out of his open mouth. Sweets looked over at the girl, his mouth open, and she leaned her head back against the wall. Her eyes lolled with passion. The girl was good. Sweets felt his hardness pushing against the cool steel of the .38 revolver tucked in his waistband.

"I'll be back," he whispered to her. He wanted to remember her like this, flush with sex, waiting on him. He did not want to tell her that he had no money left. He did not want to see that fire go out of her eye like a light switched off. He started down the stairs to Crawdaddy's bar, broke, coming down, a useless dick going soft in his pants.

Bridgett's silver Mazda clattered across the wooden bridge leading to Crawdaddy's. She wore a short black dress that swooped along the curves of her waist and hips. Jackson tried his best not to gawk at her legs as they worked the clutch.

"Some things never change," Jackson said as they pulled into the dirt parking lot. The red neon Crawdaddy's sign glowed in the stream out front. The water wound under the bridge and made a wide arc around the left side of the nightclub before flowing into Snelly's Pond. On the right side of the club, a red plank pier stretched out across the pond, bending to the right and cutting across the cattails at the water's eastern end. Two small motorboats were pulled up onto the bank beside the pier. A street lamp at the base of the pier pooled an orb of bright light across the boats. Heavy blues music rose out of the open windows of the club, and clouds of moths and mosquitoes encircled the outdoor lights that rimmed the aluminum gutters. A cacophony of boisterous voices, catcalls, breaking glass, wild laughter, and heated arguments rose above the steamy music. The smell of beer and cigarette smoke flavored the damp mossy air blowing in from the pond. Below a stand of pines, a large leather-clad biker with hairy arms the size of rolled-up sleeping bags poked a thick finger in the chest of a second man. The second man, his pocked face hardened in a fierce frown, squeezed his beer can until it crimped. Jackie took Bridgett by the arm and led her up the ramp and into the bar.

The screen door slammed behind them, and the couple moved to the side, standing beneath a flight of rickety stairs at the back of the bar as if momentarily shell-shocked by the barrage of sound. People danced in front of the stage. They bobbed and swayed but could hardly move in the crush of other dancers. The music reached a deafening crescendo then closed with a cymbal blast. A smattering of applause rippled through the crowd, but the roar of voices did not diminish. A triumphant cheer erupted from a rowdy party sitting at the edge of the dance floor, one man standing up, his arms thrust over his head.

"Jackson Moon!" called a deep voice from the front of the club. Jackie waved to Longneck Slim, the large black man who sat in the center of the stage, his guitar resting on one leg. Jackie took Bridgett's hand and snaked through the crowd until reaching the stage.

"Hi, Slim," Jackie said with a smile. "Long time."

"Where you been hiding out? I hardly recognized you, son."

Jackson shrugged. "Here and there. In and out."

The big man laughed merrily.

"Slim, this is Bridgett Baines, another old friend of mine."

The bluesman extended a huge paw down from the stage and

Bridgett took it. "I love hearing you play, Mr. Slim," she said.

The man laughed again. "Just call me Longneck or Slim. I ain't no Mister." His big sleepy eyes took in Bridgett. His ceaseless smile worked against the weight of his jowls. A scar creased his right eyebrow and arced up under his brown derby. Even in the heat, he wore a black suit coat.

"I've missed you, my friend," Slim went on, turning back to Jackson. "I cain't keep track of my favorite stool."

Jackson smiled. He used to help Crawdaddy out at the bar and would tuck Slim's stool away in a broom closet so no one would claim it. He also set aside a longneck bar bottle that Slim used to play his slide guitar.

"You got a request for me?" Slim asked. "I got to start playing again or this crowd may start throwing things." Jackson looked at a long-haired white man, a left arm casually crooked over his guitar neck, who waited patiently on stage for the music to start up again. The bass player absently strummed notes with his long fingers, filtering a catchy beat through the crowd noise.

"How about some John Lee?" Jackie said. "I love your *haw*."

"You got it," said the man. He took off his hat and bowed his head to Bridgett. "Nice to meet you, Miss Baines."

"Same to you, Slim."

The big man laughed again, then announced the song to his band mates, counted off, and broke into John Lee Hooker's *Boogie Chillen*. Howls of delight rose up from the crowd, and the dancers packed back onto the dance floor as Jackie and Bridgett squeezed their way through. Jackson led Bridgett under a flashing Budweiser sign and into the bar on the other side of the club. The music was not so loud and the crowd thinner. The bar ran along the left side of the room; on the right side, a line of round wooden tables hunched beneath screened windows looking out on the pond.

Jackson offered Bridgett a stool at the bar then sat down beside her. Crawdaddy was loading a tray with drinks at the far end of the counter. He was six-foot-five, over three hundred pounds, and had been known to throw the toughest biker off the club's front porch. His substantial gut stretched his red suspenders, and wispy white hair seemed to float around his head like puffs of smoke. As he turned from the drink tray, heading to the other end of the bar, he stopped cold.

"Well, I'll be fangdangled," he said. "My eyes must be deceivin' me."

"Hi, Craw," Jackson called over the music. "How's it hanging?"

"Clear down the pant leg," he replied with a wink. "Same as always." He then nodded to Bridgett. "Please pardon me, Miss Baines."

Bridgett smiled. "Quite all right," she said, then added: "Maybe you should drag for crappie with that thing."

Crawdaddy laughed and slapped his palm on the counter. "Might as well. Sure as hell ain't nothin' else bitin' on it."

Jackie smiled. He was having fun, probably for the first time since starting his prison sentence. "Slim sounds juiced tonight," he said.

"Oh yeah. They love him around here. I've got 'em booked for three weeks."

"Maybe I should stop by every night to store his stool in the broom closet."

"He still talks about that," Craw said, shaking his head. "He thought it was a perk that came with the contract. You spoiled him good."

Jackson turned to Bridgett. "I started helping out Crawdaddy in grammar school. Can you believe that? He'd hide me in a space up under the bar and hand me glasses to wipe clean. By high school, I was serving beer from the tap and sweeping up broken glass."

"Best worker I ever had," Craw said before excusing himself for a moment. He drew two beers and mixed a Vodka Collins, then pointed at a black man at the far end of the bar. "You gonna drink something, Sweets, or are you just here for the conversation?" The black man frowned as he rose up from his stool, then he turned an eye to Jackson. Jackie wondered why the man looked as if he had a grudge against him.

The hard eyes turned away, and Sweets walked out of the bar.

"What's his beef?" Jackson asked when Craw came back to them.

"Who knows? Maybe he gets ornery when mixing booze with the crack."

"Lovely," Jackson said.

"What can I say? I run a nightclub, not a convent."

"With you running things, even the nuns would be whooping it up."

Crawdaddy smiled as he poured two more drafts and three shots of whiskey.

"You need a hand back there?" Jackie asked, and Crawdaddy held out a palm in offering. Jackson asked Bridgett if she would mind, then he worked his way behind the bar. He found a clean rag and began wiping glasses. He bent over toward Crawdaddy. "Could I ask you a personal question?"

Crawdaddy didn't look up from the two Black Russians he was preparing. "I already gave up intimate details about my pecker. How much more personal could it get?"

"I was wondering about Michael Grant."

Crawdaddy stopped mixing drinks and stood with his head bowed. "I bought the asshole out a couple of years back, but you can't run a club around here without his say-so. He leases the upstairs rooms. I don't care much for his dirty money, but if I made a stink, he'd close my ass down. Or worse."

Jackson nodded. "You know why I ran off?"

Crawdaddy went back to work. He put the drinks on a tray and placed them on the bar for a waitress. "It happened the same night that colored bar burnt to ground. I figured that wasn't a coincidence."

"I want to know why those folks died, Craw. I need to find out what was going on."

Crawdaddy turned to Jackie. "The way I figure it," he said, "folks get killed around here for three reasons: Money, power, and land. It could be all three, but I bet at least one of them things figures into it."

"But I don't understand why...." Craw held up a finger, and

Jackson stopped talking.

"And that's all I got to say about it," Crawdaddy said. He rubbed his palms together as if ridding himself of the dirty subject. Then he clapped his hands together and turned away.

Jackson was back in front of the bar, sitting next to Bridgett, when the man called Sweets stepped up behind him and yelled into his ear. "Your name Moon?"

Jackie turned. "Who wants to know?"

"You got a phone call," the black man said.

"Who is it?"

Sweets sneered. "Do I look like yo' fucking secretary?"

Jackson leaned back, taken by the vitriol in his voice. He excused himself and followed Sweets to the far end of the bar, away from the music, and along a narrow hallway to the back of the club. They emerged in an open space at the end of the long hall where a light dangled from loose wire.

"They put in a phone back here?" Jackie asked, but he didn't get an answer. A man tucked in a corner behind him slammed into Jackson's back, shoving him through a panel door. Sweets closed the door from the outside as Jackson fell to a concrete floor. The sharp smell of kerosene and oil flared in his nose. He knew he had been shoved into a tool shed attached to the back of the club. A hand reached up and pulled a string hanging down from the center of the shed. A row of fluorescent bulbs blinked on, and Jackson looked up, shielding his eyes with his right hand.

"Hiya, Stomp," Jackie said cordially. "How you been doing?"

Stomp frowned. "Not so good after you stuck my head in the mud."

Jackson took his hand down and stood up. "I just needed to talk to you, that's all."

"Next time use a telephone," Stomp told him.

Jackson surveyed the three other men in the shed, one black and two whites. One of the white men removed a set of dentures from his mouth and set them on a worktable. He offered Jackie a tooth-less smile. The black man wore a tank top that showed off ropes of muscles coursing down his arms. Jackson wondered what type of mutant the third man was. Below a shiny bald head, two huge eyes sank in their sockets, blackness encircling them like eye shadow. A black T-shirt hung long on him, almost to his knees.

"Look, fellas," Jackson said. "There's been a little misunderstanding here."

"You're damn right," snapped Stomp. "Like I told you before, you been messin' with the wrong people."

Stomp nodded to his cronies, and the muscled black man stepped up. A huge grin appearing on his face, he rubbed his fist as he approached Jackson. Jackie stooped into a boxer's stance, fists below his eyes.

The black man looked at Jackie as if he were standing on his head. "Look at this shit," he said, turning to his buddies. "We got us Sugar Ray here."

As soon as the man turned back to him, Jackson launched two quick left jabs to the black man's face, standing him up straight. Jackson then punched him hard in the belly. The man bent over but didn't fall. He rushed Jackson, burying a shoulder into Jackie's ribs and driving him against the door. Jackson lifted a knee into the man's nose, sending him reeling across the floor. He knocked over a wheel-barrow and ended up sitting on his ass. He popped back up, the eyes flaring with anger. Toothless still wore his silly grin, as if anxious for his turn. The mutant stood with his arms to his sides like a gunfight-er ready to draw.

Jackson started to circle away from the door, but the black man rushed him again, bowling him into a row of rakes. The combatants scrambled up. The man grabbed Jackson from behind and thrust him onto the surface of a table saw. He shoved Jackie's face onto the metal, but Jackson spun loose and buried an elbow into the man's kidney. The man fell across the table and Jackie threw the switch. The saw buzzed to life, and the man screamed just as Toothless lunged into Jackson, throwing him against the table saw. The table flew over backwards, and the black man rolled away. Jackson fell to the floor, rising back up with a pair of hedge clippers in his hands.

Toothless looked at the tool. "What you go'n do, trim my sideburns?"

"I was thinking of aiming a little lower," Jackson said. He snapped the clippers at the crotch of Toothless. The blade tore into the fabric of his pants and swathed a gash into the man's upper thigh. Toothless screamed and fell away. When Jackson looked back up, it was the mutant's turn. Jackson watched the man approach slowly. He held a sledgehammer in his hands.

"Now c'mon, Uncle Fester," said Jackie. "Let's fight fair."

The big man just grunted as he took a swing at Jackson. Jackson leapt backwards as the head of the hammer whooshed by him. He pulled in his gut to avoid the second swing. Then Fester lifted the sledge above his head and bore down on Jackie with three loping steps. Jackson, his back flat against the far wall, bent into Fester as the hammer punched through the wall behind them. Fester worked the hammer out of the wall, tearing loose a pair of boards. Jackson pummeled the giant with alternating right and left shots to the body. He heard an "oof" blow out of Fester, but the man did not go down. He raised the hammer back up, ready to swing again, but Jackie poked three quick left jabs into Fester's face, and the mutant teetered. A straight right-cross to the chin drove Fester back across the shed.

Fester regained his balance and stood seven feet from Jackie. He held the sledgehammer across his body, eyes bulging. Then Fester charged. All Jackson could do was brace himself as the full weight of the huge man slammed into him, driving them both through the wooden wall and out into the night.

They tumbled across the ground. Jackson tried to get up but Fester pawed him like a drowning man clutching the reeds. He grabbed Jackie's collar and slapped him with the back of his hand. Jackie's face sloshed down into the mud, and he heard someone let loose a whoop down by the lake. Fester grabbed Jackie's shirt with both hands and lifted him from the ground as if he were a grocery sack, then the big man wrapped his arms around Jackie's waist and began to squeeze. Jackson felt the air rush out of him. Fester squeezed harder and laughed like a child with a new toy. Jackie's feet were dangling down, inches from the ground, and his ears burned from the pressure around his gut.

Stomp stepped through the hole in the wall. "Don't kill him now," he said. "We ain't s'posed to kill him."

A crowd by the pier moved along the bank of the lake to get a better view of the fight. A man and woman on the back porch stood up from their table and came to the railing. A few people began to cheer.

"What's wrong, Sugar Ray?" Fester crooned. "Can't do much boxing with your hands pinned down, now can ya?"

"I still got the Tyson move," Jackie managed to wheeze before bending into the big man and clamping Fester's cauliflower ear between his teeth. Fester screamed, and his grip on Jackie lessened, but Jackson kept grinding his teeth through the man's upper ear until he tasted blood in his mouth and felt the tissue giving away. Finally Fester dropped Jackson to the ground. The goon bent over in pain, clutching what was left of his left ear.

But Fester wasn't done. He picked up the sledgehammer again. The crowd by the bank backed away, and the woman on the porch screamed. Jackson bolted to a boat by the pier. As Fester approached, Jackie unclamped the small fifteen-horsepower motor and pulled it off of the boat. He stroked up the motor with a single pull, and it roared alive. The motor head vibrated in the crook of Jackie's right arm, and he tried to steady the spinning blade by holding the fifteen-inch shaft of the motor in his left hand. Fester challenged him with the hammer. When he took a swing, the head of the hammer clanked into the motor blade, jarring the sledge out of Fester's hand. The motor twisted violently in Jackie's arms and died abruptly. Jackie fell to his knee, still clutching the motor, with Fester looming above him.

The crowd was cheering as if it were a stunt show. Fester actually looked around at them grinning, acknowledging their appreciation. Jackson wrapped both hands around the shaft of the motor and swung the engine at Fester. Fester turned just as the motor head was coming at him. He brought a hand up, but the engine slammed into his left ribs. The hand came down, pinning the motor between Fester's body and his arm. Jackson slid his right hand down the shaft of the motor and shoved the blade up into Fester's head. The goon's eyes rolled as a jagged line of dark blood appeared across his pale forehead. He stumbled across the ground like a drunkard.

Then a gunshot roared in the yard. Jackson turned to see Stomp, a revolver pointed in the air. He lowered the sights to bear on Jackie. "I ain't s'posed to kill you, but accidents do happen."

Somehow Fester found his balance and he came back at Jackie slowly, his eyes still swimming in the sockets. Four streams of blood rolled down from the crack in his forehead and clumped in his eyebrows.

"No hard feelings," Jackson said to Fester. He held up his hands in surrender. "You know I always loved the thing you did with the light bulb in your mouth."

Fester took a swing as Jackie covered himself, hands over his face and elbows over his ribs. But Fester grabbed both of Jackie's wrists, pulled them apart, and landed a solid head butt between Jackie's eyes. Jackson hit the earth and felt consciousness slipping away as Fester kicked him over and over in the ribs.

A shotgun cocked up on the porch, and all eyes turned to Crawdaddy. He pointed the sawed-off weapon at Stomp. "That's enough," he growled.

"Hey now, Craw, we work for the same boss, right?"

"I said that's enough," Crawdaddy stated.

Stomp turned his gun to the big man up on the porch. "Don't mess with me, man." His pistol trembled as he held it up against the shotgun. Craw, his right eye shut, sighted the left eye on Stomp.

"Don't make me shoot you, goddamn it." Stomp poked the gun

forward.

Crawdaddy said nothing. He just kept the gun leveled at the black man.

It was then that Bridgett's Mazda raced out of the parking lot, through a pair of pines, and down along the side of the club. Stomp turned to the onrushing car and dove away as it barreled past him. Bridgett jerked the wheel to her left, swerving the Mazda sideways. Fester looked up into the wave of mud thrown from the car's wheels just as the car's side panel slammed into him, tossing his huge body eight feet through the air.

Bridgett shoved the car into park and got out. She ran to Jackie and helped him up. He leaned heavily on her as she guided him into the back seat of the car. No music was playing in the bar, and the buzz of talk had died out. A bulging crowd had formed on the porch and the entrance ramp. They watched Bridgett lay Jackie onto the back seat. She leered at the porcine figure of Fester now lying prostrate in the mud. She ran down to him, kicked the body as hard as she could, then rushed back to her car, climbed in behind the wheel, and bolted the Mazda back along the side of the club, through the two pines, across the parking lot, and over the wooden bridge.

They were three miles down the road when she looked over at Jackie. "You okay?"

Jackson groaned. "I think that last kick might have gotten a rib or two."

Suddenly, a black 1989 Cadillac was roaring up behind them. It slammed into the back of the Mazda. Bridgett screamed as the big automobile rammed them again. The black car then pulled into the left lane and sped up alongside the Mazda.

"Don't slow down!" Jackson yelled. They shot past the Cadillac for a moment, but the big car worked its way back alongside and swerved into them. The Mazda hit a soft shoulder and started to spin. It slid off the road and banked hard into a row of new pine, teetering for a moment on its two passenger-side wheels before slamming back down. The engine conked out.

Just as Bridgett got her door locked, her side window exploded into shards of glass. Stomp stuck his gun in at her.

"Word is you got nothing to lose," the black man said to Jackson. "But I think I just found something." He stuck the gun barrel in Bridgett's face.

Jackson nodded. "I get the point," he said.

"You better," Stomp said. "Cause you won't get another warning." He left the gun in Bridgett's face for a long moment, but kept a bloodshot eye on Jackie. "I want you to take a good look at this pretty little thing," the man went on. "Think about that sweet face with the skull blown open. Imagine that sexy neck with a gash sliced across it, blood pouring out. You think about that real hard."

Then the black man pulled the gun away and walked back to the Cadillac. He got in and the car rolled away.

"Where are you taking us?" Jackson asked after Bridgett had the Mazda back out on the road.

"You need some help," she said.

"Hospital?"

"Those guys, they could show up there. No, I'm taking you to Leola's."

Jackson worked his way up in the backseat. "Leola? What the hell will she do about it?"

Bridgett looked into the pained eyes. "You really don't know?"

"What are you talking about?"

"Leola's a nurse. You know that, don't you? She used to be a midwife. A damn good one, too. I guess she's kind of retired now, but I heard she was training some other woman there, a Miss Lucy, a younger woman."

"Midwife? Leola? Not my Leola."

"Jesus. You really didn't know?"

"She never did any midwiving for my mama, not that I ever heard about."

"Of course not. She only worked with poor folk, black folk, people who needed done what no self-respecting doctor would do around here."

Could it be possible? Leola? "No. Where did you hear about that?" Bridgett shook her head. "I didn't just hear it, Jackie. I know."

Jackie bent over and grabbed his ribs. "I don't understand."

"She helps people, okay? People in trouble."

The pain was rising in Jackson. It took a minute to force some thoughts through his head. "An abortion," he said.

She looked at him now through the rearview mirror. "Senior year in high school. You were long gone. I fell in with a jerk, a tight-end of the football team. One night, I went to tell him that he was the father. He was drunk as hell. I guess he decided he didn't like the idea that I was pregnant. He knocked me around a little, kicked me. I don't know if he damaged the fetus, but something wasn't right. I decided to take care of it. I'm not proud of it, but I didn't see any other way out at the time."

"And it was Leola? My Leola?"

But his question was already answered. Bridgett pulled up along the railroad track, down an overgrown path as far as she could go: the back way to the Moon property, to Leola's cabin in the woods.

25

As soon as Cecil found a table, up close to the runway, he asked for Starry. He was glad to hear she was working. It was the only reason he had told Moon to meet him at the Back Room. Starry's eyes lit up when she saw him. She had bundles of bronze hair, full sensuous lips, and a firm body. Her breast implants defied gravity, holding up her short silver-sparkled dress. Cecil bought her a drink.

"This visit is business, sweetheart," he told her, and she seemed disappointed.

"What kind of business?" she asked.

"Business business," Cecil said. "What else is there?"

Cecil noticed that she looked a little more dolled up than the last time he had seen her. Her hair not as wild. "You're Indian," he said. "Ain't that what you told me?"

"Yes, on my mother's side."

"But not like tomahawk Indian. From-India Indian."

"Yes," she said with a smile. "My mother was from India."

"You don't look like a girl from India," he said. "I mean you don't look like one of them gals with dark hair and a dot on the forehead."

Starry shrugged. "What can I say? My daddy was Irish."

Cecil looked around the joint, checking out the other girls. "That black stripper here?" he asked.

"You'll have to be a little more specific," Starry replied.

"I don't know her name," Cecil said. "She was passed out on the curb last time. I gave her a ride."

Starry laughed. "That was you? She said you kidnapped her."

"Crazy broad," Cecil grumbled.

Twenty minutes went by and Moon didn't show. Starry got up to leave, but Cecil grabbed the short dress and pulled her back. He gave her ten bucks to start off. He refused a lap dance and just asked for a little warm-up. Waiting for Moon to show up, he could hardly enjoy it, even with Starry performing. He kept eyeing the entrance, to see who came in whenever the door swung open. He didn't want Moon to appear at his table while Cecil was gawking at the stripper.

Starry took two dances and sat back down next to Cecil. He bought her another drink and looked around the bar.

"I told that girl up front I was here, asked her to keep an eye out for Moon."

Starry looked disappointed, sorry that Cecil wasn't having a good time. "You know what I told her?" Cecil asked, smiling. "I said to tell him Shark was in the house." The young girl laughed.

They had a few more drinks, a couple more dances, Cecil giving her fifteen on the last one so she'd leave her top off. She asked if she could sit in his lap. He said sure and they started to party. Cecil figured he might as well have some fun if Moon was going to make him wait all night.

When Cecil got up to twenty dollars, the girl laid her back fully against him on the chair and wrapped her arms up around the back of his neck. Moving, always moving, pressing her full body against his, the back of her head – all that muss of hair – against his cheek, his neck, his chest, as her back slid down his front, Cecil looking down at her upturned face, the hollow of her neck, the erect breasts, the flat tummy.

"Do you want another?" she asked, as if willing to grant his every desire.

And all he had to do was nod.

She sat on his lap after the seventh or eighth dance. "I hate when they stare at me," she said in her slow, half-drunken voice, a voice oozing with sex. "I mean when I'm dancing for you and they watch."

"I hadn't noticed," Cecil said, and she laughed, elbowing him, liking the compliment. Cecil wondered why he could never come up with anything charming like that to say to regular girls. At a club, the smooth words just slipped out.

"You think I dance okay?" she asked.

"You dance like a dream," he said.

"I'm clumsy sometimes, but guys seem to like it when I fall into them. You know what I mean?"

"Yeah," said Cecil. "I like it when you fall into me."

"I bet," she said, elbowing him again. "Especially when my hand lands a certain place."

"Right," he said. "Especially then."

She watched Cecil over her shoulder, smiling down at him. Cecil was drawn to the shoulder. It was thin and delicate, a little bony. He could cup her entire shoulder in his palm. He brought a hand along it, then up the side of her neck. She pulled her hair up off the neck, bundles of hair, and cocked her head forward, knowing just what the customer wanted. He touched four fingers to the back of her neck and traced them downward. Slowly. Between the shoulder blades, then a single finger down her spine as she arched her back. Cecil's favorite place to touch a woman – down the center of her back – along the spine, a perfect line to the ...

Starry rose up as he touched the top of her g-string, her way of playing when he came close to breaking rules. She smiled now, facing him. Brought the hair – it was brunette but with a bronze highlight; a strange color, Cecil thought, like Tina Turner used to have – up into a bundle on top of her head, both arms up, the wrists crossing over her head. The eyes gazed at him, heavy with sex, almost closing. Next, she placed her hands solidly on his chest, pushing against his muscles, and she moved her body between his legs, forcing them apart, sliding slowly down to her knees, drawing the delicate fingers across his thigh; then up again, the body coming up, straddling him on the chair, pulling his head into her, to a spot just above the left breast. He felt her nipple at the base of his neck, and he hugged her, brought her fully into his arms. She seemed so tiny to him, the body taut and soft at the same time.

"This is my favorite song," Starry said. It was a Latino number with a fast beat.

"Will you dance for me?" he asked, and she was up again, swaying, arms up high, the body moving like a belly dancer. Cecil watched her face as she concentrated on the movements, then she would see that he was watching her face, not her body, and she would smile shyly, the concentration breaking. Cecil could tell that it was a real smile, like she was breaking out of a shell, the smile lighting up her whole face. She knew how much he could appreciate her beauty. He would pay just to look at her face all night.

But he could not help but follow the hands as they moved down the sides of her breasts, the palms flat against her tummy, moving down, the fingers slipping under the g-string....

S tarry told Cecil she needed to freshen up, then she headed up the stairs to a private room. Ellis Moon wanted her to check in with him to report on how the plan was going. They had all met earlier – Starry, Moon, James, and Mitch, the bouncer who was going to play the heavy in the Moon scheme. The idea was to get Cecil to take Starry back to Solomon's Rock with him so that she could keep a close eye on Cecil.

Ellis was upstairs with Belle. She was sitting on a red leather couch fully naked, her dark brown hair tumbling over her breasts. She bit Ellis playfully on the earlobe, grinding her breasts into his upper arm, her hand stroking his thigh.

"How's it going?" Moon asked Starry.

"He likes me," she said.

"What's not to like?" The lawyer was looser than he had been ear-
lier. He had a few drinks in him. He lifted his shoeless foot up into
Belle's lap, and she started massaging it gently. She was watching
Moon's reaction with a hint of a smile on her lips.

"Yeah well, that don't mean I can get him to take me home with
him."

"Sure you can," he said. "You two have become good friends."

"It's only the second time we've met."

"Yeah, but you took your top off for him. For a man, that's a real
intimate moment."

"Right," Starry scoffed.

"I'm not kidding you," said Ellis. "I bet he thinks you two got a
good thing going on. He's got the love in his eye."

"It's lust," said Starry.

"Even better," Moon said. "That's what we're banking on."

"Everything set up with Mitch?" Starry asked.

"Yeah," Moon said. "We're ready to go. He'll be the ex-boyfriend.
Maybe he'll push you around a little. You act scared, give this Cecil a
chance to be the hero. You know the rest. It's pie, baby. A piece of pie."

"I don't know. This guy, he's been around the block a few times."

Ellis thought about it. "The way I figure this guy, you get him by
the dick, the body follows. The mind doesn't even play into it."

Starry had to smile. She had Cecil figured the same way.

"Did I give you enough money?" he asked.

"Yes, it's plenty."

Moon pulled some bills out of his shirt pocket. "Here's some more.
You stay out there at the Rock as long as you need to. If you run out
of cash, let us know."

On her way back downstairs, Starry wondered what she was getting herself into. Cecil seemed like an okay guy, a lot of fun, but he
wouldn't like being spied on, she was sure of that. She might not be

able to sweet-talk her way out of a tight situation.

She watched Cecil through the curtain now. He was a funny guy. She could tell he was checking out for her before he stuck a bill down another girl's string. He didn't want to hurt his own girl's feelings. As if she were his main squeeze.

Earlier in the evening, Cecil had made this whole thing more interesting. Starry wondered if he had just been talking big when he brought up this big score. A sure hit, he had said. He claimed he could take care of her, get her out of this place. He was one of those guys that thought she needed saving. She probably should have told Moon about this "hit" – whatever it was – but maybe that information would be worth a little extra later on. There were a lot of ways to play the situation out. Obviously, the lawyer had important connections and he was worried about Cecil. He wanted to know what Cecil was up to. If Cecil planned to hit the lawyer, or maybe one of the lawyer's high-society clients – was he smart enough to pull it off? And if he was smart enough to pull it off, was he dumb enough to let a stripper named Starry cut in on it? He could be street-smart, but with other weaknesses. Easily led by the dick, as the lawyer pointed out. Lots of possibilities here, lots of angles, as long as Cecil wasn't just blowing air. He was definitely the type to spout off.

It was just before two when she finished the last dance, and the lights came up. She had given Cecil the five hundred dollars from Moon. She told Cecil that Moon had called to apologize about missing the appointment but that Cecil should go ahead with what they had talked about. He was to keep an eye on the situation in Solomon's Rock. The money was an advance.

"Could you do me a favor?" she asked Cecil as the customers started to file out of the club. "Wait with me until my cab comes?"

"I'll do you one better," Cecil said. "I'll give you a ride home."

Starry changed into jeans and a tank top, started to brush her hair and gave up, then met Cecil at the side door. They were crossing the parking lot when Mitch came out from behind the building.

"I need to talk to you, Starry!" he called out. The bouncer was all puffed up, walking fast, playing the part.

"Who's this clown?" Cecil asked Starry, but Mitch grabbed her arm before she could answer.

"This ain't any of your fuckin' business, dickhead. I…"

And then Cecil hit him. Before Mitch could get half his story out, before the setup was really even on, Cecil hit him hard, right in the pit of the stomach. Then again, same spot, and Mitch hit the pavement. Starry was so taken aback by Cecil's sudden fury that she found herself just watching the onslaught. Cecil started kicking the bouncer, first to the body, then to the face. Blood spurted out across the black asphalt.

"Cecil!" Starry cried, pulling him away from the body. "You're gonna kill him."

"He touches you again, I'll kill him for sure. Break both his arms first."

"Come on," she said, tugging him along. "Where's your car? Let's get the fuck out of here."

They loaded into Cecil's black New Yorker and headed out of the parking lot. "He's an old boyfriend," Starry said. "Can't seem to take 'no' for an answer." Cecil could tell she was scared of him.

"Well, let's go back and teach him some English," Cecil said. "Make sure he gets the fucking message. He best keep away from you or I'll rip his goddamn head off, feed it to the dogs."

"Goddamn it, Cecil! You're just making it worse. He'll come back with a gun. He doesn't fuck around."

Cecil had to laugh at that. He knew he could handle the punk. "If he gets a gun, I'll get a bigger one," he said. "We'll see who's left standing." That just made Starry madder.

"Don't you get it, Cecil? This is my job. I've got to live around here. I've got to go home. I'll be wondering if he's out in the parking lot, waiting for me. Now you went and got him so pissed off, who knows what he'll do?"

Starry started crying. "Why don't you get a hotel for a coupla days?" Cecil suggested.

"For how long, Cecil? I have to live. I have to work. I have to go home sometime."

"You want I could hang out a few days, sleep on the couch or somethin'? The asshole shows up, it'll be the last fucking time."

"Would you cut the badass routine?" she said. "Jesus. The last thing I need is two guys getting rough in my damn living room. The landlord already has me on notice."

Cecil was seeing a different Starry now, fiery but scared. Cecil realized that staying with her wouldn't work anyway. He couldn't hang out in Atlanta. He had to get back to the hick town, stay close to the action.

"Why don't you come home with me then?" Cecil offered. "I got a nice room at the General Lee. I can drive you back up here whenever you want."

Starry pretended to think it over. "Would that be all right?" she asked.

"Well sure, honey. Hell, I got me a queen-size bed and everything. Cable television. Free muffins in the morning. We'll live it up for a while."

A smile broke out on Starry's face. She put Cecil's boombox on the floor and slid across the seat next to him. Cecil draped one arm over the top of the steering wheel, one arm around his girl, and let loose a rebel yell as he rolled down the ramp onto Interstate 85 South.

26

Sweets Malloy watched the Moon boy getting beat up. Somehow, he knew the man wouldn't give up. He was after something, and to stop him, they were going to have to kill him. He – Durlen Malloy – would have to kill him. That's how it would end up. Sweets could already see the figure of Commissioner Sump, hunched in the shadows of Sweets's small room, telling his little black errand boy how it would go. Sweets could already smell the acrid cigar smoke, a stale stench that would rot in his room for days.

Durlen decided he couldn't do it again. He couldn't kill again. He reached in his pants, felt the gun in there, and began to walk.

Sweets walked until the blues music from the bar faded into the distance, replaced by the natural sounds of the night – crickets chirping, frogs croaking, dogs howling far away, the crunch of his footsteps on pine needles. He went to his favorite spot, sat with his back against a tall pine tree, and looked out over Snelly's Pond. The water was still; the moonlight paled across it. Everything here was calm and peaceful. Sweets had come to this spot many times before – to free his mind, to dream, to pretend his life had come out differently than it had.

But even now, in this place of utter escape, he saw the ruined eye of Red Eye Barnes snapping open, piercing Sweets in the coal tower above the railroad tracks where Red Eye lay. Sweets knew he would see the eye each night when he fell asleep and again in the morning when he woke up. He would see it in his nightmares. He would see it in the mirror. He saw it now, in a swath of moonlight, as he peered out over the still water.

There was only one way to make the eye go away. He leaned his head back against the tree and, for a fleeting moment, his mind fell quiet and his spirit was at rest.

"Forgive me, Billy," the black man whispered into the night, just before he placed the barrel of the revolver into his mouth and blew away the back of his head.

The last thing Durlen Malloy saw was not the eye of Billy Barnes. Sweets saw himself, as if from above, falling backward – slow motion – onto the ground. His body bounced once then settled easily onto the bed of pine needles. Time seemed to pass slowly as he lay there dying, eyes open to the stars, red blood seeping into the earth like mother's milk. Beside the fallen body, a glint in the moonlight, sat the snub-nose .38 given to him by County Commissioner William T. Sump. The same gun he had used to shoot Billy Barnes. The very gun that had been carefully placed – twenty years earlier – into the lifeless fingers of Lonnie Brim, suspected mass murderer and proprietor of Bosco's Bar and Grille.

27

Jackson emerged from a fitful sleep. It took a few moments for him to realize where he was – on the bed in Leola's cabin. He saw Bridgett sitting on a chair, leaning back against the wall, sleeping. The lamplight softened her features and danced in her long blonde hair. One hand rested above the right breast of her green blouse. Even in his weakened condition, the woman aroused him. His ribs ached, and when he looked down, he saw his midsection wrapped in gauze. He grimaced from strong Mercurochrome vapors. There was a young black woman in the room, early twenties, smooth cream-colored face, large brown eyes, her hair pinned up on top of her head with a few long strands straggling down the side of her face. She was one of those women who always seemed to glow from the inside. She wrung a washcloth over a small silver basin.

Leola walked into the room and saw that Jackson was awake. She moved over to a second chair, directly across from the bed, and settled down into it. The girl turned now, the washcloth in her hand, and smiled at Jackie. She wiped his forehead with the cool damp cloth.

"This here's Lucy," Leola said as the woman turned toward him. "She been tendin' to you."

"Hi, Lucy," Jackson wheezed. "I guess I ought to thank you."

"Damn right you should," Leola snapped.

"Now Leola," Lucy said softly. "Let the man be."

Leola grunted and peered over at Jackie. "How you feelin'?" she asked him.

"A little woozy," he said. "My ribs hurt."

"Next time, maybe you ought to think 'fore you go out and get yo'self all beat up."

"Why are you mad at me? You should be mad at the guys who hit me."

"Now how'm I s'posed to know they didn't have theyselves a good reason?"

"Maybe they did at that."

"Wouldn't surprise me none. If I was you, I'd stay clear of Crawdaddy's bar. Go there and you go'n get what they's servin'.""

"I've got to admit that's some good advice. I'll steer clear from now on."

"I got plenty of good advice. You just got to open up yo' ears. Take my words to heart."

Jackson nodded over at Bridgett. "She okay?"

"She's fine. Been all worried about you is all. Good to see she's gettin' herself some rest. Fine place to take a classy woman like her, out to a roughneck bar. What was you thinkin'?"

"It was her idea."

"That ain't no kind of excuse, boy. No kind of excuse at all."

"Well, it's the only one I can come up with."

"Crawdaddy's bar. Ain't nothin' but trouble waitin' to happen."

Jackson looked over at Leola and studied his former maid. "Why didn't you ever tell me that you were a midwife?"

Leola looked hard at him. "Yo' parents, they didn't want you knowin'. They didn't much like what went on back in they own wood. They let it go, long as I kept you chirren out of it."

Jackson nodded. If only his father had been as careful about keeping his children out of his own business.

"I got a story for you, boy," Leola said. "Story I think it's time for you to hear of."

"A story?"

"That's right. And you go'n hear it whether you'd like to or not, so hush up now and listen good."

Leola leaned back in the chair and began to speak....

Leola strained against the heaviness of Angel as they walked out of the cabin and into the warm night. Leola had roped the pregnant woman's arm around her shoulder and forced her up off of the bed. The girl needed to walk now, get on her feet. It would help keep the pains regular. Leola figured the girl would be tough, being a whore, but she whined about walking, cried out in misery with every birthing cramp, and now she clung onto Leola and dragged her feet across the hard dirt. Sweat poured down the woman's pretty face. She had delicate features: a small button nose, beautiful dreamy eyes, full soft lips, and silky black hair that hung straight down along her high cheekbones. But now the eyes rolled up into her head, and the hair was matted with perspiration.

"C'mon girl," Leola pleaded. "You needs to walk now. You gots to listen to me, child."

Leola saw the senator over by his big red car, sucking on a peppermint drop like a scared child. She wished that old boy would just leave. A birthing house was no place for a frightened white man. He glanced over at the two women walking. He seemed to wince each time Angel moaned. He had a funny look in his eye. He had removed his red bow tie and unclasped the top three buttons of his shirt, but he still wore a dark vest and suit coat. The senator had confessed his love to the whore, but Leola wondered if his mind was beginning to turn, seeing the hard truth of it right in front of his eyes. Birthing time can do strange things to men, especially to a white man who's put a baby in a black whore's belly. Leola noticed Malcolm Wright, the man who would raise Angel's child, over on the other side of the house, also watching the two women walk, his eyes wide.

Leola managed to walk the woman out to the Longley's field and then along a dried-up creek bed. Back in the cabin, Leola sat her down in a chair and told her to breathe. "Now it ain't time to push yet, girl. I'm go'n tell you when. Don't you be pushin' yet." She leaned in close to the woman, who had fallen into a trance to back down the pain. "You hear me now?" Leola barked, and the woman nodded, looking up at Leola with contempt. "I'll tell you when. We close now, child. Real close. Ain't much longer 'fore you can push that baby right outta you."

"You look after her," Leola told Lucinda Wright. "Keep her mind calm. I'm go'n check on Sally now." The midwife walked out of the back room and closed the curtain on it. Out in the yard, Sally – a young black girl who had begged Leola to teach her – was boiling water over a fire, preparing hot rags.

The senator rushed up to Leola as she emerged from the cabin. "What's goin' on in there?" he wanted to know, as if it were Leola's job to report to him. She ignored him, checked the water instead, and told Sally where some more rags were kept. The white man was impatient, jittery, making things worse. "You tell me what's goin' on in there now, Leola."

Leola glared up at him. "What you mean, Mr. Sachs? They's a woman in there 'bout to have a baby."

"Well, I know that," he said.

"What more you need to know?" Leola noticed Malcolm Wright edging closer to the conversation. Wright had his own interest. The baby would be his, the way Sachs had worked it out. Malcolm and Lucinda Wright would raise the child as their own. Leola was happy about the arrangement. Malcolm and Lucinda had a suitable house to raise the child in, and Lucinda would be a good mother. Lucinda Wright had always wanted children, but none of Leola's remedies had worked on Lucinda's barrenness. She and Malcolm were heartbroken and desperate. They had prayed in cornfields laced with manure, eaten fish heads and frog eggs and raw veal patties, applied exotic oils and herbs and strong potions that soaked overnight through the skin, but a child would not come. Leola was glad they could now have the child they had ached for.

The only question was how Angel would take it. She had agreed to give up the child, but Leola knew women could have a change of heart once the baby came into the world. She had seen it mostly with the very young girls who suffered childbirth in secret, agreeing to give up the baby to a good family. Young girls – no more than babies themselves – who would go crazy with grief when it came time for Leola to take the child from the mama's arms.

Sachs looked at Wright, as if pleading for help, then turned back to Leola. "Well, how is she? When's the baby go'n come?"

"She's fine," Leola said. "Baby will be here directly."

That didn't satisfy him. He looked like he might break into tears.

"Why don't you get yo'self on home?" Leola said. "You ain't a bit of good here. You get on home, now."

Sachs did not waver. The stubborn look in his eye told Leola that the man wasn't going anywhere.

Leola met the gaze, then shook her head. Next, she turned to Malcolm Wright and put a hand on his shoulder. "You get on home now, Malcolm," she told him. "This ain't no bidness for a man. You get on back and wait for Lucinda to bring yo' child home."

Wright looked over at the cabin as Sally emerged with more rags. "You tell Lucinda I be waitin'," he said. "You tell her I be waitin' for our baby."

It was little more than an hour later when Angel got to push. Lucinda Wright held her on one side, Sally on the other. Leola had a hand on the inside of Angel's right knee, pushing the woman open. With the other hand she felt for the baby. "You gots to push," Leola demanded.

Angel grunted then screamed as she forced the baby from the womb. Sweat streamed down her face. Sally tried to wipe the mother's forehead, but Angel shot her a stare that scared Sally so much, it was all she could do not to run out of the room.

"Push!" barked Leola.

Angel glared down at the midwife, clenched her teeth, and pushed with all her might. Her face flared red, at first as bright as crimson, then a darker red, like wet blood. She let loose a whoosh of air and burst into tears.

Leola felt the crown of the baby's head. "One more push, girl."

"I cain't," she moaned, her voice drained of energy. "I cain't do it no more."

"You gots to, girl. You want to get this baby out of you now? You gots to push. One more good 'un, child."

Angel puffed out her cheeks, shot out three quick breaths, then she seemed to suck the air out of the room as she drew in every bit of breath she could take. She pushed until she swore that blood burst out of her ears. She could not believe the last primal scream that came out of her own mouth. The next thing she heard was the sharp slap of Leola's hand on the baby's bottom and the shrill cry of a child, seconds old.

"It's a girl," Leola told her, handing it over. Angel cried along with the baby, along with Lucinda Wright, who leaned in to look at the tiny, bunched-up face. "You got yo'self a little girl."

Sachs heard the cries and rushed in. Leola had cut the cord and was handing the child to Lucinda when Sachs reached in and cradled the baby in his own arms. Blood and afterbirth stained his white shirt and dark vest, but he didn't notice. The baby was the most amazing thing he had ever seen in his life. He had only been married three years when his wife died. They had never had children. He realized now that this child was all the family he had. Lucinda stood back, scared of the look in the senator's eyes.

Sachs was sitting in Leola's front room, the baby still in his arms, when Angel came out an hour later. Leola was telling her to lay down, to get off her feet, but Angel wouldn't listen. She smiled at Sachs and he handed the baby over. Angel was crying. Sachs got up and put an arm around Angel. He led her out the door and across the yard. When he opened the passenger door of his car, Angel asked no questions. She just got in. Leola came out of the cabin, leaving Lucinda in the doorway. Lucinda knew the baby would not be hers after all.

"Where you goin' with that baby?" Leola asked Sachs.

He turned and looked at her as if the question was a silly one.

"We goin' home," he said.

And that's just the way it was. The old senator took his little girl and he took that little girl's mama, and he brought them both right on home with him. Took them right on over to his big gray house. Nobody would have believed it possible, but that's just what he did. Took them home just as if they was his very own family. Left Lucinda crying on my do'step and Malcolm with a anger wild and abidin'. I looked on that man when I took Lucinda home, and I knew as surely as nightfall that his anger would never die out.

28

It was hours later when Jackson came awake again in Leola's small cabin. He was on his back on the bed, and as his eyes adjusted to the soft lamplight, he saw Bridgett above him. She was stroking his right cheek.

Jackie tried to sit up but his ribs still ached.

"Lay back, Jackie. It's okay. You'll be fine. Leola says you got some sore ribs, that's all."

"You okay?"

She smiled. "I'm fine."

Jackson looked around the small room. It was empty but for the bed, a single wooden chair, and a bedside table. Jackie wondered if he had dreamed up the story of Alfred Sachs and the baby. The table had an oil lamp on it and a wash basin with a sponge soaking in it. The lamp flickered shadows off the walls. Jackie looked back up at Bridgett. She wore a light green blouse that brought out the color of her deep green eyes. The light softened her features. God, she was beautiful.

"Where's Leola?" Jackson asked.

"She went to Fayetteville with Lucy. They went to talk with Lucy's mama. I don't know what about. They'll be back in the morning.

Leola told me to keep your wounds clean and to not let you out of bed." It was then that Bridgett picked up the sponge from the basin and rubbed it across Jackson's chest. Cool water in the night heat. At first he thought his groan was from the pain, then he realized it was something else.

In silence, Bridgett moved the sponge across him. He wore a robe that someone had fetched from the house. He realized that he was naked beneath the robe. He wondered who had stripped him. Bridgett moved the sponge across his shoulders, down along the edge of the gauze.

"Do you remember that night, back before you ran off?"

Jackson knew the night well. All he could do was nod.

"You took me out to Fallows Pond. You made me lay back on the cool grass. At first I thought you were up to something, but you just kept making me look up at the stars. There was no moon. Millions of stars out. 'Look at the stars', you'd say. Then I saw the first one: A star streaked right down out of the sky. It had this beautiful tail behind it – a smoky streak of bluish-white light. I had never seen a shooting star before. You told me it was a meteor. You remember?"

"Of course I do," he said. "I remember it just about every night."

She smiled at that, then dipped the sponge back in the basin. She started moving it below the wrapping around his ribs. Desire coursed through Jackie. He was lost in the talk of that night, the soft light, Bridgett moving the sponge over him, just above his erection.

Bridgett was whispering now, almost reverent. "The stars fell out of the heavens. One after another. Sometimes I'd catch them out of the corner of my eye, streaking to the rim of the earth. Sometimes they'd blaze across the very top of the sky. It took my breath away."

Jackie laughed and felt it in his sore ribs. "You thought it was the place I had brought you. Like the stars always fell there."

She laughed, too. "And you told me it was a meteor shower that you could see every year around that time, but it was especially bright because there was no moon."

"Just like this year," Jackie said. "No moon."

"We ended up skinny dipping," Bridgett said, staring into Jackson's eyes. "The water was so warm, luxurious. Felt like a sauna. I brought you back to the bank of the pond...."

"God," Jackson moaned. "I was under your spell, Bridgett Baines."

Bridgett moved away from the bed now. Jackie noticed that she wore only the blouse. Lamplight glimmered off the smoothness of her bare legs. She was standing in the middle of the room, staring at Jackson on the bed. Her fingers played with the top button on her shirt.

"Do you remember in the water, when I took off my blouse for you?"

"I'll remember it until they lay me in the earth," Jackson said.

"Did you like that?" she asked coyly.

Jackson just nodded as she unclasped the top button of the blouse and moved her fingers slowly down to the next one. "I want you as badly as I did that night," she told him. "You can have me any way you'd like."

Bridgett unclasped each button and stood in the lamplight, the blouse coming open to reveal the outline of her breasts. She walked back toward Jackson.

"I don't want to hurt you," she said.

"You couldn't possibly hurt me," he told her.

"But the ribs..."

"I will feel no pain. Trust me."

She smiled, and picked up the sponge again. She moved it back down over the gauze, below the gauze. Jackson's eyes rolled as she moved the sponge along his erection. Then she took him in her mouth. Jackson wondered if he was crying. Maybe hallucinating. He closed his eyes and was back on the bank of Fallows Pond, Bridgett holding his hand, stars reflected in the pond, stars above him and below him, meteors falling in perfect symmetry, streaking arcs of light in the sky and on the pond's still surface.

Bridgett carefully got up onto the bed, placing one knee beside each of Jackie's hips. She bent forward and they kissed. Jackson brought his hands up behind her head. She kissed his mouth, his chin, his neck, his chest. He brought his hands up under the unbuttoned blouse and caressed her firm breasts, the erect nipples. Bridgett moved her hips slowly, wetness brushing the tip of Jackie's penis. He moaned again, remembered the night at Fallows Pond, a lone dog howling in the distance.

Bridgett sat on him, taking the length of him into her. Her soft moans filled the air. She traced her fingers across her own breasts and the blouse fell away. Jackson leaned his head backward, closing his eyes again, recalling the magical night when Bridgett first gave herself to him. He opened his eyes back up to make sure the woman in his bed was real. The lamplight wiggled across her belly, pooled on the arc of her breast. He tried to speak as she moved above him, but Bridgett ran a finger across his lips then leaned in to kiss him deeply.

Jackie rolled her over and she laughed. She started to mention his damaged ribs when he came up on top of her, but he kissed her on the mouth whenever she tried to speak and her warnings turned to helpless giggles. Her breasts tingled as every part of his body moved skillfully over her and into her. Small gasps of breath escaped from her mouth. Her eyes glazed over. And the stars fell like confetti.

Jackie was wavering between wakefulness and dreams. Bridgett was gone, but he could still smell her scent on him. His mind was hazy. His dreams had begun by the banks of a pond, but had somehow sailed through fiery nights, aimless flights, and finally to a small cell in Gainesville, Florida. The final dream was dark and disjointed, but Jackson's memories were still sharp. He was in a cage in the dream, and it ushered in thoughts of his early days in jail.

"So you're Jackson Moon." It was Jackie's new cellmate. A statement, not a question.

Jackson looked over at the man, then continued reading.

"The name's Cecil," the con told him. "Cecil Blanks."

Jackson looked back up and nodded slightly.

"You've got some connection to Michael Grant, right?" Cecil said, his eyes lighting up. "Your father is his lawyer, something like that?"

That got Jackie's attention. "Where'd you hear that?"

The man smiled. "Word gets around in here. I used to work for this guy, he wanted to take over Grant's business something fierce."

"Guy got a name?"

Cecil peered over at Jackie, gauging him. "Marston," he said. "Jake Marston."

Jackson nodded.

"You heard of him?" the man prodded.

"I'll take the fifth on that one."

Cecil seemed to assume that Jackson taking part in a conversation was some sort of an invitation. The con came over and sat at the foot of Jackie's bed. "You need anything in here? Some candy, maybe?" Cecil held one of his nostrils closed and made a snorting gesture. "I've got connections."

"Candy is the last thing I need," Jackson said.

"I thought you were in here for drugs."

"You got some bad information there, friend."

The man looked at Jackie, waiting. "So?"

Jackson lifted a brow.

"So how did you end up in here?"

Jackie shrugged. "Long story," he said.

"In here," Cecil said, "that's the best kind."

That made Jackson smile. "I was down in Fort Lauderdale," he said. "How I got there, that's the long part. Anyway, I was in a bar down there, basically crying in my beer about how my life was turning out, and there was this guy at a table nearby. This bastard had an opinion on everything from capital punishment to baking bread. The damn guy would not shut up."

"I know the type."

"Yeah, well. I finally had enough. My mood was pretty lousy when I walked in the door, and this guy just made it worse. I walked over and kindly asked him to shut the fuck up. He opened his mouth again, maybe to get some clarification – I'm not sure – but that was enough for me. I punched him right in the face, the idea being to break his jaw. I figured that would shut the asshole up."

Cecil laughed. "Did it work?"

Jackson looked away, shaking his head some more. "Well, the way I see it, three things went wrong. First of all, I missed his mouth and busted his nose open. Sure as hell didn't shut him up. The guy was screaming like a banshee, blood pouring out of his nose and all over the white tablecloth. It was a mess. Second thing that went wrong, I jammed my goddamn finger. Thing was bent over crooked. So I was hopping around, cursing up a storm, trying to find somebody to pull my finger, you know, pop it back in place. Of course, the people in the bar are freaked out. One guy is bleeding all over the place, and the guy who punched him is trying to get his finger pulled. It was absolute panic."

"Sounds like a trick of my dad's," Cecil said. "You know, pull my finger and see what happens."

"Exactly," Jackie said.

There was a moment of silence. "So what was the third thing went wrong?" Cecil asked.

Jackson looked at the con for a second and sighed. "The third thing was that the man turned out to be Senior Judge of the Eighth Circuit Court of Appeals. Probably not the best man to punch out in a bar."

Cecil was laughing now. "Holy shit. That's some rotten fucking luck. You mean to tell me they put you in here for that?"

"Sure looks that way, doesn't it?"

"Jesus. You got a tough break, partner."

Jackson nodded. "The way I see it, I've done enough shit to

deserve being here. I guess it all comes out in the wash."

"If you say so," Cecil said. Now he was shaking his head. "Well, anyway. You let me know if you need anything. I can help you out, you know. Teach you how to fight, whatever you need to survive in here."

Jackson surveyed the man. He was pudgy and small. If they were both standing, this Cecil would be no taller than Jackie's chest. "You're going to teach me how to fight?"

"Sure I will, if that's what you want."

Jackie went back to his book. "I know how to fight. I've been in plenty of scuffles."

"What? Schoolyard shit? I'm talking about street fighting, prison fighting. Nothing like you've ever been into. I'll show you something right now. Stand up."

Jackson looked at the man, then decided he had nothing better to do, so he stood up.

Cecil was all smiles now, like they were playing games together. "Now go ahead and choke me."

"Choke you?"

"Yeah. You know, put your hands around my throat here."

Jackson put his hands around Cecil's thick neck.

"Now, what I do, little guy like me, is lean into you like this." Cecil moved into Jackson so that his face was almost flat against Jackie's chest, then he bit him.

Jackson pushed him away. "What the fuck? You bit me!"

"Course I did. That's what I'm teaching you here. Folks don't understand. Teeth are powerful weapons, rarely used."

"Where I come from, biting is against the rules."

"That's what I'm trying to tell you. You ain't in Topeka no more. First rule of prison fighting? There ain't no rules. You use whatever you got. We ain't talking about schoolboy tussles. In here, only one of you gets to walk away."

Jackson sat back down on the bed and picked up his book. "I'll just keep to myself. I don't want to be a tough guy in here."

"Ain't no keeping to yourself, Jack. There's two kind of cons in here: fighters and bitches. You get my meaning?"

"I get it."

"If you really want to learn some technique, I'll set you up with Clarence when we go out to the yard. He used to be a boxer. He'll really teach you how to fight."

"I took some boxing at school. The gym coach taught me a thing or two."

"Now there you go again. Schoolboy shit. I ain't talking about fighting with big puffy gloves and a fucking helmet. I'm talking about punching, scratching, biting, kicking. Whatever it takes. Ain't no gym coach go'n teach you that style."

"You never met my gym coach."

Cecil smiled. "Is that right? My gym coach was a freaking girl. Can you beat that? A woman. She was teaching me some wrestling moves so I figured – what the hell – might as well cop me a feel. Bitch busted my lip open."

"Well, did you bite her?"

"Fuck no, I didn't bite her. Bitch woulda killed my sorry ass, ripped my heart out and ate it. The woman was a fucking monster, for Christ's sake."

They both laughed at that.

Jackson asked, "So this Clarence, why would he want to teach me anything?"

"Like I told you, I got connections. My boy Clarence knows a good friend when he meets one."

Clarence was a big black man, late-forties, with close-cropped hair, big droopy eyes, and a crooked nose. He never seemed to smile, and he always looked wary, almost paranoid, as if he thought everyone he met was trying to take something from him. The first thing Jackson noticed about Clarence was his huge hands. They were so big, they looked comical, as if drawn by a caricature artist.

Cecil told Jackie that Clarence Hoffman had been working the fields for a white man when he caught the white guy raping Clarence's wife, who worked as the man's cook. Clarence came into the third-story bedroom of the white man's house, plucked the man off his wife as if the guy were a rag doll, and tossed him unceremoniously out the window. The man broke his neck on the ground below. When the local sheriff came looking for Clarence, he was at home with his wife, casually eating a home-cooked meal. When Cecil asked Clarence why he went home to eat, Clarence simply said he was hungry.

Clarence ended up getting a life sentence without parole. Over time, the story had circulated that the white rapist had not died from the fall but that Clarence had first squeezed the guy's head with his giant hands, bursting the man's skull like a pumpkin. They called him Big Hands Hoffman, and if anyone ever got the notion to challenge Clarence, the fool would need only take a glimpse at the hands to recover his senses.

Cecil introduced Jackson to Clarence. Jackie put out a hand but Clarence ignored it. He circled Jackie, appraising his new student.

"If a boxer and a wrestler was to fight, who you think would win?" Clarence asked him.

Jackson shrugged. "The boxer?"

"Wrong," Cecil jumped in, proud of himself for knowing the answer.

"Neither one of them," Clarence said. "'Cause both of them got a limited view. The boxer, he think like a boxer. The wrestler, he think like a wrestler. The one who go'n win the fight, he ain't got no limitations. He's go'n do whatever he got to do to take his man out. You understand my meaning? You got to think like a savage. You got to fight like the caveman used to fight when he needed food to eat or a woman to fuck. He didn't think 'I got to box' or 'I got to wrestle.' Motherfucker just went at it."

Jackson nodded.

"You in good condition, boy?" Clarence asked.

"You should see my man in the morning," Cecil put in. "Sit-ups, push-ups. I can't even keep count of them."

Clarence stuck a meaty finger at Cecil. "You want me to teach this boy, you go'n have to keep your mouth shut. You got that, Cecil?"

Cecil put up his hands as if warding off a battle.

"You been in many fights before?" Clarence asked Jackie.

"Schoolboy shit," Cecil said. Clarence glared over at him. Clearly, you couldn't shut Cecil up; you could only hope to contain him.

"You need a tough gut," Clarence said.

Jackson patted his stomach. "I've been working on..."

As Jackie said the words, Clarence buried a quick left into Jackson's midsection. Jackie crumbled to the ground as Cecil giggled. Jackson tried to find a breath.

"You got to make it tougher," Clarence said, and as he helped Jackson from the ground, Jackie threw his head up, catching Clarence under the chin. Clarence fell back a step, and Jackson threw a punch that Clarence casually avoided by pulling his head away. The big man looked disinterested as Jackie struck again. Clarence swatted the punch away as if it were a minor annoyance. Then Jackson tried his best move. He came at Clarence with a right hook that he knew the big man would block. But Clarence wasn't expecting Moon's quickness when he followed the blocked right with a left jab and a second straight-a-way left to the face. Clarence's lip split open.

Clarence wiped his mouth, then looked at the blood on his hand with amazement. He smiled for the first time, then sent a raging roundhouse right at Jackson. Jackie got a hand up but he had no chance of deflecting the blow. Clarence's huge fist slammed into Jackson's left temple. When Jackson came to, Clarence was helping him up. "You got some promise, boy," he said.

29

When Jackson finally emerged from Leola's cabin, it felt like he had been in a cave for a few weeks. The sunlight stung his eyes and made him see spots. He wasn't sure at first who he saw leaving his parent's house, but he slowly made out his mother, lugging a suitcase in her hand. He began to run across the yard.

"Ma?"

His mother turned. "Why, there you are, Jackson. I been wonderin' where you got off to."

"What's going on?" he asked, motioning to the suitcase in her hand.

"It's my sister. Aunt Holly? She's come down with somethin' awful, to hear Uncle Josh tell it. He needs me there to help." She started walking down the driveway. "Now I figger you can keep an eye on yo' daddy. If you need some help, you talk to Leola. She'll help you out."

Jackson couldn't believe his mother's gait. Even with the heavy suitcase, he practically had to jog to keep up with her. He assumed that his daddy had set all this up. He had probably gotten Uncle Josh to call, make it sound like it was life or death. His father had gotten his wish. His wife was leaving the house. She would not have to watch him die. It occurred to Jackson, at first, to tell her the truth, but he remembered how spiritless she had seemed when he had first seen her again. Now she had a bounce in her step and a purpose in her pace. She was racing down the sidewalk along Greenville Street.

"But where are you headed right now?" Jackson asked.

"Why, I'm going to the bus station. Got to catch the 12:40."

"You're going to walk there with that heavy suitcase? Let me give you a lift."

"No time now. I'll be fine."

"Well, let me at least carry the suitcase." He tried to take it out of her hand but she wrestled it away.

"You leave me be. I'm fine. You best go see to yo' Aunt Frank. She needs yo' help more'n me."

"What's wrong with Frank?"

"They took her down to Oakdale. Put her in the home. Pro'bly for the best."

Jackson stopped cold. "Oakdale? Who put her there?"

"Bailey picked her up again. Says he ain't go'n let her go home this time 'til she gets her wits about her." His mother didn't even turn to look at him. She continued to race down the sidewalk, clutching the suitcase in her right hand, her white sneakers padding the sidewalk, her legs churning like a pump, her blue print dress billowing out behind her. "There should be plenty to eat in the house," she called back to him without turning around. "If you need anything, the number to the grocer is right by the phone. The druggist, too. He'll tell you when yo' daddy needs more medicine...."

But Jackson no longer heard her. He was still stopped in his tracks, shaken by the news of Aunt Frank being committed. As he stood there in a daze, his mother becoming a blur, Cecil pulled up in the black New Yorker.

"Where the hell you been?" he asked.

Jackson looked over at him, his mind trying to comprehend everything that was going on. He got into the car. "C'mon," he told Cecil. "We're going to see my aunt."

"Oh yeah?" said Cecil. "They got that broad in a straitjacket yet?"

Jackie opened the passenger door and climbed in. "As a matter of fact," he said, "they just might."

Aunt Frank glared at the large black man who walked into the room to change her mattress. She had been complaining that it was too bumpy. Frank's new room at Oakdale was small with a white tile floor, yellow walls, and a single window looking out on the front lawn. The bedside table held a clock, a vase of tulips, and a brass lamp. A Monet print was on the wall across from the single bed. Cecil sat on a folding chair next to the bed. Jackson stood with his hands on his hips. There was a sour smell in the air, like milk gone bad.

"This is the softest mattress I could find, Miss Frances," the orderly told her. He had large, caring eyes and a soft voice. Jackie liked him right away, but Frank watched him closely as if he might grab her at any time. "I checked the whole building just to make sure. I know you will sleep comfortable tonight."

Frank's eyes rose, as if the words contained some secret meaning. "I never sleep too comfortable," she warned him.

"Well, maybe you should talk to the doctor. He might help you to sleep better."

"Why you so worried about how good I sleep?" Frank snapped.

The black man just smiled and chuckled. "Because I want you to be happy. I like you. I want yo' stay with us to be as comfortable as possible."

"Thanks," Jackie put in. "I'm sure she'll sleep just fine."

"Long as you ain't got no thought of throwin' me up in the air at night," Aunt Frank pointed out.

"They throw you up in the air at night?" asked Cecil.

"Of course they don't," Jackson said.

"And how would you know?" Frank protested. "I was there."

The orderly looked over at Jackie and Cecil with a look of helplessness. "Miss Frances, no one wants to throw you up in the air. I have no notion where you got that idea." Obviously, the orderly had already been trying to convince Frank that no one had an interest in tossing her into the air at night.

"She'll be okay," Jackie said. "Thanks for your help."

When the orderly left the room, Frank got up, shuffled across the floor, and watched the black man walk down the hallway.

"He's only nice when you boys are here," Frank claimed. "When it's just me, he calls me an old witch and pokes me with a stick."

Cecil laughed until Jackie glared him down. "Now, Frank. That man just wants to make you comfortable. Please stop giving him such a hard time. He's not the problem here." Jackson put a hand to the quilt of gauze under his shirt.

She looked over at Jackie as if he had totally lost his wits. "Nobody knows what goes on in this place. We are here for their pleasure. Last night, you know, they took us by our feet and walked us around on our hands. Raced us down the hall just like the chirren on field day at the YMCA."

Jackson had tried to explain to Frank that she would only have to stay for a while to let the doctors check her out. She ignored him. "Pooh" and "Pooh-pooh" were the only two responses he could get out of her. Jackie went to find the doctor who was supposed to talk to them in Frank's room. He was already a half hour late.

With Jackie gone, Aunt Frank leaned over to Cecil. "You've got to get me out of here," she whispered. "You've got to get me out 'fore they kill me."

Cecil laughed. "No one's go'n kill you."

"I can pay you," Frank urged. "I got lots of money. Cash dollar. No one has to know a thing. We can take the money and hide out at the Grand Canyon. They have donkeys you can ride right down into it. I seen 'em."

Cecil stopped laughing. Cash? Was this another delusion? Cecil thought about it. He looked into the woman's wide, imploring eyes. "I cain't get you out of here. The sheriff committed you. He's not go'n let you out 'til he's sure you ain't crazy. That could be a long time, if you ask me."

"You can bust me out," Frank whispered. "They let me walk out in the yard ever day. You could walk with me, right out the front gate. Just leave the car running nearby."

"Bust out? What you talkin' 'bout? Sounds like you in some kinda prison, for god's sake."

"Might as well be," said Frank. "They sure won't let me leave."

Cecil had a hard time coming up with a rebuttal to her point. Luckily, the doctor walked in. He wore a white lab coat, a red tie, and thick black glasses.

"Jackson Moon?" the doctor asked.

"No, I'm Cecil."

"Oh," the doctor said, checking his notes. He seemed confused.

"I think he went looking for you," Cecil said, trying to help out.

The doctor was clearly in a hurry. He shuffled his feet as if wanting to move, but his assignment here could not be completed. He checked the clipboard crooked in his right arm and tapped a pen against it. "I'll be back then," he decided and bounded out of the room.

As soon as the doctor disappeared, Frank poked Cecil's tummy. It made him giggle. "He's the one that's crazy," Frank said.

Cecil looked down at her, smiling broadly. "I think you may be right."

She nodded her head proudly. "What's go'n drive me crazy is bein' here. If they'd just keep my house in one place, none of this business woulda happened."

"Yo' house ain't goin' nowhere else. They done moved it, and they ain't go'n move it again. It's over on Maple Street, I think, and that's where it will be from now on."

Deep lines creased Frank's forehead as she tried to plant the information in her brain. "Maple Street," she said. "I thought it was Mayhill."

Jackie rushed into the room. "Damn doctor," he said.

"He was just here," Cecil told him. "He left again when you didn't show up. Said he would be back."

"Damn," Jackson cursed. He was out the door again and almost bumped into the doctor in the doorway.

"Jackson Moon?" the doctor asked.

"Yes, that's me."

"I was asked to give you a prognosis," the doctor monotoned, his eyes fixed on his clipboard. "Not much I can tell you right now. Your aunt is definitely suffering from some serious memory lapses. We're afraid it's related to a dementia disorder."

Jackie didn't get it. Dementia disorder? But it was Cecil who made the point.

"Holy Christ, doc. She's fucking senile. That's a pretty safe guess you came up with there, you ask me."

The doctor looked up from his notes. He wondered why he was now talking to the man who had dismissed him before. He turned back to Jackie to speak. "Your aunt's case is more serious than simple senility, we believe. It is a disorder that we are just starting to understand. Similar to Alzheimer's disease. Her symptoms are consistent."

"Consistent with what?" Jackie asked.

"With this disorder. Possibly it is multiple disorders. It sounds, from what I've heard, that she is handling the situation fairly well."

"Fairly well?" Jackie challenged. "She keeps running off to find her house."

"Oh, well, yes. There is that." The doctor scribbled some notes. This seemed a bit absent-minded to Jackie. How could he not take such an incident into account? "But overall, I think she is learning to cope with her disease. She seems to stay well-organized. That's important. She pays bills as soon as they come to her, things like that. She tracks her money well. Finds ways to take care of the important details."

"Important details," Jackie repeated, trying to keep up. "Like the location of her house? Isn't that a fairly important detail, doc?"

"Well, yes. I suppose it is," the doctor conceded. "But, you see, I think it was the house that grounded her. It kept everything else steady. This disease your aunt suffers from, well, it's like every once in a while everything sort of flies off into space. All her thoughts scatter, and she has to pull them back together. But she needs somewhere to start, something that's constant, something she can count on. I think her world centered around her house. She kept everything very ordered there. She kept bills laid out neat, kept her change laid out on the table, everything in its place. Things like that are vitally important to her. When you uprooted her house, it was as if the earth itself went spinning off into space. She no longer has a reference point. If you notice, most of her episodes occur when she leaves the house. The house is her reference point, if you will, the point from which everything else assumes its order."

"So we put her back in her house," Jackson suggested. "It's all back together now, just like she left it. It's just on a different street. We told the movers that everything had to be put back just like it was. We knew Frank needed that."

The doctor nodded, thought it over.

"How about the Grand Canyon?" Cecil asked.

Both the doctor and Jackie turned a wondering gaze to him.

"Pardon me?" It was the doctor. He had no idea what it was about the Grand Canyon that concerned Cecil.

"She wants to go to the Grand Canyon. Take a donkey down in there. Maybe that could be it, you know, the reference thing."

"The Grand Canyon?" the doctor asked.

Cecil shrugged. "Why not?" he said. "It's where she wants to go. She must relate to it somehow. Hell, this reference shit, maybe it's the donkey."

The doctor cleared his throat. "I don't think riding a donkey into the Grand Canyon would be the best remedy for Mrs. Helms."

"Hell," Cecil said. "I don't see what it could hurt. Give the woman her last wish. Live it up for a while 'fore she keels over."

Jackie flashed a glance at Aunt Frank to gauge her response to

Cecil's thoughtless words, but Frank was nodding her head in agreement. The doctor studied Cecil for a moment before deciding to dis-
miss him. He turned back to Jackson. "In any case, Sheriff Sump told
me to keep her here for at least a week to make sure she's stable. I cannot release her without his authority."

Jackie didn't like that. "What the hell are you talking about?" he
demanded. "Are you saying she's a prisoner?"

The doctor smiled, trying to remain patient. "Of course, I'm not
saying..."

"You're saying she can't leave here," Jackie snapped.

"I'm saying she needs to remain here for a short while. For her own
good. We need to complete a thorough analysis of her condition. At
this time, she is not fit to live on her own."

"Well, we'll take her with us, then. She won't be on her own."

"I'm afraid not," the doctor informed him. "The sheriff has issued
an order to this facility. You'll have to take up your request with him.
Now if there aren't any other questions, I really must be tending to
other patients."

"Hell, yea, I got a question," Cecil blurted. "How'd you get that bug
so far up your ass?"

Frank broke into laughter and clapped her hands together. Cecil
turned to her and smiled. He was pleased that he had given her some
enjoyment. The doctor merely raised an eyebrow.

Jackie tried to ignore Cecil. "When will you know more about my
aunt's condition?"

The doctor cleared his throat, considering whether to answer the
question or leave the room. He gazed at Cecil, then turned his eye
back to Jackie. "I've got some other tests to run. Some questions to
ask your aunt. Further research. We really know very little about
this particular illness. I should have a more complete diagnosis in a
few days."

Jackie turned back to Frank. "We'll be back real soon to visit," he
told her. "You hang in there."

Frank just frowned. Cecil patted her on the shoulder as he got up to leave. He followed Jackson out of the room, glaring at the doctor as he left.

30

Out in the New Yorker, Jackie slumped in his seat. Cecil started up the engine and stuck a cigarette in his mouth.

"You know," Jackson said, "sometimes I miss the simplicity of prison. At least you knew where you stood."

Cecil shook his head. "You just need to have yourself some fun. That's your problem. Head down to the strip club I was telling you about, have a few shots of bourbon."

Jackson rubbed his temple with his left hand, his right arm wrapped over his ribs. Cecil noticed the bulk under Jackson's shirt. He reached over and lifted the shirt up.

"What the hell happened to you?" he asked.

"I was on the bad end of a beating," Jackie said.

"Musta been a big bastard," said Cecil. "I've seen you fight."

"Guy looked like Uncle Fester."

Cecil laughed. "Well, he couldn'ta been bigger than Riso."

"No," Jackson said. "Riso was even bigger." Jackie thought back to the huge specimen who had been his first boxing opponent at the Gainesville prison.

Jackson wondered what the hell he was doing in the ring. It wasn't much of a ring, really. Strings dipped toward the floor on four sides, blocking off an eight-by-eight-foot square in the rec room. Cons stood around the strings, barking and hooting, anxious for some blood. Two guards stood close by with their sticks drawn, and four or five other guards sat and stood in the room just to watch the action. The smell of sweat wafted through the hot room. The oppressive air and intense smell made Jackie feel as if he were buried in the towel bin of a men's locker room.

Clarence rubbed Jackson's shoulders. He had convinced Jackson that he was ready to box; now Jackson wondered why he ever decided that he wanted to do it.

"This guy's big, but look at the gut. It's weak. Remember what I told you. Work the body. Head shots are for glamour, body shots do the damage."

The two fighters met at the center of the stringed-off ring. Clarence stood behind Jackson. Across the ring, the opponent's trainer, an old thin man with a scarred neck, stood beside his fighter. Riso stood six-four and weighed two-eighty. He had a fat squashed nose, dull eyes, and arms the size of pylons. His gut hung over the elastic band of his shorts. A smile curled on his lips that suggested how much he was going to enjoy knocking Jackie's head off. Clarence had told Jackson he would start him off with an easy mark, and this man is what Clarence came up with. Jackie wondered what a tougher mark would look like.

Cecil crossed over the drooped strings and came up between the fighters. Clarence had told Jackie to look dead in the eye of his opponent during the introduction. "Let him know he don't scare you," Clarence had said. Jackson doubted he could look at Riso without relaying the exact emotion Clarence wanted him to deny. Instead, Jackie's eyes wandered across the excited crowd. They cheered and laughed, bulged as a group in toward the strings. Jackson had the uneasy notion of being a combatant in a cock fight.

"Nothing below the belt," Cecil commanded over the roar of the cons. "No elbows, no head butts, no biting. If a man goes down, you back off or I won't start the count. We'll box eight three-minute rounds. Now touch gloves and come out fighting at the bell." Jackson noted that Cecil crossed back over the strings, pushing back the cons who had surged into his spot. The referee had no intention of staying in the ring.

Jackson went back to his corner, and Clarence stepped over the strings behind him. Jackie looked at the three-ounce gloves on his hands. They were old and worn, the right one patched over at the wrist with duct tape. It would be like fighting with gardening gloves on.

Cecil lifted a cowbell up over his head and hit it with a spoon. Riso bolted out of his corner like a bull with red in his sights. Jackie froze and Riso slammed into him, jolting him backward into the wall of cons. They pushed him back at Riso and the big man swung wildly, cupping Jackson's left ear. Jackie went to a knee to a chorus of deafening boos. "Back off now, Riz," Cecil barked. "Your man is down."

Riso grunted and walked back to his corner. Jackie got up and shook his head. "You've got to move!" Clarence barked.

Jackson started bobbing on his toes, moving side to side. There wasn't much room to dance. The ring had started out small and it was now made smaller by the surge of the crowd. Riso came again, his smile full of confidence. This time he simply walked right at Jackie with long, purposeful strides. When he got close, Jackie threw his first punch, pounding a right jab to Riso's chin. Riso's smile evaporated. He rubbed his chin with a glove, then looked at Jackie with rage. He screamed and came at Jackie with his gloved hands out wide. Jackson tried to move but Riso caught him in a bear hug, picked Jackie up off the ground, and squeezed him until Jackson had no air left in his lungs. He heard the crowd roaring, the mad banging of the cowbell, Clarence crying foul from the corner. Finally, someone pulled the monster off of Jackson, and he found himself on the floor again, this time full-out on his back, looking up at the ugly sneers of the convicts. "Get up, you bum!" they roared.

Jackie rolled over and got up. He saw Clarence in the ring, yelling at Riso and his trainer, then at Cecil, who threw up his hands in reply. Clarence came over and got his fighter, tugged him back over to his corner.

"You're doing okay," Clarence told him.

"I am?" said Jackie.

"Well, you survived the first round. That's a start."

"The guy picked me up," Jackson pointed out.

"Yeah, and if he does it again, you'll win by default."

The words didn't comfort Jackson much. He could only imagine Riso hugging him again until Jackie dropped to the floor for good.

"If he does it again," Jackson said, "tell the guard to shoot him. Or shoot me."

Clarence smiled, but Jackie didn't mean it as a joke.

"You remember what I told you?"

Jackson nodded. "Go to the body."

"That's right. So what did you do? You hit him on the chin. Next time, he comes at you like that, put a fist in his belly. You got it?"

Jackie nodded as the cowbell sounded for the second round.

Jackson turned just as Riso was throwing a roundhouse right at him. Somehow, he ducked away as the punch sailed over his head. Jackie stepped to the left of the big man, and rammed a fist dead into Riso's stomach. The man's gut was more solid than Jackson had suspected. Riso swung his left hand back, like swatting at a bee, caught Jackie in the back of the head and sent him stumbling across the ring. He landed against the crowd, and a legion of hands pushed at him – against his stomach, his legs, one even jammed up into his face – shoving him back out into the ring. Riso was there, throwing a mean uppercut, but Jackie reacted instinctively, balling up with his elbows covering his mid-section. The blow landed hard against his arms. Jackie jerked a hard right into Riso's gut. He heard air whoosh out of

Riso, and the big man clutched onto Jackson, wrapping the two fighters up. Jackie crouched down, working Riso's huge arms up over
Jackson's shoulders, then Jackie started delivering kidney punches –
left, right, left, right, left, right.

"Back off!" Cecil screamed, and as Jackie did, he pounded another left
into Riso's gut. Riso stumbled and looked at Jackson with confusion.

Jackie bobbed in the far corner, waiting for Riso to charge again,
but the big man held back, eyeing his assailant with new wariness.
Riso brought his gloves up under his chin, the black eyes peering
over them. For a moment, he actually resembled a boxer instead of a
goon with gloves.

They circled the ring, with Riso's huge presence dominating.
Jackson bowed his head and stepped into Riso. He felt his forehead
against Riso's chest as he went back to work on the gut, slamming five
straight punches to the midsection. Riso brought both of his gloved
hands up and slammed them down on the back of Jackie's head.
Jackson was down again when the cowbell sounded.

"Was that legal?" Jackie asked Clarence.

"In here it is."

Jackie looked over at Riso. His hands were on his trainer's shoulders. The old trainer could barely hold up the weight. He was screaming at his man.

"Next time you come in like that," Clarence ordered, "deliver your
punches, then throw up your head, catch him on the chin."

"Cecil said no head-butting."

Clarence gave him a long wry look.

The bell sounded, and Jackson started to circle. Riso stood in the
middle of the ring, his legs only moving to shift his body so he
remained eye-to-eye with Jackson. The eyes blinked from the sweat
pouring from his forehead. Jackson made a quick feint to the right,
and Riso shifted to the side; then Jackie bolted left and landed a hard
hook to Riso's kidney. Riso groaned and turned. Then Jackson
straightened up and jerked his head forward, busting Riso's nose

open. Riso flopped backward and landed flat on his ass. His rolls of fat waved as he hit the floor.

"Hey!" Cecil roared. "I told you no head-butting."

"The guy had me in a bear hug before. I'd say anything goes."

"He got warned for that. Now I'm warning you. Any more of that shit and you default."

Jackson nodded as Riso worked himself up from the floor. He looked irritated now, like a boy who was being made fun of by the neighborhood kids. Jackie felt a little sorry for the big guy. He was pouting.

"I'm gonna fucking kill you," he yelled at Jackson with unbridled rage. Then he came at him with a wild roundhouse right. Jackson skirted out of the way, and as the punch flew by him, Riso lost his balance and slammed into the crowd. He pushed the entire row of cons back and some of them fell on top of each other. The first row tried to push Riso back into the ring but he moved sluggishly. When he finally turned around, Jackson was there, landing a series of punches to the gut and the kidneys. He felt the huge mass of flesh moving downward as he continued to land punches. When he backed off, Riso was back on his ass, his eyes rolling up into his head. He rolled over on his side as if going to sleep. He even put one glove under his head as a pillow. He wrapped the other arm around his stomach and curled his knees up. He looked like a 280-pound baby sleeping in a crib.

31

Noxie watched Judge Tomey cast his line out into the pond. The judge stood in front of a fold-up beach chair, his canvas fishing cap pulled over his eyes, an unlit cigar between his lips. He wore tan slacks, a blue polo shirt, and blue canvas tennis shoes. A large metal tackle box lay open at his feet. Noxie crouched low in a row of thick brush thirty feet behind the judge. He watched as Tomey reeled the line in slowly. He was trying to catch a sly fish, probably a small bass, and it was starting to annoy him. He cursed every time the fish hit and the hook didn't set. Noxie felt like climbing out of the bushes and showing him how to land a bass.

It was always a funny thing, watching the victim. They never had any idea. Here was the judge, in the last moments of his life, worrying over a fish. If he only knew. You could bet a fish wouldn't be any big deal to him then. If only he could take the chance to enjoy the pond, the breeze, the summer sky. Savor his final moments. Maybe, one of these days, Noxie would let a victim know that he was going to die. Maybe take him out fishing and let him appreciate his last few hours on earth. Of course the man would spend all his time trying to talk Noxie out of it, worrying about his family, his kids, who would pay off the mortgage, whatever. Folks just didn't know how to die right.

Noxie liked the judge. He was a tough guy. Had that rugged face with the long scar. The judge always claimed he got the scar in a knife fight, back in his reckless youth. Too bad Tomey had been talking to Jackie Moon. Nobody knew what the two had talked about, but no sense taking any chances. His daddy was shutting everyone up, once and for all. That was the way his daddy did things – thorough – and he needed Noxie to do it right. Judge Tomey had been a friend of Jackie's, they were together the night of the big fire, shared some secrets. Now it was time for Noxie to bury the secrets: first the judge, then Jackson Moon.

Noxie backed out of the bushes and took the gravel road to the judge's cabin. He needed some time to set things up. The hit would be a good one. The kind people would talk about. The kind his father would brag about one day.

Judge Tomey put away his gear and made himself a glass of whiskey. He walked toward the porch of the large fishing cabin. Sun streamed across the pond and in through the sliding-glass window, pouring into a large clay pot of red geraniums. The judge loved to sit out on the porch in early evening as the sun dropped below the horizon, casting the clouds in red and orange and purple. The reflected colors slithered through the darkening water like oil paints rising to the surface. The porch hung out over the water, and the judge would sit on his padded wooden lounger, savoring the cool night breezes as they gathered, listening to the bass jump and the tree frogs chirp, sipping his drink and enjoying a cigar. It was his favorite time of the day.

The judge checked the phone on his black-cherry desk to see if he had any messages. That's when he saw the note. He wondered where it had come from. He lived alone in the cabin, and the note was not his, although the handwriting was similar. He picked the note up from the desk blotter and read.

"I cannot bear to be without you any longer," the note said. "You are dearer to me than life itself. I have waited long enough, my dearest Alison...."

Alison, the judge's late wife. She had been dead almost seven years, but the judge still thought about her every day. It was a note he had even thought about writing. A suicide note. But he could never do it. How had it gotten there? Why? Had he written it in some state of loneliness and delusion?

No. It had to be something else. Someone was threatening him. Tomey opened the top drawer of his desk and reached to the back of it. He withdrew a key and opened another drawer of the desk. He reached in, expecting to feel the cool metal of his revolver, but all he felt were papers. He shuffled madly through the papers until every one of them was on the floor. The drawer was empty. Where the hell was his gun? What the fuck was going on?

The judge turned to see a man rising out of the floor like an apparition. It stunned him for a moment, a moment he could not afford to waste, the last moment before his dying. He would never have believed the man could move so fast, across the floor in a heartbeat, the gun – the judge's own pistol – rising up, the barrel pressed flat against the judge's forehead.

He never even heard the shot.

As Noxie walked slowly up the road toward the Moon house, memories flooded back to him. Jackson Moon had been a good friend for three years. Jackie had been one of the few boys who didn't treat him like dirt. They fished together, hunted for crawdads and salamanders at the creek, played ball at the park, watched television while their fathers discussed business on the porch or drank and laughed in the kitchen. This, then, was the ultimate test of Noxie's resolve. This would prove that he could ignore his emotions and take care of business. Not even his father, especially not his father, could deny how good Noxie had become. He was a pro. The job was the thing. The only thing.

"Yeah?" Jackson said when he opened the door, before recognition hit him. "Edward?" he said, hardly believing it.

"Hi, Jackie."

Noxie put a hand out but Jackie ignored it and gave Noxie a big hug. "I'll be damned. You're a sight for sore eyes." Noxie was taken aback by the warmth of the greeting. They had been good friends, but twenty-five years had passed.

Noxie worried about the feelings that welled up in him as Jackie held him back at arm's length, sizing him up.

"You grew right up, now didn't you, Edward?"

"Reckon so," said Noxie, and he felt himself blushing. Jackie had always been nice to Edward, and it felt good to see him again. But he had to remember what he was here for. The job was the thing.

"Why don't we go sit on the back porch?" Jackie said. "I'll pour us some iced tea."

Noxie nodded and walked through the house with Jackson. This was the boy who had been Noxie's friend even when the other kids gave Jackie shit for it. He had stood by Noxie and had even stood up for him when he had to. Only now did Noxie think about what it took for Jackie to do that. To stand up for the boy that the other kids hated. It confused Noxie, thinking about it. He could convince himself that maybe Jackie hadn't really saved his life. Maybe it was just a story that got blown up out of proportion, like Noxie's father said. But Noxie couldn't deny that Jackie had been a good friend. He had been a friend to Noxie when no one else would.

This was clearly it then. Noxie's chance to prove to himself, to his father, to everyone, that he was the best. The very best. In the name of his father, Noxie would sacrifice his one true friend.

They sipped tea and watched the shadows lengthen across the long backyard. Noxie told Jackie that he worked at a restaurant. A cook. Jackie suggested he fix them up a dinner. "Try out your specialty on me," Jackie said. Noxie knew he should have stuck to his regular story. He was on welfare. His father sent him some money....

"I can't believe you just showed up at my door. I've wanted to stop by and see you in Atlanta. I just never knew how to do it."

Noxie nodded and smiled. They both looked out at the rows of pecan trees that lined both sides of the lawn. Yellow daffodils sprayed through the deep green grass. "Jackie," Noxie said. "I always wanted to thank you, you know, for being my friend. I know it was hard sometimes...."

Jackie waved it off. "Hell, you were always a good friend to me. We had fun, didn't we?"

Noxie smiled. "Yeah," he said. "We always had fun."

"It was great."

Noxie shrugged and stared at the floor. "I was just talkin' 'bout the other kids. I know they gave you a hard time 'cause you hung out with me."

"Now that was just because of your daddy. You know that. You know how they talked."

"Yeah, I know," Noxie said darkly. Then he looked up into Jackie's eyes. "I want you to tell me about that day," he said.

Jackie sighed. "Now why would you...?"

"I need to know. I want to know the truth. I don't remember much of nothin'. I jes' know I lost a chunk of my brain that day." Noxie felt himself pushing back tears. He hated himself for being so goddamn weak, but he had to hear the story. "You think it was my daddy?"

Jackie studied Noxie for a long moment, the flat forehead and widely spaced eyes, the crewcut like his father's, the pale skin and dark lips. "I really don't know about that. Hell, I was just a kid like you. We were still in grade school, for god's sake."

"I just want to hear the story," Noxie said. "I want to hear it from you."

Jackie nodded slowly. He understood this need that his friend had. Old stories. The truth.

Jackie came upon the Grant house from the rear. It was easier that way. You could make your way through the woods and climb the elevation slowly, instead of tackling the steep, grassy hill that was the Grant front yard. Edward's father, the one they called the porn king, once hired Jackie and his brother Ellis to mow the yard. After mowing about a quarter of the yard and flipping the lawn mower a half dozen times, they gave up and went swimming in the Grant pool out back. Grant ended up running them off with a stick, screaming about his fucked-up lawn.

Jackie emerged slowly from the woods behind the Grant home. It was the biggest house in the neighborhood, appearing castlelike perched on the huge hill. Jackie walked alongside the house and threw a handful of berries at Edward's window. No one came to the window. Music blared inside the house. Jackie wondered if perhaps Edward's parents were out and Edward had commandeered the stereo system.

Jackie walked back around the far side of the house, then came around front to the carport. He checked for the family cars. Edward's father drove a silver Mercedes, his mother a Pontiac station wagon. Both cars were parked in the garage.

Jackie started to walk back to the woods when he heard the rumble of an engine. He ducked off to the side of the house again, waiting for the car to emerge from the carport and drive off. He waited, but nothing happened. Carefully, he went back to the garage window and peeked inside. The station wagon was running. He could see the smoke coming out of the exhaust. It was a nice day, late spring. No reason to warm the car up.

Then Jackie saw Mrs. Grant propped up in the front seat of the Pontiac, her head cocked back over the seat so that she was staring straight up at the roof. Something was wrong. Something was damn sure wrong.

Jackie rushed to the front door and banged on it. The stereo blared. It sounded like some kind of jazz music. He had never heard the music so loud before, not with Edward's parents home. Sometimes Edward cranked it up when his parents were gone but never when they were around.

Jackie banged the door again, then tried to open it. Locked. He went back to the carport and tried to open the garage door but it wouldn't budge. He looked back in the garage. Mrs. Grant was still there, her head cocked back over the seat, her mouth open. Smoke poured from the exhaust as the engine rumbled. The music blared from inside the house. Jackie knocked hard on the glass but the woman in the car didn't move a muscle.

Jackie turned to the road and screamed for help. He thought about running down the hill and crossing the street to the neighbor's door, but there wasn't time. Something was terribly wrong. He had heard of how people would kill themselves sometimes by piping exhaust fumes into a car.

Jackie screamed for help again and realized he was crying. His heart raced. Finally, he grabbed a rock beside the driveway and smashed the garage window.

"Mrs. Grant!" He screamed through the window, but the woman did not move. The acrid exhaust fumes rushed up Jackie's nose and made him gag, then cough. He pulled himself up through the small garage window, scraping his thigh with the broken glass, and fell through to the other side. The exhaust fumes stung his eyes and the car engine sounded as loud as a diesel train. He worked on the garage door from the inside but he couldn't open it. He jerked the handle with all his might but it wouldn't budge. Finally, he squeezed between the far wall of the garage and the station wagon until he came alongside the driver's side window. Mrs. Grant was there, her head cocked back, eyes closed. That's when Jackie saw Edward, his head face-down in his mother's lap.

Jackie tried to open the car door but it, too, was locked. He rushed around to the passenger door. Locked. Jackie was frantic. Tears streamed down his face and neck. The fumes made him dizzy. He grabbed an ax from the garage wall and shattered the back window of the station wagon and scrambled into the car. He made his way to the front seat and moved Mrs. Grant aside so he could turn off the car.

But maybe it was too late. Too late for them all. Turning the car off wasn't enough. They needed fresh air.

Jackie jammed the station wagon into reverse and the car bolted backward, slamming through the garage door as glass shattered and wood cracked. Shards of the door exploded outward as the car bolted out of the garage and off the driveway, darting sideways across the steep front yard. Then they began to roll. Once, twice, three times. Jackie would never forget the feeling. He remembered tumbling as if in slow motion, upside-down then right-side up, upside-down, right-side up. He thought of his mother and his father and his brother Ellis. He thought of his mangled body in a hospital room, his family beside the bed mourning as Jackie sucked his last breaths through a tube.

Then it was over. The car thumped down on the grass at the bottom of the hill, right-side up, and the engine died.

Jackie didn't know how long he sat there in stunned silence. Mrs. Grant's feet were now beside him, her body wedged between the dash and the passenger floorboard. Edward had been tossed into the very back of the station wagon, face-up on the shattered glass. He looked comfortable now, lying on this back, his legs kicked up on the back seat.

The next thing Jackie remembered was Michael Grant dashing down the hill in his bathrobe, waving a cane over his head.

"What the hell have you done?" he screamed, but Jackie was too disoriented to realize that Mr. Grant was yelling at him. He sat in the driver's seat, clutching the wheel so hard that his knuckles were pearl white.

Grant reached the car and slammed the cane against the roof, just over Jackie's head. Not even the crack of the cane could snap Jackie out of his daze. He turned slowly and saw Grant's head taking up the space of the driver's side window. The man's mouth was moving madly and spit was flying from it, but Jackie could hear none of the words rushing out.

"You goddamn maniac! What have you done? You wrecked my goddamn car!"

It was then that the first policeman arrived. The neighbor across the street had heard Jackie's cry, watched the boy frantically smash the garage window, and had called for the cops.

The policeman radioed for an ambulance, then bounced from his car. Grant was still railing: "Look what the maniac did! He wrecked my goddamn car!"

It was always amazing to Jackie, whenever he thought back on it, that Grant's wife and son could have been dead in that station wagon, and all Grant yelled about was how Jackie had wrecked the car.

Edward's mother died of carbon monoxide poisoning. Edward somehow survived, but he had lost some of the functioning of his brain. That was how the paper put it. Grant claimed he had been in the bedroom, getting dressed and listening to the stereo. Apparently, his wife planned to kill herself and her son, too. "She hadn't been herself lately," the paper quoted Grant as saying.

It was the first time Noxie had heard the story directly from Jackson Moon. But it didn't matter, one way or the other. It couldn't matter. Noxie had a job to do. He couldn't fail now. He couldn't fail himself or his father.

"You okay, Edward?" Jackie asked, his own voice cracking.

Noxie nodded. "Yeah," he said. "I'm all right."

Jackie went up the stairs to check on his father, so Noxie followed along behind. Noxie was on one side of the bed, Jackie on the other, as the father slept. Noxie figured the old man was already wasted away. It was hardly worth killing him. The phone rang in the hallway. Jackie said, "Be right back," leaving Noxie alone in the room. He watched old Moon gasp for breath. Hell, he'd be doing the guy a favor. Put him out of his misery.

Noxie pulled the razor out of his back pocket. As Jackie talked on the phone downstairs, Noxie bent over the sleeping figure. He held the blade over the body. The power of the weapon surged through the muscles in Noxie's right arm. He felt a tingle in his elbow and heard a giggle rise out of his throat.

He hovered the blade over the old man's head, then touched the blade edge against his bony throat. The father's breath slackened, clattering out his throat with a deathly rattle. Noxie clenched his teeth and his arm trembled. This will be different, he told himself, the thought coming out of nowhere. Killing Jackie's father. It was different. This was the test. Another test.

Noxie wondered how it would happen. He would slit the old man's throat, and then Jackson would come in, see the blood on the white sheets, the slit across his father's neck. He might run for it.

Or maybe Noxie could cut the father, then meet Jackie as he came through the doorway, bury the blade in the son's gut, whisper in his ear as the razor dug in, tell Jackie he was sorry, thank him again for being such a good friend....

Jackie hung up the phone, and his footsteps echoed up the stairwell. Noxie pulled the razor away from the father's neck. The old man would have to wait. He would kill Jackie first, then come back for the father.

Noxie told Jackie he had to leave. "Why don't you walk with me to the bus stop?" he asked, knowing the best path led through the woods behind the Moon house. Jackie was glad to go with Noxie. They could talk some more.

They had entered the path through the woods, and Noxie again slipped the razor out of his back pocket. He felt the charge course through him. The charge Cracks had always harped about. This was the moment. For the first time, Noxie felt nausea welling in his stomach. What was wrong with him? Goddamn it, he was losing his nerve. This was the fucking moment. The test. His father would know now. He would have to admit how good Noxie had become.

Again, Noxie imagined how it would go. Swinging the blade out from behind his right leg, Jackson turning as the blade plunged into the side of his neck. He would look at Noxie with surprise and wonder. He would bleed to death on the path behind his father's house, the wonder frozen in his wide-open eyes. Noxie brought the blade up now, gritted his teeth, pushed every thought out of his brain.

"Jackson!" a voice called out from behind them. They both turned. It was the Moons' maid, the one that lived in the house out back. She walked up to them briskly.

"Hey, Leola. You remember Edward?"

The maid glared at Noxie. "I remember," she said. "You remember me, boy?"

Noxie remembered. It was the woman who cut him. He had been out in the woods with Emily, a little girl from down the street. He had the girl down, his dick out, pulling up her dress, when the maid appeared with a goddamn butcher knife.

Maybe even the same butcher knife she had now, dangling down from her right hand, flat against her apron. Noxie began to back away from Jackson and Leola, then he turned and ran for the tracks.

"What the hell...?" Jackie said, walking after Noxie.

"Let him go," Leola said.

"Why'd he run off?" Jackie wanted to know. When he turned to Leola, he saw the knife. "And what are you doing with that thing?"

Leola held the blade up, studying it. "I was doin' me some cookin' when I saw you boys out here. Guess I forgot to put my utensil down."

Jackson eyed her suspiciously. "Why was Edward so scared of you?"

She shrugged. "I caught that boy out here one day, tryin' to force hisself on a little girl. I taught him a lesson."

"What'd you do?"

Leola looked over at Jackie, then shrugged. "I just nipped off a bit of his pecker."

"You did not!"

"Just a little nick. Didn't hurt him none. Scared the boy more'n anything else."

"Leola! You cut that boy's penis with a knife?"

"Just the very tip, child. He had plenty of it left."

"Jesus," said Jackie, covering himself instinctively. "That's not something you take just a nick of and act like it's okay. That's his manhood, for Christ's sake."

Leola thought back to the day. "I reckon that boy still recollects ever time he whips that nasty thing out. Pro'bly kept that old pecker out of some places it had no business goin'." Leola nodded her head with assurance and turned back toward the cabin.

Commissioner Sump looked up from his desk, saw the young man who had tramped into his office and closed the door behind him, then he looked back down at his magazine. It took a long moment for recognition to dawn on Sump. Slowly, he brought the hooded eyes back up, taking in the figure before him.

"What the hell're you doin' 'round here?" Sump snarled. He couldn't stand the Grant boy. The little weasel.

"I got some orders for you," Noxie said.

Sump bellowed. It was a deep, hearty laughter that made Noxie cringe with hatred and resentment.

"Now ain't that somethin'," Sump roared, slapping the magazine against his knee. "The Grant boy has got some orders for me. Now that's a good one, boy."

"You best listen to me, Sheriff," Noxie growled. "We got to clean up the mess around here."

Suddenly Sump got serious. His eyes glowered. "I ain't the sheriff no more, boy. I am the commissioner of this county. And don't you be tellin' me about my bidness. This ain't yo' daddy's concern. This here is my territory."

"Bullshit," Noxie snapped. "You know damn well it's my daddy's concern, and whether you like it or not, he's go'n take care of it."

Sump snarled, kept his eye on the boy. "I got this situation under control, boy. You can tell yo' daddy that. We got no problems 'round here."

"No?" taunted Noxie. "You think it's all under control, do you?"

Slowly, he walked around the side of the desk and faced the former sheriff in his chair.

"I'm tellin' you, boy. We got no problems."

"No problems?" Noxie said, his hatred of this man starting to seethe. "No fucking problems, Sump? Well, let's start with the judge then. How you go'n explain that?"

"The judge?"

"Judge Tomey," Noxie said. "He's laying on the floor in that cabin of his on Clearwater Pond. Got a hole clean through his head. It's a real fucking mess over there, Mr. Commissioner."

Sump's eyes widened. "You crazy bastard. They won't no need..."

"No need?" Noxie broke in, his body now inches from the old man. "He's been talkin' to Jackson Moon."

"Arguin'," the sheriff pointed out. "That's the way I heard it."

"Talkin', arguin'. Either way, it's bad news. They ain't scared of you, Sheriff. Not no more. You just a old has-been 'round here. A stupid, careless, limp-dick. We got to put the fear back in these folks."

Sump started to bolt up out of the chair, but Noxie was too quick. He drew his razor and had the point pressed against Sump's throat before the commissioner could get his feet flat on the floor.

Now Noxie had the commissioner's attention. The old man drew his head back and stared at the blade. "Let's just take it easy now, boy," he said.

"I want you to shut the fuck up," Noxie snarled, inches from Sump's ear. It was funny how a razor could make even a big shot like Sump take notice. "I wouldn't think twice 'bout cuttin' yo' throat out. I would love it. I would just love to watch you writhin' on the floor like the snake you are."

Sump started to speak but the boy pressed the blade harder against his throat.

"Don't say a fucking word," Noxie demanded. "I got to give you these orders, and I don't want to end up killin' yo' ass 'fore the message gets delivered." Noxie eased up a little, but kept the tip of the blade against the old man's Adam's apple.

"You go'n take care of the Moon boy," Noxie told the commissioner. "Ain't no two ways about it. You take care of him, Sump. Him and the old man. They both have to die. You understand me?"

Sump nodded slowly. Noxie felt renewed. He had failed to take out the father. He had failed to kill Jackson in the woods. But now he felt the power again. He saw the fear in Sump's eyes.

"You take care of them," Noxie stated. "Or I'll be back to take care of you."

32

The eyes weren't darting. They focused on Ellis – dead on – when he came into the small room. As usual, Grant was smoking a Pall Mall, blowing smoke out of his nose, but this time the eyes didn't dance and dodge and circle the room. They were on Ellis, following him as he came in and sat down. Ellis nodded.

"Michael," he said cautiously. Something was wrong.

"Moon," said Grant.

"Ummm...this thing – the change of venue thing – it went through, you know. They'll be moving you soon, north of here."

Grant nodded but kept his eyes glued to Ellis. Ellis tried to keep the conversation going.

"I still don't get it. Seems like a bad idea to me. City folk, they're going to be more tolerant of porn, sex, alternative lifestyles. You get out in these backwater towns, they're not as accustomed to it. You show them folks a Picasso and they'll call it obscene. I still say it doesn't make sense, this change of venue."

Michael just kept his eyes steady, tugged on the cigarette, and glared at Moon. "It's done, right?"

Ellis nodded. "Yeah. It's done."

Michael turned up a palm. Case closed.

Moon searched for another topic. "I'm lining up your character witnesses. That's going well. We got just about anybody we need from Solomon's Rock. We have some respected businessmen from Atlanta, a couple of politicians. Hell, you'll come out looking like a true prince. No problem there."

The Moon smile got no response from Ghost Grant.

"Is something wrong, Michael?"

The eyes narrowed, held to their target. "I don't know. Is there?"

Moon shrugged. "Everything's fine on this end."

Grant nodded slowly. "What about that brother of yours? I hear he's causin' a big ruckus down there at the Rock."

Was that it? Grant was worried about Jackie? "He's harmless. The man's just a little confused. Don't worry about him."

"Must be a common Moon trait," said Grant. "This confusion."

Moon leaned in and furrowed his brow. "What do you mean? I don't get where this is headed."

"I don't like confusion. I don't understand it. When you have complete loyalty, there is no confusion. That's what I expect. Complete loyalty."

Now Ellis studied the eyes. "What's going on here? You falling for this prosecution ploy? They're setting me up. Don't you get it? They're pulling some sort of bullshit."

"Is that right? What kind of bullshit?"

"I'm not sure," said Moon. "I just know they've been acting awfully strange. Something's up. Maybe they want you to dump me. Maybe they want you to think I've turned."

"Have you?"

"Hell no! Jesus Christ. What do you think?"

"I'm not sure what to think. Yo' daddy, he won't talk to me no more. Yo' brother is stirrin' up the pot. I need to know where you stand."

"I stand with you, just like I always have."

Grant studied him as the smoke rose in front of the eyes. "I don't like confusion," he said.

"No confusion. None. I'm with you all the way."

Grant nodded and, for the first time, averted his eyes. He took another long draw of the cigarette and crushed it into a tin ashtray, then he got up. "Okay then," he said, heading for the door.

At the door, Moon hesitated. It was scary as hell, wondering where Grant's head was. "So we're okay?" Ellis asked.

The guard opened the door, and Grant led Moon out. "I just want to leave you with three things to think about."

"Yeah? What's that?"

"Salvador Creeks, Jason Farmer, and Casey Hart."

"Jesus, what's that supposed to mean?"

Grant held a single finger to his lip, and Moon shut up. "I just want you to think. That's all. Understand. Now get on out of here."

As he headed out of the prison, Ellis realized that he had started to run.

The guard, stone-faced, towered above Grant. The pornographer spoke.

"So you're sure about this?"

The guard nodded, the barest movement.

"Moon has turned."

Again, the slight nod.

"Son-of-a-bitch."

The guard stood, staring straight ahead, emotionless.

"And they'll be moving me to Waynesburgh."

No response from the guard.

"You'll need to contact my wife, let her know the spot. And she'll need to get that crazy son of mine in on it. Cover the bases."

The guard listened.

Grant headed through the door and stopped.

"And tell Monster it's time," he said.

And above him, the guard nodded as the corners of his lip turned up.

33

They were in the New Yorker again, Jackie and Cecil, driving along 121. Jackson was at the wheel of the car, and Cecil was smoking a Camel. They were talking about Gainesville, and whenever the subject of Gainesville came up, it always came around to Jackie's boxing matches. Cecil took pride in Jackson's skills, since he had introduced him to Clarence. Cecil was convinced Jackson could turn pro, even on the outside, and make some money in the ring.

"C'mon, Cecil. I was beating up a bunch of cons. A real fighter would knock me silly."

"What about Magee?" Cecil offered. "The guy was an ex-boxer, man."

Jackson nodded. The fight against Magee was not something he was proud of.

The fights had become a big hit on the cellblock and throughout the prison. The warden believed it was a positive social activity and helped release some of the tension in the penitentiary. Besides, he had his money on Jackson and had won four times already. Jackie was becoming a celebrity. They called him Moondog and howled when he was introduced. They even moved the fights out to the yard and set up actual ropes. The warden watched from the tower. "Jab, Moondog, jab and feint," he would urge his fighter from his exclusive perch. Moondog had won seven straight fights, all by knockout, when he went up against Rock Magee, a former welterweight from C-Block. It became an all-out event. The warden even invited guests to sit with him in the tower, including a local sports columnist.

"The guy was a professional boxer," Jackson pointed out to Clarence.

"So it's time for your first real test."

"My first real test? What have I been doing for the last seven bouts?"

"Developing your skills."

"This guy could kill me," Jackie said.

Clarence shrugged.

"Damn, Clarence. Is that all you have to say about it?"

"You better just make sure he don't. You've trained hard. Listen to what I tell you. Be smart in the ring. Rock has some skills but he's slow and obvious. He's a fighter, not a boxer. You fight smart, you'll take him. You won't knock him out, but you can take him on points."

"Why don't you think I can knock him out?"

"That's where he got the nickname. The guy's a rock. You can hit him 'til the cows come home and that boy will just take it. He won't go down. But if you hurt him, he'll drop his hands and you can pound away, rack up the points, work on him like a damn punching bag. You've got to get him into the later rounds for that. He'll be strong the first five, six rounds. He'll cover up well, throw some hard stuff. And he can fight either way, left or right, so you've got to watch that. Sometimes he leads with the right jab, follows with the left, sometimes the other way around. He's a tricky bastard."

Jackie stared at Clarence and wondered how it had come to this. He was going into the ring with a professional boxer. "Maybe it's time for me to take a dive," Jackson suggested.

At first, Jackson was disoriented by the big sky above him. It was bright blue, dotted with thin clouds that hovered at the horizon. The sun blared down on the dirt ring, and Jackson could feel the heat on his skin as Clarence rubbed his shoulders. He had grown used to the confined quarters of the rec room and now, with the bigger ring, the open air, and the crowd roped off five feet back from the ring itself, he felt strangely vulnerable. Rock had protested about Jackie's cellmate being the referee, so a guard had agreed to do it. He even had a striped shirt and stood inside the ring instead of out of it. The ref was tall and square-jawed. He looked like a fighter himself. It all seemed a little too official for Jackson. For the first time, he felt like he was in an actual boxing match.

"Remember what I taught you," said Clarence. "Counterpunch, counterpunch, counterpunch. It's the only way you're going to hit him in the early rounds. He's got good defenses, but he's slow. He'll leave himself open when he jabs, but you've got to be quick to get away with it. Anticipate the jab and counterpunch. You understand me?"

Jackson didn't answer. He was admiring the protruding abs of his opponent, the sleek brown body that already glistened from a thin film of sweat. Magee tossed sharp, tight uppercuts into the air and glared at Jackson with controlled menace.

"You know that dive I told you about?" Jackie said to his corner man. "I told you the third round, right?"

"Don't talk like that, man."

"I've moved it up to the first."

They even had a real bell now. It sounded, and the fight was on.

Jackson danced around the ring. He had more room to move, and he felt light on his feet. Rock stood firm in the center of the ring, gloves up and eyes hard. He watched Jackson like a bird of prey, waiting to swoop with claws bared. Jackie danced left, then right, staying clear of the man scowling at him. The crowd began to boo. Rock took three measured steps toward Jackson, trying to quarter him off, but Jackie scooted by him and backpedaled toward his own corner. He took two quick feints, just for show, and danced away along the ropes. The boos grew louder.

Rock dropped his gloves. "What is this, the fucking prom?"

"Just remember, I don't fuck on the first date," Jackie replied.

Rock grunted and stepped more quickly. They weren't dancing steps, more like the hunched plod of a bear. He tried to quarter Jackson again, then he took a step to his right, blocking Jackie's movement, and as Jackie backpedaled left, Rock lunged, faster than Jackson expected, and threw an overhand right into Jackie's chin. Jackson felt the blow cock his head back, then he bounced once on the ropes and covered. Rock threw a pair of uppercuts into Jackie's gut, then a right to his jaw. Jackson heard his teeth slap together, and he fell back on the ropes, gloves over his face. Rock pummeled him with sharp cracks to the body and arms as Jackie tried to grab on. Finally, he got hold of Rock and tied him up. Magee threw a kidney punch as the referee separated the fighters.

Rock backed off to the center of the ring. He was smiling. He had expected more from his adversary. Jackie's feet didn't feel so light, and the pang of a cramp was already growing on his right side. In his mind echoed the freeing words "*No Mas.*" Rock stalked him, biding his time, looking for another opening. He dropped his left tauntingly, then slammed Jackie with two right jabs as the bell rang.

"What the hell are you doing out there?" Clarence barked in the corner.

"I'm getting the shit kicked out of me," Jackie replied.

"Why is it you forget everything I tell you when you step between the ropes?"

"Goddamn it, Clarence. The guy knocked every thought out of my brain."

"Well, he's gonna knock your brain out your ear if you don't buck up."

"All right, all right. Counterpunch. Counterpunch."

"You've got to focus. Anticipate the jab. Keep your right up and counterpunch with the left when he's leading with his right. Left up and counterpunch right when he's leading with the left."

"Jesus Christ. Could you write all that down?"

"Just keep moving, damn it. Look for the opening. Let it flow."

"Right. When he cracks my lip open, I'll let it flow."

Clarence screamed out, "Believe in yourself, goddamn it," just as the bell rang.

Moondog started to move better in the second round. He felt himself focusing and landed his first few punches. Magee caught him with a left jab, but Jackie countered with a right cross that snapped Rock's head to the side. Jackie heard the crowd roar, and it revived him. He ducked under the next jab, slid right, landed two quick right jabs, pulled back, faked a left, and landed another hard right to the face. The crowd began to chant "Moon-dog, Moon-dog," as Jackson danced back out, then in, out and in. Rock switched over to a right lead, but Jackie was ready with a left hook that stunned Rock for a moment. Jackson reacted with another right cross, two left jabs, and a right uppercut that sent Rock to the ropes. Rock wrapped Jackie up, but Moondog landed a series of body shots, and a hard blow to the left kidney. Just before the bell, Jackie came in with his hands down, ready to pull back and counter, but Rock unleashed a wild roundhouse right that caught Jackie square on the jaw, and Moondog went down. He managed to get up after the bell and staggered to his corner.

"You can't play with this guy," Clarence warned. "None of that cute shit. Keep your guard up, fool."

Magee methodically took the third and fourth rounds with crisp jabs and solid defense. He was slow, but he moved strategically, cutting off the ring, landing punches, and pulling out. At the end of the fourth round, Rock ducked Jackson's right hook, moved into the body, then delivered a vicious head butt that split open Jackson's lip.

Clarence worked on the cut as he warned Jackson not to punch wildly. He had to stay focused, controlled. Pick his openings.

"Hey ref, you see that head butt?" Jackson called as the ref neared the corner.

"Yeah, pretty damn good one, wadn't it?"

The action slowed in the fifth round. Jackson wrapped up his opponent every time Rock tried to come in. He pinned Magee's arms and leaned into him, trying to find his strength and his wind. The ref pulled them apart and Jackson circled the ring until Rock came in again. Rock landed a punch or two before Jackson wrapped him up again, pinning the arms and hearing the boos wash over him. He got a warning from the ref toward the end of the round and then made a show of it, landing an artful counter before the bell rang.

Moondog felt strangely rejuvenated midway through the sixth. Rock had gotten lax, and the left hand started to drop. Jackie landed some solid right crosses before Rock switched styles again, leading with the right and keeping the left up. The two fighters stood toe-to-toe at the center of the ring, the crowd roaring its approval, and matched flurries. Magee's right jab was landing consistently, but Jackie was able to throw enough jabs and sweeping hooks to keep Rock off-balance. As the round closed, Jackie had a moment of supreme focus like he had never experienced before. He had heard baseball hitters talk about how big a pitched ball looked when they were in a groove. Jackie understood what they were talking about when he saw a right cross coming from Rock. It seemed to come at him in slow motion. Jackie bored his sights on the ridge beneath Magee's right eye socket. He delivered a straight left to the spot as he spun his chin to the side, glancing away Rock's blow. Moondog's left landed hard, driving Rock backwards. The fighter landed on the ropes and his knees buckled. Jackson pounded Rock's body as the fighter tried to hold on. Jackie no longer heard the roaring crowd. He heard only the sound of his fists slapping into Rock's ribs. He wailed away like a motorized pump: left, right, left, right, left, right as Rock wheezed above him. Jackson did not realize the round had ended until the referee wrapped his arms around him and pulled him away.

"Keep landing those body blows, boy," Clarence crooned in the corner. "You got him now. You got him good."

Early in the seventh, Jackson caught Rock with another perfect counterpunch and went back to the body, pounding away as Rock tried to tie him up. No sooner had the ref separated them than Moondog came back like a fighting machine with a tight uppercut to the chin and another series of killer body punches. At the end of the round, Rock staggered to his corner and went down on one knee as his trainer tried to encourage him on. Clarence kept preaching body blows. Victory was at hand. "You need these last three rounds to win on points. Just keep landing the punches, Moondog." Jackson noticed the blood from his knuckles seeping through the worn gloves. Luckily, his hands were numb.

Magee came out for the eighth, and Jackson saw blood pooling up in his opponent's mouth. It wasn't from a split lip or a cut tongue. Jackie could see it came from inside the fighter. The dark blood gurgled up Rock's throat, drooled down over his chin, and streamed down his neck.

"You've got to stop this, ref," Jackie urged, but the guard ignored him. Magee stood like some blank-eyed zombie, taking the fighter's stance by pure rote. Jackson approached and landed an easy right jab. Rock didn't even bring the gloves up. His head snapped back then bobbed into position like one of those baseball dolls with the spring heads. Jackie landed another defenseless right, then another. He turned to the ref again. "He's done," he said.

"You gonna talk or are you gonna fight?" the ref told him.

Moondog moved in close to Rock. He kept his gloves down, but Rock refused to punch. Instead, he stood with his gloves curled up by his chest. The blood spurted out of his mouth as he bounced to an eerie rhythm. "This is a slaughter," Jackson told the ref.

The ref then held up a hand, penalizing Jackson for refusing to fight. Jackson approached Rock again, landed another soft jab. The blood spat out onto Jackson's right cheek. Rock seemed to lose his balance. He staggered once toward Jackson, somehow flailing out his left arm. The weak punch glanced across Jackie's right ear, and Jackson fell to the dirt. He rolled over on his stomach and listened, fully conscious, as the referee counted to ten.

The ref held up the winner's right arm, but Magee didn't seem to know what was happening. They took him to the infirmary, then to the city hospital. He had two broken ribs, one of which missed piercing his lung by less than an inch.

Clarence clapped his fighter on the back. "You beat a pro," he told Jackson, but it wasn't much of a consolation. As he left the ring, the convicts threw punches at him, slapped his head, spit on him, and jeered as he passed through.

"You cost me quite a chunk of change, Moondog," the warden said. He had summoned Jackson three days after the fight. Jackie stood before him with a left eye almost swollen shut, bruised forearms, and a bottom lip that looked like a sausage wrapped in thick dough.

"The name's Jackson Moon."

The warden looked at him from behind the oak desk. The room smelled like dust and old books. A single window looked out on the yard. The day had turned dark. Rain tapped against the windowpane.

"The boys call you Moondog."

"I'm not a fighter anymore."

"Is that so?"

"Yes, sir."

"And why is that?"

"I'm retired. Besides, my parole is coming up. I'll be out of here soon."

"You think so?"

Jackson looked over at the warden. "My record's clean."

"Oh, but I have substantial pull on the parole board. You might say your parole is at my discretion, and in my view, you seem to lack a certain amount of contrition."

Jackson glared at the warden through the damaged eye. The man didn't flinch. His steel blue eyes held the assured look of someone in absolute authority. His gray suit was crisp, the white shirt starched, the trouser crease razor-sharp, and the black hair was molded to his head. The warden rose up and walked around his desk, straightening his maroon tie.

"But I've got a deal for you to consider, Moondog." The warden brushed off a spot on the edge of his desk and sat on it. "That stunt you pulled didn't fool anyone. My mother could've taken that last punch. You ask me, you're a coward and a fool. But I had this sportswriter up in the tower and he saw it another way. Wrote this lyrical column about the convict boxer who took a fall to save his opponent's life. Quite touching, really. Seems you've become something of a local hero. The boxer with a golden heart."

Jackson peered out the window. The rain picked up, pattering the window like marbles across a tin roof.

"We've got an offer to showcase your talents. They want you to box down at the gym in Canterback. Lots of civic interest. There would be some folks there that could help this prison out. Bring badly needed funds our way. It would be good for the community, good for this prison. But you're the one they want to see, Moondog."

Jackson watched the rain while the warden watched Jackson.

"If I fight," Jackson said slowly, "will I get my parole?"

"If you fight and you give it your all – no dives, no phantom punches – you'll get your parole. But you've got to give a hundred percent until the last bell sounds. Nothing less."

"And you'll promise to get me out of here."

"I guarantee it," said the warden.

Jackson considered the offer.

"And I'm a man of my word," the warden said.

Jackson eyed him cautiously. "I guess we'll find out."

"So," Cecil said, coaxing Jackie out of his daydreams, "you know what you go'n do now?"

Jackie looked over at him. "What are you talking about?"

"I'm just wonderin' what you go'n do, that's all."

"About what? What the hell are you getting at?"

"About yo' brother, goddamn it. You know what I mean. About all this shit goin' down."

Jackson didn't say anything. He wondered where the conversation was going, what Cecil had in mind.

Cecil was talking again. "You know why yo' aunt is losing her property," he said. "It's this fucking theme park. It's expanding, man, and I ain't talking a new parking lot. Hotels, rides, trams. They're even trying to build a casino on the Cherokee land west of here. You know that, don't you? It's drivin' yo' aunt clear out her mind. They gonna plop a interstate right on her land, done shoved her poor ass off to a half-acre lot. How does that make yo' little girlfriend feel?"

Jackson scowled at him. "What's Bridgett got to do with this?"

"She's got everything to do with it. Her daddy lost his land the same way, drove him crazy, too. That's how these folks is about the land. It's like the blood in they veins." Cecil studied Jackie. "The girl, does she know what's goin' on? She happy about it?"

"Of course she's not happy. She doesn't want the theme park coming this way. She sent a clip to me in prison. From the newspaper. A letter she wrote about the park."

"A letter," Cecil scoffed. "Might as well write it on toilet paper and wipe yo' ass with it."

Jackson watched the road and waited.

"You know who built that fucking theme park, don't you? Same bastards behind all this expansion. You hear of Twelve Oaks International?"

Jackson thought about Aunt Frank in his father's office. TOI. Twelve Oaks International. Awful generous folks.

Cecil kept going. "It's a front company for Grant. He built it to clean up his money, never guessin' what a hit it'd be. Now it's a legit investment, rakin' in the cash, drawin' the kiddies from all over, all them rednecks longin' for the good ole days of the Civil War. But the dirty money, it still goes through. Comes out all shiny clean. You know that, don't ya, Jackie? You ain't foolin' me."

Jackie glanced at Cecil. His frown deepened. "Who have you been talking to?"

Cecil shrugged. "I was down at the library a while. Talked to that librarian about it."

"Librarian? You expect me to believe that bullshit? You haven't set foot in a library your whole life."

"Goddamn it. Why does it matter who I hear it from? It ain't no secret. Everybody knows it. It's in the paper ever other day, for Christ's sake. They buildin' up the park and Grant's behind it. Don't take no brains to figger that shit out."

Jackson sighed. "I was in my daddy's office the other day," he said. "Aunt Frank, she mentioned some things."

Jackson fell silent, so Cecil prodded him. "Mentioned what?"

Jackie looked over at him, then back at the road. "Payoffs," he said. "A common occurrence, really. Anybody who wanted a business in Solomon's Rock paid off the planning commission. It was simply a cost of doing business. TOI, it was a generous contributor."

"So TOI paid off these guys so they could build."

"Looks that way," said Jackson. "The payoffs were never that big, except the ones from TOI." He looked over.

It took Cecil a minute. "Michael Grant had them all hooked."

Jackson thought about it. The commissioners – his father, other lawyers and judges, town councilmen, Frank's late husband – they must have counted on the extra cash. Grant had them where he wanted them, dependent on him, vulnerable to blackmail. "This town built a monster," Jackson said. "And now it's going to swallow them up."

"That old girlfriend of yours, she's got to know what's what, workin' the money like she does. She must run across Twelve Oaks all the time. Movin' the money in, takin' it out. She knows Oaks is behind the park, and Grant is behind Oaks. She ain't a stupid girl."

"You're right, she's not stupid. That's why she's staying out of this."

"She's already in the middle of it, man. She works for the accountant. Don't you get it?"

Jackson gave up. "Why don't you just tell me what you have in mind, Cecil?"

Cecil smiled, his brain turning. "There's a big transfer goin' down, Jackie. It's time for Grant to go to the laundry. He's movin' the money into Twelve Oaks. He gets to unload some dirty cash and finance the new development at the same time. It's all ready to go down. He's movin' the money in."

Jackson jerked the car onto the shoulder and hit the brakes. Gravel flew as the car slid to a hard stop. He threw the car into park and grabbed Cecil by the collar.

"You didn't get that tidbit from a goddamn librarian!" Jackie roared.

"Fuck, man. What you gettin' all riled about?"

"Goddamn it, don't fuck with me. Who are you working for?"

Cecil slapped Jackson's hand from his collar and glared back at him. "Who gives a fuck? I'm workin' with you now. Me and you. We can pull this thing off. Me, you, and the girl. Fuck everybody else. It's up to you now, man. You either with me or I figger out some other way to get my hands on the money."

"That's all you care about," Jackson growled.

"Fuck yeah. What else is there? Ruinin' Grant, bustin' up TOI, that's all gravy."

Jackson settled back down in his seat and shook his head. He had to laugh a little as he gazed out the driver's-side window. After a few moments, he turned back to Cecil and considered him carefully. "Are you sure about this? The transfer?"

Cecil straightened his collar and tried to look put out. "I'm sure. I wouldn't be tellin' you if I wadn't sure."

"And you think Bridgett can get her hands on it?"

Cecil nodded. "She works in the office with the accountant. Thomas Dade."

"That doesn't mean she can get the money."

"Goddamn it. She works the computers. It's a lock."

"I don't know," Jackie said.

Cecil decided it was time for his trump card. "Listen to me, Jackson. The accountant – he's workin' for Jake Marston. They plan to strip Grant clean."

Jackson leaned back, taking it all in. He ran a hand through his hair. "So Dade has turned on Grant?"

"That's right," Cecil said, his eyes flaring with excitement. "He works for fucking Marston. Don't you see? If we don't take the money, Marston will. Everything's all set. All we got to do is throw the switch, head the train down another track."

Jackson stared out the window. "You're up to something, Cecil. You're playing both ends of this thing."

"Damn right, Jackie. And now I'm givin' you a chance to get in on the action. Think about it. All we need is the girl. She holds the key to all of it."

"You don't know if she can even do this...."

"I know," Cecil said. "I know she can do it."

"Even if she can," Jackson said, looking over at Cecil, "you don't know if she will."

"That's yo' job," Cecil said, tapping Jackie on the chest. "You got to convince her."

"I don't know, man."

"Think about it. The park is gonna destroy this town. If you lucky, they'll bulldoze the whole town over and throw a couple of hotels smack dab on top of it. They leave it standing? You ever been in a town caught between a theme park and a casino? That'll be some ugly shit. Trash city, man." Cecil leaned in toward Jackie, driving home his pitch. "But we can stop it. You, me, and Miss Baines. We can stop the park dead in its tracks. Take the money and stop the machine. Save the town of Solomon's Rock, Georgia. Get a measure of revenge for yo' aunt and Bridgett's poor old daddy. It's beautiful."

"What are we talking about here? A couple million?"

"A couple million? This is a major expansion of a theme park. Hotels. Restaurants. Fucking roller coasters. Ten million easy. Maybe more."

"Ten million dollars?"

"It's the big one, man. I know it is. With all this legal shit, Grant's havin' some serious cash-flow problems. He needs clean money. Lots of it."

Jackie looked out at the road and beyond. Distant lightning veined through dark clouds that were gathering in the southeastern sky. He smelled ozone in the raw air. He shook his head as if shaking loose the thoughts that were cobbled there. Then he shoved the New Yorker in gear, spun a U-turn in the highway, and headed back toward the General Lee.

"I'll get back to you," he said.

Cecil and Starry were sitting on the couch at the General Lee. Cecil was bored, watching some sitcom that Starry liked, so he tried out his TV show idea on Starry.

"It's about these two guys living together. The place is a pigsty, beer cans everywhere, piles of dirty clothes. They eat peanut butter sandwiches every night. So they hire this strip girl to look out after them, keep the apartment clean, that kind of thing."

"You can't have strip girls on television," Starry pointed out.

"She ain't naked," Cecil said. "She wears a g-string and one of them little cut-off shirts. Hot as hell."

"That's what she walks around in?"

"Yeah, sure," said Cecil. "She's one of them girls, likes lookin' sexy all the time. Likes driving men wild."

"And in this show, she's cleanin', cookin', what?"

"Nah," Cecil said. "I mean that's her job but that ain't the show. You have fucked-up situations, you know. One of the guy's parents comes over to dinner and she dances on the table, not knowin' no better."

"Why wouldn't she know no better than that?"

"She's a strip girl, for Christ's sake."

"What do you think? Girl like that goes home and can't help but dance on the table? You ever seen me do that?"

"Well, this girl, the one on the TV show, she's different. She was born to be a stripper. It's all she knows. Besides, the guys pay her for that: serve up dinner and dance on the table while they're chowin' down."

"Sounds disgusting," Starry said.

"It would be a hit, I'm tellin' you that. You got your sex, you got what you call your situations, you got your love element. One of the guys, he's in love with her but can't tell her. She starts datin' some guy down the hall so you never know if she's gonna make it with her master. She's always doing stupid shit but they can't get rid of her 'cause she's just one of the family after while."

"Family? If I was her, I'd run off soon as I had the chance."

"There you go. That could be a show. The strip girl keeps runnin' off, so they tie her up, put her away in the closet or somethin'."

"That's a show?"

"Sure it is. That's the situation. The mom comes over, she wants to hang up her coat, but all the guys, they go spaz tryin' to keep her away from the fuckin' closet. One guy grabs the coat, throws open the closet door and there you see the strip girl all tied up and gagged. He throws the coat in there and slams the door. That's some funny shit."

"And that's a whole show? The girl tied up in the closet?"

"It ain't the whole show. You got the guys dealin' with other shit. Maybe the landlord comes over, he's heard some complaints about a strip girl in the house. He's trying to find her and they keep movin' the girl around, takin' her out of the closet, stickin' her under the bed, tyin' her to the porch out back. Shit like that."

"I don't know, Cecil. From then on, you got to keep the girl tied up. Every show, you got the girl tied up somewhere."

"Nah, man. You know how it works. End of the show, she figgers she likes the guys again, says she won't run off no more if they let her go. Maybe she says she'll make them up some eggs and she comes out the kitchen throwin' eggs at the guys. You know, she gets the last laugh. Everybody cuttin' up at the end, back to normal. Next week, you got some other situation."

Starry thought about it. "It might work," she said.

Cecil had been in the room at the General Lee for almost two hours. He had gotten his way with the television once Starry's show was done. They were watching a cartoon – an old Yogi Bear one – when the phone rang. Cecil answered it on the first ring.

"Yeah?"

There was silence at the other end. Cecil knew it was Jackson. He waited, giving Jackie plenty of time. No rush. Cecil knew he had him.

"We're on," Jackson said.

"Fucking right!" Cecil roared, but before he could celebrate with Jackie, the phone went dead. Cecil hung up the receiver and slapped the couch.

"Who was that?" Starry asked.

"That was our boat," said Cecil.

"Our boat? What boat?"

"The one that just came in."

34

Bill Sump drove his silver Lincoln along the red dirt road. On either side of him, the earth spread out in miles of flat, shadeless fields. Cows hunkered beneath solitary trees or beside small mud patches that had held pools of water in early spring. In the distance he saw a mound of rusted metal. It resembled one of the creations that today passed for modern art. A fender protruded from one side. A roll of barbed wire swirled out the back. The bent hood of an old Buick tee-peed over a stack of steel pipe.

As he came closer, he noticed a young dirty-faced girl sitting on a wood beam in front of the metal pile. Twelve, maybe thirteen. She wore a simple knee-length cotton dress. The dress had been white at one time, but it was now stained and worn. White trash, Sump thought as he turned into the driveway, making sure to navigate around the metal mound and the shattered glass that sprayed out around the pile and shimmered in the bright sunlight.

It was still morning but the hot sun had already burned away the early breezes. It was even hotter out here, Sump thought, in the flatlands. No shade to speak of. Nothing to combat the endless waves of heat. He drove up the dirt driveway and parked the Continental close to the small house where Marvin Slats lived. A gray barn stood thirty yards to the west. Between the barn and the house, a row of clothes hung from a thin wire, stagnant and damp in the still, humid air.

The little girl came up along Sump. "You used to be the sheriff," she said. "Didn't you?"

"That's right," said Sump.

"You here to arrest my granddaddy?" the girl asked.

"No ma'am," Sump replied. "You know somethin' I should be arrestin' him for?"

The girl gave him a look as if everyone knew what Marvin Slats should be arrested for. "He makes his own whiskey," she pointed out. "That's one thing."

Sump walked past the girl, toward the house. The little girl was a pain in the ass. Slats's daughter, at only age fourteen, had gotten pregnant with the girl, and she couldn't say who the father was. Two years later she took off, leaving the baby girl with Slats and his wife. Slats had tried to get Sump to come get the girl since he wasn't beholden to her. That's what Slats had said. He figured it was Sump's job to track down the daughter and give her baby back to her. Lately, he hadn't heard much from Slats about the girl, so as he was driving over, he found himself hoping that Slats wouldn't bring the girl up. Now he wasn't so sure that Slats wouldn't.

"He beats up on me sometimes, too," the girl said to Sump's back. "He'd pro'bly do more than that, but he gets so drunk he can't catch me. He falls flat on his fat ass."

Sump turned around, considered the little girl in the dirty dress. "You best not be talkin' 'bout yo' granddaddy like that," he said, pointing a finger at her. "Yo' granddaddy loves you."

"Not if I can help it, he won't," the girl said.

Sump dropped the finger and shook his head. "He will whup you good, girlie, if he catches you tellin' the law about his still."

The girl shrugged. *Defiant little shit*, thought Sump.

"You best be a good little girl 'cause you got nowhere else to go. They will put you in one of them homes for chirren ain't got no family. You lucky yo' granddaddy and grandma are willin' to take you in."

Now the girl shook her head and veered around Sump, into the house. "Grandma!" she shouted out as the door swung open. "The sheriff's here!"

Bill Sump stayed put in the doorway even though the door was now wide open. He looked over the front room: an old black-and-white television that looked like it hadn't worked in a few years, a beat-up couch, beer cans on the coffee table. The girl reappeared in the room. "Grandma wants to know what you want."

Sump entered the house. The girl turned around and led the commissioner to the kitchen. Slats's wife was standing over an old wood stove. There was a pot on the stove, and on the table nearby lay piles of roots and spices, herbs and berries. And there were some live insects in a jar.

The smell in the kitchen rushed at Sump and stole away his breath. "Good God, Elma, what the hell are you cookin'?"

Elma just stared at him with big black eyes. Her gray hair was tied back but strands of it wiggled out and up like shocks of electricity. "Child tole me it was the sheriff," she said in an accusatory tone. "You ain't the sheriff no more."

"Well, I know that," Bill Sump said.

Elma nodded firmly, as if she had put the old man in his place. She studied him for a moment with her probing eyes. Sump was amazed how sharp the eyes were, considering the woman's advancing years.

"It smells like holy hell in here," Sump said.

Elma stirred the contents of the pot, ignoring him.

"You go'n eat that stuff?" Sump asked.

She looked at him like he was a pure idiot. "'Course not, you fool," she said. "It's for the chickens. They ain't layin' they eggs."

Sump stared at the pot as if it were giving off deadly fumes. "Not even a goddamn chicken is go'n eat that mess."

Elma ignored him again. She sat down at the table and began chopping up some roots.

"She put slugs in it," the girl said.

"You hush up, now," Elma told her. "Go tell yo' granddaddy that Bill Sump is here to see him. He ain't the sheriff no more. Don't be tellin' yo' granddaddy that. He likely do somethin' crazy."

The girl ran out, and Elma worked on the roots. Sump had never put much stock in Elma's various potions and remedies, although he knew many of the townfolk did. One story had it that Elma had given Louise Mays an elixir to get rid of her husband. The husband left on a business trip and never came back. They say he got to Chicago and plumb forgot everything – who he was, where he was from, every-thing. Sump figured it was just a way for Louise to save face after her husband left her for another woman. Another story had it that Elma cured a young boy who was sick with consumption. Gave him a potion and he hopped up out of bed a few hours later. She also got credit for killing a man, Josh Givens, who had sold her a sick rooster. Three days later Josh was drunk on 'shine and fell face first in a mud puddle, drowning himself in five inches of water.

As Sump studied the old woman, she looked up at him and turned the cutting blade so a shaft of light stung his eye. He cringed away and the old woman cackled. "You need somebody dead," she told Sump, "I can do it a whole lot better than that no-account husband of mine."

Sump shook his head but he felt beads of sweat on his face. How did she know this shit? "I don't need nobody dead," he lied.

She just smiled knowingly and went back to cutting her roots.

The little girl came back in and told Sump to follow her. They went out the back door and walked over to the barn. It was so rickety that Sump didn't like going into it. Streams of light speared down through holes in the tin roof high above him. The girl led him to the back of the barn where Marvin Slats stood with his back to them. The girl pointed, then turned around and ran off.

Slats had one of his mouse cages open. He was prodding one of his mice, trying to get it to go through a tunnel made of bean cans. It was something else. This crotchety, bitter man who would just as soon spit at you as shake your hand, playing with a bunch of mice. Sump once had made the mistake of calling them rats, and he thought Slats was going to plug him with his shotgun. One of the mice had a huge lump on his neck, as big as the mouse itself. "I should put that poor thing out of his misery," Slats would say, but he never seemed to have the gumption to actually do it. Would kill a man with his bare hands, but couldn't kill a rat with an ugly tumor growing out of its neck.

"What you want?" Slats snapped, not even turning around.

"Well, I'm doing just fine, Marvin," Sump replied. "And how are you?"

Slats closed the door to the mouse cage and turned around slowly. Sump could tell he was already drunk. He walked as if balancing on a wood beam. "This a social visit?" Slats asked.

"A little bit social," Sump said. "A little bit business."

Slats grunted. He sat down on a stool and pointed at another one for the commissioner. Sump walked over to it, but decided against testing his weight on it.

Slats looked up at Sump. Slats's eyes were still steady and tough, unrelenting, even after all the hard years and the hard liquor. A fine scar ran from the corner of Slats's right eye down to his jaw line. He had sold some moonshine to a group of teenage boys one winter. Three of them ended up in the hospital, one of them in the ground. A week later, Slats was down at the pit in Easton, betting on the cocks, when the dead boy's mother showed up. Slats turned around and looked at the woman who had said his name just as a steak knife flashed in his eye and sliced the side of his face. The right eye remained bloodshot to this day.

The knife scar cut across another scar on Slats's right cheek. This was the one Sump studied, as if trying to read a sign there. The scar from 1978. Teeth marks. It was a reminder that seemed to mock Slats wherever he went. The bite mark of Lonnie Brim.

"Elma, she's cooking up somethin' nasty in there," Sump reported. "Says it's for the chickens."

Slats held his stare on Sump. "I used to think them potions was a bunch of horseshit. But that woman, she can surprise you."

Sump shot up an eyebrow.

"Coupla springs ago, I was havin' myself some awful nightmares. I'd wake up screamin' in the middle of the night. I'd be dreaming about my daddy – he's dead, o'course – whippin' up on me good. Elma tole me it was my daddy's spirit. Said his spirit was restless, said it was after somethin' and I best find out what it was. She gave me three stones to go put on his grave, tole me to listen up when I was down there. I won't there no more than five minutes 'fore it came to me. You see my daddy's brother, he had gone off with my daddy's shotgun, said my daddy wanted him to have it. Now I know that won't true, cause my daddy hated that bubba of his.

"Turns out it's that shotgun my daddy wants back, so I tracked down that no-good brother, beat him senseless, and took back the shotgun. I thought I had me a new shotgun, but Elma tole me I gots to bury it right on top of my daddy. Now, I don't do it at first and I had me the worst nightmare yet. The next mo'nin, I got my sorry self down to that graveyard and gave my daddy his shotgun back. Buried it right there in the ground. Ain't heard from my daddy again since that day. No more nightmares, no nothin'. He just wanted that shotgun, the stubborn old coot. That's all he wanted."

Sump nodded. "That gun still buried down there?" he asked.

Slats stared at him suspiciously. "Anybody try to take that gun, both me and my daddy go'n be after him."

Sump held up his hands. "I ain't goin' after the gun, Marvin. I's just wonderin'. Seems kind of funny, that's all. Havin' a shotgun buried in the churchyard."

"One time some women from Atlanta heard stories about Elma," Slats went on. "They was witches or somethin', least ways that's how they tole it. Came here askin' Elma about her spells and such. 'Course, Elma don't take none to that shit. She is a God-fearin' woman, you know that. So here's them girls, sayin' they chants to

Satan or some such garbage, and Elma throws them right out the door. She was chasin' them off, throwin' some kind of potion at them and they was screamin' out to God almighty. Yes siree, they had found theyselves the lawd on that night. I figgered that was some powerful potion. Turns out it was just plain ol' bacon grease that Elma had put out on the stove. It was funny, though, watchin' them Satan girls find the Good Lord as soon as the bacon fat was flying."

Sump laughed and Slats tried to. Slats's laugh came out as a grunt, then he held his side as if the laughter pained him. "Got me some stomach trouble," he explained.

"Maybe you should lay off that stuff you been cookin' up."

Slats peered at him.

"I hear you got yo'self a good batch goin'."

Slats nodded. "Strong enough to make you see things that ain't there," he said. "But not quite strong enough to kill nobody. Least ways I hope not." He fingered the scar running down his face.

Sump hoped not, too. He used to hate having to investigate such deaths and didn't wish it on his son. Every year, it seemed, there were one or two liquor deaths back this way. It was never the old men whose systems had built up immunity to the rotgut, but always a younger man, one trying to prove himself by guzzling too much of the white lightning. The stuff would tear the boy's stomach clean out. The poor victim would retch until his insides were lying on the ground.

"What's this business you talkin' 'bout?" Slats asked. He wanted to get off the subject of his homemade liquor. He knew it could be a sore spot with the commissioner. One year, when he was still sheriff, Sump had gone so far as to bust up Marvin's still.

Sump looked down at him. "It's the man," he said. "He needs yo' help."

Slats looked away. Grant. Somehow he knew this was about Grant. Two nights ago he had dreamed about him. Grant was in a big car, talking to Slats out on the street. Grant's eyes like balls of fire.

"What's he want?" Slats asked.

"There's this goddamn kid, Moon's boy, been stirrin' up some trouble, talkin' about Lonnie Brim, Bosco's bar, crap like that."

Slats turned to Sump. He had not heard that name spoken in some time. "Lonnie Brim?" he said as if the name were from some ancient story he could not quite remember.

"That's right. He's got to be shut up, Marvin. That's all there is to it."

Slats nodded. Something stirred deep inside of him. It made him feel alive. "That Jackson Moon's boy?" he asked.

"That's right."

"I thought he was some hot-shot lawyer, workin' for the man."

"It's Moon's other boy we talkin' 'bout here. The one what was with you that night."

Slats scowled. "That little fuck? Sat hisself in the shadow while that nigger bit half my face off?"

"That's him."

Slats nodded. It looked like he had thought about killing the boy before.

"Grant wants the father dead, too. Bury this shit once and for all."

It sounded good to Slats. Bury it. "Why me?" Slats asked. An old man now. Twenty years since Bosco's.

Good goddamn question, Sump thought. He wasn't sure himself why he had come back to Slats. Probably because Sump liked his loyalty. Liked how Slats had kept his mouth shut all these years. He had stayed quiet and out of the way. Never asked for more money, never asked for more work. Just did the job and went away.

"I like yo' work," Sump told him. "I don't want nobody else involved. That way, I won't have no new problem to fret over. You kept yo'self quiet all these years. I'm the kind of man appreciates that."

Slats nodded.

"It's got to look like a accident," Sump went on. "Somethin' we can explain away easy enough. Like before."

Like before, Slats thought. Fire.

"You take care of it," Sump said. "We shut the punk up and send a good strong message at the same time. Put this Brim business back in the past, where it belongs."

Slats didn't hear him. He was still nodding. His eyes had grown wide and hungry. Fire.

35

Cecil was watching a talk show, something about women who imagined killing their partners during sex, when the phone rang.

"Yeah?"

"Hello, Mr. Blanks."

"Why, hello. Looks like we all set."

"I must say I underestimated you."

"Now see, I told you I'd take care of it."

"You did a good job. We have Mr. Moon in the fold."

"You bet we do. I thought he was go'n beat the shit out of me, but I made him see the light."

"Very good."

"So he talked to you? Asked if you'd get in on the scam?"

"He talked to me, yes."

"What a hoot. You were mullin' it over, right? Actin' all worried and shit. The whole time, you thinkin' 'We got the motherfucker.'"

"Something like that."

"So now we take the money, right? Make it look like Jackson?"

"We have to wait for the transfer, then we'll move."

"Soon, right?"

"Soon, Mr. Blanks. Stay patient. We're almost home."

"What next?"

"I'll need an account number to transfer your cut into."

"Yeah, right. You hold on." Cecil put the phone down and dug into Starry's pocketbook. She was in the shower, the water still running. He pulled out her checkbook, got back on the phone, and read the number. "You sho' you can't drop me the cash?"

"I'm sure. I can only transfer funds."

Cecil laughed, thinking about the switch. "You know, Jackson really has a thing for you. You hooked him good. He swallowed the fucking bait, the hook, the sinker, the goddamn bobber, too."

"I suppose that's true."

"How's it feel? Fucking over a guy like that?"

"The Moon family has been dancing with the devil for a long time. They protected the man who destroyed my father. They defended Grant, got rich off of him. You think I give a damn about any of them?"

"You go'n enjoy fuckin' 'em, that would be my guess."

"I'll do what I have to do."

"Well, listen here, I just want you to know, seein' as how you go'n lose yo' honey and all, I would be happy to offer my services, if you get my meanin'. You got needs to fulfill, I got just the tonic."

"As tempting as that sounds, I think I'll be all right."

"Your loss."

"I'll just have to live with it," Bridgett Baines said, and then she hung up.

36

Two FBI agents had brought the prisoner to Waynesburgh and then left to stay at the only hotel in town. Two other agents were out in a car, keeping an eye on the jail. Thomas Sands, the regular night-duty officer, had signed the papers and locked Grant in one of the two holding cells they had. It was part of the plan: to transfer Grant to a small, no-name town for a few days. It would get the press off the track and, hopefully, keep Grant out of the limelight for a while. Then, they would transfer him to a local facility in the town where the trial would take place. The final trial location hadn't been decided yet, at least as far as Sands knew.

Grant struck up a conversation with Lamar Hatley, the other officer on duty. The prisoner knew a surprising amount about Waynesburgh, a small Georgia town that most folks had never even heard of. Grant knew the mayor and a couple of the town commissioners. Hatley didn't care much for Mayor Rodum, and he laughed when Grant told the story about Rodum at a fancy black-tie fundraiser in Atlanta with his fly down.

Thomas Sands sat at the front desk, occasionally looking over at Hatley and Grant. Sands was quiet, but didn't mind that the two were talking. It was good to have some company. They had no other prisoners in custody, and Hatley had been called in so there would be a second officer watching Grant. Any other night and Sands would be at the desk alone, waiting for a call about an intruder that would end up being the neighbor's cat or a call from Mrs. Bailey, inquiring about her drunk husband's whereabouts. That's if he was lucky. Normally, the biggest challenge was staying awake through the night. Sands got up to make a new pot of coffee. He checked his watch: 2 A.M.

The back room was dimly lit but a bit more homey than the outer office. There was a sink and a small refrigerator. The floor was carpeted, and a sofa and a cushioned chair hunched in the corner. The only official-looking item was the tall filing cabinet against the wall. Sands dumped the old coffee in the sink, rinsed the pot and ran fresh water into it, loaded a filter and new coffee, then he poured the water into the coffee maker and turned it on to brew. He listened to the voices from the outer room. Grant was talking big, bragging about the people he knew, saying how all men liked dirty pictures, so what was the big deal about him giving the people what they wanted.

Sands thought about that. To him, it wasn't as bad as killing someone or robbing them. Grant said he was just a businessman. That was one way of looking at it. In fact, he had been arrested not for the materials he was selling, but because he transported the materials across a state line. They had got him on a technicality, that's how Grant saw it. They were out to get him. He brought up Stevens, the black man that had shot a white over in Cawlings. They had let him off on some legal technicality.

"Now how does that figger?" Grant wanted to know. "That nigger is walking the streets, ready to kill more innocent white folk, and they got me in jail for some girlie pictures."

Hatley agreed with Grant. He liked hobnobbing with the criminal who got his name in the papers. Since his divorce, Hatley had been getting pretty wild. Sands had even thought about saying something to Hatley about it. Drinking on the job, carousing about. One time,

Sands was with him when they pulled over this young girl who couldn't have been older than seventeen, eighteen. She had been drinking, the car wasn't registered, and she was scared about her parents finding out about it. Hatley told Sands to go back on patrol. Hatley said he would take care of the situation. A little while later, Sands cruised back by, just to check on things, and the car was still there, pulled over to the side of the road. All he saw was Hatley's head, lolled back on the passenger side seat. Sands figured the girl's head was down there somewhere.

But Sands was not the one to straighten out Hatley. Someone senior should take care of it. By all talk, Hatley would be the next sheriff. Folks liked him, liked his style, the way he talked. They liked a man who would bust heads if he had to. They liked a man who took charge. And that was okay with Sands. He didn't mind laying low, staying out of the limelight. He would work the all-night shift, do the grunt work. Sure as hell, he did not want to be sheriff. He couldn't take all the politicking. Sands would just as soon lay low, pick up his paycheck on Friday, and go fishing. Let Hatley have all the headaches.

The coffee brewed. Sands poured himself a cup and called out to Hatley, "More coffee?"

"Yeah," Hatley called back, "Bring a couple cups. How you like yours, Mike?"

The pornographer was "Mike" now.

"Two cups," Hatley ordered. "One black, one with cream and sugar."

Sands grunted. So the pornographer liked cream and sugar, and it was Sands's job to make it up. That was the worst part of laying low: people taking advantage, getting you to do a bunch of crap that didn't have anything to do with law enforcement. Last month he had to go out to the middle school to get the faucet working. Call a plumber, Sands had thought, but he went out and did it. Used a pair of pliers to turn the knob. That was all it took.

Sands came out of the room with the two cups. He handed both cups to Hatley. Let him serve his new buddy. When Sands got back to the desk and put his own cup on it, the buzzer sounded. They kept the door locked at night, but there was a buzzer for civilians. Sands wondered who it could be at two o'clock in the morning.

He looked out on the stoop through the door pane. There were three girls out there. Good-looking women. Two of them had on short dresses. Real short. The one in the pantsuit was a little older, a redhead, but still a looker. Sands opened the door.

"Can I help you ladies?"

Sands swore the blonde giggled. The redhead said, "I sure hope so, officer. We're here to see Mr. Grant."

That set off alarms in Sands's head. Nobody was even supposed to know Grant was in Waynesburgh.

"What you want with him?" he asked the girls.

"I'm his wife," the redhead told him. "I just want to see him for a few minutes."

Sands looked over at the other two women. The blonde had a zipper on the front of her dress. It ran from her neckline clear down to her waist, right between her breasts. Sands loved those kind of zippers.

"Who are they?" Sands asked, nodding at the other two women.

"They're just here to..."

"Who is it, Tommy?" It was Hatley. Walking up to the door. Taking over.

"Some girls," Sands said, as Hatley barged in and threw open the door.

Hatley howled. "These ain't girls!" he bellowed. "These here are women. Cain't you see good, boy?"

Hatley, big-timing it as usual, invited the girls right in.

"Hey, Lamar," Sands said, trying to pull Hatley aside. He didn't want to show Hatley up. That would just make things worse. "These girls, they're here for Grant. How would they even know...?"

"Hell, Tommy. They're women, for Christ's sake. What you think, they go'n overpower us or somethin'? Shit, man, we cain't look out over a coupla women, we got no business in law enforcement."

"We're not here to cause any trouble," the redhead said. "I just want to see my husband, that's all. They haven't let me see him in over..."

"Well, ain't that a shame now," Hatley said. "Man ought be able to see his wife, 'specially if she's a pretty little thing like you."

Hatley showed the ladies into the office. "Hey, Mikey. You got yo'-self some visitors!"

Now the pornographer was "Mikey." Sands kept a close eye on the women. Something was up. But what could he do about Hatley? There was no way to deter him, that was clear enough. No sense in burning bridges. Sands put a hand to his pistol.

"Marie!" Grant called out and his wife ran to him. They started holding each other through the bars.

"How'd you girls know Mr. Grant was here?" Sands asked, as casually as he could. Hatley shot him a look. Hatley was hungry for a party. Clearly, the two girls were dressed for one.

"I got a call," Marie Grant said, still holding Michael and looking into his eyes like she was too in love to look away. "I don't know who. Somebody sympathetic to my husband, I guess. He told me my husband would be in Waynesburgh. That's all he said."

Sands shook his head at the idea of a sympathetic official. Bought off, more like it.

"Well, sometimes you just got to have some compassion," Hatley spouted. "That's how I play it. Sometimes you got to bend the rules a little, comes to a man and his wife. Ain't that right, Tommy?"

Sands shrugged. "I hope those FBI boys don't come in. They musta seen these girls...."

"Oh, we took care of them FBI boys," the blonde put in, smiling coyly. "They were out in the car, right? You don't have to worry about them. Not for a little while anyway."

Hatley whooped. "You hear that now? They already took care of them FBI boys. See how it works, son?" Big-timing it, calling Sands "son."

"I don't know, Lamar. This don't seem..."

"C'mon now, lighten up. Look at these two lovebirds. You go'n break these two up?"

Sands just shook his head. He couldn't win this one, he knew that. "A few minutes then," he said. "Then you girls will have to be on yo' way."

Hatley clapped his hands. The party was under way. "Could I get you girls a drink?" he asked.

The blonde smiled broadly and looked at the brunette. She shrugged and nodded.

"I ain't got much," Hatley said, heading to the back room. "I keep a little in the cabinet for special occasions, you get my drift."

Sands heard Hatley opening the file cabinet in back. He reappeared in the outer office holding a bottle of Johnny Walker and two shot glasses. "We'll have to share the glasses," Hatley said, clinking the two shot glasses together in his hands.

"Shit, Lamar," Sands said helplessly.

"My friend here, he don't like to drink on duty," Hatley explained. "Normally, I'm the same way, but I can't stand to see pretty women drinkin' alone." He handed a shot glass to each of the girls and poured them a drink. The blonde took a small sip and shuddered as if the drink was too much for her to handle. The brunette tossed the drink down her throat in one gulp and handed the glass back to Hatley.

"Now there's a girl after my own heart," he told her. He poured himself a shot and tossed it down. The blonde took another sip and wiggled. She walked over to Sands, but he stepped back, keeping his eyes sharp, a hand on his pistol.

"Don't you want to have some fun?" the blonde asked Sands.

"No, ma'am," Sands replied. "I am on duty now, and this is highly irregular. We have ourselves a federal prisoner in custody and..."

"We're just here for a little visit," the girl said. "We won't hurt you."

Hatley laughed. "She ain't go'n hurt you." He was already on his second shot. The brunette was all over him.

"Hey, Lamar." It was Grant now, from inside the cage. He was on a first-name basis with Hatley. "How about a little conjugal visit? I need something to hold me over all those lonely nights behind bars."

"Conju-what?" Hatley called back.

"Conjugal," said Sands. "He means sex. He wants to have sex with his wife."

Hatley hooted. All part of the fun. "Well, shit, they is married, ain't they?"

"C'mon now, you know we can't be letting this prisoner out for no..."

The redhead, Grant's wife, spun around, her back to the bars. "I'll go in," she said. "I just want to be with my husband for a few minutes. It could be years before we have another chance."

"Now I cain't see one thing wrong with that," Hatley said. A full shot was in his hand. "Hell, it ain't like they don't have sex in prison. Least ways we'll have it the proper way, man and woman." He laughed hard at his own joke. The blonde, still standing close to Sands, giggled. "You know what I mean," Hatley said with a wink.

"I can't allow this," Sands said.

Hatley spun around. Sands had gone too far. He had threatened Hatley's authority.

"It ain't for you to allow," Hatley said, all puffed up. "I am the senior officer here, in case you have forgot."

"I ain't forgot," Sands said. "It's just this whole thing, it's out of control."

"Out of control?" Hatley boomed. "She's go'n be in the goddamn cage. How much control you want?"

Sands hated the position he was in. Either way, he was screwed. He could take a chance getting caught with the girls, or he could make an enemy out of Hatley.

"I'll have to search her first," Sands said, looking directly at Grant. Grant looked at his wife. "That all right with you, darlin'?"

She looked over at Sands with some skepticism. "If it will get me in there with my husband," she said, "I'll do whatever it takes."

So Sands went over to the redhead. He felt like a pervert, especially with Grant watching. He patted down the legs of her pantsuit, up under her arms, her waist. Nothing. He unlocked the door and put the redhead in the cell with Grant, then he locked it back up.

"Now see?" Hatley sang out. "We all set now."

Grant and his wife were already kissing deeply and touching each other all over. Sands looked away for a few seconds, then peered back, keeping his eye on the situation.

Hatley acted coy. "Now I understand why Mrs. Grant is here," he said, "but what I cain't quite figger out is why you two pretty girls have paid us a visit tonight."

The blonde giggled, and the brunette snuggled up next to Hatley. "Marie's here to take care of Mikey," the brunette said. "And we're here to take care of you...."

"Is that right?" Hatley said.

"That's right," said the blonde. "One of us for each of you, but if your friend isn't interested...." She looked over at Sands with a pout. "I guess you got us both to yo'self."

"And it ain't even my birthday," Hatley said. "Well, I tell you what, ladies. We got ourselves a private room right back here. Got a sofa and some..."

"Lamar," Sands said. "I need to talk to you."

Hatley grunted, then excused himself from the girls.

Sands kept an eye on the women as he talked to Hatley. "You know what you gettin' yo'self into? You know what Grant is. These girls, they's pro'bly whores or somethin'."

Hatley laughed heartily. "Nothin' gets by you, does it? 'Course they whores. Shit, you think I don't know that?"

"They might be setting us up, Lamar."

"Look at them two girls," Hatley said. Sands didn't have to look. He was already staring at the women. He wouldn't take his eyes off of them, except to check on Grant. The blonde waved at him. "What you think they go'n do? Two little women."

Tom studied the women some more, then looked at Grant and his

wife in the cell. Grant had his wife's shirt unbuttoned and was kissing her breast. Sands felt a red flush across his face, and he turned
away. "This is crazy, Lamar."

"I tell you what it is. When I was just a boy in high school, I saw
me a falling star." Hatley's lips turned into a huge, silly smile. "My
wish has finally come true. It took all these years, but it has finally
come true."

"Why would he give us these girls? You tell me that."

"Well goddamn, you got to have everything spelled out for you?
The wife, she wants a night with her husband. She has some desires
what need fulfilling. She figgered these girls, well, they is our reward,
so to speak."

"A bribe, you mean."

"Shit, it ain't like we takin' money."

"I don't know. I don't like it one bit."

"Goddamn it. Don't ruin this for me. Hell, you got yo'self a woman
to come home to ever'night. You get it any time you want. Me, I'm
hurting, man. You know that. I need me some tang somethin' awful.
Shit, a man'll go crazy."

Sands sure as hell didn't get it whenever he wanted, but he wasn't
going to get into that right now.

"You got to leave yo' gun with me," Sands said. "And keep them in
back. If the buzzer goes off, you make sho' you respectable. We'll be
in so much trouble...."

Lamar already had his holster off. He didn't want Tom backpedal-
ing now. He put the holster and gun on the desk. "I owe you, my
friend." He looked over at the girls again, held up his finger to let
them know he was almost ready. "That blonde, she got a hankerin' for
you. You think about that. When I'm done, I'll keep watch. You have
yo' turn." Hatley held up his hands. "If you want. No pressure. But
you don't get many chances in this life. Not like this." He smiled at
Sands as he walked back to the ladies. He took one under each arm
and led them out back.

"You search them," Sands called back to him. "You search them first, Lamar. You hear?"

"I hear you," Hatley called back.

Sands sat down at the desk. What a mess. The wife was naked now from the waist up. Grant was kissing her and had one hand clamped to her breast. Sands looked away.

Better than a fucking dream, Hatley was thinking. This was flesh and blood. The girls were as pretty as models. Tight bodies, big round breasts, perfect figures. The three of them were standing on the carpet, in the dim light, close to the couch. The brunette was all over him, a leg rubbing his crotch. Hatley could barely catch his breath.

"Now, you heard the man," Hatley said. "I got to search the both of you." The blonde giggled.

Hatley started with the brunette. She nibbled his ear lobe as he ran his hands along each side of her sheer dress, down the stockings. He got to her feet and started up the inside of her calves.

"I can make it easy on you," the blonde said, and she tugged at the zipper running down the front of her dress. Her full breasts pulled the fabric open as she pulled the zipper down. The zipper stopped just above her waist. Hatley, still kneeling with his hands on the inside of the brunette's calf, watched the dress fall open. He saw the roundness of her breasts and her flat tummy below them. The dress opened up enough for him to see a hint of the girl's nipples. Hatley swallowed hard.

He stood up and walked over to the blonde. She was licking her lips. Hatley placed his hands inside the dress, touching the soft skin of her waist. She wore no panties. He reached down, pulled her to him as he passed his hands over her ass, and up the sides of her body. As he reached under the dress, pulling his hands upward, the dress came open. He brought his hands up to her breasts and felt them. They filled each hand, the nipples hard.

"Nothing here of any danger," he said, making the blonde giggle again. Hatley brought his hands up to the girl's neck, then down along her shoulders, moving the dress off her arms. The dress slipped off of her and fell to the floor. The girl stood naked. Standing there for Hatley to do with as he pleased. A fucking dream, Hatley thought, only flesh. Flesh, true to the touch.

Now he felt the brunette rubbing his crotch. Hatley moaned. The brunette was working his zipper. He heard it unzip. The blonde was rubbing her breasts against him, kissing his neck, while the brunette loosened his pants, dropped them down to his knees. She pulled him out of his boxers and held his hardness in her soft hand, wrapping the fingers around him. He held his breath in anticipation. The brunette's tongue flickered on him, then he was in her mouth. The blonde moved around behind him, her breasts against his back. He felt the brunette's wet mouth on him, taking him in....

Then he felt something cold and hard and metallic. Up under his scrotum. The gun had been hidden in the brunette's garter belt. Later, Hatley would come to realize how the blonde had expertly co-opted his search of the brunette. Now the brunette had a gun crammed up under his dick.

The blonde whispered in his ear. "Move a muscle, say a word, first she bites, then she fires."

"Oh, fuck," Hatley moaned, but the brunette shoved the gun up against him harder and he shut up.

"Not a word, asshole. Not one fucking word, or she'll blow your balls up into your throat."

Hatley tried to nod, but he was scared. He knew the girls meant business.

The brunette pulled away from him, the gun held in both her hands. The gun was tiny. A derringer. She pointed it right at Hatley's head. Her eyes were cold and purposeful. Hatley knew she would do it. She would blow his brains out if she had to.

The blonde took Hatley's handcuffs, then put his hands behind him. "I want you to say 'You are bad girls,'" the blonde told him. "Say it loud enough for your friend to hear, say it like you're having a grand o'l time. Say it right or you're fucking dead."

"You are bad girls," Hatley said loudly.

"Now say, 'You know what we do with bad girls.'"

Hatley felt the sweat on his face. The brunette took a step toward him with the gun. "You know what we do with bad girls...." Hatley called out.

Just then, the blonde snapped the handcuffs on Hatley. "Now lay down on your stomach," she ordered, her voice low but no-nonsense. Hatley did it. He didn't see the blonde as she pulled on her dress, took the gun from the brunette, and headed out of the room.

Goddamn Lamar, Sands thought. Playing with the hand-cuffs again. He claimed girls loved it, being locked up like that. They all loved it, according to Hatley. Apparently, he had never asked Sands's wife about it. Sands had mentioned it to her once, all in good fun, and she said she'd twist his neck off if he ever tried putting handcuffs on her. Didn't sound much like something she looked forward to.

Sands looked over at Grant. He was sitting on the bench, his pants around his ankles and his wife straddling him. The Waynesburgh jail had become a peep show.

He turned back and saw the blonde. Her dress was unzipped to the waist. "I don't think they need me in there," she said sadly. "Three's a crowd, I guess."

Sands studied the girl's naked skin between the two rows of zipper teeth. He moved his eyes up from the waist to the round firmness of her breasts. His eyes were scanning downward again when he saw the gun. A tiny thing.

The shot sounded like a pop gun. The bullet thudded into Sands's chest and rammed him backward in the chair. Then came another pop. The next bullet cracked the officer's skull open. Blood splattered onto the floor, and Sands followed as the chair toppled backward, dumping him onto the hard white tiles. One last thought flashed in his mind.

Goddamn that Hatley.

37

Jackson sat on his father's porch. He had taken a beer and a cigar up to the old man and sat down to watch him drink and smoke. He didn't like to leave his father alone when he was smoking in bed, but his father barked at Jackie for treating him like an adolescent. Jackie gave up and retreated to the porch, listening for the occasional hacking cough that descended from the upstairs bedroom.

Jackson watched rain seep through the cover of pecan trees. Jays squabbled in the upper limbs, and two chipmunks chased each other across the back lawn. Jackson rubbed his mouth and considered Cecil Blanks. He hoped he had the guy figured right. Cecil had been predictable, but Jackson knew he might turn squirrelly before this thing was over and done with. He remembered his talk with Clarence when Jackie had first learned that Cecil worked for Jake Marston.

Jackie was out in the yard with Clarence. His trainer held the big bag while Jackson pummeled it. The bout at Canterback gym was on, but they had yet to announce Moondog's opponent.

The two men settled down on a bench, the workout over. The day was cloudy but warm. Sweat streaked across Jackie's hardened body. He gulped from a water jug. "You lookin' good," Clarence told him.

Jackson looked over at his trainer, then surveyed the yard. "You talk to Cecil a lot, don't you, Clarence?"

Clarence's laugh was not audible. It came as slight shake in his stomach. "You know Cecil. That boy love to talk."

Jackie nodded slowly, then turned a dead-on stare to Clarence. "So what's he up to?"

Clarence closed his left eye and leveled the right one at Jackson. "What you mean?"

"You know what I mean. I see him sneaking around, dealing with these cons. When we get back to the cell, all he wants to talk about is Michael Grant. He's after something. He's trying to draw some information out of me, but I've got nothing to tell him even if I wanted to. So what does he want?"

Clarence looked at the ground. "I don't get messed up in those affairs," he said. "It ain't healthy."

"Hell, you're in here for the duration. What do you care?"

"Just cause I'm inside, it don't mean I'm safe."

Jackson nodded. "Maybe you'd be safer outside, then."

That got Clarence's attention. His eyes came back up to meet Jackie's. "What you got in mind?"

"It would be pretty tough – damn near impossible – to make a break out of this prison. But I've got to think you might have a chance of breaking out of the Canterback gym."

The laugh came again, a rumble deep in the tummy. "Yeah, right. I'm sure a big black man sneaking away from the ring and slipping out the door wouldn't cause a single head to turn. You ain't got that much magnetism, Moondog."

"What if you weren't in my corner? What if you were in your own?"

"What you talkin' about?"

"Think of it. Moondog going against his trainer, Big Hands Hoffman. Fight of the century."

"Well, that's gonna make it a whole lot easier for me to slip out, being one of the damn fighters. What the hell you thinking about, boy?"

"I got a plan, Clarence. I can't guarantee anything, but what have you got to lose? It just might work."

"Well then, let's hear it," Clarence demanded.

"You first," said Jackie.

Clarence rubbed his chin with one mammoth hand, then sighed.

"You ever hear of Jake Marston?"

"Yeah, I've heard of him. Runs numbers around here, stuff like that."

"He's a lot bigger than that. He runs most everything around here. Numbers, drugs, some unions. Lots of influence, that man. Lots of powerful folks under his thumb."

"Yeah, so?"

"So Cecil is in with the man. He acts like he's Marston's first lieutenant. I'm sure he's full of it, but he knows a lot, so I think he's in pretty tight with the whole operation."

Jackson thought about it. Things were already falling into place in his mind. "And Marston wants to cut in on Grant's operation."

"Especially with Grant in so much law trouble. Marston figures the time is right to move in."

"And what does Cecil have to do with it?"

"Marston has a lot of pull at the prison. Not sure how, but he's got it. He's the one that got Cecil as your cellmate."

Jackie snickered. "I'll have to thank him someday."

"Cecil got put there to keep an eye on you, find out all he could about Grant. Cecil reports to some flunky inside, Malone Dragg, lets him know what he finds out about you and Grant."

"Well, he hasn't found out much. There's not much to find out from me."

"Cecil probably makes shit up as he goes along, just to keep it interesting, make it look like he's got a line on something."

Jackson nodded.

"Sounds like Cecil's getting more interested in some old girlfriend of yours. She works the computers for some accountant in your old stomping grounds."

Jackson perked up. "Bridgett Baines? What's she got to do with this?"

Clarence gazed over at Jackson for a moment, then looked away. "This accountant – I forget his name if Cecil ever mentioned it – he handles Grant's front accounts. There's some big company Grant runs his money through and this accountant does the dirty work."

Jackson sat up straight, tumbling the information through his mind. "The guy's name is Thomas Dade. Bridgett works on the computers. She's not into the dirty stuff. I'm sure of it."

Big Hands shrugged. "I don't know. Cecil never said nothing about the girl being dirty."

"So Cecil knows about Grant's accountant," Jackie said.

"It gets better," Clarence said.

Jackson was all ears.

"Turns out Marston has his hooks in this accountant. Old gambling debts or something. Marston's about ready to call in his marker."

Jackson rubbed his temples. He couldn't believe Bridgett was caught in the middle of all this. "So the accountant handles Grant's money, but he owes favors to Marston."

"That's right. And Cecil got word that Grant is about to move a big load into the front account. I guess Grant's legal bills are piling up and he needs the cash."

"So Grant pulls the money into the account, and Marston nabs it through the accountant?"

"I think that's the score. Of course, Cecil has other plans."

"What plans?"

"Cecil says Marston is going to get him out of here about the same time you get out. I guess you told him you plan to go back home. Cecil thinks you're hot for some revenge on Grant. He didn't really get into that end of it, just that you were heading back with a chip on your shoulder. Cecil plans to meet up with you back there. He can keep one eye on you, one eye on the accountant. I guess Marston liked the idea. The guy doesn't seem to be the best judge of character."

"In his business, you can't be too picky when it comes to character."

"Guess not," said Clarence. "Anyway, Cecil is supposed to take instructions to this accountant, tell him how to divert the funds to Marston when the big transfer comes through."

"Don't tell me Cecil is going after the money. He's not brave enough to go up against Marston."

"I don't think he's that brave, but he is that stupid."

"Cecil's going for the cash?"

"Once he found out how this girl of yours runs the computers for the accountant, he figured he could team up with her and divert the funds his way."

"Jesus Christ," Jackson said. "He told you all that?"

Clarence shrugged. "That boy, he sure do love to talk."

38

Leola had come to get Jackson at the big house. Fetched him was how it seemed to Jackie. She took him back to the cabin. Lucy, the girl Leola was teaching, the one who had helped bandage Jackie, was there, along with another woman. Lucy had a round, pretty face and a gentle smile. She wore a white cotton dress that hung to her knees. The dress glowed in the muted light of the cabin, and the girl seemed to float like a spirit. The cabin smelled of vanilla extract and cinnamon sticks.

"How're those ribs?" asked the young woman, the one named Lucy.

"I'm all right," Jackie said softly. "I never got a chance to thank you. You do good work."

"It was Leola mostly. I just help out."

"Don't you be modest, child," said Leola. "You did the work. I jes' got in the way."

The third woman stood back against the wall. She was early fifties, maybe. It was hard to tell with dark glasses covering her eyes and the brown turban wrapped around her head. The face was weathered and creased, but the body sturdy. She wore a mottled afghan about her shoulders.

"Was you two properly introduced?" the woman asked, gesturing to Jackie and Lucy.

"No, ma'am," Jackie said. "Bridgett told me her name is Lucy."

"That's what we tell folks," the woman said, then she sauntered slowly across the room.

"What you *tell* folks?" Jackson asked.

The older woman sat down in the rocking chair. Leola brought a wooden chair out of the bedroom. "Her real name is Alfreda," Leola said as she sat down. Slowly, she rose her head up, resting her eyes firmly on Jackson. Jackie turned to Leola, and a light came on in his eye.

"Alfreda?" he said. "Alfreda Sachs?"

The girl was smiling when Jackson looked over at her. "And this is my mama," she said, holding out a hand to the rocking chair.

Jackson looked over. "Angel," he said, his knees suddenly feeling weak.

Now the older woman smiled. "Tha's right. You gettin' it now, ain't ya, son?"

"He's a smart boy," Leola said. "Just takes him a little while."

Jackson didn't even hear her. He was looking at the woman, remembering the story Leola had told about the prostitute that Senator Sachs had fallen in love with, about the baby Leola had delivered to them, about the two of them taking the baby home.

"Don't you look so goddamned disbelievin'," Angel snapped. "I was a looker once, you know. Jes' like my daughter here."

"It's not that," Jackie said. "It's just that I ... Well, I just ..." Jackson's mouth was open but nothing came out. He walked over to the small couch and collapsed into it. He imagined pieces of a puzzle jumbled on the floor in front of him. "You weren't in the bar that night," he said, sorting it through. "You must have been with the senator. You know he wasn't killed at Bosco's. He was carried there." He looked up to see if she held a piece of the puzzle in her hand.

Angel leaned back in the rocker, a smile on her face. She began to rock slowly as her story came out....

It had been almost a year since Angel and Alfred had brought the baby home. They had just sat down to eat at the table in the kitchen, where they always took supper. Angel had made up pork chops, rice, green beans, and cornbread. Pecan pie for dessert. The baby was in her high chair, sucking on green beans and laughing. She was the best-tempered baby Angel had ever seen. Alfred was in a good mood, playful. He still had on his white business shirt but he had slipped off his tie and changed into some tan slacks and loafers. Angel felt strangely uneasy and off kilter somehow. It was a feeling that something wasn't right, that something was about to happen.

A knock rapped on the screen door to the porch. Alfred got up to answer it while Angel moved to the kitchen window and looked out into the darkness. Michael Grant stood on the stoop. Angel could see the devil eyes flashing in the night. Grant wore a dark suit coat, no tie, a white shirt and gray slacks, and shiny black boots. Alfred let the man in.

"Well, sir, how are you doin' this fine night?"

Grant nodded. "Just fine, Senator. Mighty nice night."

"It sho' is. Angel and me were just sittin' down to supper. Can I get you a plate?"

"Nah, nah," Grant said, looking around the place with his darting eyes. "I ain't got a whole lotta time. I just need to talk at you for a little while."

"Is that so?" Alfred said. "Well, I hope it ain't about my land. You got my answer on that. I ain't interested in sellin'."

That man had been after my husband's land for months and months. He had the crazy notion to build hisself up a Civil War park. We figgered him for daffy, but damned if that boy didn't end up buildin' his park. Can you beat that? A Civil War park with rides and shows and riverboats. Turn't out, that park rose up just like the man had it figgered. But on that night, my husband was the only thing standin' in Mr. Grant's way. The one and

only thing. And Mr. Grant was not a man to let things stand between him
and what his black heart desired.

"Can we sit down, Alfred? I just got a coupla things to say."

They headed through the house to the back parlor. There were four red-velvet antique chairs in the center of the room, placed in a circle with a small marble-top table and a stand-up ash tray beside each one. Grant sat in the chair with its back to the large picture window that opened to the gardens behind the house. More chairs lined the wall on the far side of the room. It was the room where Senator Sachs had hosted many meetings over the years. Many decisions had been made over whiskey and cigars. On this night, Alfred offered neither. He sat down across from Grant, facing the picture window.

"Now, Alfred, you know this theme park is a good thing for this town."

Sachs just smiled. "I don't believe I do know that. I am in no way convinced. To my mind, it could well be the destruction of this town, and I don't intend to be a party to that."

"You go'n stand in the way of ever other man who matters in this town? The people want this thing."

"You mean the people you got in yo' pocket. They say they want it 'cause they don't dare say anything less. When I talk to 'em, they got a different notion."

"That so?" Grant sneered.

"I believe it is. They think this Civil War park is malarkey. 'Course, they been takin' money from you for so long that they can hardly tell wrong from right anymore, but this theme park – they don't much like the idea. I can tell you that, all right."

"Right from wrong? You the one go'n tell them that? Old man livin' with a colored woman, a whore, just as if they was man and wife. You tellin' me that's right?"

Alfred seemed to think about it. "Maybe it ain't. I cain't rightly say."

"Well, plenty of folk got their own ideas on that."

"I'm sure they do. I hold no illusions about that."

Grant looked hard at the senator, then sighed. He was getting nowhere. "You ought know better than to fight against me," he muttered.

Sachs leaned toward Grant. "I don't owe you one goddamn thing," he said. "I never once took yo' dirty money. Never once asked you for a thing. I never even took a contribution, and you know it. You got yo' hooks into lots of folk, Mr. Grant, but I ain't one of 'em."

"That might be so," Grant conceded. "But that don't mean I got no leverage."

"What you talkin' 'bout now?"

"I'm talkin' about this nigger you're holin' up with. What if you have to choose between yo' job and yo' family and the land I need?"

"I guess folks are gonna make they choice about that," Sachs said, "come election time. I know they don't much care for what I done, but I'm bettin' they go'n look at the whole picture. They know I try to be a honest man. They know I work hard for the good folk. I think they go'n let me stay on."

"I think you overestimate the people's charity. I'm sure there's parts of this country where a white senator can claim him a colored whore for his wife, but it sure as hell ain't here. Not in South Georgia. Ain't no question of right and wrong around here. It is wrong. Capital 'W'."

"Like I said, I'll leave that up to the people and to the Good Lord. The folks will vote, and the Lord will judge." Sachs smiled wryly. "You know, Michael, some folks claim you are the Devil hisself. Now, I don't cotton much to that notion, but contrary to your own opinion, you are not the Lord either. You ain't the one to be judgin' me."

"You may be wrong about that."

Sachs peered over at the pornographer. Grant was here to make trouble.

"I got a man ready to make a claim," Grant said. "A claim on that baby of yours. A colored man. He's go'n say that he had Miss Angel when she was whorin'. He's go'n say that little girl belongs to him."

Sachs scoffed. "That's nonsense. I was the only…"

"Who's go'n believe that bullshit? You were the only one? She's a goddamn whore. Things may be changing, Senator, but the courts still would rather see a colored baby with colored parents, and that baby don't look like she got a single white drop of blood in her."

"You are one sorry…"

"Them NAACP folk, they don't like seein' white folks takin' they babies. You been readin' the papers, ain't ya? They think the little black babies should learn about they culture. I bet they'll take a inter- est, too. The sparks'll be flyin' 'round here, you can bet yo' dollar on that." Grant laughed. "It surely will make the Atlanta papers. Hell, it'll be a national story. A state senator shacked up with a colored whore, claimin' her black baby belongs to him, fightin' agin' a poor helpless colored man who just wants his baby girl back. They'll eat the shit up. If that's not front page, then I really am the sorry bastard you think I am."

Sachs sat back in the chair, eyeing the man who was threatening to ruin him. Losing an election was one thing; losing his family was something else altogether.

I heard ever' word of it, that evil man threatenin' my husband like that. I had snuck up into the hallway outside the parlor. That man was go'n take everything from Alfred – everything he loved. He was go'n ruin my hus- band and take away my child. And I was not go'n have it. I knew I had to stop him. They won't two ways about it. I got myself a key from the kitchen drawer and opened up the dining cabinet. Alfred, he sto'd his pistol in there, back behind the good silver. He had took me out back on occasion, learn't me how to shoot. At the time, I had no notion why I should learn me such a thing, but as I held that gun in my hand, it came to me that Alfred, he had been preparin' me for the day. Preparin' me for this very moment. I got my mind set on what I had to do. I did not want to break the Lord's com- mandment, but it was God's work that I was fixin' to do. I knew my hus-

band could bury that body where not one soul would ever find it, and that him and the Lord would both forgive me.

Michael Grant pulled a cigarette from his shirt pocket and lit it with a gold lighter. He rose out of the chair and turned to the picture window. "I ain't tryin' to run you out of your own place, Alfred. You know that. Hell, you got it set aside for the museum. That's all fine and dandy. But tell me this – what folk are go'n wanna come to a museum dedicated to a scoundrel?" He looked over his shoulder at Sachs, then turned back to the window. "You can stay here with your colored girl and yo' little black baby, live out yo' final days in peace...."

Sachs said, almost to himself: "You really don't have a soul."

Grant laughed at that. It was a hearty laugh. "I've been blamed of many things," he said. "But having a soul..."

Grant turned from the picture window as he said the words, and when he first saw the black woman standing behind Sachs, the vision of her – appearing as if from nowhere – yanked every thought out of his head. She stood there granite-faced, her eyes set hard on him, a woman of medicine casting her spell. A coldness, like frozen metal, shivered down his spine. Grant started to speak, but then the black woman lifted the pistol up, shoulder-high. Her medicine would fly by gunpowder. The blood drained out of Grant's face. His stunned look made Sachs twist in his chair. Only then did Sachs see her with the gun.

"Angel!" Alfred cried. "What in God's name...?"

But before Sachs could stop her, Angel squeezed the trigger firmly, just as her husband had taught her, and the pistol roared. A single bullet thumped into Grant, just above his right breast, and a blossom of crimson bloomed on the white shirt. The crazy eyes widened in horror and pain. He dropped back a step, then another, until he was pressed against the glass. Then Angel squeezed the trigger again. Another deafening roar. The second bullet struck Grant just above the first one and bolted him through the picture window. The glass exploded as he crashed through it and disappeared into the night.

Sachs was too stunned to say anything. He stood up from the chair and stared at the shattered window. A large piece of glass, dangling from above, broke loose and fell. Slowly, he went to the window and looked down to the earth three feet below. The body of Ghost Grant lay in a bed of tulips, the bright red blossom of blood staining the right breast of his white shirt.

And there was something else. Grant's arms were rising up together. Sachs squinted at the scene, noticing – too late – that Grant held a gun in his right hand. He fired a single shot that pierced the soft flesh on the underside of the senator's chin. Blood spouted from the top of his head and he flopped over onto the floor.

I knew he was dead right off. But somehow he found a way to speak his last words to me. He tol' me to run. Tol' me to take his baby and run far, far away. So that's what I did. I heeded the last words of my dyin' husband. I took our child and I ran. I ran as hard as my legs could carry me. And I did not stop 'til I was clear past Grantville.

39

Noxie felt the questions searing through his mind. How could he have not known? How could he have never guessed it? All these years, going by the name "Noxie," people calling him that, laughing behind his back. Carbon monoxide. It had killed his mother and destroyed part of his brain. His daddy, his own father, had come up with the nickname.

And it was the woman who had called him that, up there in Waynesburgh when they broke his father out. She said it to his face, then told the other girls what it meant. Like it was all a big joke. She said she was his father's wife, but they were never really married. She was a slut, that's how Noxie saw it. He had done all the dirty work, crawling up to the car on his belly, sliding across the wet pavement to get below the driver's side door. Then the sluts came by, wagging their asses and bouncing their tits so the FBI guys would look their way.

Then the car came by. Two A.M., in the middle of nowhere, and a car happened by. Noxie had to roll up under the FBI car and wait until it was clear again. Then he just said fuck it, rose up and shot the driver first, then the passenger. Two head shots. Then the fucking bitch is yelling at him, asking why he didn't shoot when they were walking by – that was the whole plan. Then she's bitching about the goddamn mess. Like you can shoot two guys in a car and not get blood all over the place. What did she care anyway? It was Noxie who had to hide the car, get it off the street.

But what really ripped Noxie was when she told him where to meet his daddy. She gave Noxie the day, the time, the directions. He wanted to see his father get out, help blow away the hillbilly deputies if he had to. But the bitch barked at him, told him to follow orders, asking him if he was dense. Then she starts telling these other girls – sluts just like her – about the nickname. About his mother. About the car in the garage. Carbon monoxide. Noxie. He should have shot the bitch right in the face. That would have shut those girls up, blood all over their pretty little dresses.

Noxie took a right on North River Road. She had given him written directions, like he was too stupid to remember, but now he was glad she did. He was somewhere around Alpharetta, just east of bumblefuck. The road turned to red dirt and banked along the river to Noxie's left. He drove the old Ford pickup just about as fast as it could go. Noxie was sure that the beat-up truck had been another big joke on him, the Ford pickup in the parking lot where he was sent to dump the FBI men. Noxie could hear them laughing about the dense kid putt-putting away in the beat-up old truck.

Where to now? The directions just said North River Road. The road seemed to go on and on, deeper into the woods, and with each twist and turn, the ruts in the road got deeper and the road itself narrower. How was he supposed to meet up with his father when he could be anywhere along this river?

And there he was. Standing right in the middle of the road. Noxie hit the brakes, skidding the truck across the dirt. He gripped the wheel hard and hugged the riverbank as the truck careened off a large boulder. "Fuck!" Noxie screamed as the pickup slid to a stop only feet from his father, who stood ramrod straight in the middle of the road. The man didn't budge an inch as the truck barreled down on him and came to a stop in a billow of red dust.

"Fucking idiot," Michael Grant said.

Noxie stared at the man on the other side of his windshield as the dust settled. It had been four and a half years since he had last seen him in person. The eyes were hard and disapproving, disgusted.

Only then did Noxie fully realize what he had to do. There was only one way left to prove to his father that he had become the very best at what he did.

"Park it over there," his father barked, waving at an open patch of dirt on the far side of the road.

Noxie swung the pickup around and planted it up off the road. His father turned around and walked back to the silver Mercedes hunched around a bend. Noxie got out of the truck, wrapping a black leather strap around his right fist.

His father was in the driver's side of the car as Noxie approached. The window came down. "Get in."

"Where we goin'?" Noxie asked.

"Where you think, you fucking idiot? We're going to Solomon's Rock to deal with those assholes."

"It's already taken care of."

"What are you talkin' 'bout?"

"I told Sump. Ordered him to take care of the Moons."

Grant exploded. "Where you come off orderin' anybody? That was your job. And what was that shit with the judge? Jesus Christ. You don't think they gonna know he didn't write the goddamn suicide note? They got experts can tell it wadn't him. You fucking idiot. Just get in the goddamn car."

"I told Sump to take care of it," Noxie said.

"You think I cain't hear good? That was yo' job, Noxie. You understand me? It ain't yo' place to be orderin' folks around. You do as you're told. You just got soft on me, boy. Felt all queasy about the Moon boy. He was yo' buddy and shit. Didn't matter that he was takin' your old man down. Didn't matter what you were told. You were buds. You had to get someone else to do the dirty work."

"I ain't soft."

"You didn't take care of the boy 'cause he was yo' friend. You let yo' feelings get in the way of the job. Now c'mon, Noxie...."

"Don't call me that," Noxie snapped.

Grant took a long look up at the boy, then he burst into laughter. "You finally figgered that shit out. Holy fuck. Only took you, what, about ten fucking years."

He was still laughing, his hands on the steering wheel, when Noxie reached through the window and slapped the leather strap around his father's wrists.

"What the fuck?" his father grunted, as Noxie tightened the strap in his right hand. Noxie cracked open the door of the Mercedes, reached in and grabbed the strap with his left hand, and then threw the door open wide.

"Get out," Noxie demanded.

"What the hell are you doing?"

Noxie pulled out his razor. "Get out."

Grant snickered and got up out of the car. "What's spinnin' 'round in that head of yours now, Noxie?"

"I told you not to call me that no more!" Noxie roared.

"You go'n stab me with a knife, that the idea here?"

Noxie closed the door of the car as his father stepped out onto the dirt road. "I love you more than anything on this earth, Daddy. You go'n find out now who's soft."

Grant laughed. "Jesus. You are one fucked-up boy, son."

"Just shut up. Shut the fuck up." Noxie was getting mean, putting the voice on. He wanted to see the fear in his father's eyes. Like he saw it in Creeks, like he saw it in Farmer, like he saw it in his own mentor. Even Sump showed the fear. Now his father would know it. He would know the fear that Noxie could drive into people.

Noxie walked him out in front of the car, over by the riverbank.

"Calling me 'Noxie' like that. Your own son."

Grant looked out at the water. "To tell you the truth, we cain't be too sure about that. The father thing I mean. Yo' mama, she got around, if you know what I mean. In plain language, son, she was a fucking whore. Could be yo' daddy is some bum beggin' change in Five Points Park." He laughed. "Truth is, boy, you never favored me much, and I always figgered you was too goddamn stupid to be my son."

"It was you who did that. You took away part of my brain. You don't think I figgered that out?"

Grant looked over at Noxie and laughed again. "Boy, you were plenty stupid 'fore you ever sucked in them fumes. You were always a dense boy, since the day you were born. A natural idiot right out the chute."

Noxie felt tears burning under his eyes. He had to hold them back. No emotion. No remorse. Only the job. It was his last chance to prove himself. The best chance. He had to see the fear in his father's eyes, and even then, even despite his love, even despite his daddy's pleas, he would have to kill him. It would be the final proof.

"You cain't kill me, boy," Grant stated.

"Bullshit I cain't. You know how many men I killed? Blood just as red as yours."

"But they were faceless. You couldn't kill the Moon boy. Couldn't even kill the old man. They had a face."

"I killed Cracks."

Grant nodded. "Yeah, I got to give that one to you. That was good. I thought you had finally made it. Then you fucked up the Moon job."

"I told Sump to take care of it," Noxie insisted.

Grant shrugged. "It was your job, Edward."

Edward. Noxie's first triumph. His daddy called him Edward.

"Now this is my job," Noxie said.

"What job?"

"Proving to you that I ain't soft. Letting you see just how good I am."

Grant shook his head sadly.

"Get on yo' knees," Noxie demanded.

Grant looked up and smiled. "I don't get on my knees, son. Not for you or anybody else."

Noxie stepped closer, waved the razor. "Get on yo' fuckin' knees!" he barked.

Grant simply shook his head.

"Do it now!" Noxie shouted, trying to sound dangerous, but the words cracked out of his throat and he felt a hot tear on his cheek.

"Go ahead, boy. Do it."

"Get on yo' knees, goddamn it." The tears were flowing now.

"Kill me, you fucking idiot. C'mon. Let's see what you got."

"Just get on yo' knees." Noxie was whining now. He heard himself moaning.

"C'mon, goddamn it. Do it!"

Noxie's arm came down. He was sobbing now. This was not how he had imagined it. He had seen his father kneeling before him, begging for his life, spilling his fear out like vomit, clutching Noxie's feet. It was then that Noxie would lift his daddy's head, drink in the fear from the terrified eyes, and stab the man in the center of his heart.

"Do it!" his father roared, right up into Noxie's face, the father's eyes filling Noxie's world.

One more time, enraged, his father screamed "Do it!" Then he was behind Noxie, the leather strap around Noxie's throat. Noxie gasped for air but found none. The razor dropped from his hand as the strap tightened around his neck, choking back every breath. His eyes bulged and the hot tears felt like blood draining out of his head. Noxie clutched at the strap, felt the world spinning away. There was no air to breathe. He recalled clearly, for the first time in his life, lying in his mother's lap as the station wagon rumbled in the garage. In his head, Noxie screamed, but only a sick gurgle emerged from his throat. The world went black and all he heard was the sound of his own death, a rattle somewhere in his chest, his lungs exploding, a last panic that held no hope.

Grant held the boy many moments longer, yanking at the strap, then he let Edward fall down the bank of the river. The body rolled twice, then splashed down into the water, the head sliding to a rest at the river's edge.

Grant stood at the bank, watching his son hit the water, and he shook his head again. Somewhere, in that place between dying and death, words drifted through to Edward Grant, the last words he would hear from the living world, the words he had come to know so well: his father calling him a stupid fuck.

40

Ellis Moon had sent away his secretary, called a cab, and packed a briefcase. He looked once around the office before pulling the door shut. Then he paused a moment. He felt the need to bring something else along. What? He unlocked the office door and walked across the room to his desk. He grabbed the electronic calculator out of his desk drawer and then the small brass clock off the bookshelf. He put the clock and calculator into the briefcase and turned back to the door.

A figure loomed in the doorway, almost filling it. Billy "Monster" Cobb. As usual, his suit coat looked like the arms would rip out the first time he stretched. The tie was askew. He had thick knobs over each of his dark eyes, and black hair slicked back from his face. His nose was swollen and crooked, his lips thick, his jaw square. He stood six-four, two-eighty.

"Going somewhere?" he asked.

"Yeah," Moon said. "I got an appointment over at the courthouse."

Monster Cobb's eyes surveyed the office. "You got no appointments at the court," he said, sure of it.

"Judge Rowell," Moon lied. "He asked me to come see him. Can't keep a judge waiting, you know. Bad business." Moon tried on a smile.

"I'll walk on over with you," Monster stated. "We got some business to discuss."

"Business?"

"I guess you heard the news. About Michael."

Moon pretended to think that over. "Michael? You mean the change of venue? I know they're moving him now."

Monster studied Moon for a moment. Moon looked back at the big man and shrugged.

"Let's go," Cobb said. "Don't want to keep the judge waiting, right?"

"Right," Moon agreed, trying the smile again. Monster held out a hand and Moon walked past him, out of the office. His mind was racing. He could go on to Judge Rowell's chambers, if he had to, and take sanctuary there. Make a deal. He wondered if they would actually make it to the courthouse. He couldn't see Monster escorting him to the judge's office. He had something else in mind.

"This really Hank's bat?" Monster Cobb asked from behind him. He was studying the bat that Moon had racked on the wall.

"Sure is," Moon said, putting his briefcase on the floor and taking the bat down off the wall. "See here?" He showed him the signature. "Signed it in 1957. The last year the Braves won a World Series."

"No shit?" Monster said, studying Hank Aaron's signature and the year "'57" scrawled below it. "I didn't know the Braves won a World Series."

"Well, they were in Milwaukee then. They didn't come here 'til 1966."

"No kiddin'? They were in Milwaukee before that, huh?"

"That's right," Moon said. "Before that, they were the Boston Braves. See over here?" Moon led him over to a pair of pictures on the far wall. "That's the Boston Braves on the left – 'Spahn and Sain and pray for rain.'" Monster looked at him without comprehension, then he glanced at the picture. He had to know Moon was still holding the bat. But the big man didn't seem to be wary of Moon at all. "And the

Milwaukee Braves there on the right: Warren Spahn, Lew Burdette, Eddie Mathews..."

Monster looked over at the picture of the 1954 Milwaukee Braves. Moon tightened his grip on the bat. Monster started to turn away from the picture. "See there," Moon pointed again, keeping Cobb directed at the wall. "Henry Aaron. That was his rookie year."

Monster bent over. "Well, I'll be damned. He sure was a skinny...."

The big man turned just as the bat was sailing at his head. He got an arm up and deflected the blow. The bat shattered the crystal of Monster's wristwatch as he fell back against the wall. One of the pictures fell to the carpeted floor. Ellis swung again, from the left side, but this time Cobb turned and the bat pounded him hard on the back, just below his right shoulder blade. Moon brought the bat back a third time but Monster twisted around, swinging out his arm as he did and catching Ellis on the side of the head with the back of his hand. The lawyer heaved backward and slammed into his secretary's desk. He tried to recover but Monster was on him, slapping the bat out of his hand with an effortless swat, then he grabbed Moon by the collar and rammed him up against the wall.

"You're pretty scrappy for a dead man," Monster said, his face glowering over Moon's, the breath hot. He punched Ellis once in the stomach, driving the air out of him. When Monster let go of the collar, Moon sank to the floor and rolled over. Cobb kicked him in the side.

Monster Cobb tried to stretch his back. The blow had struck him hard. He checked his watch. "Motherfucker broke my watch," he said to himself.

Clutching his stomach, Moon saw the bat. On the floor. Five, six feet away. He groaned and rolled madly across the carpet. He grabbed the bat, scrambled up, and fell back against the curtains on the far wall. He held the bat out in front of him. Monster looked over at him, as if the sight of the lawyer with a bat in his hand was only vaguely interesting.

"You won't get a jump on me this time," Cobb told him. "I never thought you'd be stupid enough to go after me the first time."

Ellis felt the bat shaking in his hand. Monster casually took off his watch and tossed it in the trashcan by the desk. Then he reached in under his suit coat and pulled out a pistol. Game over.

Monster smiled. The big body shook with silent laughter. "You are a stupid fuck, you know that? You was gonna make a deal? Against Ghost Grant? And I thought lawyers was s'posed to be smart."

Ellis didn't even hear the words. He was focused squarely on a spot at the bridge of the big man's nose. He brought the bat up over his head, like a samurai sword, stretched it back behind his neck. He saw only the one spot.

"What the fuck are you...?"

In one quick motion, Ellis sent the bat hurtling end-over-end through the air, across the room, smack dab at the target. The throw was perfect. It cracked into the big man's face just as the thick barrel of the bat came around the third time. The nose exploded, splattering blood across the stunned face, into the air, even onto the wall behind Monster. The head jerked back in a violent twitch. The words coming out of Monster Cobb's mouth ended in a strange yelp as his body arched backward. Monster slammed against the wall, teetered there for a moment, then came forward, eyes rolled back and body limp. He plopped onto the carpet in front of Moon, the gun still clutched in his right hand.

For a moment, Ellis was paralyzed, but when a distant moan rose up from the body on the floor, he scooped up his briefcase and rushed from the outer office. He closed the door and looked around. Some other workers in the building had stepped out into the hall. He started to offer an explanation for the noise they had obviously heard, but nothing came out of him. He headed down the steps in a gallop.

41

Thomas Dade walked into the offices of Dade and Sanders, the accounting firm for Michael Grant. Sanders, his former partner, had died fourteen years ago, strangled – it was said – by Grant's own hand. Grant had insisted that the Sanders name stay with the firm: A reminder that nobody messed with Grant's money. Dade remembered the story – and the message – as he mounted a single flight of steps. He tried to push the fear out of his mind, but it was getting harder to do as the time came nearer. The time when he would mess with Ghost Grant's money.

Dade checked Bridgett's office to make sure she was gone, then he opened the door to his own office and entered. He put his briefcase on the oak desk and sat on the leather chair. He looked at the phone for a few moments, then the accountant drew a deep breath. He picked up the receiver and dialed the number Jake Marston had given him.

"Hello, Mr. Marston," Dade said when Marston answered.

"Mr. Dade. Good to hear from you. How are we doing?"

"Everything's a go," Dade said.

"Great. That's fine to hear. You're a good man."

"I don't think Mr. Grant would agree with you on that."

Marston laughed heartily. "You got that right. The little fucker's gonna split a gut. But let me tell you, he's had this comin', goddamn it. About time that asshole gets fucked."

"I just better be in another time zone when he finds out."

"Don't you fret. Everything's taken care of."

"Good. That's what I wanted to hear."

"So what're we looking at now? How much is coming through?"

"Looks like twelve million and some change."

"We can live with that," Marston said. "Course it ain't just about the money. It's about bringin' Grant down. He won't survive this."

Dade wasn't so sure. He had heard the stories about Ghost Grant. Stories about the man getting shot, stabbed, poisoned, all kinds of crazy rumors. Some folks were convinced he really was a ghost who could take a human form. Dade didn't believe half the stories, but if only a tenth of them were true, it would take a stake to the heart to kill Michael Grant, and as long as he was alive, he'd remain a man to be reckoned with.

"I'll call you when it's done," Dade told Grant's rival.

"You do that."

"Yes, sir. Goodbye now."

"You take care."

Dade hung up the phone and found himself staring at it again. He had tried not to think about what he was doing. He had gotten squeezed between Marston and Grant. There was no way to stay on the good side of one without making an enemy of the other. Dade had figured that being a friend of Grant's and being his enemy weren't that much different. Either way, you were playing with fire.

42

Marvin Slats worked his way up from the railroad tracks and through the woods with only a penlight he had won at Wednesday Night Bingo. The can of gasoline sloshed beside him. It was getting heavy in his right hand. He cut the light as he came up to the clearing and saw the house looming against the moonlight across the long backyard. He had noticed the small cabin at the edge of the wood, but decided no one would be living in it anymore. The windows were dark.

Fire. His body tingled at the thought of it. It was fire that cleansed him, brought him alive. He needed to feel that surge of power again. Lately, he had been feeling so drained, weak, deadened. It was fire that revived him, sent a rush of energy through his veins.

There were probably easier ways to get rid of the boy and his father, he realized. Scare the old man enough and he'd probably die of a heart attack. You could pump the son full of drugs. The way things were these days, no one would doubt an overdose. But Slats ached to see the huge old house engulfed in flames. He longed to step back as the fire ripped through the wood and licked the sky. His breath quickened as he imagined it. A fire he had brought into creation, the raging power that belonged to him, that was part of him.

He understood the irony of it all. His lust had emerged, after all, on the night that they had set the nigger bar aflame. Old man Moon had been there that very night, a part of the whole thing, and his son had been there with Slats, the two of them crouching in the shadows, watching Lonnie Brim from the darkness. The lawyer Moon had come from the other direction, all gussied up in his fine three-piece suit, and collected the money from Lonnie Brim. The weekly profits from the bar. Moon had run the place through Brim, taking the money and spreading it out to Grant, Sump, and a few other upstanding citizens.

Slats remembered the lawyer walking off. The older Moon wouldn't be there, of course, to help subdue Brim and set him up for what was to follow. He had left it up to his own son and Slats to do the dirty work, to knock the nigger out and set the fire. And what a fire it had been, as magnificent a work as he had ever seen. There had been other fires since then. Burning Aaron Naley's barn after the asshole built his own still and cut in on a business Slats had worked hard to establish. The nigger church they put up over on Trestle Street. He had nothing against niggers having a church, but they kept building them all over the goddamn place, practically in Slats's own neighborhood. Slats may not be much, not some highfalutin lawyer, but he sure deserved more respect than a bunch of dirty niggers. The church fire had been a disappointment. They had put it out before it caught on good. They even fixed that church up again, and then they kept an eye out. One day, Slats knew, he would go back and do that one right.

The Bosco fire was still the best. It had flared up in the night, rising up like a flock of birds, consuming the whole place in minutes. He would set up the Moon house the same way they had done the bar. Douse it first upstairs and light the fire from the bottom. He moaned as he thought of the flames racing upward, catching the gasoline on the second floor, bursting up through the roof, a sudden fireball in the black night. It would be glorious.

Jackie had never seen the sight before: Leola asleep in a chair by the stove. The poor woman was so exhausted, she had dropped off before finishing up the dishes. She had come to the big house to help watch after Jackson's father.

Jackie got a blanket from the hall linen closet and covered Leola up with it.

Slats carried the can of gas along the edge of the backyard. There was a tool shed off to his right, so he headed toward it. The shed belonged to the house next door. He came to the edge of the shed and sat down against its wooden wall. He loved this old stuff. Pure wood. None of that goddamn aluminum shit they sold today.

Slats placed the can a few feet from him and fired up a cigarette with his Zippo lighter. The red ember lit up his face as he drew in a deep lungful of smoke. He exhaled up into the night, then edged over to the end of the shed, peering at the Moon house. He would set the fire and get out of there fast, back across the yard and out to the railroad tracks. His car was maybe a hundred yards down the tracks, tucked up on an old dirt road that nobody used anymore. He would get the car and drive it around the old depot, up along Greenville Street. By then, people would be out of their homes. A few cars would have pulled over. He could easily park his car along the road to watch the spectacle of flames. Everyone loved to watch the magnificence and power of a raging, out-of-control fire, eating away an old house.

As Jackie mounted the steps to the second floor, he felt the aches in his body, a tiredness that sank down into his bones. He came to his father's door and looked in. Jackson Moon Jr. was sleeping. It was that disturbed sleep he often fell into, his face strained and his mouth partly open. It made Jackie want to wake him or perhaps try to change the face by running a hand over it, clop the mouth shut by pushing up on the old man's chin.

His father moaned as he twisted in his bed. It looked like he wanted to turn over but lacked the energy. Jackie wondered about his father's dreams. Were they dark and foreboding, images of his past sins come back to haunt him, perhaps even of that fire so many years ago and the murder that followed? Or maybe the dreams were of simple things: walking up stairs, catching up to a bus at a curbside, getting out of bed to go pee. Maybe it was the simple things that caused his greatest nightmares, the things that were no longer so easy. Jackie thought of the dream he often had when he needed to run fast but his legs wouldn't move for him. They would lay paralyzed or move as if stuck in deep mud. For his father, just getting out of bed could be his greatest struggle. Perhaps he would strain in his sleep, wondering how his body had ever gotten so weak.

Slats stubbed out his cigarette in the grass. It was time. He took up the can and worked his way back across the yard, his eyes alert. A window upstairs was full of light and on the lower floor, there was a dim glow, maybe a nightlight. He came up to the back of the house and crouched below a row of windows. He peeked into a dark day room. It was empty and quiet.

"Be unlocked," he urged in a whisper as he reached up to the door handle. It turned and clicked. Slowly, he pulled the door open and stepped into the house.

Jackie was sitting beside his father's bed. It had become a familiar, comfortable spot. He had this strange urge to read to the sleeping old man. Maybe *Goodnight Moon* or some Dr. Seuss. He laughed aloud at the thought. Not tonight anyway. It would take all of his energy just to get up out of the chair.

Slats heard the laughter up on the second floor. He froze in the hallway and listened. Nothing. He stood still for long moments, waiting for snatches of a conversation or more laughter to reach him. Nothing. Perhaps someone had laughed out loud in their sleep. He stepped slowly, keeping the gas can as steady as he could. The gas made soft sounds of liquid swirling in the can. Slats came to the bottom of the stairs and took one step up. Toward the laughter.

At some point, Jackie's thoughts drifted into waking dreams and he began to nod off. He fell into deep rhythmic breathing. Young, healthy breathing, unlike the old man's strained and halting inhalations. Jackie thought of Bridgett Baines, of a spot by a pond, of stars streaming endlessly across a moonless sky.

Slats was halfway up. On the landing. The gas can was getting heavy. It was hard to carry it up and keep the gas in the can from sloshing around. Slowly, he placed the can down on the landing for a moment and massaged his right arm. This, he realized, would be his swan song. His last masterpiece. It was time for him to retire. He picked the can back up and started up the second set of stairs. Too fast. The can caught the railing with a metallic thunk and the gas sloshed in the can. Slats froze on the stairwell.

Jackie sprang awake. He had heard something, hadn't he? What had it been? He thought of Leola downstairs, sleeping in the kitchen. Had she fallen out of the chair? Jackie shook sleep out of his head and rose up slowly. Blurry-eyed, he checked his father one more time, pulling a light blanket up over the old man's body.

Slats heard someone walking around in the room. He stood still and listened. It was time to make his move. He bolted up the last steps, swinging the can furiously at his side.

Just as Jackson came into the doorway of his father's room, he saw a man – a man he vaguely recognized – dashing up the stairs. He came at Jackie furiously, carrying something – a large can – in his right hand. Jackson ducked back into the room, tried to get the door closed, but the man slammed into it hard, knocking Jackson to the floor. The can slung madly in the man's hand, splashing its contents up through the spout. Gasoline. The harsh fumes blew up into Jackie's nose.

Jackie tried to get up, tried to yell out, but now the man swung the can at him. It struck the side of his face, knocking him back against the bed. His father jolted awake. "What the hell?" he demanded as the intruder swung the gas can back around, cracking Jackie again on the side of his head. Jackie went down and lay still on the floor.

Jackson Moon Jr. sat upright in his bed. "What the hell is going on here?" Then he saw the face, the scar, the eyes glowing below heavy brows. "Slats?" Moon asked, not believing the sight of this man from his past, standing above his bed.

Slats smiled at him. The scars along his right cheek glared in the pale lamplight. "I'm here to finish the job, Mr. Moon. I always finish what I start."

Moon looked at the gas can in Slats's hand. "Leave my son out of this, Slats."

Slats laughed heartily. "Too late for that. He's already into it, up to his goddamn neck. I'm here for him. You're just along for the ride."

Slats tossed gas onto the bed. Moon tried to shrink away from it as the gas doused the sheets. The old man rolled over with effort, off the bed and onto the floor. Slats was already there. He put the can down, grabbed the old man by his arm, and shoved him back toward the wall. Then Slats flung open a closet and shoved the old man in.

Jackie was working his way up from the floor when Slats reached him. The madman grabbed Jackie and drove him across the room. Before he knew what was happening, Jackie found himself in the closet with his father. A sliver of light stabbed in beneath the door. His father was on the floor, in the corner, groaning. Jackie had slammed into him and knocked him over. He tried to get up off the old man, but there was not enough room in the closet to maneuver. Jackie found the doorknob, but it wouldn't turn. They were locked in the closet. He heard Slats moving the bed now, sliding it up against the closet door.

As Jackie struggled to get his father up off the floor, he heard Slats pouring gas on the floor of the bedroom. Then Slats moved out into the hall and down the stairs as the sound of splashing gasoline followed along behind him. "Jesus God" was all Jackie could say. He worked himself up, then pulled his father up off the floor. The old man leaned in a corner, gasping for breath. Jackie worked the locked knob, slammed against the heavy closet door. It was hard to get any leverage. He couldn't draw up any force to propel against the door. He turned around and pushed against the back wall, slamming his back against the door again and again. He couldn't help thinking about those people in Bosco's bar, locked up in the attic, waiting to die.

At the bottom of the stairs, Slats finished pouring the gas and threw the can aside. He had to work fast, before they got the door open. He pulled out his Zippo and struck up a flame. He watched the small flame flicker for a moment. It was a remarkable sight. This tiny flame would soon grow into a roaring two-story fire. It even looked like the huge flame in miniature, dancing above the black wick.

A voice, behind him. "Don't do it," it said evenly.

Slats turned. It was a wiry colored woman. Probably the maid. She still had her apron on. In her hand was a butcher knife. She held it up resolutely. "Don't do it," she said again.

Slats looked at the flame, heard the son upstairs, slamming against the door. The maid moved closer to him. She was no more than eight feet away now. "You hold on right there, missy," he told her.

She paused, then took another step. "You put out that light," she said.

What could an old woman do? He was ashamed for even considering the danger. He smiled broadly and dropped the lighter on a pool of gas. Whoosh. The blast of fire rocked him backward and he fell against Leola. It was when Slats turned to grab her that he felt a terrible, searing shock of pain explode at the base of his throat. The woman had driven the knife blade into his neck, as deeply as it would go. Slats heard an awful gurgle rumble from the wound in his throat. The pain shattered every thought in his head. The scream he heard in his own mind filled his consciousness as the fire raced up the stairway and blasted into a mushroom of flame and smoke.

Slats grabbed Leola by her hair and pulled her down as he fell at the edge of the flames. He clutched the hair in a death grip as he fought for breath that was not there. With his other hand, he felt the knife, jammed into his neck up to its wooden hilt. It was then that he heard another strange gurgle rising up from somewhere deep inside of him. It rattled up his throat like a spoon slapping against the bones in his neck. His life flashed by him, a rush of images and memories and fire. Always fire. He knew, as the world spun away, that he was meant to die here. In a holocaust of flames. In fire.

L eola worked against the unearthly grip of the madman who had lit the house on fire. She screeched and trembled, actually pulling the man over the floor with her hair. Some of the strands came out at the roots.

Leola could hear screaming above her. She worked on the hand that clutched her hair, prying loose the fingers. They wouldn't give. Finally, she reached up to the knife buried in the madman's throat and worked it out. She slashed at her hair with the blade until she fell back free. Her cut hair was still clutched in the man's hand. She looked at his scarred face as the flames began to eat him.

Leola rose up. The fire was everywhere now. Smoke stung her eyes and blocked out her sight. She drew in torrents of the black air, then dropped to her knees gasping. She could not hear Mr. Moon anymore. She could not hear Jackie. All she could hear was the cackle of the flames all around her. She would not remember crawling for the door. Later, she knew, it was some primal instinct that drew her there. Instinct, nothing more. As always, she did what she had to. She survived.

J ackie heard the terrible whoosh of the fire rushing up the steps. The heat of it rolled over him like a huge ocean wave. He was holding his father up in the closet. Jackie felt the gasoline seeping under the closet door just before both of them were suddenly standing in a rage of flames. It was as if the world had fallen away, as if everything he knew had become nothing but a blaze of angry, hot fire. He felt himself fainting, falling, then the floor gave way.

His father was still in Jackie's arms when they both slammed onto the dining room table below his father's bedroom.

His father was barely conscious, half his body scorched, as Jackson tugged him across the floor, crawling madly toward a large window. He reached the sill, pulled himself up, and drew his father up over one shoulder. On both sides of him, the window's curtains suddenly billowed up in flames like a cheap magician's trick, and the window behind the drapes exploded, shattering glass into Jackie and blowing him backward. He hit the floor hard, his father rolling across him, and he saw fire no more, only black.

Jackson's father saw a blurry vision before him as he grasped at consciousness. In fact, he thought it was a dream: the huge black man now filling the shattered window. The man came into the burning house, the fiery curtains on each side of him, intent eyes reflecting the savage flames. He scooped Jackie up over his shoulder then knelt down for the old man. Jackie's father noticed the hands, impossibly huge, as the black man cradled him up and carried both he and his son back toward the window.

The father looked out at the night beyond the flames. He seemed to float through the window. An explosion of fire and heat followed after them, Jackie draped over the black man's shoulder and his father cradled in the savior's arms. Flames seared up the wall behind them, and the porch overhang burst into fire. It seemed as if the inferno had engulfed the very earth itself. Jackie's father saw the black man kick the porch railing once. The wood cracked, and the three bodies surged over the edge, hitting the shrubbery and sinking into it, the house exploding, the porch overhang collapsing, everything going black.

43

He saw red lights swirling around him, but it wasn't fire. The heat was gone. Jackie sat up and felt a strap tighten at his waist. He was moving now in a vehicle. His eyes focused on a young man sitting close to him. The man was dressed in white. The swirling red lights came from the direction of the siren above them.

Jackie was in an ambulance.

The man was looking off through the back window, unaware that Jackie was awake. Jackson looked past the man to the scene the man was watching. Filling the back window was a towering fire. Flames blazed out of the Moon house, burning out of the walls and rising in gushes from the windows. It seemed dreamlike to Jackie. As the ambulance moved away from the fire, the frame of the house appeared to Jackie as a giant cross, burning in the night. Then the upper structure collapsed, and the hungry flames rejoiced, roaring up higher and spewing a swirling ball of red and black smoke into the sky.

"Everything's okay." It was the young man in white. He had turned around and was facing Jackie.

"My father," Jackie managed to say.

The young man's eyes could not conceal his concern. "He's alive," he reported. "But he's in bad shape. The first ambulance took him to the hospital. It was a lot of trauma for a man his age to handle. Especially the fall. You both got burned pretty bad."

"What about Leola?" The pain of his burns was becoming real to Jackie. He fought for consciousness.

The young man thought for a second. "Oh," he said. "The colored woman. Yeah, she made it out, too. Through the back door. She suffered from bad smoke inhalation. We wanted to bring her in, but she wouldn't let us."

Jackie tried to focus his thoughts.

"We gave you some sedatives and a painkiller. You got some nasty burns on your shoulders." He eased Jackie back down on the stretcher. "You should just relax now."

Jackie dropped down against the stretcher's firm mattress. He felt as if he were still falling. Free-falling. Drifting in space. He closed his eyes and saw, fused onto the inside of his eyelids, the vision of fire, of the huge burning cross, of his father's beautiful house falling in on itself.

Jackie wasn't sure how long he had slept. His hospital room was shrouded in twilight and he felt the sting of the burns on his shoulder. He saw the face of a nurse and another figure behind her, the nurse rubbing a cool ointment on his wounds. He felt a needle prick and slid off again into a sleep that was more like a dreamy daze.

When he came back awake, Bridgett seemed to appear out of the hazy, curtained light of the room. She held Jackie's hand in hers. The hand was as soft and as warm as a hot biscuit. Jackie managed to smile.

"What day is it?" he asked.

"It's Thursday," Bridgett said.

Thursday. It meant nothing to him. He struggled for a reference.

"You just rest." Bridgett's voice was so soothing that he could feel his confusion lilting away. "Everything's all right now."

"How's Daddy?" asked Jackie.

"I'll answer your questions when you're better. You need to rest now."

"Is he dead?"

"No, Jackson. He's alive."

A glass of water appeared in Bridgett's hand and she eased it up to his lips. She held his head up and he swallowed heavily. Then she placed his head back down on the pillow.

"Your father is hanging in there. He's awake now, but he's weak. His breathing is very strained. His burns are bad. They want to put him on a respirator, but he won't let them. He says he doesn't want some machine keeping him alive. Stubborn to the end."

Jackie tried to smile again but couldn't. "And Leola?"

Bridgett nodded. "Leola's just fine," she assured him. "Alfreda is seeing after her. She's back at her house."

"And she's going to be okay?"

"Yes, Jackie. Leola's stronger than all of us put together. She may lose a step, but that'll probably be good for her. She'll be fine."

A short silence followed.

"I feel like I've been sleeping for a month."

"Just two days," she said. "It's Thursday. The fire was Tuesday night."

Two days. He struggled for other questions he knew hung in his mind. "Did we miss it?" he asked.

W hen Jackie's eyes opened again, Leola appeared before him, drawing herself from the slivers of light and shadow. Her hair was cut short, almost to the scalp, and a dark red burn streaked over her left ear. The haircut made her look sad and strangely vulnerable, like a lion without his mane. Her eyes stared at Jackie, but they didn't seem to focus.

"Hello, boy," she said.

"You okay?"

"Looks like I's better'n you."

"I'm all right," said Jackson. "If they'd just stop pumping drugs into me, I could walk right out of here."

There was a silence as Leola studied the injured man. Finally, she said, "It was Clarence, you know. The boxer from prison."

Jackson tried to remember. "Big Hands?"

"I caught him out back a few days ago, keeping an eye on you. I reckon it was a good thing he was about."

"He saved us?" Jackson said, finding the memory nowhere within him. He looked up at Leola. "Is he safe?"

Leola nodded. "We got him hid out. He'll be okay."

"He saved us," Jackie said, his words tinged with wonder.

Leola looked at him, her frown deepening.

"What's wrong?" Jackson asked her.

Leola shook her head very slowly. Jackson watched her eyes glaze over. He slowly rose up out of the bed.

"No, boy," Leola said. "You ain't s'posed to...."

But Jackie was already to her, reaching out to her. He folded her into his arms, wrapping her up and reaching his right arm around her neck, three fingers upon her right cheek.

"I killed that man," Leola said, as if trying to believe it.

"He was there to kill us all."

"That don't matter. I killed him. I stole away his soul."

Jackson didn't know what to say to the woman. Her understanding of what it meant to kill a man was deeper than anything he could possibly grasp. All he could do was hold her tight. Her body began to shake. He felt hot tears streaming between his fingers as he slowly stroked her cheek.

"I love you, Leola. You know that, don't you? I love you like my own mama...."

44

Jackson dreamed he was in a boxing ring, facing a huge heavyweight who kept pummeling Jackie's ribs. The bell was ringing and the big boxer wouldn't stop hitting him. Jackie lifted his eyes over his raised right glove and saw the fighter he was facing. It was Big Hands Hoffman.

Jackson sprang awake. His head was spinning and his shoulders burned. The memory of his last bout swirled in his head.

Canterback Gym was packed. Thick smoke from cigars and cigarettes filled the air. The crowd was buzzing with anticipation. A ring had been set up at the center of the gymnasium with rows of bleachers on all four sides. The warden had a special stand at ringside, filled with councilmen and bureaucrats. They had passed a special ordinance to sell beer and allow smoking in the gym for this special night. The small community had rarely seen an event like it. There had been protests, but they were largely ignored. Bleacher seats had been gobbled up at forty dollars a head; ringside seats went even faster at seventy-five, with the proceeds going to a proposed playground and to the prison activity fund. A former heavyweight contender from St. Charles had been recruited to referee, and a local doctor took a ringside seat to monitor the action and prevent the kind of damage that had befallen Rock Magee.

The crowd cheered when Moondog entered from the locker room, his fists raised high. They even took up the chant of *Moon-dog, Moon-dog, Moon-dog*. They jeered at Big Hands Hoffman, the huge black man who had thrown a defenseless white from the third-story window of his own home. The crowd longed to see him punished, but the sight of his massive frame and the huge hands fueled a growing doubt. Moondog suddenly seemed awfully small.

Jackie danced in his corner. Cecil was his new trainer. Moondog peeled his robe off, and the crowd was heartened to see his honed body. The town had sprung for all the trappings: the local beauty queen set to carry placards announcing the round, a shiny brass bell with an official timekeeper to ring it, three judges at a ringside table to tally the scores, two sportswriters at the same table with their pens ready, and an American flag hanging from rafters above the center of the ring.

Moondog and Big Hands walked to the middle of the ring, and the referee checked their gloves. He nodded his approval and explained the rules. "This will be a civil boxing match, gentlemen, and I will be strict in the enforcement of the rules. You back off when I tell you to or you will lose a scoring point after one warning. Low blows and head butts are grounds for immediate default. You will drop your fists at the sound of the bell ending a round and go directly to your corner. In the case of a knockdown, you must proceed immediately to an opposite corner. Standing eight counts and doctor inspections are at my sole discretion. I will end the fight if at any time a boxer is incapable of defending himself or is not fully cognizant. A three knockdown rule is in effect. If any boxer goes down three times in one round, it will be ruled as a knockout. Do you understand?"

Both men nodded.

"Now touch gloves, go to your corners, and prepare to come out fighting."

Moondog held out his gloves but Big Hands knocked them violently away. It was great theater. The crowd booed with passion.

"Watch yourself, Jackie," Cecil told him. "I don't know what you were thinking. Clarence is gonna knock your head off."

Jackson looked at his trainer. "Thanks for the pep talk," he said.

The bell rang and the boxers rushed to the center of the ring and immediately started punching. The crowd roared its approval. Clarence unleashed a barrage of left jabs, but Moondog ducked and bobbed, avoiding the punches with deft movements. Twice he countered with right crosses, then danced backward, arms raised as the crowd cheered. Big Hands was stoic and purposeful, stalking his showboating prey, but Moondog continued to elude punches with expert timing and quickness. Jackie came inside, rattled off a series of body blows, then danced away. They ended the round toe-to-toe with Moondog again getting the better of the rally.

Cecil was ecstatic in the corner. "You got skills, Moondog," he gushed. "You got skills."

The second round was more of the same, with Big Hands prowling and Moondog dancing. Big Hands landed with a strong hook, but Moondog stood his ground and landed consistent jabs and crosses. The crowd broke into the Moondog chant again as the round came to a close.

A hush fell on the crowd in the middle of the third round, when – in the midst of the Moondog chant – Big Hands shoved a straight right hand between Moondog's gloves. The blow struck Jackie dead on the chin. It felt like the strike of a hammer, and he didn't remember falling down. He came to on the canvas. The crowd was silent except for a few fans urging Moondog to get up. He struggled to his feet as the referee reached the count of eight. Big Hands had hovered over him for a good five seconds before the referee forced Clarence to the opposite corner and then started the count.

"You hear me?" the referee yelled at Jackie. He nodded.

"Where are you?" he asked.

Jackson looked around at the apprehensive crowd and up at the flag dangling above him. "I'm in a boxing ring," Jackie answered.

"Close enough," the referee said and waved the fighters on.

Jackie stumbled forward and threw a weak punch to the gut of the big black man, then he tied him up and leaned in.

"Jesus, Clarence, you really hit me."

"I had to make it look good," Clarence told him.

"You make it look any better and I'll end up six feet under."

The bell rang. "You just keep your feet," Clarence said. "Don't go down on me."

"I told you he'd knock your head off," Cecil said from the corner.

If Jackson had the strength, he would have put a left hook to Cecil's jaw. Instead, he shook his head and tried to find his breath. The ring swam below him, and the crowd spun in circles.'

Jackson came out for the fourth round flat-footed. He kept his gloves up and tried to keep his feet moving. Big Hands dodged his head back and forth and tossed some weak jabs into Jackie's gloves. The crowd booed at the lack of action, and the referee stepped in. "We aren't playing patty-cake here, gentlemen," he said.

Moondog ducked into Big Hands, and began landing hard body blows. Big Hands bent over him, his gloves on Moondog's shoulders, as Jackie continued to work over the body. "You got to beat me up good," Clarence said in Jackson's ear. Motivated by the urgings of his former trainer, Moondog threw a hard kidney punch, then released a breathtaking right uppercut that flung back the head of Big Hands Hoffman. The crowd erupted as Moondog tracked down his foe, who stumbled into the ropes. Jackie threw a pair of punches that jerked Clarence's head violently, first to the left, then to the right. A straight-armed left sent the sickening echo of Big Hand's groan up into the rafters. Jackson pulled back and landed a hard right hook to Hoffman's jaw, followed by two left jabs and a thunderous right uppercut. Clarence's head flew back over the top rope, blood flying out of his mouth. Moondog ducked into the body as it lunged from the ropes. Jackson crouched low and landed blow after blow to the

big man's ribs and abs. As the referee pulled Jackie away, Clarence tot-
tered on the ropes, his eyes rolling away and blood spilling down his
chin. Then Big Hands Hoffman fell forward to the canvas with a
deathly thump. He didn't move at all through the count. The fight
was over. The roar of the crowd was deafening. The referee summoned the doctor.

"Oh, God," Jackson screamed. "What have I done?"

The doctor shook Clarence but he didn't move. The crowd was surging into the ring to congratulate their hero for his unlikely win, but
Jackie called after Clarence. "Help him, Doc. You've got to help him."

The doctor ordered the referee and two of the judges to help carry
Clarence through the surging crowd. They took him down a hall to
the gym's small infirmary. They laid Clarence on a cot, and the doctor shoved the other men out of the room. "Call the emergency
room," he ordered. "Get an ambulance here fast." The guard refused
to leave the infirmary, so the doctor let him stay, closing the door on
the others.

Even through the closed door, the chant of the crowd was loud and
frenzied. The muffled roar of *Moon-dog* thumped the walls and shook
the windows. The doctor reached into his bag and pulled out
smelling salts. He put them to Clarence's nose. The big man shook
violently on the cot, then reared awake, rolling off the cot and to the
floor. The doctor helped him up as Clarence slowly came to his feet.
The guard stood against the wall, watching the fighter's knees buck-
le. The doctor was between Clarence and the guard as he strained
against the weight of the big boxer.

Big Hands Hoffman moved with a lightning quickness he never
revealed in the ring. He threw the doctor up against the guard, pinning the guard's rifle against his chest. Big Hands delivered a single
straight-arm right to the guard's jaw, thrusting the guard's head against
the cement wall. Clarence's huge left hand covered the stunned doctor's mouth. "Sorry, Doc," Clarence whispered as he brought an elbow
down to the back of the doctor's head. Clarence stripped away the

doctor's smock and tried to wrap it around him. He jumped up on the cot, slid open a window, and rolled out to the ground.

Clarence dashed along the side of the building, then through the woods and down Route 11 for twenty yards until he came to a small pond. He ducked back into the woods, following the bank of the pond, running full-out until he had made a three-quarter circle around it. He came to a dirt road and dashed down it until he saw Bridgett Baines standing by the opened trunk of her Mazda. He tumbled into the trunk and she threw a blanket over him.

Bridgett started to close the trunk, then she peeled back the blanket. "Jackie said no home-cooking this time," she told Big Hands Hoffman. Even through his heavy gasps, Bridgett saw the man's tummy rumble with laughter.

Bridgett closed the trunk, spun the car around, and headed for the highway.

45

When he woke back up, Jackson realized the phone was ringing by his hospital bed. He shook sleep from his head and picked up the receiver.

"Jackson?" The voice was intimately familiar, but very strange to hear. "Ellis?"

"Jesus Christ. I tried to call the house and the phone was dead. I couldn't get hold of anybody. I finally called Jimmy over at the store. He said you and Daddy were in a fire. Said the whole house burned down."

"That about sums it up," Jackson said. His mind was still groggy. Everything seemed so unreal: the fire, being in the hospital, and now his little brother on the phone.

"You okay?"

"Yeah, I'm all right. I plan to walk out of here as soon as the pesky nurse turns her back. My ribs are a little sore, that's all."

"How'd you hurt your ribs?"

"I fell through the floor and landed on the dining room table. It probably wouldn't have hurt so badly if I hadn't had the shit kicked out of me over at Crawdaddy's."

"Crawdaddy's? What's that all about?"

"It's a long story. It concerns your good buddy Ghost Grant."

"He's not my buddy anymore. I'd say I'm at the top of his enemies list."

"How did that happen?"

"Goddamn prosecutor set me up. Got Grant believing I had turned on him. State's witness or something. I've got to run. I should have enough money to make it to South America. Maybe I'll rob a bank down there."

"Makes sense," said Jackson. "A lawyer for Grant, you should be used to a life of crime."

"Touché."

"Looks like we both got screwed."

"You know what they say, you play with fire…"

"Yeah," said Jackson, "I know all about that."

"I guess you would."

Jackson took a deep breath. Despite everything, it was nice to talk to his only brother. "We'll have a drink some time. Fill each other in."

"It'll have to be a place where Grant can't find me. East Mongolia, maybe."

Jackson thought about it for a few moments.

"Hey, Ellis?"

"Yeah?"

"How about the Grand Canyon? I bet they wouldn't look for you in there."

46

It was Monday when Jackson walked past the rubble of his family's house, across the long backyard, and into the wood. He remembered his first visit to Leola's cabin only days earlier: the small hills that appeared to him as sacred burial mounds, the way he stood frozen in his tracks, at first unable to approach the tiny house. He felt that same uneasiness now, the strange feeling that he was facing something ancient, even sacred. This time, he understood the feeling. It was time for his own confession.

He knocked once on the door, and Leola opened it. She moved out of the doorway, reading the look on Jackie's face and saying nothing. Angel was sitting in the rocker, as if she had been there waiting for Jackson to return.

Jackson sat on the wooden chair across from the old woman in dark glasses. Leola came over to Jackson and peeled back his collar. Jackie moaned. "What they put on them burns?" Leola asked.

"Hell, I don't know. They gave me some pills. Whatever it was, it didn't do much good."

"Pills? For a skin burn? Those doctors ain't got no common sense a'tall." Leola shook her head sadly. "Alfreda, go on in the back room and get my salve."

Alfreda disappeared into the room where she had treated Jackie and came back with a dark brown bottle. She unbuttoned Jackson's shirt and pulled it down around his waist. When she unscrewed the bottle cap, a rich aroma filled the air. It was the smell of earth and mint and something else Jackie couldn't quite identify. The smells seemed to draw him into a trance, sending him back to another place, another time. He was drifting.

"Peppermint," he said dreamily as Alfreda placed three fingers on the back of his neck. The fingers were damp with the salve, and at the very touch of them, the pain evaporated. Alfreda was moving her fingers down along his neck, across the left shoulder, and as the fingers lightly massaged his skin, the burning went numb. His neck and shoulders tingled. The peppermint scent conjured the distant memory of Senator Alfred Sachs with his pocketful of gumdrops, the children happily dipping their hands into the sack.

Jackson could see the four of them huddled in Leola's cabin. They were below him, as if he were floating up around the ceiling. He saw Leola with a red bandana wrapped around her head, Angel revealing a look of patience and expectation as she removed the glasses, the young black woman slowly stroking the white man's shoulders and neck, the white man's head lolled back, his mouth moving....

My daddy had got a call earlier that night, and he left the house right away. I ran outside after him. I could tell something important was up. I asked him if I could come along, but as usual, he wouldn't let me. But then, a little while later, he pulled back up into the driveway and waited there with the engine idling. I went out to the old Belvedere, and my father opened the passenger-side door from his seat behind the wheel. I walked over and got in. Daddy just sat there for a while, his head crooked down, not saying a single thing. I looked out of the windshield and stayed quiet, happy just to be there in the car with him. Finally, his head came up and he turned to me. He told me that if I came, it would mean that I was a man, that I had to put away the things of a child. And he said I had to do exactly what I was told, and tell no one about anything I heard or saw. I was seventeen years old. I had just finished my junior year of high school.

His father drove Jackson past Bosco's bar and turned right onto a side road. He stopped at a railroad crossing. A big rugged man came up to the window. He had a pockmarked face and sagging jowls. There was a club hanging from his belt. His father told Jackson that the man's name was Marvin Slats and that Jackson should do just what the man told him to do. Jackson got out of the car. His father drove the Belvedere over the railroad crossing, took an immediate left, and headed down a road that paralleled the tracks. He would keep his regular appointment with Lonnie Brim.

Jackson and Slats crouched behind some blackberry bushes close to the tracks. They waited there, Slats slurping thirstily from a whiskey bottle and wiping his mouth with the back of his hand. The sickly sweet smell of the blackberries and whiskey fluttered in Jackie's stomach along with tingling anticipation. The night seemed charged with electricity. Jackie knew he would always remember this time, the raw energy of it.

"What are we waiting for?" Jackson asked, but Slats ignored him. He took another long pull from the whiskey.

"What are we going to do?" Jackie tried again.

"Shut up," Slats growled. "You listen to me and do what I tell you, jes' like yo' daddy tole you."

Slats had smoked two cigarettes and swallowed most of the whiskey when Jackson saw the black man emerge from a path leading down from Bosco's bar. The man came out by the tracks and stood there waiting, a brown paper sack in his hand. Jackie tried to rise up to get a better view of the man, but Slats put a hand on his shoulders to keep him down.

"Hold onto your horses," he said. "We got to wait for your old man first."

Jackson waited until he could make out his father, appearing at the far end of the track as if forming from the swirls of darkness. He walked crisply in his gray three-piece suit, moonlight catching the chain of his pocket watch. Jackson rose up, intending to meet his father out on the track, but Slats pushed him down with one slap of the hand. "Stay down, goddamn it," he said, his voice now slurred from the whiskey. "We're s'posed to wait 'til your old man is done. We want Brim alone."

Jackson's father did not say a word to the black man. He simply took the brown paper bag, turned on his heels, and headed back the way he had come, the vision of him dispersing as mystically as it had formed. The black man rolled a cigarette from a pouch of tobacco and struck a match on the rail.

"You wait here," Slats ordered. He pulled the wooden club from his belt and handed it to Jackie. "I'm gonna take care of the nigger. Once he's down, you come on out."

The black man was smoking his cigarette when Slats came up to him on the railroad tracks. They passed some words that Jackson couldn't make out. Slats lifted the whiskey bottle up as if offering the black man a toast. The black man started to say something else but he never got the words out. Slats lunged into the black man, swinging the whiskey bottle in a wide arc with his right hand. The bottle exploded against the side of the black man's face, the glass popping like a balloon, the whiskey splattering against the tracks, drenching the black man's shirt. Brim stumbled backward, somehow keeping his balance. Slats then kicked him in the stomach and slammed a fist into his temple. Brim thudded onto the rail bed, face-first, his head bouncing once against the wooden ties. Slats stood over him, brushing off his hands. He kicked the man to see if he would move. Jackie wondered if the black man was dead.

Slats nudged the man with his foot again. It looked like Slats was trying to turn him over onto his back. But then the black man rose up with Slats's foot in his hand. He drove Slats over backwards, down onto the track. Brim tried to run but Slats got up and dove on the black man's back. They rolled off the track and down a bank. Jackie stood up behind the blackberry bush, wondering what to do. Slats had told him to stay put. Jackson crept out from behind the shrubs and started walking toward the two men. The club dangled from his right hand.

Jackson saw Slats rise up over the black man again. He grabbed Brim by the hair, saying something an inch from the man's ear. That's when the black man bit Marvin Slats. Jackie heard the scream tear across the tracks and echo in the night. When Jackson came up to the men, Brim's jaws were still clamped down on the fat of Slats's cheek. Jackie cracked the club across the back of Lonnie Brim's neck.

Slats told Jackie to keep an eye on Brim. "Make sure he don't get up before the fire's going good."

"What fire?"

"Just do what you're tol't," Slats snapped. "I'm goin' up to the bar. You stay here."

Jackson got scared waiting alone with the unconscious black man. He slowly made his way back up the hill behind the bar. He heard a shotgun blast and it stopped him cold. He stayed in the shadows of an elm tree at the top of the hill. He saw men rushing out of the bar. He saw Sheriff Sump. Jackie's head was racing. He gasped as the bar erupted into flames. Fire tore up the sides of the building and roiled up into the sky. The heat rushed against Jackie's face, and hot ash began to fall like black snow. Jackson was watching the flames when Lonnie Brim walked within ten feet of him. The black man was oblivious of everything but the burning bar. He walked right up into the doorway and stepped into the fire.

Jackson came up behind him, shielding his eyes from the glaring light. He had stepped up into the doorway, a few feet behind Brim, when he saw the small boy stranded on the stairs in the bar.

"Goddamn it, Billy. You won't make it!" Brim screamed just as the stairway collapsed. A blast of flame knocked Brim over. He lay supine on the floor, black smoke pouring over him. Jackie stood motionless, not knowing what he should do. Then his feet began to move. He worked his way into the bar. The smoke seared his eyes and clotted in his throat. He made it to Brim's body and began dragging the man out of the bar. He strained against the dead weight and spewing flames. He let go of Brim when he was back outside, the legs still crossing the doorway, and retreated back into a stand of trees.

Brim sat up and gazed around dreamily. He began to crawl away from the building. Jackie heard sirens whirring up in the distance. Brim rose to his feet and began to run, across Donovan Street and down Shady Lane.

As Jackson stood there, transfixed by what had happened, the sheriff's cruiser roared up beside him, screeching to a halt. The back door opened. Inside sat his father and his Uncle Rufus. Sump and Doctor James sat in front, Sump at the wheel.

"Get in, boy," his father said, but Jackson was so dazed that he didn't recognize the words. His uncle lunged out of the car, grabbed Jackson by the arm, and pulled him in. The car rolled out of Bosco's parking lot and turned slowly down Shady Lane. Sump cut the cruiser's headlights.

The cruiser pulled up to the curb across from Brim's wooden blue house just as the black man frantically stumbled through his doorway. The front door slammed shut. You could hear the lock turning, the chain being mounted. The men got out of the cruiser and Sump opened the trunk. He handed a pistol to Jackie's father and to Doctor James, a shotgun to Uncle Rufus, then he picked up a shotgun himself and loaded it up. Another car pulled up, then another. More armed men piled out, some Jackson recognized, some he didn't. Slats was there with a shotgun and a cigarette. His face was covered in soot. He saw Jackie and winked.

Sump walked across the street, over the curb, and into Brim's yard, cocking the shotgun as he walked. The lawn was well tended. Red roses bloomed from a bush by the door. Honeysuckle lined the front wall, the long pink pistils poking up over windowsills. Sump stopped twenty feet from the house and then waved the other men over. They made a crooked line along the yard, on either side of the sheriff. Jackson waited for Sump to order Brim out, but the command never came. Instead, the sheriff nodded and the men opened fire.

The volley of gunfire shocked Jackson. He stumbled backward to the ground as bullets riddled the house, blew out every window. The pistols popped, *rat-a-tat-tat*, a chatter overwhelmed by the intermittent roar of the shotguns that tore the night open. Smoke rose above the line of men until Sump held up a hand. The shooting stopped. The yard fell silent. Jackson wondered if he had lost his hearing. All he could make out was a loud buzz in his head.

Sump said nothing. He just waited. He slowly brought the hand down but the men did not start shooting again. The house was quiet except for pieces of glass that continued to drop down from the windows.

A voice hollered from the house, down below one of the blown-out windows. Somehow, crouched behind the red-brick chimney, the Brims had survived. Lonnie was screaming now.

"I'm comin' out!" he yelled. "I'm comin' out right now! I didn't do nothin' wrong! I swear it! I ain't armed! My wife, she's in here with me! Don't shoot! I'm comin' out!"

Seconds later, the door started to open. Jackie crooked his head around one of the armed men to watch Brim as he emerged. But he never saw Brim. He fell back, shocked, as the gunfire started up again without warning. The door exploded into shards and splinters. Behind it, a body writhed and wiggled, held up by the rally of gunshots. Finally, a shotgun blast blew the body off its feet, backward into the house. The gunfire died out again. The door dangled from a single hinge, then fell forward out into the yard.

Sump approached, the men close behind him. As he came to the door, he saw Mary Brim, her body riddled by bullets, her yellow dress soaked red, her shoulder shorn off by the last shotgun blast. The other men gathered around the sheriff. Jackson couldn't help but approach and stare at the scene, the dead woman planted in a pile of wood shards, glass, and shreds of drywall. White powder drifted in the air above her. Blood bubbled up out of the maze of bullet holes.

From the front hall rose the cries of Lonnie Brim. He dragged himself from the wreckage and over to his wife. His bleeding leg dangled behind him as he pulled himself across the floor. He was screaming insanely, crying uncontrollably, so distraught he could only screech. The helpless eyes glared up at the men in his doorway. "You killed her!" he screamed until his voice broke. "You bastards killed my Mary!"

Sump looked at the dead woman. "What kinda man uses his wife to save his own skin?" he asked.

Brim couldn't answer. He pulled his wife into his lap and looked down at her bloody face, as if she might know the reason for all that had happened. "She said she would come out," he whispered. "She said they would never shoot a woman."

"Tough break," Sump said, then he lifted the shotgun up from his hip and blew away the top of Brim's head. The head exploded, splattering blood down the ruined hallway. Even the armed men reared back. "Shit!" blurted Jackie's uncle. Sump just turned away and started back across the yard. He stopped midway, disgruntled. "Well, let's get it on, boys. That nigger needs a few more holes in him." The men turned back to the house, looked at each other, raised their guns, and rolled off another round of fire as the two lifeless bodies jumped and jiggled.

Sump went out to the cruiser, got another gun – a pistol – from under the spare tire in his trunk. He wrapped Brim's hand around it. He told two of the men to drag the woman out back, into the woods. Then he pointed at me and Bill Tomey.

"You two, come on back here," Sump was in command now. There was no denying him and no mistaking the sense of urgency in his voice.

Bill Tomey, the future judge, and Jackson Moon, the lawyer's son, stood by the murdered woman who lay in a heap at the edge of the wood.

"Folks will be here directly," Sump said. "Reporters, firemen, ambulance. Billy, you go and pull yo' daddy's car around. Park it right up there, as close to those trees as you can get. Open up the trunk and wait for us. Go on now!" Tomey ran off in a dash. "You boys pick up the body. Jake, you get her legs; Marty, you get the arms. Come on now. We got no time to dally here."

They were carrying Mary Brim's body through the woods, toward the road, when Jackie's father came up alongside Sump. "What you doin' with that body, Sheriff?"

"I'm gettin' rid of the damn thing, what you think? We got us a situation here. Folks, they go'n understand us shootin' down a arsonist, but they ain't go'n take to us killin' a woman, even a nigger one."

"What do you want with Jackson?"

"He's goin' with the Tomey boy. They got to take care of this body."

"Take care of it?"

"Bury it. What the hell you think? Don't be goin' soft on me, now."

"I was just thinkin' maybe one of the men would be better…"

Sump stopped and glared at Jackson Moon Jr. "Now you said you wanted to bring this boy in, ain't that right? You said it was time. Well, he's either in or he ain't. They's no halfway. And they ain't no goin' back neither. The boy is in it now, and I got a job for him to do. Now you go on back and talk to the newspaper boys when they show up. You tell 'em how that crazy nigger burnt up his bar, kill't a senator, and started into shooting at us when we showed up at the house. I'll be there directly."

Jackie's father hesitated another moment, then Sump exploded. "Go!" he roared, and Jackson Moon Jr. was off through the woods.

We loaded Mary Brim's body into the trunk. Tomey and I drove it out to the Rock. We stopped by Tomey's house first to pick up a shovel. It happened so damn fast, I couldn't get my brain to think.

I n the car, Tomey drove. He lit up a cigarette. He was sur-
prisingly at ease.

"Where are we taking the body?" Jackie asked.

Tomey glanced over at him and laughed. "Jesus, you got to calm yo'self down. Looks like you bound for a heart attack. We don't want no one else dyin' tonight."

"What happened, man? I can understand burning down that bar, but why'd we have to blow away the woman?"

Tomey looked over at Jackie again, gauging him. "You don't have a fucking clue, do you, Moon? Jesus Christ." Tomey hooted as he screeched around a curve. "You got a lot to learn, my friend. A whole lot to learn."

Jackson stared at Tomey, tried to figure out what the hell was happening. "Jesus, Bill! We blew that woman away. Sump shot that man right in the head."

"Shit, boy, you right off the turnip truck, now ain't ya?" Tomey took another drag and flicked the cigarette butt out the window.

Jackson watched the road rush by. This was the night he was to become a man. He had felt okay about destroying the bar where whoring was going on right under the noses of Solomon's Rock. Beating up Lonnie Brim got his blood rushing, and the fire excited him, made his heart race. But then something went wrong. He had never expected to be in a car with Bill Tomey, a colored woman in the trunk, her body shot full of holes. Here he was, deep into the night, headed for a place to put Mary Brim in the ground.

We got to the Rock and Tomey drove the car to a mossy spot out behind it. Tomey told me I had to dig. He claimed it was my initiation. Bastard handed me the shovel, then sat on the car, smoking cigarettes and rattling on about how good it would be for me now that I was on the inside, now that I knew the score.

It took Jackson almost an hour to dig the hole deep enough. After awhile, he didn't even hear Tomey. He heard only the strike of metal against the earth, the buzz still ringing in his ear from the roaring gunfire, and the memory of the fire cackling.

It was after midnight when Jackson dragged the woman's body into the pit. Mary Brim fell flat on her back with a heavy thud. When Jackson looked down in the hole, Mary's eyes stared up at him, taunting him, damning him. He threw the first shovelful of dirt over her face, trying to blot out the eyes, but the dirt slid off and the eyes still glared up in defiance. Jackson realized he was crying. The tears burned out of his eyes as he slammed the shovel into the pile of dirt, tossing on load after load, as fast as he could go. Maniacally. He could still see a single eye, blacker than the dirt around it, mocking him, promising vengeance. A whine squealed from Jackie's throat as he madly tossed dirt into the hole.

"Jesus Christ," said Tomey as he approached Jackson. "Chill out, man. I can dig for…"

In a lightning motion, Jackie whipped the shovel up, slamming it into Tomey's head. The sharp edge of the shovel sliced Tomey's face from his right eye to the jaw line. "Goddamn it!" he yelled as he scrambled back, blood spurting out of the wound. "You are one crazy fuck! You see what you did? You sliced me right open. I'm gonna need a doctor now." But Jackson just kept throwing dirt on the grave. "You ain't got the balls for this kind of shit. Next time, you should stay at home with the women. Goddamn you!"

But Jackie didn't hear. He filled the hole as the tears continued to strain out. The tears felt like the slice of a razor streaking down his face. Finally, he was finished. He backed away from the grave, dropped the shovel, and started walking.

I didn't know where I was headed. I just started walking. Walking just as fast as I could. Tomey was screaming at me, asking me what the hell I was doing. The side of his face was still all bloody. But I just kept on walking.

Didn't say a damn thing. Didn't even slow down. I just got out to the highway and headed south.

Jackson was still walking fast, his eyes straight ahead, when Tomey pulled the car alongside him.

"C'mon, Jackie. Get in the car, man." He was holding a towel, now soaked red, against the side of his face.

But Jackson didn't even acknowledge Tomey. He just kept walking.

"Goddamn it. Get yo' ass in the car! What am I s'posed to tell yo' daddy now? Stop this bullshit and get the fuck in." He swung open the passenger door, but Jackson just kept walking.

"You are a fool. Don't you get it? This is how it works. You play the game now and you get the power later. You want to change things? Work on it then. The old men, they get tired. They want to retire and fish all fucking day. Then we move in, man. Don't you see that? Then it's our turn. We get to be the lawyers and the judges and the doctors and the chiefs. C'mon now. Get in the goddamn car and we'll talk about it."

But Jackson just walked.

Finally, Tomey slammed on the brakes and got out of the car. "Fuck you, then!" he yelled at the figure heading down Route 106. The towel was now nothing but a bloody mass that Tomey pressed against the side of his head. "Fuck you! You can go straight to hell! You're out now, Moon. You know that? You cain't ever come back! Never! Goddamn it, you might as well be dead yo'self!"

The voice kept raging as Jackie walked on. He crested a hill and turned onto Junction 13. In the distance, he could still hear the screeching voice, cracking now, telling Jackson how he could never come back....

47

Aunt Frank looked up to see Ellis ducking into her room. He closed the door behind him.

"Well, hello, boy," she said.

"Do you know who I am?" Ellis asked.

"Do *you* know who you are?"

Ellis laughed. "Sure sounds to me like you got your wits about you."

"That's what I been tryin' to tell these folks."

"I've been talking to Jackson," Ellis said. "He wants me to get you out of here."

Frank got up and walked toward the door. "Let's go," she said.

"Hold on a second," said Ellis, but Frank already had the door open and was walking out into the hall. Ellis followed her along the hallway, peering around nervously. He was whispering to her, "We can't just walk out of here. Bailey signed some kind of order."

"Pooh on that Bailey Sump. He's as bad as that no-account daddy of his."

"We need some kind of plan, Frank."

"Plan is, we act like we goin' for a walk and we don't never come back."

"But I don't even have a car. I took a cab here."

"I got a car," Frank said.

"Do you have the keys with you?" he asked.

Aunt Frank gave him a suspicious look. She might be crazy, but she was no fool. "You get me out of here," she said. "And I'll get you the keys."

Ellis smiled. "We'll need the car to get away," he said. "You give me the keys and I'll park out back. You know, wait for you."

"I can't get out of here by myself," she said. "They won't even let me outside without an escort. I got to be with family or one of the nurses."

Ellis rubbed his chin.

"You can walk me out," Frank went on. "Take me out the gates and hide me in the bushes by the wall. Then you can go get the car and pick me up."

"I'm not going to hide you in the bushes," Ellis said.

Aunt Frank looked at him. "I'd rather be in the bushes than flyin' through the air, waitin' for them colored boys to catch me."

"I suppose, if that were the choice, I'd rather be in the bushes, too."

"I'm duckin' in the bushes," Frank said, "if you like it or not."

Ellis had to follow his aunt down the hall. He was surprised how fast her gait was. "This is crazy," he said.

"Ain't you heard?" Frank replied. "That's me. Crazier'n a March hare." They walked down the steps and out the front door.

"You'll have to sign her out," a nurse told Ellis. She was sitting at a reception desk across from the front door. Ellis looked back at the door Frank had just walked through, then went over to the desk to sign her out. By the time Ellis was out in the yard, Frank was heading down the red cobblestone walk toward the front gate. He ran to catch up to her.

"Are you really going to hide in the bushes?" Ellis asked.

Frank stopped on the walk, considering. "The keys are at the house. In the desk drawer by the back door." She shook her head. "Waitin' for you to find 'em, I could be in them bushes for days."

"I think I could find a set of keys in a drawer."

Frank looked back at the doors she had walked out of, then ahead to the gate. It was her only clear opportunity. She had to take it. She started walking again, toward the gate, toward freedom.

Ellis laughed. "What the fuck?" he said, throwing up his hands.

"You watch yo' mouth," Frank told him.

"So where are we going?"

"We got to get to my house. Get the keys."

"Then what?"

She peered over at him. "Didn't Jackson tell you?"

"The Grand Canyon?"

A smile rising to her lips, Frank just kept walking – right out the front gate.

They were walking beside the outer wall, along Oakdale Drive, Frank's eyes wide with excitement. She was out.

"We can't just walk down the road, Frank. They're going to be looking for you any minute now."

Frank stopped. She turned around and walked back to the entrance of the grounds. There was a bicycle rack there. She looked over the three bikes in the rack. Two of them were locked up. She grabbed the one that wasn't and rolled it away from the rack.

Ellis laughed again. "You stealing a bicycle now?"

Frank looked over at Ellis. "Borrowin' it," she said. Slowly, she brought her feet up over the bar and sat on the seat. She started rolling down the side of the street. Her arms trembled and the bike swayed, but she was riding it. She started to pedal. Ellis jogged beside her.

"Are you going to ride this bike to the Grand Canyon? Is that your plan now?"

Frank said nothing. All her energies were focused on the bike, on steering it down the road. She ran through a stop light, and a car braked hard as she rolled in front of it. Ellis was running faster now, trying to keep up with the bicycle.

"Jesus, you're really doing it. You're really going to take off."

She said nothing. Her eyes were pinned to the road ahead. She tried to keep the front wheel straight. Suddenly, she was slowing down. She tried to pedal, but the bike kept slowing. Ellis was holding onto the middle bar, stopping her.

"Let me go now!" Frank cried.

"Move back," Ellis said, hopping over the bar and putting his feet on the pedals. "You just sit up on the seat."

And so Ellis took over. A grown man, still dressed in his one-thousand-dollar pinstriped suit, pedaling down the road as fast as he could. He stood up to get better leverage, then took off his tie and threw it to the wind. Frank was amazed at how expert her nephew was on a bicycle. He shot across the street, veered through a parking lot, and swung out onto a side street.

Frank cried out with joy. She held her hands out to her sides, as if pretending to be an airplane. "Hold onto my waist now," Ellis implored. His aunt was having entirely too much fun. They turned right, up over a bridge that ran across the railroad tracks. Halfway home.

Frank made a joyous sound. It reminded Ellis of the sound the little wiener whistle made, the kind that used to come in the Oscar Mayer hot dog package. Now Frank was holding out her two arms and her two legs, a regular daredevil. "C'mon now," Ellis cried out, "Please hold onto me." But apparently Frank intended to enjoy her newfound freedom. Perhaps she no longer took her freedom for granted, or maybe she figured she didn't have much freedom left and wanted to savor it. In any case, she made it hard for Ellis to steer the bike. He wove across the road.

They turned up Lancaster Street and bumped up over a curb. Frank screamed with excitement as Ellis steered expertly through the woods, even when leaves slapped against his face. Frank hunched up against him, holding tight. They came out in her backyard, and the bike rolled to a stop. Ellis tried to put a foot down on one side but Frank lunged the other way, sending the bike crashing to the ground. Frank and Ellis tumbled across the grass.

Frank laughed so hard she couldn't get up. It was the ride of her life.

"We don't have much time," Ellis told her. This was his chance at freedom, too. They could sell the car, maybe get something for it as an antique. It was in good shape, and he could actually show the salesman the little old lady that had driven the thing only on Sundays. Of course, they would never have enough money to make it to the Grand Canyon, but they could head south, towards Florida, try to reach the ocean. He had some friends in Fort Lauderdale, and there was a large elderly community in Florida, wasn't there? Maybe he could clean the rooms at one of those elderly condo complexes, and then they would take Frank in and give her the care she would need.

Aunt Frank was struggling with the bicycle now, pulling it across the yard instead of rolling it. Ellis gave her a hand.

"What are you doing?"

Frank wheezed as she pulled on the handlebars. "We got to get this bicycle hid away, case somebody comes lookin' for it."

"If somebody comes now, the jig's up."

Ellis and Frank stuffed the bike under some hedges. Ellis headed for the back door, but when he turned back to his aunt, she was studying the house with awe.

"What now?" asked Ellis.

Frank looked at Ellis, her eyes wide. "They really did move my house," she said.

"Of course they moved it. What did you think?"

"I figgered it was all a trick," she said.

Ellis threw up his hands. "Where are the car keys, Frank?"

Frank peered at her nephew quizzically. The house, now safely tucked in a new location, threw her for a loop. "We still in Georgia?" she asked.

"Of course we're in Georgia. We're still in Solomon's Rock, for God's sake."

Frank looked back up at the house, then surveyed the surroundings. "We must be in Alabama," she said.

Ellis sighed. "Does that make any sense? You think I drove that bike all the way to Alabama?"

Frank considered. "I reckon not," she conceded.

"We're in Solomon's Rock, and we've got to get a move on if we want to make it out of here. Where are the car keys?"

Ellis could see Frank concentrating, trying to make her brain shift gears. "The car keys," she said. "Yes, the car keys."

She walked up the back steps and into the house. She looked around the room and up at the ceiling. "They put it back just how it was," she said in awe. The car keys were in a drawer by the door, exactly where she had left them. She pulled the keys out and looked at them as if she had found some secret treasure. They walked together to the old Chrysler. Ellis wanted the keys but Frank wouldn't give them to him. She insisted on driving.

When they were on the road, Ellis asked Frank where they were going. "Shouldn't we be heading for the interstate?"

"I got to go by the property first."

"The property? What the fuck?"

"Now, I done tole you about that mouth," she said. "I got to pick up somethin'."

"Pick up something? There's nothing left over there." But Frank ignored Ellis. She casually drove to the spot where her house once stood. She got out of the car and walked through the back yard, into a stand of trees. Ellis came after her, throwing his arms into the air.

"We really don't have time for a summer stroll."

"Hush up" was all Frank said.

She stopped in the middle of a small clearing and looked up at the trees, then at the ground. She bent over and brushed aside some pine needles to reveal what looked like a pair of iron handles clasped together with a Master lock.

"What the hell...?" said Ellis as Frank pulled a necklace over her head. There were two keys on the necklace. Frank used one to open the lock on the handles. She stepped back.

"Pull that on open," she told Ellis.

Ellis reached down and tugged on one of the handles. A three-by-five metal door appeared out of the pine needles as he pulled the handle up. The door swung open, and Frank stepped down onto a small set of concrete steps that descended into the earth.

Ellis watched, slack jawed, as his aunt disappeared into the hole. "Are we going to hide away in there?" he asked.

"Don't be silly," said Frank as she shuffled around in the pit. She emerged on the steps with a large lockbox, which she handed up to Ellis. He took the box and set it on the ground next to the bulkhead.

Frank came back out of the shelter and used the second key on the necklace to unlock the box.

When the box opened, Ellis almost fainted. Packets of neatly wrapped bills were stacked in the box, hundred dollar bills on top.

"Holy God in heaven," he said, but Frank wasn't listening. She pulled some folders out of an organizer on the other side of the box and flipped through them.

"How much is in here?" Ellis asked in amazement.

"That ain't a proper question in polite company," said Frank.

"Asking your salary or how much you got in the bank, that's not polite. Somebody pulls out a box full of cash, it's the most proper question I can come up with."

Frank said nothing. She was studying the cash ledger; Ellis was staring at the bundles of cash.

Frank said, "We got to send these records to Jackson, once we're on the road."

"The records? But why...?"

"He says he needs them. Somethin' 'bout a property dispute." Frank smiled. "Course he's fibbin' me about that."

"Fibbin' you?"

"He thinks I don't know the truth about the money."

"What do you know, Frank?"

Aunt Frances said nothing.

Ellis understood now. "That's from the payoffs," he said. "The payoffs for building permits, contracts."

Frank looked down at the ledger. "Them TOI folks, they took my land from me. I figger they can pay me off, pay me for the land, and then I can get them in a whole heap of trouble for it."

Ellis raised an eyebrow.

Frank looked back up. "Seems fair to me," she said.

Ellis smiled. His aunt could be a surprising woman. "So you know it's dirty money?"

Frank was putting the records back in the box. She closed it up, locked the box, then stood up straight and peered at her nephew. "If me and you go'n run off together, we gots to set us some ground rules."

"Ground rules?"

"First off, this is my money, free and clear. My husband worked hard all his life, and he left me this money as my inheritance. I won't abide by you slanderin' his name, nor your daddy's neither. Fact, I don't wanna hear one bad word 'bout nobody in this family. You hear me?"

Ellis nodded. "Yes ma'am."

"And we are goin' to the Grand Canyon and gettin' us some donkeys to ride." Frank turned and walked back toward the car. "You bring that box on along," she said to Ellis.

Ellis picked up the lockbox. "Jackie didn't say anything about donkeys."

Frank ignored him.

O ut in the driveway, Aunt Frank pulled out the pins that she always kept in her hair. The long gray locks tumbled down below her waist. Ellis had never seen her hair down before. It was striking.

"We've got to dump the car," Ellis said. "They'll be looking for it."

Frank thought about that. "I want me a red car," she announced. "The kind where the top comes down."

"Well, I don't know if we can find...."

"I know where it is," she said. "Out on the Powell lot. Shiny red with a black top. That's the one I want."

Ellis hiked his shoulders. "Okay," he said.

It would be the time of her life, driving to the Grand Canyon with her nephew. She could already feel the wind in her hair.

"And my donkey," said Frank, "I want to name her Mabel."

48

Jackie had to drive all the way to the town of Columbus to find what he was looking for. The house was set back from a winding road, the green front lawn dipping down at its center into a small fish pond like a cereal bowl with a few spoonfuls of milk left in it. Jackson parked on the road and walked up the gravel driveway. As he passed the large white house, he saw – behind the house and off to the left – an old man working a hoe in the midst of a small garden. Jackie veered off the driveway and approached the man. He stopped at the edge of an elm shadow. "Mr. Stone?" Jackie asked.

The old man stopped hoeing and looked up into the hot sun. His light blue cotton slacks were held up by red suspenders. Ovals of sweat soaked the white shirt around his armpits. He pulled down the brim of his straw hat against the bright morning light. Gnats swirled around the wisps of white hair that poked from under the hat. The corners of his blue eyes turned down, and his thin lips quivered. The smell of green vines and fertilizer wafted in the air.

"Can I help you?" the old man asked.

"I'm looking for a Mr. Virgil Stone."

"Well, I reckon you found him then."

Jackson bowed his head in greeting. "You used to own Martin and Stone Construction. That right?"

The man squinted his eyes at Jackson, then resumed his work with the hoe. "That was a long time ago."

"Yes, sir. I understand. I just had some questions about it."

"Is that right?" The man pulled clumps of weeds away from a patch of cucumber plants. The leaves were yellowed. He bent down and picked a cucumber from a vine, placing it carefully in a basket at his feet. Red tomatoes bobbed among the row of green plants at the garden's far edge.

"The company was investigated by the Sachs Commission a few years back. Something about fraud of county construction contracts?"

The man didn't look up. He chopped at the earth with his hoe. "It was more than a few years back, young man. And the company was cleared by that commission."

"Yes, sir, I know. But I found some articles from a few years later, after the company went under. Turns out, the county had to hire another construction firm to clean up the mess. Faulty wiring, cheap materials. One of the buildings was even dumping sewage into a local stream."

"If you're looking for some kind of settlement, son, you've come to the wrong place. I cain't hardly pay my own bills."

"I'm not looking for a settlement," Jackson said. "I'm just looking for the truth."

The man bent over his hoe and laughed. Everyone in Solomon's Rock seemed to have the same reaction when Jackson brought up the subject of truth.

Jackie went on. "I just can't figure out how a powerful investigating committee could have missed such obvious abuses. When the senator closed the investigation, he said it had been thorough and rigorous."

"If he said that, I would have to believe him. He was an honest man."

"Except, maybe, when it came to his crusade against Twelve Oaks."

The old man stopped working the hoe, but his eyes remained on the ground.

. "You owned the land right next to the senator's," Jackson said. "You were the last refuge, you might say. Senator Sachs must have been pretty worried about TOI getting hold of that plot."

"Reckon so," the man said softly.

"Is that how it worked, Mr. Stone?" Jackson asked outright. "The senator agreed not to expose the construction fraud if you refused to sell your land to the theme park?"

The old man leaned heavily on the handle of the hoe. The straw hat sagged over his eyes. Rivulets of sweat poured down the deep wells in Stone's neck.

Stone looked over at Jackson, cocking the hat back out of his eyes. "You got this all figgered out, son. What you need me for?"

"I just wanted to run it by someone who would know. Make sure I've got all the facts right."

Stone looked off to the north as if seeking a refuge. "Talk about being betwixt a rock and a hard place," he said, shaking his head slowly. "Mr. Grant threatened to kill me if I didn't sell him the land; Senator Sachs was going to ruin me if I did sell it."

"Why didn't Grant just kill you anyway, if he wanted the land?" ·

Stone shrugged. "I had heirs. My wife. Two daughters. The only way Grant could get the land was if I sold it to him. Hell, I wanted to sell it off anyway. Who wants to look out the kitchen window at a damn roller coaster? A roller coaster ride through the burning of Atlanta. Can you beat that? What will they come up with next?"

"So you told Grant you would sell, but only if Sachs disappeared."

Stone's eyes dimmed. He seemed resigned to telling the story, as if he had expected this moment to come: When a young man would appear in his garden, asking for the truth. He began to move the hoe absently across the earth.

"I had to be sure that Sachs wouldn't send me to prison," Stone said in a low tone. "That's all I told Grant. I told him that I had to be sure."

"Well," said Jackie. "Grant sure found a way for you to be sure."

"I didn't think Grant would kill him," Stone insisted. "Sachs was holed up with that nigra woman. Grant was going to threaten to expose him. I told Grant I didn't think that would work. Sachs was as crazy to stop that theme park as Grant was crazy 'bout building it. I didn't think Sachs would give in to blackmail over the woman. Grant said he had something else. Something worse."

"He threatened to take the child," Jackson told Stone. "Grant had a black man that would claim to be the father of the little girl. Sachs was faced with losing the family he had made, losing his only daughter."

Stone nodded as one of the last details from the dark episode clicked into place for him.

"I didn't think he would kill him," Stone said again. Perhaps he thought that if he said the words enough, he might actually come to believe them. "I just told Grant that I had to be sure. I had to be sure that Sachs wouldn't talk." A strained frown bent Stone's lips, and his chin slumped onto his chest.

"You can never be sure what a man might do," Jackson said. "Not until he's buried in the ground."

Virgil Stone nodded solemnly. "I reckon that's true," he said. The old man made a sour face as his mind dealt with the things it had tried to stash away.

"I didn't come here to hurt you, Mr. Stone. I just needed to find out some things for myself."

"You cain't hurt me," the old man said dully. "Nothin' can hurt me no more."

Jackie looked into the creased eyes that turned up to him. He tried to look into the soul of a man whose spirit had died.

After a moment, Stone shook the dirt off of his hoe. "I best be gettin' in the house," he said. "Doctor says I shouldn't get too much sun."

Jackson watched as the man walked between the rows of cucumbers and tomato plants. He had a hitch in his step as he walked toward the house. He carried the pain nobly, the way a man will once he has learned to live with injury. Stone came to a stop in the middle of the gravel driveway. He took off his hat and ran a hand through his thin white hair. As he went to put the hat back on his head, he fumbled it, and the hat fell to the gravel. Stone just looked down at it for a moment, then walked away toward the house, leaving the hat behind like a lost thought.

Jackson had stopped back by the hospital on his way home from Columbus. It was early evening, but the sun still burned high in the sky, and heat settled on the ground like a thick fog. Jackie took the elevator to his father's floor and walked slowly down the hallway, passing a nurse with a food cart. Jackson stood in the hallway by his father's room for a moment, still sorting through the thoughts in his head, before he lifted his fist and tapped gently on the door. When no one answered the knock, he entered the room quietly, peeking around the door as he opened it.

His father was sleeping. In spite of the oxygen tubes feeding his nose, his breath was labored, as if he were trying to breath beneath a wet blanket. Three yellow carnations drooped on a nearby table. Brownish liquid from a bag beside the bed drained down through a clear tube to the needle in his father's left arm. The right side of his father's head was seared with dark red burns, the hair on that side shorn away and the corner of the lip misshapen. Jackie wondered how much time his father had left. The doctor had said he was in stable condition, but Jackie remembered the solemn tone to the doctor's voice and the doubt in his eyes. It was almost time to make a move on the accountant, but Jackie was wondering if he was up to the task.

The door to the hospital room opened, and Bailey Sump walked in. He held his trooper hat in his hand, and his uniform was freshly pressed. Bailey turned a stern look on Jackson.

"What's wrong, Bailey?"

"Why don't you step on out into the hallway. Let yo' daddy sleep in peace."

"What's going on?"

"Just come on out here," Bailey said as he turned and walked out into the hall.

Jackson put a hand on his father's leg for a moment, then stepped out into the hallway. The sheriff's deputy, Aaron Coop, was standing behind Bailey's right arm, hat also in his hand, his uniform rumpled, a coffee stain beside the smudged star. Deputy Coop's black hair was slicked back, away from his long face and over his elongated ears. Dark eyebrows hung over droopy brown eyes.

"What are you doing here?" Jackson's eyes were still on the deputy, but his question was for the sheriff.

Bailey nodded at the deputy, and Coop walked around behind Jackie. "Put your hands behind your back," the deputy said.

"What the hell?"

"Jackson Ezekial Moon," Bailey intoned, "you are under the arrest for the murder of Mary Brim."

"What?" Jackson barked as the deputy clamped on the handcuffs.

"You have the right to remain silent. Anything you do say can and will be used against you in a court of law."

"What the hell is going on here? Mary Brim?"

"You have the right to an attorney. If you cannot afford an attorney, one will be appointed to you free of charge."

"Goddamn it, Bailey."

The sheriff stopped talking, sighed heavily, and looked into Jackson's eyes. "Judge Tomey is dead," he said.

"Tomey? When? How?" Jackie was trying to slow the spinning thoughts in his head. "What does that have to do with me? I don't..."

"His suicide note says the two of you buried Mary Brim out by the Rock," Bailey said. "The body was right where he said it would be."

"Jesus Christ," Jackson said as the deputy pushed him forward, guiding him down the hallway of the hospital. Two nurses stopped talking when they saw the spectacle of the arrest in progress. "There's a lot more to it than that," Deputy Coop put in.

"The shovel you used was still in the judge's basement, Jackie. It had Mary Brim's blood on it, and your fingerprints were all over the handle."

Jackson remembered his heated conversation in the judge's chambers at the courthouse. Tomey's ace in the hole. He had kept the shovel that implicated Jackson. "Jesus, Bailey, c'mon. I did not kill Mary Brim."

"We have three witnesses. They say that twenty years ago, you picked up Lonnie Brim's gun and shot his wife with it. Said you laughed about it."

"Witnesses? Your father, right? Your father and a couple of his cronies."

"Don't say anything more," Bailey warned. "You need an attorney."

"Where am I supposed to find an attorney that Grant and your father don't have stuffed in their pockets?"

"Shut up, Jackie."

"Listen to me, goddamn it. There must have been a half dozen bullets in that body."

"The body's too decomposed to make out bullet wounds. There's some broken bones, but it could have happened when you threw her in the pit."

Jackson and the two officers stepped into an elevator. Muzak played on the speaker. The doors shushed closed.

"The bullets must still be down in the grave," Jackson said. "I'm telling you, they've got to be. Her body was all shot up. There must be a whole assortment of bullet types."

A look of concern crossed Bailey's face. "If they're there, we'll find them."

"We? Who is 'we'?" Jackson demanded. Bailey kept his eyes focused on the floor numbers counting down over the elevator door. "Your damn father is at the burial site, isn't he? You think there'll be any credible evidence after he's done? He's setting me up, goddamn it. Can't you see that? The bastard is setting me up."

"Just don't talk anymore," Bailey pleaded. "You're making things worse for yourself."

"How much worse can they get? You're arresting me for murder!"

The elevator eased to a stop, and Bailey took Jackson under the arm, leading him past the admissions desk and through the automatic exit doors. The deputy placed Jackson into the backseat of the police cruiser, putting a hand on Jackie's head as he did it. The door thumped shut, and for a moment, Jackson was alone with the silence and his worst fears. He had thought Bailey could be his ally, his one trump card on the side of the law. All his hopes were crashing down around him.

The sheriff got into the front passenger seat, his deputy behind the wheel. Coop started the engine and they pulled away from the hospital. Jackson looked at Bailey through the grid of steel bars that separated the front seat from the back.

"You've got to listen to me, Bailey. I know why they took out Sachs. His neighbor, Virgil Stone, was defrauding county construction contracts. Sachs ran a commission investigating it. He got some dirt on Stone and threatened to ruin him if he sold off his land. Grant needed that land for the theme park. Stone agreed to sell, *if* Grant could keep Sachs quiet. It's in the public record, for Christ's sake. Stone was using faulty materials, dumping waste. There's no way that commission could have missed it. Sachs closed the investigation and cleared Stone's name. Check it out, goddamn you."

While Jackson spoke, Bailey kept his eyes squarely on the road ahead.

"Keep your mouth shut back there," Deputy Coop commanded.

Bailey stuck a finger at his deputy. "Shut up, Aaron."

"Why're you snapping at me? I was just…"

"Just shut up and drive."

Jackie's mouth fell open. He couldn't process what was happening to him. They had found the body of Mary Brim and a shovel with her blood and Jackie's fingerprints on it. Bill Sump was out at the Rock, sifting through the evidence, lining up the witnesses, making everything nice and tidy for the county prosecutor. Sump was burying Jackson just as surely as Jackie had buried Mary Brim.

Both men sat quietly in the front seat as the cruiser stopped at a red light and idled. Coop glanced over his shoulder at the prisoner, then turned his head back to the road.

"I buried that woman," Jackie blurted. "But I didn't kill her. I swear to it."

"Anything you say can and will be used against you in a court of law," Coop pointed out.

"I done told you to shut up," Bailey said.

"I'm just letting this boy know his rights."

"We told him his rights already. You just go on and drive."

Bailey waved at the light that had changed to green. Coop eased across the intersection.

"You don't really believe Tomey killed himself," Jackson said. "C'mon. That old bastard? No way."

"Just hush up," said Bailey. "We'll be to the courthouse directly."

"Who are these fucking witnesses? They're lying. You must know they're lying."

The sheriff didn't respond. Jackie collapsed back against the seat, the handcuffs grating against his wrists. He felt scared and utterly alone. A pain throbbed at the base of his throat as if someone had slammed a hammer against his breastbone. The cruiser pulled up into the sheriff's reserved spot. Two boys on bicycles stared in at the prisoner in the backseat of the police car, gawking at the man who had just been charged with murder.

49

B ridgett moved into the doorway of Thomas Dade's office. She savored the look on the man's face. He was in a panic, madly punching the keys of his computer, his eyes darting across the screen. Bridgett had dressed up for the occasion. She wore a sleek white dress, sleeveless, and low white heels. She leaned a shoulder against Dade's door frame.

"Looking for something?" Bridgett asked.

He looked up, his eyes flooded with confusion. The sleeves of his white shirt were rolled up to the elbow, the blue tie loose and askew, his suit coat draped across the desk. Sweat beaded on his high forehead, and his designer glasses were starting to fog up.

"I don't know. I…" Dade stammered. "Something's gone wrong. It must be the computer. Maybe the network … Has anyone been messing with the accounts?"

"The Twelve Oaks investment?" Bridgett asked casually.

That stopped him. He looked up at her.

"It isn't there," she said.

"What are you talking about?"

"It isn't there," she said again.

"What do you mean, 'It isn't there'? Where the hell is it?"

Bridgett stepped slowly into the accountant's office and up to his desk. She put her purse on the desk and leaned over so her arms were on either side of the purse. She precisely placed the tips of her fingers on the polished oak finish. She wanted to be close to the gun that Jackson had given her, the pistol tucked safely in her purse, the safety clicked off.

"Do you know that Grant took away my daddy's land?" she asked. "He didn't want to sell it. It drove him out of his mind, losing that property. He died six months after moving out."

Dade looked at Bridgett like she had lost her wits. He held up his sweaty palms. "What the hell are you babbling about?"

"I'm telling you about my daddy," she said.

"Your daddy?" Dade said. "What in God's name does your daddy have to do with this funds transfer? I'm telling you the money's not..." He stopped in mid-sentence as recognition passed in the panicked eyes. His hands dropped to his sides, and the shoulders slumped down. He looked steadily at his assistant for a long moment. "You?"

Bridgett looked back at her boss. "You were always so careless with your accounts, Thomas. Writing your passwords down, sharing access codes with your coworkers. Leaving electronic files open. I guess I owe you my thanks. After all, you set everything up. All I had to do was grab the money before you did."

His mouth fell open, then the awe in his eyes clouded over with anger. "I trusted you," he said.

That made Bridgett laugh. "Oh, I'm sorry that I took the money before you and Marston got a chance to steal it."

Dade's eyebrows shot up. Bridgett knew about Marston.

"You can't do this," he said.

She shrugged. "It's done."

"Bullshit, it's done. You can't do this to me, goddamn it. This is my life we're talking about."

He bolted out of the chair and started across the office. Bridgett reached into her purse and pulled out Jackson's .38 revolver. The accountant stopped cold.

"What the...?"

"We all need to stay calm here," Bridgett said.

"You bitch."

"Now, now," Bridgett said. "There's no call for that kind of language. Why don't you just head on back to your side of the desk?" Bridgett pointed the gun at Dade's chair. The accountant walked back around the desk.

"You won't get away with this," Dade said, but he knew it sounded desperate.

"You mean *you* won't get away with it," said Bridgett.

"What are you talking about now?"

Bridgett shrugged. "It was your log-in, your password, your access codes, your transfer. Turns out you were in cahoots with this ex-con in town – Cecil Blanks? You've been making calls from that phone there on your desk, setting it all up. You called him in his room over at the General Lee, just before you transferred some of the stolen money into his girlfriend's bank account. Some stripper down in Atlanta."

"Cecil Blanks?" Dade said, trying to sort it out. "He was that goon who came into my office. The one who works for Marston."

"He was the one who first called me. He had this slick idea about stealing Grant's money before Marston could. Poor Cecil didn't realize that Jackson had set him up. Jackie told me Cecil would call to recruit me for his scheme. Turns out, Mr. Blanks was an easy fish to play."

The accountant sank down in his chair. "Jackie Moon?" he said. "He was in on this, too?" He said it as if his best friend had betrayed him. Dade's face seemed to crack with confusion and defeat. Bridgett almost felt sorry for him. Almost.

"The way I see it," Bridgett explained, "you have three choices here. You can go to Marston and explain to him how your assistant stole the money right out from under your nose. He may kill you because he doesn't believe such a story, or he may kill you because he does believe it, or he may kill you just because I hear he has an awful temper. On the other hand, you could always go to Grant's people, tell them how you were planning to steal the money but someone else beat you to it. That might work."

Dade looked up wearily. "And the third choice?"

Bridgett pulled an envelope out of her purse. She placed it on the desk and slid it over to Dade. "You have an electronic plane ticket in your name. A one-way flight from Atlanta to the Grand Caymans. You'll have to hurry if you want to make the trip. No time for phone calls, no time for reflection. In that envelope is an anonymous account number. Keep your mouth shut, lay low, and you'll get regular transfers. You can live a nice life. Enjoy the sun. Bop around the islands. You will be comfortable, as long as you don't get careless."

Dade looked into Bridgett's eyes. "Once I run, they'll think I have all the money. They'll think I took it."

"They're going to think that anyway," Bridgett said. "You can either take the plane trip or hang out here and take your chances with Marston and Grant. That's a tough squeeze."

Dade shook his head and turned to his window. He took off his glasses and rubbed his eyes, then heaved a huge sigh before putting the glasses back on. "I never cared much for this town anyway," he said.

Bridgett drove her silver Mazda down Greenville Street. She was heading out to the General Lee. She was thinking about that first phone call from Cecil Blanks. She had been waiting for it. Jackson told her what Cecil had planned. She had answered the phone after three rings.

"Hello?"

"Hello. Is this Bridgett Baines?"

"Who is this?"

"My name is Cecil Blanks. I'm at the prison down here in Florida. I share a cell with your boyfriend."

"My boyfriend?"

"Your old flame, whatever. Jackson Moon."

"I see."

"Well, you know, sharing a cell and all, we get to talking about all kinds of stuff, and he happened to mention you."

"Is that so? And do you make it a habit to telephone the people Jackson mentions to you in prison?"

"A habit? Well, no. I wouldn't call it a habit."

"Are you lonely? Did you just need someone to talk to?"

"Lonely? Well hell, I'm in prison. Kind of hard not to get lonely sometimes."

Bridgett decided that sarcasm was lost on this man. "What is it you want from me?"

Cecil cleared his throat. "It's just that Jackie mentioned how you went to work for this accountant – Dade, is it? – and I happen to know a thing or two about the guy."

"Such as?"

"Well, for starters, he handles money for Michael Grant."

There was a long silence on the other end of the line. Finally Bridgett spoke up. "That's none of my business and certainly none of yours."

"You just might be wrong about that, missy."

"I'm hanging up now."

"Hold on there. You ever hear of Jake Marston? You might call him a business rival of Michael Grant's."

"I've heard of him," Bridgett said tentatively.

"Well, I got some very interesting information about Marston, Grant, and that accountant of yours."

Bridgett didn't respond, so Cecil went on: "It also involves a whole hell of a lot of money."

Still more silence.

"Hello?" Cecil prompted. "You still there?"

"I'm here."

"You interested?"

There was another short pause from Bridgett. "I'm listening," she said.

"It's pretty simple really," Cecil said. "Grant needs to move some money through the accounts. Marston knows it, and he's got your accountant by the balls. He's gonna make Dade transfer Grant's money to a different offshore account. The way I see it, with you working the computers for Dade, we just need to get to the money before Marston does, move the cash to an account of our own."

Cecil waited. This was the moment. Would the girl go for it?

"I'm not sure," she said. "You're messing with some dangerous people."

"That's why we have to cover our tracks," Cecil said. "Seems to me, you should be able to pin it on the accountant."

Bridgett made it sound as if she were warming to the idea. "That could be arranged."

Cecil was getting excited. "That's what I'm tellin' ya. It could be arranged. Slicker than shit. We're talking about a gold mine here."

"Slow down now, Mr. Blanks. We need to think this thing through."

"I already thought it through. It's cake, baby."

"Stealing money from Michael Grant isn't cake. We need to be very careful."

"Sure we do," said Cecil, trying to stay calm so he didn't scare the Baines girl off. "That's my motto. You gotta be careful."

There was silence on the line as Bridgett pretended to think the scheme through. "What about Jackson Moon?"

"Jackie? Hell, I don't know. I guess we could pull him in on it if you want. The way I figgered it, why bring in another partner? He ain't got nothin' to offer us."

"I was thinking more in terms of setting him up for the fall," Bridgett said. It had been Jackson's idea. It would keep Cecil close by so Jackson could keep track of him, and it would be a good diversion to keep Cecil's mind busy, channel his thoughts to a bogus setup so he didn't notice the trap he was falling into. Bridgett believed Jackie wanted to be the fall guy so he wouldn't feel so bad when he turned the tables back on Cecil. If Cecil were willing to set up Jackie, then Cecil couldn't very well blame Jackson for doing the same thing.

"Setting up Jackie?" said Cecil. "Sounds like you two had a little falling out."

"His family has always worked for Grant – first his father, then his brother. The man is a scourge. Besides, he dumped me without so much as a word. We were two high school kids in love and he just took off. Next time I heard from him was from a prison phone."

"I guess it's true what they say," Cecil said. "There's no hell like a pissed-off woman."

"I've never heard that one," said Bridgett.

Cecil was still smiling. "So maybe we can get rich and you can have a little revenge on the side."

Bridgett didn't respond.

"You hear what I'm saying?"

"I hear you, Mr. Blanks."

"And about this 'Mr. Blanks' shit. Just call me Cecil."

"I'll be back in touch, Mr. Blanks. Don't do anything stupid before then."

Cecil didn't like the way the conversation was turning. "Just so we're clear here, missy: I'm running this operation."

"Is that so?" said Bridgett. "I work for the accountant. I know the computers. I have access to the accounts. And you're probably going to need some money, unless the pay for making license plates has gone up. I'd say I'm the one in charge here."

She had him there. Cecil grimaced. "Hey, the way I see it, we're partners. I ain't into power trips."

"That's good to hear. Like I said, I'll be in touch."

The phone line went dead.

"C'mon, baby," Cecil pleaded. "Let me see a little dance. Maybe slip out of them jeans."

Starry shook her head but she couldn't help smiling. She sat on a padded chair across from the queen-size bed, looking out the sliding glass doors to the pool below their balcony. Cecil had put on some music, thinking maybe it would get her in the mood to strip. He was sitting on the bed, a cigarette in his left hand, the right hand on his thigh. She thought he was funny, but she kept her clothes on.

Cecil said, "C'mon, just a quick peek at yo' titties" when the doorbell rang. He looked at her with pleading puppy-dog eyes as he walked over to the door.

It was Bridgett Baines. "What the hell you doin' here?" Cecil asked.

Bridgett didn't answer. She simply walked into the hotel room and nodded at Starry. The bed in the middle of the room, slightly mussed, had a picture of fruit over it. Across from the bed, there was a television set with a boombox on top of it. The set was bolted to its stand. Latin music blared from the small speakers of the boombox, and cigarette smoke wafted around the ceiling light. A thick moldy smell hung in the air.

Cecil closed the door and held a hand out to Bridgett. "Starry," he said. "This is Bridgett. Bridgett, Starry."

They looked at each other with equal discomfort. Bridgett pulled out a wooden chair close to the door and sat in it. There was a small desk wedged into the corner beside her. She put her purse on the desk, then moved it next to her on the chair. Cecil went back over to the bed and sat on the edge of it.

"What's going on?" Cecil asked, his eyes looking hungry. "Are we all set now? Is that what this is about?"

"Sort of," said Bridgett. "But I need you to listen closely. Try to concentrate on what I'm going to tell you." She felt like a mother trying to focus a child with attention deficit disorder. She walked over to the boombox, turned it off, and walked back to her chair. She folded her hands in her lap.

"I'm listening," Cecil said.

"This thing we've been working on," Bridgett began, her eyes shifting to Starry. "It isn't exactly what you imagined it to be."

"What are you talking about?" said Cecil.

"You know how we were going to set up Jackson?"

"Yeah, sure. You got him to set up an account. The plan is to pass the money through Jackie's account, make it look like he was working with the accountant."

"That's the right idea," said Bridgett, "but the details are a little different."

"The details?"

"The money passed through your account, Mr. Blanks. Or, technically, I guess it was your friend Starry's account. You were the mark, not Jackie."

At first, Cecil's eyes were blank, then – slowly – they closed. "Fuck."

"What's goin' on, Cecil?" asked Starry.

"Hold on a minute, honey."

"Don' t tell me to hold on. What's this got to do with me? Why is she talking about my checking account?"

Cecil looked over at her. "It's kind of complicated, sugar."

"You didn't even tell her?" Bridgett asked. "Did you steal the checkbook while the poor girl was asleep?"

"She wasn't sleeping," Cecil said. "She was in the shower."

Starry stared at Cecil. "You little bastard."

"Hold on, honey. I can explain all this. I thought we was go'n be drownin' in cash. I wanted you in on it. You woulda been happy, right? All of a sudden, you got six figures in yo' checkbook? It was go'n be a surprise. One hell of a surprise."

The stripper didn't know what to say. She just glared at Cecil.

Cecil looked back at Bridgett. "What happened with Jackson? We had him cold."

"Jackie's with me," Bridgett told him.

"He's with you? Since when?"

"Since the very beginning."

Cecil squinted his eyes. His mind was trying to go to work.

Bridgett laid it out for him. "Jackson knew what you had planned before you called me the first time. He found out from Clarence. I was waiting for your invitation to rip off Grant. We had you pegged from the start."

"But you can't hang this on me. You worked for the guy."

"The phone calls I made to you were from Dade's phone. The transfer was from his computer, and it went through your girlfriend's account. Everything points to you and Dade."

"Mother…" Cecil was up off the bed, but Bridgett had the .38 out before he had taken two complete steps. She pointed the barrel at Cecil.

Cecil froze. "You wouldn't shoot me," he said.

Bridgett shrugged. "We could blame that on Dade, too. He decided to cut out his partner and take all the money himself."

Cecil's mouth gaped. He stepped back slowly, his eyes pinned to the gun. He collapsed back on the bed.

"I don't get it," Cecil said. "The three of us could've been in on this from the beginning. We could've pinned it all on the accountant…."

"We couldn't trust you," Bridgett explained. "You have a big mouth, Mr. Blanks. That's what got you into this trouble in the first place. We couldn't have you hanging out at some strip joint, talking about your big score and throwing C-notes at the girls. We had to find a way to keep you quiet."

"Who says I'm gonna be quiet?"

"I guess that's up to you," Bridgett said. "But keeping quiet would be a lot safer for you."

Cecil's mind was still turning. His brow furrowed, and he worked his lips in and out, in and out. "So what I'm hearing," he said after a long moment, "is that Marston and Grant will be hunting me down, and I don't even get any of the fucking cash?"

"Who's Marston?" Starry asked.

"There's a way out," said Bridgett.

Cecil and Starry looked over at her. With the revolver still clutched in her right hand, she reached into her purse with the left and pulled out a small mailing envelope. She placed it carefully on the desk beside her.

"Both of you have a plane ticket waiting at Hartsfield International. The flight is bound for the Cayman Islands. You'll have to leave immediately to make it. In the envelope is a number to an anonymous account. You keep quiet, stay lost, and the account will take care of you both."

"The Cayman Islands? Where the fuck is that?"

"It's in the Caribbean. You'll like it."

Cecil thought about it. "How much money do we get?" he asked. To the very end, he was still wheeling and dealing. Despite herself, Bridgett had to admire the little man. He went up against Marston and Grant without flinching, used the girl's account number without the slightest ping from his conscience, and now – with his life on the line – he was bucking for the best terms he could get. The man had balls, she had to give him that. No brains, but the guy had balls you could bowl with.

"Enough" was Bridgett's answer. "You'll have enough to be comfortable."

The mind was still working, but the sour look on Cecil's face told Bridgett that the message was getting through. Running was his only choice. "If I run, I'm gonna look guilty as hell."

"You never struck me as the innocent type," Bridgett said.

Cecil cocked a smile. "You got yourself a point there," he had to admit.

Cecil rocked on the bed, his feet tapping the floor. He searched his brain for options, but he couldn't come up with any. "I'm not gonna let this happen," he said.

Bridgett shrugged. "You don't have much time to catch that flight," she said, then she got up and opened the door. She stuck Jackie's gun back in her purse, stepped out into the hall, and pulled the door closed behind her.

Thomas Dade came down the steps from the second floor of his two-story ranch, a packed suitcase in each hand. At the bottom of the stairs, he put the suitcases down and opened his front door. He turned to take one last look at the home he would leave behind. That's when he saw the figure sitting on the overstuffed leather lounger. Dade's stomach turned like a winch in his gut. He wondered if his heart was still beating.

"Are we taking a trip?" Michael Grant asked casually. He held a huge pistol in his right hand. The barrel seemed to stretch across the length of the room.

"I... I... My mother's sick," Dade said. "I'm going to visit her in Florida."

Grant rose up out of the chair and stepped across the living room, toward the entrance hall where Dade stood. He waved his gun at the two suitcases at the accountant's feet. "Were you planning on long-term care?" he asked.

Dade looked down at the suitcases, then back up at the Colt Anaconda in Grant's fist. He felt the panic racing up his throat. "I... She..." His mouth was wide open, but he could muster no words. "It wasn't me, Mr. Grant. I didn't steal your money. I swear to God."

Grant's eyes went cold. "Are you saying someone *did* steal my money?"

"It was the Baines girl. She took it right out from under my nose. Her and that old boyfriend of hers. The Moon fellow."

"Jackie Moon?" said Grant, the name like a poison in his mouth.

"Jackson Moon. Yes. They didn't give me any choice. They were going to pin it all on me. I had to run. I swear. I had to."

"You could've come to me, Thomas."

Dade didn't have a good answer for that. His mind wouldn't settle down, and his breath came in bursts, as if Grant were feeding air to him in gusts. "I was scared, Mr. Grant. I didn't know what else to do."

"You were scared," Grant said. "As scared as you are right now."

"No, sir."

"Then you understand my point," said Grant.

"You're on the run," Dade rattled on as a desperate idea leapt into his mind. "You've got to get away. They gave me an account, Mr. Grant. We can go to the Cayman Islands. You can hide out there, and we'll have plenty of money to work with."

Grant looked at the accountant doubtfully. "So you think I should run off with you so these assholes can dole out my own money to me?"

"You could get away. You wouldn't have to go to jail...."

Grant smiled. "I'll tell you what," he said. "I'll think about it."

Grant looked down at the floor, feigning deep thought. Dade held his breath. Sweat poured off his face. He felt his legs quiver, and a freshet of tears welled up out of his eyes. He dropped to one knee, as if proposing to the pornographer.

"Nah," said Grant, then he shot Thomas Dade in the face.

After Bridgett left, Cecil threw a few things in his duffel bag. "It's up to you, baby. I can say I'm sorry 'til the cows come on home, but it ain't go'n change a single thing. All you can do now is come with me or stick around here and get yo'self shot." Cecil stopped packing for a moment and laughed to himself. "You know, I wanted that Baines broad. Wanted her somethin' awful. Turns out she fucked me good."

Cecil went back to packing. Starry sat on the padded chair, arms crossed, trying to stay mad at Cecil, but she couldn't help thinking he was kind of cute and a whole lot of fun. There were worse things in life than spending it in the Caribbean with Cecil Blanks. Sure had to beat dancing naked for a bunch of dirty old men.

"I tell you what," she said as she got up off the chair. "Once we get to our hotel on the islands, you put that strip music back on."

That got a big smile out of Cecil. "That's my girl," he said.

Starry could only shake her head. "You little shit."

50

Jackson asked to make a phone call, so Bailey carried the desk phone into Jackie's cell and placed it on the floor. He locked the cell behind him. Jackie called Bridgett's house.

"Hello?"

"It's me," said Jackson.

"Jackie, where are you? Everything's all set. I've been waiting for you."

"There's a small problem," he said. He wasn't sure how he should broach the topic of his incarceration. He decided it would be best not to worry her yet. "I just need a little time, okay? I'll call you this evening."

"What's wrong?"

"I can't explain it to you right now. I'll call you later. You took care of everything else?"

"I did just what you told me. It went like clockwork. They're going to run, Jackie, I'm sure of it. The money's already offshore."

"Don't say anything else, okay? You've done great."

"Why can't you talk? Tell me what's going on."

"I just need you to hold out a little longer. Can you do that?"

"Okay," Bridgett said. "But you tell me if you need my help."

"There is one thing."

"Yes?"

"I need you to keep an eye on my father. I don't want him to be alone."

"Sure, Jackie. I'll go out to the hospital."

"I'll call you there. How's that?"

"Okay. I'll be waiting."

"And Bridgett?"

"Yes?"

"I love you."

He could almost see the smile break out on her face. "I know," she said.

Jackson looked up then, and he saw William Sump enter the office. In his right hand, the commissioner held a large zip-lock baggie with a gun inside of it. Jackie placed the phone receiver on its cradle.

"I hope you been talkin' to a lawyer," Sump said to Jackson. "You sure do need one about now."

"What you got there?" Bailey Sump asked his father.

The commissioner put on a shit-eating grin. "Let's just say I have Jackie Moon's death certificate." Sump put the bagged gun on the sheriff's desk. "That there is the pistol that killed Mary Brim. It was also used on the fella I told you about, the one I found with a bullet in his head down by Snelly's Pond. And those body pieces we found down below the coal tower? There was a bullet in one of them pieces. A bullet from this very same gun."

Bailey lifted the baggie up by the seal and studied the gun. Black ash had settled at the bottom of the bag. "Where did you find this?" Bailey asked, even though he already knew the answer.

"We found it in the rubble of the old Moon house," Sump said.

"Surprise, surprise," Jackson said from his cell.

Sump ignored him. "The gun had been stolen out of the evidence locker from the old Brim case. I talked to Alice Wells. She told me Jackson had been alone at the back of the deeds room. He must've snuck out the back door and gone to the evidence locker. An old con like Jackson Moon could've picked that lock in a few seconds. I had Marty dust the area for finger prints. Moon's prints were right there on the lock.

"When you engineer a setup," Jackie said, "you don't miss a trick. I've got to give you that."

"He stole the gun he used on Mary Brim," Sump went on, glaring at the man in the cage. "Musta shot some poor soul out by the railroad tracks. Then he kill't Malloy out by Crawdaddy's. He was covering his tracks. Those men probably knew something about Mary Brim. He shut them up good."

"Fascinating story," said Jackson.

Sump put the grin back on. "I suggest you keep this boy quiet," Sump told his son. "He's in a whole heap of trouble."

Bailey was still looking at the gun. His father took the bag out of the sheriff's hands. "I best go lock this up," the commissioner said. "'Fore it gets stole't again."

Bailey just nodded absently.

As the commissioner headed back out the door, he called out over his shoulder. "A triple homicide. They go'n stick a needle in you, boy." Jackie could still hear Sump's laughter out in the hallway.

"You can't let this happen, Bailey," Jackson pleaded from his cell, but the sheriff didn't appear to hear him. He followed his father out into the hall. Bailey watched his father walk to the end of the hall and turn toward the evidence room. Bailey looked into the commissioner's office for a moment before entering it. He used a key on his ring to open the top drawer of the commissioner's desk, then he slid open the bottom drawer and pulled out his father's revolver. He clicked open the chamber.

When Jackson Moon Jr. eased open his eyes, he saw the bag above him gurgle and a oval of liquid drop down the tube toward his arm. It felt like needles were stuck in his throat, needles that dragged against the skin when he took a breath. The right side of his body burned, and his eyes stung. He turned his head slowly and noticed the nurse preparing a gurney beside his bed. She moved one of the bags above him to the metal arm above the gurney. "What's going on?" Moon croaked.

The nurse didn't answer. When she looked across the room, Moon could see the fear in her eyes. Moon turned his head. In the far corner, Michael Grant stood with a gun in his hand. The pistol was the size of a small country.

"What are you doing to me?" Moon asked.

Grant smiled. "Just stay calm," he said. "We wouldn't want to cause any further complications."

Moon looked back at the nurse. She had strapped the second bag to the gurney. She lifted it up so that it was even with his bed. She looked at Moon helplessly. "We're going to move you," she said.

"What the hell is going on?"

"You're coming with me," Grant said. "Once that boy of yours gives me back my money, I'll bring you back here to die in peace."

"Coming with you?"

"Sure," said Grant. "It'll be great fun. We can talk about the old times."

Moon looked over at the nurse. She was crying. Grant came over to the bed and helped the nurse transfer Moon's body to the gurney. Moon grunted in pain as they lifted him from the bed. Grant got behind the gurney and was starting to roll it when the door opened. Grant lifted his pistol to Bridgett Baines.

"Well now," he said. "Ain't this a surprise."

Bridgett froze. Her eyes took in the scene: Grant with the huge pistol, the crying nurse, Jackie's father on the rollaway gurney.

"Just the woman I needed to see," Grant went on. "I feel like I've drawn into an inside straight."

"What do you think you're doing?" Bridgett asked.

"We're going on a little trip," Grant said. "You, me, and the vegetable here."

"What do you want?"

"First I want Jackie Moon's head above my mantle. Then I want my fucking money, every last penny of it."

"You can't just roll this man out of the hospital," said Bridgett.

"Sure I can," Grant said. "This thing's got wheels on it."

"You're insane."

The amusement on Grant's face melted into a scowl. "What's insane is a woman who thinks she can steal ten million dollars from me."

Bridgett shook her head unconvincingly. "I don't know…"

"Don't fuck with me," Grant said. "I got to Dade. He told me the whole sordid story. By the way, you don't have to worry about that little account of his. He won't be needing it."

"He must have misled you, Mr. Grant. I don't know anything about…"

"Shut up!" Grant roared, shaking the gun fiercely. "I don't even want to hear it. Jackie Moon will have to come save his father and his little girlie. You can watch me slit his scrawny-ass throat. Then if his daddy here ain't dead already, I'll stab him in the fucking heart. I'll save you for last, sweetheart. We'll have some fun first, me and you."

He pushed the gurney at Bridgett. It slammed into her thighs and drove her out into the hallway. Grant shoved Moon out after her, the gurney crashing into a wall. Moon cried out in pain. A nurse looked up and started to assist the old man until she saw Grant with the Anaconda. She shrieked. Grant put the gun against Bridgett's head. "You drive," he said.

Bridgett rolled the gurney down the hall with Grant beside her. He ground the gun into her ribs. People who had gathered in the hall after the nurse screamed now retreated into their rooms or flattened their backs against the wall. They were clearing the way for Ghost Grant.

Sheriff Sump pulled a set of keys from his top drawer and opened Jackson's cell.

"What's going on now?" Jackson asked.

"Just keep quiet," Bailey replied.

He cuffed Jackson's hands behind him and led him across the office. Deputy Aaron Coop appeared in the doorway. His eyebrow shot up.

"Where you going with the prisoner?" he asked Bailey.

"I'm taking him out to the murder scene. I need to straighten some things out."

"I don't think that's a good idea," Coop said.

Bailey stared him down. "Last I checked, the deputy works for the sheriff, not the other way around."

Coop stepped back. "Whatever you say, Bailey. You're the boss."

"That's what I'm telling you," Bailey said as he led Jackson out of the office and toward the eastern exit of the courthouse. He walked quickly, pushing Jackie ahead of him. A woman on the sidewalk gathered her two small children close to her, and two men looked up from their game of checkers. One of them looked at Jackie before spitting tobacco juice into a Dixie cup.

"Why are we going out to the murder scene? I don't understand..."

"Just keep quiet for now," Bailey said as he looked back over his shoulder. "We'll talk when we get out to the car."

Bailey led Jackson to his cruiser. Jackie was surprised when the sheriff placed him in the front passenger seat. Bailey hurried to the other side of the car and got in. He started the car and backed out of his parking spot on the square. The cruiser squealed away from the courthouse, looped across an intersection, and sped down Greenville Street. Bailey turned on the siren, and cars began to pull out of his way.

Jackie looked over at the sheriff. "You found out something, didn't you?"

"Yeah," Bailey said, keeping his eyes on the road. "I found out something."

Jackson waited.

"You remember how I told you that I'd looked into the Bosco fire a couple of years ago?" Bailey asked.

"Yeah."

"Well, I went through all the evidence back then." Bailey slowed down at an intersection, looked both ways, then dashed through a red light. "The murder weapon was missing."

Jackie looked out the windshield. "You mean the gun I supposedly stole from the locker."

Bailey nodded. "It wasn't there to steal. It was gone way back when you were still sharing a cell with your friend Cecil."

"So who else besides you had a key?"

"Deputy Coop had one," Bailey said.

"And your father had one," Jackson stated.

Bailey nodded again. "My daddy always told me I should keep an extra gun handy. One that wasn't registered in my name. In case I needed it to protect myself."

"Or in case you need to kill some people and blame it on someone else."

Bailey slammed his palm against the steering wheel. "Son of a bitch!" he roared. "I was wondering why he went out to Snelly's Pond when Malloy got shot. He took care of that himself. Said it was made to look like suicide but there was no gun around."

"You think your father shot him?"

Bailey thought about it. "I don't think so. I can't see him running around, shooting people himself. I think maybe he got Malloy to shoot the man out on the railroad tracks. Maybe Malloy really did kill himself, then my father picked up the gun. Maybe."

"I bet I know who got shot on the tracks," Jackson said. "A man by the name of William Barnes. They called him Red Eye. He survived the fire at Bosco's. I started riling things up around here. I think your father got nervous about it."

Bailey took a sharp right onto Redding Way. The siren blared.

"Where are you taking me?" Jackson asked.

Bailey didn't answer. He turned left on Maris Avenue and pulled into a driveway at the end of the road. The driveway led up to a red-brick house up on a hill. Two tall pine trees swayed in the front yard. Jackson knew it was Bailey's own house.

"What are we doing here?"

Bailey threw the car into park and reached over to take the handcuffs from Jackie's wrists. He took one of the keys off of his key ring and handed it over. "You take my truck," he told Jackie, nodding to the blue Dodge Ram at the end of the drive. "They'll be looking for your car."

"Take it where?"

"I'd go to the bus depot in Grantville, take the first bus north. Go as far away as the damn thing will take you."

"I'm not going anywhere," Jackson said.

"What the hell are you talking about? My father's going to put your ass on death row."

Jackie just shook his head. "This town is my home, Bailey. I swore I wouldn't run again."

"Goddamn it, Jackson. This isn't a game. My father can put you away. Don't think he won't."

"You can stop him," Jackie said.

"Me? What the hell am I supposed to do?"

Jackson looked squarely at his old friend. "I thought you were the sheriff of this town."

Bailey cocked his head back in surrender. Just then, the police radio cackled to life. "Sheriff Sump? This is dispatch."

Bailey picked up the handset. "Go ahead, Dottie."

"We have an incident at the hospital," the dispatcher reported.

"What sort of incident?"

"A man has kidnapped one of the patients at gunpoint."

Jackson stared at the radio. "What the...? Who is the patient?" Bailey asked.

"It's the man whose house just burned up. A Mr. Moon."

Jackie covered his mouth with a hand and looked over at Bailey.

"A man at the hospital thinks he recognized the perpetrator," the dispatcher went on. "He thought it was that pornographer on trial in Atlanta. Michael Grant? We're contacting the authorities up there now. The man is supposed to be in prison."

Jackson had no words. He just shook his head slowly, his mind in a daze.

The radio came to life again. "There was a woman with them, too," the dispatcher said.

"Bridgett," Jackie said. He remembered their phone call. Jackie had asked her to go stay with his father. He had sent her into the lair.

"Pretty woman?" Bailey asked into the handset. "Blond hair below the shoulders, green eyes?"

"That fits the description."

"Oh my god," said Jackson.

"Anything else, Dottie?"

"The perpetrator left a message with the admissions clerk."

"What kind of message?"

"He said that the patient's son was to go out to Harlow's tavern and wait by the phone booth there. No authorities. If he was alone, he would get a call from the perpetrator. That's all he said."

Bailey looked over at Jackson, but Jackie was staring at the radio as if it were about to bite him.

"Should I send a deputy to the hospital?" the dispatcher asked.

"You do that, Dottie. We need a report from any witnesses."

"Yes, sir."

The radio died. Bailey replaced the handset carefully. "Holy shit," he said.

Jackson opened the passenger door.

"Where are you going?" Bailey asked.

"You know where I'm going."

"I'm coming with you, Jackie."

"You can't. You heard what she said. I have to go alone."

"That's crazy. You know you can't trust Grant."

"I'll get him to let Bridgett and my father go. He'll take me."

"What the hell are you talking about? He'll take you, and then he'll kill all three of you. The man is out of control. He just took hostages from a goddamn hospital."

"I've got to go, Bailey. I gave Bridgett to that madman. I've got to get her out."

"I'm going with you, damn it. That's all there is to it."

Jackson turned to the sheriff. "You've got other business to tend to," he said.

Bailey thought about it. He felt his head nodding slowly.

Jackson held up a fist. "Here's to finding the balls," he said.

Bailey looked at the fist for a moment, then he punched it lightly. "Don't do anything stupid," he said. "There's a radio in the truck. Use it."

Jackie got out of the car. He closed the door and leaned into the window. "You watch your back, Sheriff. Don't underestimate him."

Bailey pulled his service revolver from its holster and pushed the gun through the passenger window to Jackson. Jackie looked at the revolver. "Take it," the sheriff said.

Jackson took the gun and stuck it in the waist of his pants. "You've got another weapon, right? You're going to need it."

"Don't you worry about me," Bailey said. He threw the cruiser into reverse as Jackie dashed up the driveway.

51

Jackson was standing in front of the phone booth at Harlow's tavern. The gravel parking lot was empty except for Bailey's pickup truck. The bar had been closed for over a year. The roof was sagging, and weeds had grown up through the walkway to the entrance. One of the front windows was broken.

A black Grand Am approached from the west and pulled into the parking lot, gravel popping under the tires. It pulled to a stop in front of Jackie and a man got out of the car. He was younger than Jackson, late twenties to early thirties, and he was built like an athlete, eclipsing six feet and weighing close to two hundred pounds. His blond hair was combed to the side with a row of strands hanging over his left eye. Rough stubble covered his chin and neck.

"Are you with Grant?" Jackie asked him.

"The man called me," he replied. "Said he needed me to take care of something for him."

"Where is he?"

"I'm here to take you to him," the man said. "But first he wants me to soften you up a little bit."

"Soften me up? C'mon, man. Let's just take care of this thing."

"That's what I'm doing. Taking care of it."

"What do you want from me?"

The man walked around Jackson as if sizing him up. "What you got there in your pants?"

Jackson didn't answer. He kept an eye on the man as he paced.

"Shoot me, and you'll never get to see Grant," the man said.

"I wasn't planning to shoot you."

"I can't take you to Grant with a gun in your pants."

Jackson pulled Bailey's revolver out and dropped it on the ground. The man then walked out in front of Jackie, reached behind his back, and pulled out his own gun, a .44. The man then dropped his gun on the ground, too.

"What's going on here?" Jackson said.

The man smiled slyly. "I hear you're some bad-ass boxer."

"Give me a fucking break. We don't have time for this."

The man brought his fists up in front of his face and started to bounce on the balls of his feet. "I happen to be a pugilist myself. Now, Grant told me to soften you up. I figured we might as well see how good you are. My personal record is unblemished."

Jackson couldn't believe it. He bowed his head down. "I will concede to your superior talents. How's that?"

"Not good enough. I want to get a taste of the great Jackson Moon."

"Let me tell you about the great Jackson Moon. I have two bruised ribs from a guy who came at me with a sledgehammer. I went to the hospital in an ambulance after nearly getting burned up in a fire. And I've spent the last several hours in a jail cell. I'm in no mood for a goddamn boxing match with a punk who has something to prove."

The man was still bouncing. He put one hand behind his back. "I'll fight you one-handed. How about that? We'll call it a handicap."

"I'm not going to box with you," Jackson said.

The man swooped in fast and landed a quick jab below Jackie's left eye. Jackson tumbled back on the gravel.

"Look at that shit," the man preened. "Put you down with one punch. I am one talented motherfucker. They call me Hammer on account of that right hand you just experienced."

Jackson held onto the gauze around his ribs as he got up slowly from the ground. "All right, Hammer. You proved your point. Now can we just...?"

The right came again, this time to the bridge of Jackie's nose. Jackie stumbled back against Bailey's pickup, but he kept his feet. Hammer kept dancing, feigning in at Jackie then retreating. Reluctantly, Jackson lifted his fists up, his elbow covering the bruised ribs.

The man who called himself Hammer looked more deliberate now. He hunched over and swayed left and right. He came into Jackson and poked another jab at him, but Jackie pulled his head back out of range.

"Hey, you're pretty quick for an old man," Hammer taunted. He then did a stutter step and landed another right jab to Jackie's chin. Jackson swung back, too late, as his right arm sailed uselessly through the air.

"You see that?" Hammer chattered. "You see that? You can't touch me. You're putty in my hands, Moon. Putty in my hands."

Jackson stood flat-footed in the parking lot. Hammer came in again. Jackie threw a left jab, but Hammer blocked it and slammed a hard straight-hand against Jackson's mouth. He followed with a left hook that cracked against Jackson's temple. Jackie hit the gravel again.

"This is pathetic. What, were you fighting women in that prison? I heard you had game. You got nothin', man. Nothin'."

"You're right," Jackson said. "Can we go now?"

"Get up and fight, or I'll take you right here, and you'll never see Grant."

Jackson got up off the ground and brought up his fists again. A line of blood dripped from his lip, across his chin, and down his neck. He heard the words of Big Hands Hoffman echoing in his head: "Use the jab, goddamn it. Set up the counter."

Hammer came again, but Jackson landed a good left jab. He saw a look of surprise flare up on the man's face as he ducked down and danced away. He started to circle Jackie, but now Jackson was moving too. Hammer ducked again and threw a tight left hook that came up short. Jackie landed two quick left jabs and Hammer's head cocked backwards. The man steadied himself and began to circle, the smile now gone. He tried a stutter step again, but Jackie leaned in and slammed a right to Hammer's kidney. The punch seemed to hurt Jackson more than his opponent. A pain shot through his aching ribs.

Jackie was leaning to his right, favoring the ribs. Hammer was smiling again. He knew Jackson was hurting. Jackie bided his time, waiting for Hammer to telegraph a right jab. The kid moved his head from side to side, taunting Jackie, then he dropped his left and launched an overhand right. Jackie spun his head sideways as he countered with a left hook. Hammer's punch glanced off Jackie's chin as Jackson's left fist pounded against Hammer's right cheek. The kid stumbled back, his eyes startled. Jackson moved in, drilling his opponent with two left jabs, then a powerful left-right combination and a right to the gut. Jackson moaned from the pain that shot through his ribs. Hammer's hands came down, his eyes glazing over. Jackie followed with a roundhouse right that sent Hammer reeling backward. He tumbled across the hood of the black Grand Am and rolled off of it, hitting the gravel in a puff of silt.

Jackson wiped his mouth with the back of his hand and walked over to the man's gun. He picked it up and tossed it into a stand of trees at the edge of the lot. Then he picked up his own gun and stuck it back in the waist of his pants. Hammer had worked himself up from the ground, but he was doubled over beside the car. Jackson grabbed the back of his collar and slammed the top of his head into the sideboard. He then opened the door of Bailey's pickup, dragged Hammer's body over to it, and lifted him up into the passenger seat. He limped around to the driver's side, his right arm wrapped around the ribs, and got in. The kid was lying across the seat, blood pouring out of his nose.

"You should stick to being Grant's errand boy," Jackie told him. "You flat-out suck as a boxer."

Jackson started the car. "Where to?" he asked.

The boy just groaned. He held his arms around his waist. Jackie took a handful of his blonde hair and lifted his face up. "Where to?" Jackson demanded.

"A right out of the parking lot," Hammer moaned.

Jackson dropped the boy's head and hit the gas. The pickup spun around in the parking lot, gravel flying, as Jackson sped out onto the highway. He grabbed Hammer by the collar again and straightened him up on the seat. Then he pulled out Bailey's service revolver and cocked it. "No more games," Jackie said. "Tell me how to get to Grant or I'll blow out your fucking knees."

The house was off the Water Works service road. Jackie drove down a long dirt lane that winded through thick woods. There was not a single house on the road. He turned the pickup truck onto a drive that had no mailbox at the end of it. "This is it," Hammer told him.

"Thanks for the guide," Jackson said, then he slammed the butt of the gun against Hammer's forehead. The man slumped over the dashboard. Jackson reached over, opened the passenger door, and shoved Hammer out. He reached behind himself, stuck the gun in the back of his pants, and took a deep breath before shoving the truck into gear.

The drive crested a hill, and the house appeared in a valley below. It was a large rust-red colonial with dark green shutters, huddled in a clearing amidst a thick clutch of trees. The drive looped in a circle in front of the house. In the middle of the circle, a fountain sprang up, the water spraying out in a majestic arc and sprinkling down into a marble-walled pool. A porch bent around three sides of the structure, flower boxes stuffed with azaleas hanging from the rails. A vegetable garden grew out back, the tomato plants carefully staked. Jackie pulled the pickup around the circle and parked it in front of the house. A silver Mercedes was stationed in the attached garage.

Jackson got out of the truck and stood looking up at the house. The curtains were drawn over every window. He felt a light mist from the fountain on his back and heard the shower pattering against the shallow water. The front door of the house opened, and Grant appeared in the doorway with Bridgett Baines in front of him. His left arm was crooked across Bridgett's throat. In his right hand, he held the Colt Anaconda against her temple.

"Hold on right there," Grant said.

Jackson stopped in the gravel walkway.

"Where's Jason?"

"You mean Hammer? He went down for the count. I left him at the top of the drive. He'll have a pretty nasty headache when he wakes up."

"Are you armed?" Grant asked.

"Let the girl go," Jackie said, "and we'll talk about it."

Grant smiled. "Oh no, we have to talk about it now. The girl stays with me until I'm sure I've got my money."

"The girl doesn't know how to get your money. I'm the only one that can get it for you."

"I may be violently insane," Grant said, "but nobody ever accused me of being stupid. I know the girl could get me the money, but it just won't be ultimately rewarding unless I get the money from you."

"Unless you get to kill me. Isn't that what you mean?"

"Nobody fucks with Michael Grant."

"Let the girl go. She can take the truck. She'll pick up your flunky on the way out and get the poor kid to a doctor."

"We're playing by my rules now," Grant said. "I want to see a weapon on the ground in front of you, or I will blow this girl's brains out her ear. I still have your daddy to bargain with."

Jackie stood for a moment, studying the impassive look on Bridgett's face. "You won't get the money until my father and Bridgett are safe," he said.

"Understood," Grant replied.

Jackson looked off to his right, then reached behind him, pulling out the gun and dropping it on the grass beside the walkway.

"Now we're getting somewhere," Grant said. "Come on in and join the party. He motioned to Jackie with the gun. Jackson walked slowly along the walk, up three steps to the porch, and through the doorway as Grant stepped aside, keeping Bridgett in front of him. Jackie walked into a large living room. A picture window, covered with a thin white curtain, looked out over the fountain. Matisse's *Rose-Colored Nude* hung over the plush sofa against the far wall. A large arched doorway opened up to a dining room. The table was elegantly set with fine china and silverware. Two ornate porcelain figures – a nude woman holding a pitcher and a man covered with only a leaf and holding a cornucopia of fruit – stood at the centerpiece below a magnificent crystal chandelier.

"Quite the digs you've got here," Jackson said.

"Oh, it doesn't belong to me. Not technically." Grant came out from behind Bridgett and walked out into the center of the living room. Black dirt trailed behind his shoes and sullied the white oriental rug. "It's owned by Twelve Oaks International. You might have heard of them. They're building that wonderful theme park to celebrate our rich Southern heritage. I'm just visiting, really. I'm in tight with the regular residents, you might say."

Grant walked under the arched doorway and around the dining table. Beyond the table was a set of white double doors. Grant stood in front of them and smiled maliciously.

"Where's my father?" Jackie demanded.

"We'll get to that," Grant said. "I want to show you something first. Something that will confound and amaze you." He bent a finger to Jackson, directing him to the dining room. Jackson walked around the table and stood in front of the two doors.

Grant put a hand on each of the brass knobs. "Get ready to blow your mind," the madman said, his eyes wide and expectant, like a ringmaster announcing the grand finale. Then Ghost Grant threw open the doors.

52

Bailey had already radioed the dispatcher, telling her to have his father meet him at the Rock. He pulled the cruiser off the road and parked behind a stand of maples and oaks. The sun was starting to set, spreading a reddish-orange streak across a high bank of purple clouds, and a breeze lifted the day's heat from the hardened ground. Bailey walked up over a knoll, the Rock rising to meet him like a sentinel guarding the sacred earth. From a base of thirty-five square feet, the granite structure sloped to a rounded peak almost fifty feet high. Some people imagined a solemn face where two depressions and a sharp jut marked the granite at its peak. Indians believed the spot to be holy, and they had buried their dead in mounds just east of the Rock. It rested on land that once belonged to Arnold Solomon, the founder of the town.

Bailey walked up to the hole where Mary Brim's skeleton had been unearthed. He crouched down and examined the grave, wondering if other bullets were still hiding in it. He assumed his father had produced the incriminating bullet without worrying about removing other evidence that might contradict the story the commissioner was selling. It probably wouldn't cross his father's mind that anyone would dare try to contradict him. He realized the whole Bosco episode was about prideful men who believed they were above the law, believed in fact that they *were* the law. He had heard his father say it more than once during his time as sheriff: "I *am* the law," he would announce without a trace of doubt. Who was Bailey then? The sheriff in name only? A man too weak to stand in the way of men who ran the town as they saw fit? A man they could count on to turn the other way?

The sheriff straightened up as the commissioner's Lincoln Continental pulled up behind the police cruiser. Sump bolted out of the car, leaving the door open, and came over the knoll with long purposeful strides. His collar was open, his shoulder holster strapped tight to his body.

"Where the hell is he?" the commissioner demanded.

Bailey just watched his father approach.

"Where is the prisoner, goddamn it?" Sump asked again.

"We'll get to that," Bailey replied. "We need to talk about some things first."

The commissioner came to a dead stop, his eyes flaring in disbelief. "We'll get to it now," he said. "We're talking about a man guilty of triple homicide."

Bailey shook his head and looked up at the reddish-orange streak that was darkening above him. "Jackie Moon didn't kill anybody. You know that."

"What in God's holy name are you jabbering about? We've got witnesses, physical evidence, the murder weapon. What more do you want?"

"I want the man responsible for this mess," said Bailey.

His father looked at him coldly. "I don't know what you're getting at, boy, and I don't want to know. I just want my prisoner, and I want him now."

Bailey studied his father's eyes for long moments, searching for some hint of guilt in them, a trace of contrition, but the eyes held no clues. "I inventoried the Bosco evidence a couple of years back,"

Bailey said. "The murder weapon was missing from the locker back then. There's no way Jackie Moon stole it last week."

Sump's frown bit into his jaw line. "You're making a mistake, son. Listen to me now. You tell me where the Moon boy is. We'll pick him up, put him away, and go have ourselves a fine meal. It ain't worth it, believe me."

"You always told me I should carry an unregistered gun for emergency situations. You sure got plenty of use from your emergency weapon, didn't you, Daddy?"

Bailey heard a growl emerge from the base of his father's throat. A pair of birds flew off from a nearby tree. "Just who the hell do you think you're talking to, boy?"

Bailey looked down at the earth for a moment, then he peered back up at the rugged old man. "I'm talking to a criminal," he said. "A man who killed at least two people in cold blood. A man who stained this town with a terrible sin for the price of a pornographer's graft."

A hot red blush flared across the commissioner's cheeks. "I'm your daddy, goddamn it. I made you everything you are. You are nothin' without me, boy, and you best not forget that. I made you and I can destroy you. This town worships me. You think they will believe your bullshit story? Even if they do, they can't touch me. This is my town, and it will be 'til the day they lay me down."

Bailey shifted his feet. The reddish-orange streak was fading in the sky. The night ate away the surrounding clouds, the darkness closing in on the last flush of dying sunlight. "Here's the story," Bailey said. "You're going to leave here, Daddy. Head on down to Florida, find yourself a nice place on the beach, live out your days in peace. I'll come visit you every now and again. But you can never come back to Solomon's Rock. That's the deal. You get in your car and head south. If I see you in this town again, I'm going to put you in jail."

Sump burst into hearty laughter. He even bent over and struck his knee. "That's the goddamnedest thing I ever heard. You serious, boy? You go'n put me in jail? You are clearly touched in the head. That's the only thing that can explain it. You've lost your mind."

Bailey removed the handcuffs from his belt and took a step toward his father. Sump stepped back and drew his revolver.

"You stay right where you are," the commissioner said.

Bailey tipped his head slightly to the right. "You're gonna shoot me now, Daddy? Your own flesh and blood?"

"You ain't my flesh and blood. No blood of mine would be taking me down like this. You think you can run me out of town like some goddamn Wild-West lawman? Bullshit. This is my town. Ain't nobody go'n run me off, and sure as hell ain't nobody go'n lock me up. Damn straight I'll shoot you, if that's what it comes down to."

Bailey looked at him. The shadows darkened with last light. "That's what it comes down to," he stated. He took another long step toward his father.

"I'm warnin' you, son. I will blow a hole clear through your belly. Don't think I won't."

The sheriff didn't answer. He took another step. His father held up the gun and closed one eye. There was no fear, no hesitation in the eye that aimed the revolver.

Bailey took one more step, and Commissioner Sump pulled the trigger. The solid *thunk* of the hammer striking echoed off the Rock. William Sump's eyes came open wide. He looked at the gun in wonderment. Bailey was less than ten feet away. Sump leveled the pistol again. Five, six, seven more times the trigger clicked and the hammer thudded, but the revolver did not fire.

"You were really gonna kill me," Bailey said, not so much out of surprise but as a simple statement of fact. "You were gonna blow away your own son."

Sump rolled out the chamber of the revolver and peered in.

"You had the keys to the evidence locker," Bailey said, "but I had keys to your desk. You should never keep your gun in a drawer like that."

"You sonovabitch," Sump growled.

"Son of an asshole, more like it."

Sump threw the gun to the ground. "Come on then," he taunted, his left hand balling into a fist, the right hand motioning his son forward. "Your old man can still whip your no-good ass. I'll tear your goddamn arms off."

Bailey shook his head sadly. He had given his gun to Jackson, knowing that he would not be able to use the weapon against his own father. Now it had come to this. Bailey sighed heavily, hiked up his trousers, and settled down into his best three-point rushing stance. He was bent fully at the waist, three knuckles of his right hand dug into the dirt below him, his left elbow cocked on his left knee. He lifted his heels and balanced on the balls of his feet. He ignored the dull ache in his left knee and remembered the long-ago day when he had assumed the same stance to stop Valdosta from claiming the state championship. Bailey had driven out of the stance at the very moment that the ball was snapped. The toss when to Curtis Hamm, a sweep to the left. Bailey pounded into the left guard, sending him flailing backwards. The fullback tried to take out Bailey with a lead block but Bailey neutralized him with a low right shoulder and spun away from him. There was nothing between Curtis Hamm and the winning touchdown except for Bailey Sump, jersey number 99. Hamm started to roll toward the sideline, but then he made his cut-back to the inside. Bailey squared his shoulders, planted his feet, and drilled Hamm with a textbook tackle. His left shoulder slammed into the running back's waist, and he kept his legs moving, driving Hamm backward four, five, six yards as the roar of the crowd rose to a deafening crescendo. Hamm finally lost his footing and fell to his back with number 99 pinning him to the turf. Bailey rose up above his prey and lifted his arms into the air. Solomon's Rock had won the Georgia state championship, and no one in the town would ever forget it.

"What the hell are you doing?" his father asked as he watched his son crouch into position. The words had barely escaped from his mouth when Bailey charged, rushing out of the stance in perfect form. William Sump rose his arms up helplessly, as if warding off a missile attack. Bailey's body rammed into him, snapping Sump's head back crazily, the arms whipping through the air like the tails of a windsock. His body sailed backward as his son's 260 pounds drove him into the hard earth. The air whooshed out of Sump's lungs, and the beady eyes bulged out of their sockets. Bailey rolled his father's slack body over, grinding Sump's face into the dirt. The sheriff then yanked Sump's arms behind him and slapped on the handcuffs. A high-pitched whine escaped from the commissioner's throat as he wheezed for air. Clods of dirt clung to his face and clumped in his mouth. Curtis Hamm never had it so rough.

"William Terrence Sump," Bailey intoned, "you are under arrest for the murders of Lonnie and Mary Brim. You have the right to remain silent...."

53

Ghost Grant led Jackson into a large sitting room at the back of the house. A set of atrium doors opened up to a wooden deck that ran the length of the back wall. There was a bar on the right side of the room, beneath a painting by Georgia O'Keeffe. The left wall was covered by floor-to-ceiling bookshelves, packed neatly with hardbound volumes. Against the wall stood a rollaway gurney with liquid bags hanging down from an extended metal arm. Two tubes ran down from the bags and into Jackson Moon Jr.'s arm. The old man turned his head to Jackson, but his eyes did not seem to focus. He was being nursed by Alfreda Sachs, the same woman who had cared for Jackie's wounds, the woman he had first known as Lucy. She looked over at Jackson, her eyes flushed with concern. He started to ask about his father's condition, but the answer came in a solemn shake of Alfreda's head.

Jackson's eyes scanned to the right. Angel was standing against a curtained window on the far wall. She wore a dark purple dress adorned with print flowers and had one arm placed on a high-backed velvet chair. Jackie immediately recognized the figure sitting in the chair. He was older, of course, and his hair was faded white. He had sickly pale skin as white as the hair. In a dark suit and bow tie, he looked like a corpse. "Hello, Jackson," he said.

Jackie couldn't answer. All he could manage was the slightest nod of his head in the direction of Senator Alfred Sachs.

Jackson stepped slowly away, keeping his eyes on the senator, until he backed into a love seat and collapsed into it. "You lied to me," he said, turning his eyes back to Angel.

"I was protecting my husband," she told him. "I didn't want it known that he was still alive. I wanted him to live out his last days in peace. I believed my lie was for a higher calling."

"You never shot Grant, did you?"

Ghost Grant laughed from the other side of the room. "Is that what she told you?" he bellowed. "Wishful thinking, huh, Angel?"

Angel stared at the pornographer. "I should have shot you. Would've saved a lot of heartache all around. I knew, soon as I pulled the trigger, that I shot the wrong man."

Jackson leaned back on the seat as Bridgett moved in behind him and put a hand on his shoulder. "Are you saying you did shoot a man?" Jackie asked.

Angel turned her eyes back, but they gazed out beyond Jackie, to some distant place. "His name was Malcolm Wright."

Jackson remembered Leola's story in the cabin. "The man who thought he was getting your child," he said.

Angel nodded. "I didn't mean to kill him. All I felt was anger and shame. The man was lying about me and my child. He was claiming it was really his baby. The way he figgered it, we had stolen the child from him and Lucinda. She always wanted a baby so bad. Grant put him up to it. He was going to use the story to blackmail my husband. I didn't know what else to do." Jackson studied the placid eyes of Senator Sachs as Angel told her story again. This time around, she was giving up the truth....

Grant had brought Macolm Wright to the Sachs home. Wright was ready to spread the story about the senator's baby. He would tell the world that it was his own child. The black man stood in front of the picture window in the sitting room, next to Grant, who sat in the red-velvet chair. Angel had heard the lie that Malcolm was ready to spread. She took the gun from the dining cabinet and walked into the sitting room.

I never meant to shoot the man. I just wanted to make him tell the truth. I wanted my husband to hear it. This man was ready to steal my Alfred's fatherhood and take away our only daughter. I wouldn't have it. I just wanted to scare him into the truth and drive this crazy plan right out his head. But the boy just looked on me like I was dirt, like I was just some wild nigger with a pistol. The rage ran through me like a shot of white lightnin'. Ran right up my fingers and tensed up my hand.

The bullet pierced Malcolm Wright's throat, the sound like that of a tomato thrown against a wall. The bullet passed through him and put a small hole through the picture window. Blood gurgled out of the throat and spat out across the floor. Wright put a hand to his neck, his stunned eyes on Angel. The blood leaked through his fingers as he stepped backward. A web of cracks splayed out from the bullet hole in the window like ice splintering beneath a man's weight. The web blossomed across the expanse of glass until touching the outer frame. Wright coughed out a knot of blood and fell back another step. The glass shuddered once, then fell like a waterfall behind the stricken black man. Perhaps he thought it was the sound of heaven opening up to him. More likely, he believed it was the sound of demons rising, because his next sensation was of falling, through the smashed window and down into the bed of tulips below. He landed there, hands still clutching his neck, eyes widened in fear, and sucked one last agonizing breath down through the hole in his throat.

"I was willing to suffer the lie about Alfreda's father," Senator Sachs said. His wife was silent now, a glint of tears on her cheek. "I was even ready to expose my cover-up of the Stone investigation. But after Wright was shot, Grant had my wife on a murder charge. I wasn't going to watch her go to prison for the rest of her life."

It was all falling into place for Jackson. "So it was Wright's body that burned up. They wrapped it in a blanket and carried it up to the attic of Bosco's bar."

"That's the beauty of having a whole town by the balls," Grant put in. "I owned the sheriff, the cops, the medical examiner. Ain't that some shit? A black boy's body is in the grave of the honorable Alfred Sachs, and no one knows any different. They didn't want to know. Everyone had heard the rumors about the senator's sinful weakness for colored whores. They knew why he would have been at that bar. They were as anxious to cover up the real story as I was. They were much better off with a dead hero than a disgraced public official."

"Why didn't you just kill the senator?" Bridgett asked.

Grant shrugged. He was sitting in a chair on the other side of the room, his leg draped casually over the chair arm. "I guess I could have. But if the senator had shown up with a bullet in his brain or if he had simply disappeared, there would have been all kinds of investigations and allegations. Who needs the aggravation? Might've even delayed the sale of Stone's land. It never occurred to me to dump Sachs in a burning nigger bar until Wright went down. It was pure inspiration at that point. Hell, we had ourselves a body to get rid of anyway. It was the perfect plan, if I must say so myself. We burn Wright and say it was the senator. Nobody wants to dig too deep and embarrass the town. Stone sells me the land and I get my theme park built. Everything fell right into place. Besides, I liked the idea of having me a kept senator. You might say he's my bitch." Grant smiled wryly.

"I didn't know he would burn all those folks up," Sachs went on. "After that happened, I should've come forward. But I did what I thought was best for my family. We took up our life in this home. I never left the house except to tend to the garden out back. Angel and

I educated Alfie. Leola taught her some medicine. She's grown up to be a fine young lady. I helped build a lot of things in my life, but I'm proudest of my little girl. She deserved the very best."

Grant hopped out of his chair. "Well, you got what you wanted," he said to Jackson. "The whole truth and nothing but. So now it's time for me to get what I want." He walked across the room and stood next to the gurney where Jackson's father lay.

"Here's how it's going to work," Grant said, rising the Anaconda to the temple of the sick man on the gurney. "I'm gonna put a hole in your daddy's head, just to prove I mean business. Then you, me, and your girlie are gonna head on over to Dade's office and get my money back. If you don't get it to me nice and quick, I'll blow out the back of the pretty girl's head."

"You don't have to kill my father," Jackie said. "I already know what you're capable of."

"That may be so," said Grant. "But you clearly have not gotten the message through that thick skull of yours. Nobody fucks with Michael Grant."

"I know how to get money." It was Jackson Moon Jr. The words croaked out of the sick man's mouth. "Lots of it."

"What are you jabbering about, old man?" Grant snapped.

Jackie's father licked his lips and tried to clear his throat. "The bribe money. From the Planning Commission payoffs. I know where it is. Lots of cash, free and clear."

Grant's eyes lit up at the prospect. He leaned into the former lawyer. "Tell me, old man."

Jackie's father mumbled something unintelligible. Grant bent over the body. "What's that? Speak up, goddamn it."

Grant never noticed that Moon had pulled the needle out of his arm. He held it in his right hand. Grant looked up just as the old man's arm swung around. Moon jabbed the needle right into Ghost Grant's left eye. He shrieked in pain as he stumbled away from the gurney and blood spurted from the eye socket.

"Run, Jackie," Moon pleaded in the loudest voice he could muster.

Grant yanked the needle out of his eye and started firing the pistol. The first shot shattered a standing lamp in the corner. The second shot popped into the sick man's hip. Alfreda screamed and fell to the floor. Angel grasped at Grant, but he backhanded her with the butt of the gun. She hit the back wall hard and fell. Sachs rose from the chair just as Grant came back around with the gun, cracking it against Sachs's forehead.

As Jackson and Bridgett dashed through the double doors and across the dining room, Grant turned and blew a bullet into the crystal chandelier. It spun around like a carousel, tearing away from its ceiling mount, and dropped to the dining table in an explosion of glass. Pieces of crystal splashed up in the air, against the walls, and across the floor. Jackson had bolted around the table before the chandelier fell. He hunched over Bridgett, who scampered in front of him. They had reached the entrance foyer when Grant's powerful gun blasted a hole through the front door. Jackie turned Bridgett toward a second door behind them. They slammed through the door and down a flight of steps into the basement. Jackson leapt up and smashed a bare light bulb as they ran past it. They collapsed in a corner and huddled behind a disassembled bed. The basement was cool and dark. Jackie sat on the cement floor, clutching Bridgett close to him, and tried to adjust his eyes to the blackness. He could see a bulkhead on the other side of the room, but there was a chain roped around the two handles of the bulkhead. A Master lock dangled from the chain.

Grant appeared on the stairwell. He turned on the light switch but nothing happened. He tried another switch, and a small light over the stairs blinked on. The madman came down the stairs with the Anaconda out in front of him. His hand covered the left eye as blood dribbled between his fingers and flowed down his left cheek.

"There's no way out, Moon," he preened, the smile looking even more sinister on the bloodied face. He turned right at the bottom of the steps and walked out to the middle of the basement floor, directly under the broken light bulb. Glass crunched beneath his feet. Jackie tried to calm his excited breathing, and Bridgett began to tremble.

Grant examined the shadows in the room. The pale light from the stairway slithered across the floor. Jackie reached over and picked up a wooden slat from the disassembled bed and cocked it over his shoulder. He moved up into a crouch as Bridgett tried to hold him back. She grabbed a fistful of his shirt, but Jackie took hold of her wrist and worked the shirt free of her grasp. He took a measured step from behind the bed mattress. Grant was looking at the bulkhead, his good eye slowly turning, when Jackie took two quick strides across the floor, swinging the slat out in front of him.

Grant fully turned just as Jackie slapped the wood across Grant's right hand. The Anaconda clattered across the cement floor, tumbled over a lawn mower, and slid against the far wall. Grant dashed after the weapon, but Jackson jumped on his back, driving him down on top of the mower. Jackson scrambled to his feet, pulling Grant up by the collar. Grant took a swing, but Jackie pulled away from it, then buried a fist into Grant's gut. Grant doubled over as Jackie brought a knee up into his face. The pornographer jerked backwards, falling over the lawn mower and into a five-gallon can of gasoline. The can rocked over, spilling gas across the floor. The gasoline soaked into Grant's shirt and spit into his eyes and mouth. He gagged violently and wretched. Jackson picked up Grant's gun and pointed it at the man on the floor.

Grant was on all fours, coughing and trying to wipe the gas out of his eyes. He couldn't focus his vision, and the fumes caught in his nose and throat. The damaged eye stung like the devil's vengeance.

"I expected more of a fight from you," Jackson told him. He held the gun inches from Grant's head.

But Ghost Grant had one more trick in him. The razorblade that he had taken from Noxie, the same knife that had originally belonged to Frank Crackson, was lodged in his boot. He hunched over and moaned, moving his hand toward his foot. Jackson was looking back at Bridgett, making sure she was okay, when Grant pulled the blade from his boot and jabbed it into Jackie's right thigh. Jackson screamed as the pain seared up his leg. He fell to the floor, realizing only then that he had dropped the gun. He clamored for the weapon, but Grant got to it first.

Grant got up with the gun. "Game over," he said. He then looked over at Senator Sachs, who had just reached the bottom of the stairs. Grant blinked his burning eyes, trying to make them focus, the left eye nothing now but a bloody mass.

"Get out of here, Sachs. This doesn't concern you now."

Sachs walked across the floor and stood in front of Grant. A red welt the size of a baseball rose from the spot on his forehead where Grant had hit him. Jackson was moaning on the floor behind the senator, the razorblade still poking out of his thigh. Bridgett was holding Jackie and trying to comfort him.

"Get out of my way, goddamn it, or I'll put a hole in you," Grant barked. "Hell, I could kill you anytime. You think they'll arrest me for killing a dead man?"

Sachs turned around to look at Jackson. His back to Grant, the senator reached into the small inner pocket of his suit coat. Jackie watched through agonized eyes as Sachs held something small and silver in his left hand. The senator turned back to Grant.

The pornographer's good eye was tearing up. He tried to wipe it with the tail of his shirt. He rubbed his free hand across his eyelids. The orbs stung as if there were needles jabbed in his iris. Blood was pouring in streams down his face.

"It's ironic, isn't it?" the senator said softly. "Everyone thought I burned up, but it turned out to be you."

Grant couldn't make out what Sachs had in his outstretched arm, but when Sachs struck a thumb across the flint wheel, Grant saw the small flame spark from the silver Zippo lighter.

Grant lifted the gun up from his hip, but it was too late. The small flame arced toward him and ignited the fumes rising from his shirt and arms. Before his one good eye, Grant saw the haze of fire bloom into a swirling fireball. He fired his gun, but it only punched a hole into the ceiling, sending down shimmers of fine white dust. As Grant threw his hands up in front of his face, the fire raced down the length of his arms like a fuse, torching the gas-soaked shirt. Grant's body erupted into flames. The pricks of hair singed and, for a moment, it looked like his head was covered with dozens of tiny birthday candles. He screeched wildly and tumbled backward over the lawn mover, into the pool of spilled gas. The fire whooshed upward, blowing Senator Sachs backward and searing the concrete wall with a black scar. Grant's body shook madly, then broke into convulsions like an old car engine conking out. The arms flailed, the legs kicked, the teeth chattered, and the gun flew from his hand, clattering across the floor. Grant shuddered once more and sat still, his back against the wall. The skin of his face began to bubble, pulling away from the bone like the burning frame of a movie reel, as the fire engulfed him.

Sachs sat up on the floor and looked into the good eye of the dying man. The eye held the look that Noxie had always longed for, a look of terror and disbelief. Sachs watched the eye until it became a smoldering red ember and burned away, leaving only the depression of an eye socket in a scorched skeleton.

Angel Sachs came halfway down the basement stairs, a hand up to the flames below her. She was still woozy from Grant's blow. "Alfred!" she cried out. "Are you all right?"

"I'm okay," he said. "Go get the fire extinguisher from the kitchen, and tell Alfie that Jackson needs her help."

She started back up the stairs. "And Angel," Sachs added, his eyes still mesmerized by the sight of Ghost Grant burning away, "no hurry on that fire extinguisher."

It was good to hear his son asking forgiveness. Moon could hear Jackie's voice echoing out: "Forgive him, forgive him, forgive him...." He was surprised at the calm he felt. Did that mean he was forgiven? It was the best moment of his life: his head resting in his firstborn's lap, Jackie stroking his hair, praying for him, the world quiet now except for the echoing voice. It seemed as sacred as a chapel. He liked it here. He felt like a child not wanting to fall asleep but unable to resist the gentle music of a mother's lullaby. He had to sleep. There was no choice now.

"I love you, Daddy," he heard Jackson say.

He tried to form the words, but he wasn't sure if they were only spoken in his own head. He wanted Jackson to hear them. He wasn't sure if he had ever said the words before. He wanted Jackson to know that he loved his boy, that he had always loved him, despite everything. He felt his hand squeezing Jackie's, and he knew his boy understood, one way or another.

54

Bright sunlight filtered down through a huge magnolia tree that grew at the edge of the Moon plot. Shadows danced through the leaves like puppets on strings, and shimmers of light shifted across the damp earth, jewel-like. Jackson watched a black man on the crest of a hill carefully watering a row of pink and white impatiens.

A large crowd huddled around the casket. Adorned with a bouquet of flowers, it hovered over the grave, held there by the pallbearers on either side. Jackson felt the weight straining his muscles and wondered how much of it belonged to his own father's body. Hundreds of people from Solomon's Rock had come to the funeral: store owners, bankers, lawyers, politicians, gas-station attendants, mill workers, farmers, and doctors. Most of them stood patiently as the pastor finished his short service at the gravesite. The pastor wore a black suit and a gray tie, a Bible open across his right palm. His words were low and reverent. Two small boys had broken loose from the crowd and tousled in the green grass.

After the pastor had finished speaking, the pallbearers lowered the casket into the grave. Jackson picked up his cane and stepped back. He put his free arm around Leola. She wept softly, a cotton handkerchief over her nose and mouth. Across from Jackie, Bailey Sump placed the end of his rope on the ground and took a single step backward. He wore his dress uniform and held the blue trooper hat over his heart. Birds chattered in the trees, and on the highway two miles east, a Mack truck downshifted, its engine straining to conquer Carlson's Hill.

Jackson picked up a handful of dirt and stepped back up to the grave. He admired the spray of white and pink carnations below. He looked down in the grave, said "Goodbye, Daddy," and dropped the dirt onto the casket. Laura Murray, an old family friend who was a teller at the bank his father used, broke into sobs. Jackie stood for a long moment, peering into the grave, then looking out to the puffy white cumulus clouds on the horizon. He nodded his head as if acknowledging a message held in a gentle breeze that swept through the grass and ruffled his hair. He turned, kissed Leola on the forehead, and walked away from his father's tomb.

He had limped halfway down the sloping hill when he heard Bailey call to him from behind. Jackson turned around and forced a smile at his old friend. Jackie was struck by the strange peacefulness he felt inside.

"Sorry about your daddy," Bailey said.

"Yours, too," said Jackson.

Bailey's face was turned toward the sun. His dress uniform was freshly pressed and starched. A slick black stripe ran down the right leg of his gray trousers. He held his cap under his left arm. His voice seemed drained of emotion. "I always thought nothing in the world could break my father. He stood up to everything that got in his way. I just never believed he would string himself up by his own belt. Never even occurred to me to take it away from him in the cell."

"It wasn't your fault, Bailey."

The sheriff nodded doubtfully. "All those boys were going with the lies for years. They said whatever my daddy told them to say. But when it came time to defend my father, not a one of them stepped forward."

Jackson watched Bailey's face in the sunlight as it seemed to drop out of a trance.

"I got the package you sent me," the sheriff said in a business-like tone.

Jackson thought about the records Aunt Frank had left behind – the meticulous logs of payoffs from town businesses to the planning Commission. "It's up to you," Jackson said, "what you want to do with them."

Bailey shrugged. "The FBI folks are interested in the TOI bribes. Between the money laundering and your friend Cecil running off with all that money, the theme park may just die in the crib."

"Now that's a shame."

"As far as the other records, most folks probably figured the pay-offs were just a cost of doing business in this town." Bailey looked Jackson in the eye. "Maybe some secrets are best left buried."

Jackson nodded, his eyes looking away.

"The rumors are flying already," Bailey said. "Some folks have it that Grant was all burned up but he still walked away from that house. Got a call just this morning. Woman said she saw the ghost of Michael Grant last night, hanging out over where Bosco's bar used to stand."

"Oh yeah? What was he doing there?"

"Hell if I know. Floating around, whatever it is ghosts do."

The gathering was breaking up and moving slowly out toward the cars at the crest of the hill.

"You and I," Jackson said. "I guess we get to be men now."

"Nah," said Bailey as he shook his head. "We're all just children, trying our damnedest to act grown up."

Jackson smiled at that. "Sounds about right to me."

They were silent again, watching the people wander away.

"Are you heading back down south?" Bailey asked.

"I don't think so," said Jackson. "I plan to stick around here for awhile. See what happens."

The sheriff nodded. "Well, you take care of yourself then. Keep out of trouble."

"Yeah, you, too."

Bailey laughed. "It's a deal." He held out a hand and Jackie shook it. The sheriff turned slowly and headed back up the hill.

"Hey, Bailey," Jackie called out. The sheriff turned back around. "Maybe we could meet up sometime. Have a cup of coffee over at the Tin Roof. Talk about old times."

"I'd like that," Bailey said. "We could even talk about the future."

"There's always that," said Jackson.

Bailey started to turn away again, then he stopped. "You know," he said, "there's one thing I can't quite figure out."

"What's that?"

"How did my truck end up at the Grantville depot?"

Jackson remembered handing over the keys in the basement of the TOI house. He imagined the sight of Alfred Sachs, his hat pulled low over his eyes, helping two black women onto a northbound train.

Jackie took a deep breath and met Bailey's eye. "Like you said, maybe some secrets are best left buried."

The sheriff nodded. He put on his trooper hat and touched the brim of it in salute to his friend. Jackson watched him walk back up the hill.

Jackson turned toward the dirt path that hugged the bottom of the hill. Bridgett Baines was walking along it. She wore a black dress and carried a single red rose. When Jackie met her on the path, she handed him the flower. A breeze brushed the hair back from her face, and she smiled tentatively.

"You okay?" she asked.

"I'm okay."

They walked for a while along the cemetery path. Bridgett moved into Jackie and held him around his left arm as he clutched the cane in his right hand. It seemed oddly formal to Jackson, as if he were an usher and she a bridesmaid.

"You know, I heard Mr. Grant had a change of heart just before he died," said Bridgett. "Or maybe it was just a show, an act of good faith for the trial."

"Oh yeah?"

"He made some big transfers. Charitable stuff. Turns out he owned a whole row of old condemned houses over on Spinner's Lane. He's funded brand-new homes for those folks and turned them over to the tenants."

"Imagine that," Jackson said. "I guess the man wasn't so bad after all."

"I guess not."

Bridgett stopped and looked up to Jackson. "What are you going to do now, Jackie?"

Jackson shrugged. "My mama's heading back to Florida after the business with Daddy is done. She wants to stay with her sister. I may build a small house on the property. We'll see."

"You should build it big enough for a family, don't you think? Just in case."

Jackson looked down at her bright green eyes. "And plenty of space for Aunt Frank, if she ever decides to come home."

"And do you think Big Hands and his wife will like it in Jamaica?"

Jackie shrugged. "They had a choice of anywhere on earth. It's an open offer."

They walked across the path, farther away from the cars that were heading out of the cemetery. Jackson was getting accustomed to walking with the cane.

"You know," said Jackson, "I used to hang out with our yardman. He was a black man named Andrew. I didn't realize it at the time, but Andrew taught me a lot. I can fix toilets, do some carpentry, maybe help the old folks plant their flowers. I just might have a gardener gene in me."

"A gardener gene?"

Jackson chuckled. "Something Senator Sachs told me once. We've all got to find out what our gene is. Me, I'm still trying to figure that one out." He looked over at Bridgett. "But I'll get by," he said. "How about you?"

She smiled back at him. "You can plant a garden for the old folks, and I'll do their taxes. Maybe play around with some small investments." Her smile widened. "I'll get by."

They were holding hands, heading for the woods that bounded the graveyard.

Bridgett looked straight ahead. "You know," she said, "if you need a place to stay while they're building your house, I have an extra room."

Jackson stopped and looked hard at her. She was too damn pretty for him, but she didn't seem to notice it. "Can I think about it?"

"Sure, the offer's open."

They walked some more. Jackson watched the cane forming impressions in the dirt.

"Maybe we can go somewhere," Bridgett suggested. "Talk about it."

"I know a place by a pond," said Jackson. "Stars fall right out of the sky."

"Is that a fact?"

"It's what I heard anyway."

"I'd like to see that."

He looked over at her and smiled. It made him think about redemption. He might not have gained it, but he sure as hell gave it his best shot. "I'll bring the champagne," he said.

"And I'll bring the stars."

— THE END —